EXPLORER INTERNAL AND EXTERNAL

A Journey beyond the Imagination

SUSAN SHAKER

Copyright © 2025

All Rights Reserved

No part of this book may be reproduced or transmitted in any form or by any means, electronic or mechanical, including photocopying, recording, or by any information storage and retrieval system without the written permission of the author, except where permitted by law.

Living Forever, Staying Young – A Dream or Reality?

For Humanity has been captivated by the idea of immortality and eternal youth for centuries. What if these long-held desires could become a reality? What if the power to control the aging process, to heal oneself, and to transform one's body were within reach? Imagine being able to erase wrinkles, restore youth, increase height, or remain in the prime of your life forever.

What would you do if this power were suddenly available? Would you embrace it or fear its consequences? Explorer, Internal and External, a world where humans have mastered their own biology, unlocking the potential to alter their bodies in ways never before imagined. But with such power comes a question: Is humanity ready for the price of eternal life? The answers are more complex than anyone could anticipate.

"Embark on this extraordinary journey with me to uncover how they achieved the impossible."

To the scientists who rose from the people and lived for the people, though history may have dimmed their names, their legacy will forever shine, unforgotten.

This book is dedicated to the countless scientists who have spent their lives striving to make the world a better place. These gifted individuals poured their intellect, passion, and relentless determination into discoveries and innovations that have shaped our lives in profound ways. Yet, despite their invaluable contributions, their names have faded into the shadows of history, unrecognized by the public and often overlooked by their own peers.

In a world where tales of ambition, rivalry, and even corruption among scientists are frequently immortalized in books and films, the silent heroes of science remain unsung. Their stories are rarely told, their achievements often claimed by others, and their legacies buried beneath layers of forgotten history. Many of these brilliant minds were not driven by fame or fortune but by an unwavering commitment to knowledge and the betterment of humanity.

Consider the case of Nicola Tesla, whose groundbreaking inventions and visionary ideas laid the foundation for modern technology. For years, his contributions were overshadowed, with many of his innovations mistakenly attributed to others, like Thomas Edison. It was only long after Tesla's death that the world began to recognize the true extent of his genius. But Tesla is just one example among countless others whose names we may never know, yet whose work quietly transformed our world.

This book seeks to honor those forgotten pioneers—the scientists whose brilliance was eclipsed by the politics of recognition, whose discoveries were credited to others, and whose passion for truth and progress never wavered, even in the face of obscurity. Their dedication continues to ripple through time, embedded in the fabric of our daily lives, silently shaping the world we know today. To these unsung heroes of science, this book is a tribute. Their legacy, though hidden from the spotlight, is etched into history, and their work lives on in every life they've touched.

- Susan Shaker

Acknowledgment

To: Professor John Zilcosky,

I extend my heartfelt thanks to a dear friend, Professor John Zilcosky. When I first began writing this novel back in 1998, we owned a restaurant, and he was one of our dearest customers. Each time he saw me working on my manuscript, he would encourage me, making me feel inspired and supported. After completing the novel, I asked if he'd be interested in reading it and sharing his thoughts. He graciously accepted, becoming the very first person to read the story. His insightful feedback—highlighting both the strengths and areas for improvement—has stayed with me, and to this day, I continue to apply his valuable suggestions. Your guidance shaped not just this book, but my journey as a writer.

I have never forgotten you or your invaluable advice. Thank you for believing in me.

Thank you, John, for being such an amazing friend.

***

My heartfelt thanks go to everyone who has been a part of my journey in writing Explorer, Internal and External. Your support has been the light that guided me through every page.

To my children, who supported me throughout the entire process—thank you for being there every step of the way.

To my dear friends, thank you for being my constant source of encouragement, inspiration, and companionship through every word and every chapter. Your presence in this journey has been nothing short of extraordinary.

I extend my deepest gratitude to my employer, Larry, and his kind and sweet wife, Lorna, for their unwavering support. A special thank you to my wonderful manager, Caroline, whose graciousness in allowing me to stay in the office and work on my novel made this dream possible. Your understanding and kindness have left an indelible mark on my heart.

To my incredible friends in the office— Jennifer, Trisha, Kayla, Natalie, Lisa C. and Bernie—thank you for your warmth, encouragement, and friendship. Your belief in me has been a source of strength, and I am truly grateful to each one of you.

To everyone who has walked beside me on this path, thank you from the bottom of my heart. This novel carries pieces of all of you within its pages.

Contents

CHAPTER ONE

The Name Sean Morgan

The sun blazed with an almost regal brilliance, its golden rays cascading through the window like molten threads of light, setting the room ablaze with a dazzling, ethereal glow. A tender breeze surged in, infused with the crisp purity of dawn, caressing Sean's face like the softest whisper of nature's breath.

The papers on his desk leapt and twirled in an elegant ballet, their edges flickering like delicate wings caught mid-flight. The air was drenched in the intoxicating essence of spring, a fragrance so vivid, so fiercely alive, it seemed to pulse with its own heartbeat—tangible, electric, as if the very spirit of the season had unfurled within those walls.

The sky unfurled in endless splendor, drenched in a shade of blue so rich and mesmerizing, it seemed capable of drawing in the soul itself and never letting go. Scattered across this celestial masterpiece were clouds, not mere wisps, but billowing, majestic sculptures of white, each more breathtaking than the last, glowing like fragments of dreams suspended in the heavens.

Birds darted and danced with wild abandon, their songs sharp and crystalline, weaving an orchestra of melodies that pierced the air with exquisite clarity. The rhythmic pulse of their wings sliced through the sky, a gentle, hypnotic cadence, echoing like the tender hush of waves kissing distant shores, while the seagulls' graceful flutters whispered secrets of the sea, as if the sky itself was breathing, alive with the poetry of flight.

The sunlight poured onto Sean's sheets like liquid gold, cascading in delicate streams as the morning unfurled with quiet grandeur. Lost in the depths of a vivid dream, he shifted slightly, the tender kiss of warmth brushing against his face like the softest fingertips of dawn.

A crisp, cool breeze drifted lazily through the open window, weaving around the room with an almost sentient grace, its gentle touch wrapping around him like an invisible cloak of serenity. It cradled him in a soothing embrace, blurring the line between sleep and wakefulness, making the pull of slumber feel like an irresistible tide, drawing him deeper into its comforting abyss.

He was adrift in a dream woven from the fragile threads of memory, haunted by the faces of his parents and his twin sister, Sharon—echoes of a past once vibrant, now dimmed by the shadow of distance. Their bond, once unbreakable, had splintered under the weight of unspoken words and simmering resentment, fractured by the sharp edges of anger that refused to dull with time.

Since leaving Toronto, the silence between them had grown louder, filling the hollow spaces of his mind as he spent countless hours unraveling the knots of guilt, questioning the selfishness that had shaped his choices. Why had he been so relentless, pushing Sharon to walk his path, to view the world through the narrow lens of his own ideals? The question gnawed at him, a restless echo in the quiet corners of his heart, where regret bloomed like a bruise that never fully faded.

Since childhood, they had been reflections of one another, bound by an unspoken pact to mirror each other in every facet of life—their studies, routines, and ambitions, as if their futures were two halves of the same design. As twins, they clung to the belief that their emotions and destinies were woven from the same thread, inseparable and eternal.

But when Sharon veered off that shared path, choosing a future that diverged from their carefully crafted symmetry, it wasn't just a decision but a rupture. The illusion shattered like glass, leaving Sean grappling with the jagged edges of betrayal and confusion. Dazed and untethered, he grasped for stability in the only way he knew—by running. Fueled by frustration, He seized the first job offer that unexpectedly came his way—not out of passion, but as a desperate attempt to drown out the dissonance. Letting his resentment steer him into unfamiliar waters.

That's why he fled to the U.S., not just to start a new life, but to escape—a self-imposed exile from the memories that clung to him like shadows and the pain that refused to fade. Yet, no distance could silence the echoes of the past. His dreams betrayed him, stitching together fragments of a childhood bathed in warmth: their laughter ringing through endless summer skies, their shared wonder beneath constellations that felt like promises written in the stars, and the unbreakable bond that once tethered their hearts without question.

Beneath the layers of pride and regret, he yearned to go back—not just in miles, but in time—to reclaim what had been lost, to bridge the gap that had grown like a chasm between them. In the stillness of those quiet reflections, when the world's noise fell away, he faced the undeniable truth: he had been wrong, blinded by his own stubbornness, and the cost of that realization weighed heavier than he'd ever imagined.

At six-thirty, the alarm clock erupted with a jarring, merciless shriek, slicing through the fragile tranquility of the morning like a blade. Sean groaned, his face contorting in protest as he pried one reluctant eye open, squinting at the unforgiving red digits glowing on the display.

"Just five more minutes," he mumbled, his voice thick with the weight of sleep, each word a fragile plea against the tyranny of time. His hand flailed blindly, fingers clumsily searching for the elusive snooze button until he managed to silence the relentless clangor. With a sigh of defeat and triumph all at once, he retreated beneath the thin sanctuary of his sheet, rolling into the golden warmth of sunlight that sprawled lazily across his bed, as if the very day conspired to lull him back into the comforting abyss of sleep.

Thirty minutes later, he jolted awake, his body snapping upright as if yanked from the depths of a restless sea. His thoughts lagged behind, sluggish and tangled, a haze of confusion clouding his mind. He rubbed his eyes with the urgency of someone trying to erase the remnants of sleep, then darted a glance toward the window, squinting against the blinding glare of the sun, its position an unspoken accusation. And then it hit him—a jarring surge of realization that crashed over him like a tidal wave.

"No! I'm late again!" he shouted, his voice ricocheting off the walls, sharp and panicked, shattering the fragile silence that had lingered in the room.

He flung the sheet aside with a frantic sweep, vaulting out of bed in a tangled rush of limbs and urgency. Half-dazed, his feet barely found their footing as he stumbled toward the bathroom, driven more by panic than coordination. The cold sting of water and the sharp scrape of the razor did little to clear the fog clinging to his mind. He dragged a brush through his unruly hair with trembling fingers, taming it just enough to feign order.

Wasting no time, he bolted to the closet, yanked the door open with a force that nearly unhinged it, and grabbed the first set of clothes his hands found—wrinkled, mismatched, it didn't matter. He dressed in a blur, each motion fueled by the relentless drumbeat of one thought: "I'm late. Again."

He snatched his car keys from the table and slung his computer case over his shoulder in one fluid motion, the door snapping shut behind him with a decisive thud. His footsteps echoed with urgency as he hurried toward his car, heart still racing from the imagined crisis. But then, he glanced at his watch. He froze mid-stride, the realization hitting him like a sudden gust of wind.

"That's ridiculous," he muttered, narrowing his eyes at the offending timepiece. "Not only am I not late, but I'm far too early."

A heavy sigh escaped his lips, part frustration, part disbelief, as he ran a hand through his already disheveled hair. Shaking his head with a wry smile tugging at the corner of his mouth, he grumbled,

"I must've done it again—set the clock earlier than I was supposed to." The absurdity of his own self-imposed panic settled over him like an invisible weight, both infuriating and faintly amusing.

He slid into his sleek, silvery BMW, the leather seats cool against his back, and with a smooth turn of the ignition, the engine purred to life like a well-fed beast. The morning sun glinted off the polished surface as he navigated the familiar streets, heading toward his favorite coffee shop—a ritual etched into the fabric of his routine, rarely disturbed. It was their usual meeting spot, a place woven with the echoes of countless conversations with Greg. But today, for the first time, Greg was late.

Unbothered and with time to spare, Sean ordered his coffee, the rich, intoxicating aroma wrapping around him like a warm embrace. He claimed his favorite corner table, the one that caught just the right amount of morning light, and unfolded his newspaper with deliberate precision. As he delved into the printed pages, each article became a small world of its own, and he savored them one by one.

The steady hum of the bustling café, the rhythmic clinking of cups, and the faint hiss of steaming milk blended seamlessly with the comforting scent of fresh brew, creating a perfect, unspoken harmony that filled the space around him.

"The President of the United States has been diagnosed with cancer," the bold headline declared, its stark words casting a heavy shadow across the page.

"The White House has relayed this somber news. All Americans are united in praying for their leader." He looked at the article with a little anger and thought: "Thousands of people die of cancer every day, and yet no one gathers to pray for them." Sean's eyes drifted over the article, absorbing the gravity of the words with detached acknowledgment, his mind already moving toward the next headline. He scanned the page with mechanical precision, determined to devour every story.

But then, a small, almost insignificant blip nestled in the "What's New" section snagged his attention. It wasn't bold or dramatic, just a modest line tucked between more prominent stories, as if it didn't demand to be read. Yet something about its quiet presence, its refusal to shout, pulled at his curiosity. His gaze anchored to it, the larger headlines fading into background noise. Sometimes, he knew, the smallest details held the biggest secrets.

"Is this a miracle or what?" the headline blared, its bold letters practically leaping off the page, demanding attention. Sean's eyes narrowed as he read on, curiosity sharpening with each word. According to a Canadian newspaper, the world was witnessing something nothing short of extraordinary—a ten-year-old boy, once shackled by the relentless grip of severe asthma, had transformed overnight into a picture of perfect health.

For years, his life had been a fragile thread, stretched thin by wheezing breaths and hospital walls. Just months ago, doctors had delivered the grim verdict: his time was slipping away, his lungs failing beyond repair. But now? His condition had reversed so completely it defied every medical explanation. Specialists were baffled, their years of expertise crumbling under the weight of the inexplicable. No treatments, no new medications—just a sudden, radiant burst of life where death had been patiently waiting. It wasn't just remarkable. It was impossible. And yet, there it was, inked into the morning paper, daring the world to believe.

One of the customers walked past Sean, who was engrossed in the newspaper he held, and remarked, "Isn't that amazing? It's bound to be a phenomenon."

Sean instantly recognized him, just as everyone else did, by his daily appearance in a sharp, expensive suit, his blue purse always carefully placed right in front of the café, as if it were part of some unspoken ritual.

Sean smiled and replied, "Yes, it's truly a miracle." Sean then spotted Greg behind the entrance door, visibly shocked to see Sean there so early.

Greg had been Sean's friend since day one on the job, a bond forged in the fires of early career chaos and countless shared moments. Handsome and effortlessly charismatic, Greg had a way of commanding attention without even trying. His wavy reddish hair caught the morning light like threads of copper flame, and his tall, broad-shouldered frame made him easy to spot in any crowd. But his eyes-those—piercing, clear blue eyes—did most of the heavy lifting, a shade so vivid they seemed to cut through noise and distraction alike, leaving more than a few hearts trailing in his wake.

As he stepped into the bustling coffee shop, the door chiming softly behind him, his gaze swept across the room with casual precision, effortlessly scanning faces until it landed on Sean, tucked away in his usual corner. A slow, easy smile curved across Greg's face, the kind that could disarm even the most guarded stranger.

Without hesitation, he made his way over, weaving through the crowd with the natural grace of someone who belonged wherever he went. Greg tugged the newspaper down with a swift, playful flick, revealing Sean's face hidden behind the rustling pages.

"Good morning, Sean," he quipped, a mischievous glint dancing in his piercing blue eyes.

Sean glanced up, momentarily startled, then broke into a wide grin, the corners of his mouth tugging upward with genuine amusement.

"Good morning, Greg," he replied, his voice tinged with mock triumph.

Leaning back slightly, he added with a smirk, "For once, I can actually say—you're late."

Greg chuckled, shaking his head as he slid into the seat opposite, the easy rhythm of their banter settling in like a well-worn habit, comfortable and familiar.

Both of them burst into laughter, the sound spilling out like an old song they'd played a thousand times, blending seamlessly with the hum of the bustling café. The easy camaraderie between them filled the air, a familiar melody woven into the fabric of their friendship.

Sean's eyes sparkled with anticipation, the grin lingering as he leaned forward, elbows resting on the table, unable to mask his excitement. "Are you starting today?" he asked eagerly, his voice a notch above the background noise, brimming with curiosity and an unspoken sense of shared purpose.

"Yes," Greg replied, his grin stretching wide, a spark of excitement flickering in his clear blue eyes. "And I'm very excited."

Sean's face lit up, his smile reflecting genuine pride and warmth."You're stepping into a higher role, and I couldn't be happier for you because you deserve it," he said, his voice rich with sincerity, every word wrapped in the warmth of true friendship. Leaning in slightly, his tone shifted to playful seriousness, the corners of his mouth twitching with amusement. "You know, I'm excited too. But you have to promise me one thing—tell me everything."

Greg chuckled, shaking his head with mock exasperation, but there was no mistaking the gratitude in his eyes. "Deal," he replied, his voice low and conspiratorial, as if they were about to share the most important secrets in the world. He chuckled, a warm, easy sound, and nodded. "I promise."

Sean leaned back, a satisfied grin tugging at the corners of his mouth, the kind that spoke of years of friendship and shared ambitions. Hired as a space researcher, Sean had carved his path with the precision of a man destined for the stars. His sharp intellect, paired with an insatiable curiosity, set him apart, propelling him toward the title of astronomer with a momentum that seemed unstoppable.

His mind burned bright, a beacon in any room, drawing both respect and admiration from his peers like gravity pulling at distant planets. It wasn't just his knowledge that set him apart—it was the way he thought, connecting the dots others couldn't even see, as if the universe itself whispered its secrets directly to him. He wrote a couple of books about his research and his ideas on space and galaxies—ideas that puzzled scientists and challenged many long-established rules. Greg's gaze drifted to the newspaper sprawled across the table, curiosity flickering in his eyes. "What's new?" he asked, nodding toward the crinkled pages.

Sean leaned back, his fingers lightly drumming the table as he recounted the story of the miracle boy, his voice tinged with a mix of skepticism and wonder. Greg listened intently, his brow furrowed in thought, the tale pulling at his imagination like a thread unraveling a larger mystery. They exchanged theories, their minds racing with possibilities—medical anomaly, undiscovered treatment, or perhaps something far beyond explanation.

The conversation flowed effortlessly, like it always did, shifting from the improbable miracle to the more tangible excitement of Greg's new position. They dissected the upcoming challenges with the same intensity, their words weaving between ambition and curiosity, painting a picture of the adventures that lay ahead, both in the universe above and the lives they were building below.

In the midst of their animated discussion, as laughter and speculation wove effortlessly between them, the door of the coffee shop swung open with a long, grating creak, slicing through the comforting hum of conversation. Instinctively, both Sean and Greg glanced up, their words trailing off mid-sentence.

A man stood in the doorway, his presence an immediate contrast to the cozy warmth of the café. His clothes were filthy, layered in grime and dust, with tattered scraps of fabric clinging loosely to his gaunt frame. The frayed edges fluttered slightly with each step he took, as if even the air recoiled from his disheveled state. His face was hollow, marked by shadows deeper than mere exhaustion, and his eyes—wild, sharp, and unnervingly clear—scanned the room with the precision of someone searching for something... or someone.

Then his gaze locked onto Sean and Greg, a sudden, unsettling focus that sent an inexplicable chill down Sean's spine. Without hesitation, as if driven by a purpose only he understood, the man began to approach their table, his footsteps uneven yet deliberate, cutting through the cafe's atmosphere like a blade through silk. Greg noticed it, glanced at Sean, and muttered, "Oh boy."

"Good morning. Would you like to buy me breakfast today?" the man asked, his voice a fragile blend of hope and hesitation, like a thread stretched thin, ready to snap. His eyes flickered between Sean and Greg, searching for something—kindness, perhaps, or just acknowledgment.

Sean exchanged a quick glance with Greg, an unspoken conversation passing between them in that brief moment. Greg raised an eyebrow, the faintest hint of a smile tugging at the corner of his mouth—not mocking, but touched with curiosity, as if wondering what twist of fate had steered this stranger to their table.

Greg lifted his head, glanced at the man, then turned to Sean. With a weary shake of his head and a hint of exasperation, he sighed, "And here we go again."

Sean turned back to the man, his expression softening slightly. The warmth of their earlier conversation lingered, but now mingled with something else—a quiet question lingering in the space between them, fragile and undefined. Finally, Sean smiled at the strange man who was inviting. The man smiled too and stood beside their table, waiting for a more formal invitation.

Sean pointed at a seat and said, "Please have a seat." The man's face lit up with a grin, the shadows of doubt and hesitation vanishing in an instant.

Sean flashed a smile at him before turning to the waitress, who was patiently waiting to take their order, and placed his own. "I'll have the number three. It looks perfect—pancakes, eggs, toast, and coffee."

Then, he turned to the man still waiting for his order. The man met Sean's gaze, his expression softening. "Pancakes sound like heaven. Thank you!" he exclaimed, his voice now carrying a warmth that hadn't been there just moments ago.

Sean smiled, leaning forward slightly, his eyes reflecting genuine kindness. "Then pancakes it is. Everyone deserves a little bit of heaven now and then."

Greg, with an easy grace, pulled out a chair and gestured for the man to sit. The man hesitated briefly, as if unfamiliar with such simple gestures of hospitality, then lowered himself into the seat, his posture easing as the tension began to slip from his shoulders.

Greg's smile was steady, warm, and disarming. "What's your name, my friend?" he asked, his tone light yet sincere, as if they'd just welcomed an old acquaintance rather than a stranger. The question hung in the air, simple but weighted, an invitation to be seen, not just noticed.

"Walter, sir," the man replied without hesitation, his tone carrying a mix of respect and eager gratitude. The name seemed to anchor him, giving him a sense of place at the table, however temporary.

As soon as the plate of warm, golden pancakes was set before him, Walter wasted no time. He dove in with an almost desperate fervor, each bite swift and hearty, as if afraid the meal might vanish if he paused for too long. The clatter of his fork against the plate was the only sound between them for a moment, punctuated by the faint hum of the café in the background. His hunger was palpable, etched into every hurried motion, yet beneath it was something more—a silent relief, the fragile comfort of being seen and fed without judgment.

Sean and Greg exchanged a quiet glance, not with pity, but with a shared understanding of how small gestures could ripple into something larger, even if just for one morning.

Sean watched Walter for a moment, his curiosity quietly stirring beneath the surface. There was something in the man's hurried bites, the gratitude woven into every motion, that felt like more than just hunger. Once the initial silence had settled and everyone was seated, Sean leaned forward slightly, resting his forearms on the table, his voice gentle but inquisitive. "So, Walter," he began, his tone casual yet warm, "Do you live around here? Or do you work in this area?"

Walter paused mid-bite, his fork hovering just inches from his plate. He swallowed, wiped his mouth with the corner of a napkin, and glanced up. His eyes, though tired, held a flicker of something— caution, perhaps, or the faintest trace of pride.

"Used to," Walter replied after a beat, his voice low but steady. "Had a place not far from here. Worked in construction. Things just… changed." His words trailed off, but the weight of what was left unsaid hung between them, lingering in the quiet space carved out by unspoken stories.

Walter paused briefly, his fork resting motionless in his hand as a flicker of uncertainty crossed his face. His eyes darted toward the window, as if searching for the right words somewhere beyond the glass.

"I... I've been around here for a while," he murmured, his voice soft, edged with something brittle—regret, perhaps, or the faint echo of a life once steady. "Used to work nearby, but... not anymore." The words slipped out quietly, fading into the ambient noise of the café like fragile threads unraveling from a worn fabric.

He didn't meet their eyes, choosing instead to focus on his plate, resuming his meal with mechanical precision. Each bite seemed more like a distraction than nourishment, as if the act of eating could keep the weight of unspoken stories at bay. Sean and Greg exchanged a brief glance, their curiosity deepening, but neither pushed. Some truths, they knew, unfolded only when the silence was ready to give them up.

When Walter finished the last bite, he set his fork down with a quiet clink, the sound oddly final against the backdrop of the bustling café. He sat there for a moment, his hands resting limply beside the empty plate, his shoulders hunched under the invisible weight he carried. Then he lifted his gaze, meeting Sean's eyes for the first time—not with the guarded glance of a stranger, but with a raw, unfiltered desperation that stripped away any pretense.

"There's nothing in this world for me to live for," he confessed, his voice barely more than a whisper, fragile and frayed around the edges. The words hung in the air like frost, chilling in their simplicity. His eyes, once darting and uncertain, were now steady, dark pools reflecting the emptiness he felt inside.

"I just try to get through each day, but honestly, the sooner I pass away, the better it'll be. That's why I don't work anymore."

The cafe's warm chatter faded into a distant hum, as if the room itself had recoiled from the starkness of his truth. Sean felt the weight of those words settle heavily between them, an invisible barrier and a bridge all at once. Greg sat in stunned silence, his usual charm stripped away, leaving only the quiet ache of someone who had just realized how deep another's pain could run. Sean swallowed hard, his mind racing for the right words, the right gesture—something to pull Walter back from the fragile edge he was standing on. But in that moment, all he could offer was presence, the simple, undeniable fact that Walter wasn't invisible, not here, not now.

His words hung in the air, raw and unfiltered, seeping into the quiet spaces between them like a shadow that refused to be ignored. Walter's eyes dropped to the empty plate, the remnants of his meal a stark contrast to the emptiness etched across his face. Every line, every hollow beneath his weary eyes, bore the weight of years spent wrestling with invisible battles—struggles woven deep into the fabric of his being, silent scars only the heart could carry.

Sean and Greg exchanged a somber glance, the echoes of their earlier laughter now distant, fragile things lost in the moment's gravity. The easy camaraderie that had filled the space just moments before was replaced by a heavy silence, thick with unspoken words and quiet concern. It was the kind of silence that didn't beg to be filled, only acknowledged—an invisible thread pulling them closer to a truth too profound to ignore.

Sean's voice was gentle, threading carefully through the fragile silence. "Are you married, Walter?" he asked, his tone soft, as if afraid the question itself might break something already delicate.

Walter's gaze remained fixed on the empty plate for a moment before he lifted his head slightly, his eyes clouded with a distant, aching grief. "Yes… I mean, no. But I was." His voice wavered, rough and uneven, like a fragile relic pulled from the depths of his chest.

"She died of cancer and left me all alone in this world." The words spilled out, heavy and raw, each syllable soaked in the weight of loss.

"She was everything to me. Without her, I want to die." His breath hitched, his shoulders slumping under the unbearable load of that truth. "I think I'm already dead."

With those final words, Walter's head dropped, his gaze sinking to the floor as if he could disappear into it, escape the reality carved into his heart. The fragile connection between them stretched taut, the room around them fading into a blur, leaving only the echo of his grief lingering like a ghost that refused to leave.

Sean sat in the stillness, their hearts heavy, knowing there were no words strong enough to mend what had been broken inside him—but sometimes, presence was the first fragile stitch while Greg's eyes met Sean's with a mix of impatience and boredom before his gaze shifted, drawn to the newspaper in Sean's hands.

Sean's heart ached at Walter's words, a heaviness settling in his chest that he couldn't quite shake. Sensing the fragile edge Walter teetered on, he gently steered the conversation toward lighter ground, hoping to ease the weight of the moment.

"So," Sean asked softly, his voice threaded with warmth and care, "do you live in this area?"

Walter shrugged, his shoulders rising and falling with the kind of weariness that went deeper than physical exhaustion. His gaze drifted somewhere distant, unfocused, as if the answer itself was lost in the haze of days gone by.

"Well, I live here or there. I don't really know," he replied, his voice low, tinged with resignation, as if the words were more a confession than an answer. The ambiguity of his reply lingered in the air, a quiet reflection of a life unmoored, drifting without anchor or destination.

Sean exchanged a glance with Greg, their silent communication speaking volumes. In Walter's words, they heard more than just uncertainty—they felt the fragile thread of a man barely holding on. Both longed to offer something, anything, that might lift his spirits, even if just a small gesture to remind him he wasn't invisible.

But then, Sean's eyes flicked to his watch, and his expression shifted instantly, the softness replaced by a flicker of urgency. He stood abruptly, the chair scraping lightly against the floor, breaking the delicate stillness that had settled over them.

"We have to go," he said, turning to Greg, his voice low but edged with a sharpness that hadn't been there before. The warmth from earlier remained, but now it was layered beneath something pressing, something unspoken, as if time itself had suddenly grown heavier.

Then, pausing for a brief moment, Sean glanced back at Walter, his expression softening. "We're here for breakfast most days. If you ever have the time or feel like joining us again, we'd be delighted to share a meal with you," he said kindly, his words carrying the warmth of genuine sincerity.

Walter looked up, his weary face touched by a flicker of something fragile yet unmistakable—gratitude. It softened the hard lines etched by years of struggle, his eyes glinting with a faint spark that hadn't been there before.

"Thank you," he murmured, his voice quiet but threaded with sincerity, as if those two simple words carried the weight of everything he couldn't say.

Sean and Greg nodded, their smiles warm and reassuring, small gestures of connection in a world that often overlooked such moments. Then, without another word, they turned and made their way toward the door and making the bell above chiming softly as it closed behind them, leaving behind the faint echo of kindness in their wake.

As they stepped outside, the crisp air hit them, but it did little to cool the tension simmering beneath Greg's composed exterior as his jaw tightened, and he shot Sean an irritated sideways glance, the warmth from moments ago replaced by a flicker of frustration. They walked a few paces in strained silence before Greg's restraint snapped, his words spilling out, sharp and unfiltered.

"How long are you going to keep helping people like that?" he blurted, his tone edged with annoyance. "He's a bum, Sean. Why did you invite him? I don't want to sit at a table with someone homeless." The dissatisfaction in Greg's voice was palpable.

The words hung heavy between them, stark and jarring against the memory of Walter's fragile gratitude. Sean's steps slowed, the sting of Greg's comment settling like a stone in his chest. The contrast between the simple act of kindness and Greg's harsh reaction created an invisible divide, thin but undeniable, as if they were suddenly standing on opposite sides of something much larger than the sidewalk beneath their feet.

Sean came to an abrupt stop, his footsteps halting with a sharp finality. He turned to face Greg, his expression carved from a mixture of disappointment and quiet, unwavering resolve. The easy camaraderie they'd shared moments ago had shifted, replaced by something heavier, something rooted deep within him.

"Greg," he said firmly, his voice steady, carrying the weight of conviction. "Everyone deserves a little kindness. You don't know his story—you don't know what he's been through." His gaze didn't waver,

holding Greg's with a quiet intensity that made the words impossible to dismiss. "And maybe, just maybe, a small gesture like this could make a difference."

The words lingered in the air, not sharp like Greg's had been, but solid, anchored in something deeper than frustration. It wasn't just about Walter anymore. It was about the kind of people they chose to be when no one was watching.

Greg sighed, the tension in his shoulders easing slightly as he shook his head, though the frustration lingered in his furrowed brow. He didn't say anything more, the weight of Sean's words settling between them like an invisible barrier, quiet but undeniable.

Sean shifted his gaze forward, his eyes fixed on the path ahead, a steady determination etched into the lines of his face. His voice, when he spoke again, was calm and unwavering, a reflection of the principles he refused to compromise.

"Don't worry," Sean said, his tone gentle yet resolute. "He's a good guy. He's just a man, like us. I think he's lost hope, and that's all."

The simplicity of his words carried a quiet power, the kind that didn't need to shout to be heard. It was a reminder, not just to Greg, but to himself, that sometimes, the smallest acts of kindness could be the only thread holding someone together. And for Sean, that was reason enough.

Greg glanced at Sean, the sharp edge of his irritation dulling, though a flicker of skepticism still lingered in his eyes. His posture eased slightly, but the crease in his brow hinted at thoughts left unspoken, questions he wasn't ready to voice. Despite the lingering tension, something in Sean's calm conviction seemed to chip away at Greg's stubbornness, if only a little.

Sean, undeterred, continued walking with steady, measured steps, his expression marked by a quiet sense of purpose. The cool morning air brushed against his face, but it was the warmth of his belief that carried him forward—that even the smallest act of kindness, a gesture as simple as sharing a meal, could plant a seed of hope in someone lost to despair. He didn't need Greg to understand, not fully. It was enough that he knew, deep in his heart, that compassion mattered, even when no one else believed it did.

They both headed to work in silence, the remnants of their conversation hanging in the air like an unspoken echo, heavy yet fragile. The hum of the city around them did little to fill the void left by the words they hadn't said. When they arrived at the towering glass building, they exchanged a quick, wordless nod—a gesture more out of habit than connection—before parting ways.

Sean made his way to the elevator, the familiar ding marking the start of another routine day. He rode up to the third floor, the doors sliding open with mechanical precision, welcoming him back to the predictable comfort of his office. He settled into his chair, the same view, the same desk, the same rhythm—but his mind drifted, the morning's encounter with Walter lingering like a faint aftertaste he couldn't shake.

Greg, meanwhile, stepped off one floor below, the elevator doors closing behind him with a soft, final hiss. The excitement of his new role felt distant, dulled by the weight of his earlier thoughts. As he entered his new office, sleek and freshly organized, he couldn't ignore the faint echo of Sean's words, replaying in the back of his mind like a song he didn't want to admit he remembered.

Sean needed to check his schedule for the day, so he walked past the secretary, barely sparing her a glance, his usual bright smile intact as he greeted everyone with a cheerful, "Good morning."

The familiar rhythm of the office greeted him—keyboards clattering, phones ringing, the soft murmur of conversation—a comforting background to the start of another routine day.

But just as he was about to settle into that rhythm, his supervisor, John—always lurking with a new challenge or deadline, eager to stretch Sean's limits—called out from down the hall. "Sean! I need you in my office when you've got a minute!"

Sean turned, ready to respond with his usual mix of professionalism and reluctant enthusiasm, when the secretary's voice cut through the din, her tone sharp and serious, slicing through the ordinary like a knife.

"Excuse me, Mr. Morgan," she said, her eyes meeting his with an intensity that made him pause mid-step. "Your father is on line one, and he says it's an urgent emergency. He insists he must speak with you immediately. Would you like to take the call, or should I tell him you'll call him back later?"

The words hit him like a sudden shift in gravity, pulling him out of the mundane flow of the morning. His heart quickened, a ripple of unease spreading through his chest as the office noise faded into a distant hum. Without hesitation, his mind raced through possibilities, none of them good.

Sean froze for a heartbeat, his mind racing through worst-case scenarios in the span of a breath. "No, I'll take it," he replied quickly, his voice firm but laced with a thread of concern.

He stepped toward the phone, his hand hovering for a brief moment before he picked up the receiver, already bracing himself for whatever news was waiting on the other end.

"Hello, Dad! What's wrong?" Sean's words tumbled out, sharp with worry, his heart thudding in his chest like a distant drumbeat growing louder.

"Hello, son," his father replied, his tone unusually calm—too calm, as if carefully measured. "I just wanted to let you know that your mother is in the hospital."

Sean's breath hitched, a sudden tightness gripping his chest. "Oh… no. Is it serious?" His voice wavered slightly, the panic creeping in despite his effort to hold it at bay.

"No, son, she's okay," his father reassured him gently, though the edges of worry still clung to his words. "At first, we thought it was a seizure, but luckily, it wasn't. She's doing much better now. I just thought you should know."

Sean exhaled, the tension loosening just a fraction, though his heart still raced. His father's next words settled over him like a quiet plea. "If you call her, it would mean a lot. It'll make her feel supported—and that support will make her stronger."

Sean swallowed hard, the weight of those words anchoring him. "Of course, Dad," he replied softly, his voice steadier now, but the undercurrent of emotion remained. "I'll call her right away."

Sean let out a breath he didn't realize he'd been holding, the tension in his chest easing just slightly. "Thank you for letting me know, Dad. I'll call her right away."

Then, with a flicker of confusion cutting through his concern, he asked, "Anyway, why didn't you call me on my cellphone?"

"I called three times and left messages," his father replied, his voice steady, though tinged with the exhaustion that comes from worry held too long. "I called your home, too, but didn't leave any message. I thought maybe it's better if I call you at work."

Sean rubbed the back of his neck, guilt creeping in for missing the calls. His father calmly recited the hospital's phone number and his mother's room number, his tone meticulous, as if anchoring himself in the facts to stay grounded.

Before hanging up, his father added reassuringly, "Don't worry, son. She's perfectly all right. The doctor just wants her to stay in the hospital as a precaution, and they want to run more tests from head to toe. Otherwise, there's nothing wrong with her. Trust me."

Sean nodded instinctively, even though his father couldn't see him, gripping the phone a little tighter. "Okay, Dad. Thanks. I'll call her now."

But despite the reassurance, his heart still felt like it was wrapped in a tight fist, the words "perfectly all right" echoing in his mind, fighting against the lingering fear that maybe, just maybe, things weren't as simple as they seemed.

Sean nodded to himself, a fragile thread of composure holding him together. "Thanks, Dad. I'll call her right away," he murmured, already reaching for his phone as if the act alone could ground him.

But as he ended the call, the weight of his father's words crashed over him like a silent wave, drowning out the familiar sounds of the office around him. The world blurred at the edges—voices faded into distant echoes, footsteps became muffled thuds against an invisible barrier. His mind, usually sharp and quick, was now a blank canvas smeared with streaks of panic. His chest tightened, breaths coming shallow and uneven, as if the air itself had thickened.

Somehow, guided more by instinct than awareness, he found his way to a chair. His legs buckled slightly as he sank into it, his hands trembling faintly, still clutching the phone like it was the only thing tethering him to reality. The room spun gently around him, not with dizziness but with the disorienting weight of fear—fear-the kind that grips you from the inside, quiet and suffocating. He stared ahead, unseeing, as his heart raced, not from exertion but from the crushing uncertainty of what if.

"Sean!" His supervisor, John, called out sharply, his voice cutting through the fog clouding Sean's mind, jolting him back to the present.

Sean blinked, his vision slowly sharpening as if someone had adjusted the focus on a lens. "Yes, I'm alright," he replied weakly, though the tremor in his voice betrayed him, thin and fragile like a thread stretched too tight.

John didn't buy it. His usual brisk, authoritative demeanor softened as he crossed the room, his footsteps steady but gentle. He rested a hand on Sean's shoulder, the gesture more paternal than professional, a quiet anchor amidst the storm swirling inside Sean's chest.

"Is there anything wrong?" John asked, his tone low, laced with genuine concern—a rare warmth from a man known more for deadlines than empathy.

Sean stared ahead, his thoughts a tangled mess, words caught somewhere between his heart and his mouth. He didn't respond immediately, his mind still racing to process the weight of the news.

Sensing the hesitation, John gave his shoulder a light squeeze and added softly, "Is there anything I can do for you, Sean?"

The simplicity of the question chipped away at the wall Sean was trying to hold up. His throat tightened, and for a moment, he wasn't an employee with tasks and deadlines—he was just a son, trying to hold himself together when everything felt like it was falling apart.

Sean looked up at John, his eyes shadowed with worry, his voice barely a whisper. "Thank you... My mother is in the hospital." Just then, his cellphone rang, making him flinch with a start. He glanced at the number, but the screen read: "The number is spam." With a sigh, he shoved the phone back into his pocket.

John's expression softened even further, the usual stern lines of his face giving way to genuine empathy. "I'm so sorry to hear that," he said quietly, his hand still resting gently on Sean's shoulder, grounding him in the moment. "Take all the time you need. Let me know how I can help."

Sean nodded faintly, his throat tight, managing to say, "Thank you for your concern."

John offered a small, reassuring smile, his voice steady but warm. "I'd be glad to help whenever you need it." With one last supportive squeeze to Sean's shoulder, he turned and made his way back to his office, leaving Sean with a fragile sense of comfort amidst the storm still brewing inside him.

Sean entered his office, closing the door softly behind him as if afraid any sudden sound might shatter the fragile calm he was trying to hold onto. He sank into his chair, his hands trembling slightly as he reached for the phone, the cool plastic grounding him in the present. His fingers hesitated for a brief second before he dialed the hospital's number, his pulse quickening with each digit pressed.

After providing the operator with his mother's room number, the line clicked, followed by a faint hum that seemed to stretch longer than it should. Each ring felt like an eternity, his heart pounding in sync with the rhythm of the unanswered call.

Then—click.

"Hi, Mom," Sean blurted out the moment he heard her voice, relief rushing through him like a tide but tangled with the stubborn knots of lingering concern.

"I heard the news. Are you okay? Dad told me what happened, and I'm so glad it wasn't serious. Do you have any pain now?" His words spilled out in a breathless rush, as if speaking them quickly enough might chase away the fear still lodged in his chest.

"Hi, sweetheart," his mother replied gently, her voice a balm, soft and familiar, though laced with a faint weariness that didn't go unnoticed.

"I asked your father not to call you, knowing it would only make you worry. But don't worry, Sean—I'll be fine." She paused, as if letting her words settle, then added with a warmth that reached through the phone and wrapped around him like a soft blanket, "I feel great today, and in a few days, I'll be going home."

Sean closed his eyes for a moment, the tightness in his chest easing just enough to breathe. Her words, simple as they were, carried the weight of reassurance he desperately needed. He exhaled deeply, the tension in his chest loosening with each of his mother's calm, reassuring words.

"I'm so glad to hear that, Mom. Just focus on getting better, okay?" His voice softened, the weight of worry shifting, but not entirely gone. Then, without thinking, the words burst out, raw and impulsive. "I'm going to see you soon. I'll take the first available flight."

There was a pause on the other end, filled only with the faint hum of the hospital room. "Oh, Sean," his mother replied gently, her voice touched with warmth and a hint of longing.

"As much as I dream of seeing you, nothing would bring me greater joy than having you close. It's been far too long." She paused, her voice shifting, a quiet attempt to offer solace in return. "But I don't want you to risk your job for me. I'll be alright."

But Sean's mind was already made up. His grip on the phone tightened, his resolve solidifying with every beat of his heart. "I'm going to see you soon," he said firmly, his voice steady and leaving no room for argument. "I'll see you soon."

The finality in his words hung in the air, undeniable and absolute, as if spoken into stone. There was nothing more to discuss—his heart had made the decision long before his words had caught up.

His mother hesitated on the other end, a mix of gratitude and concern woven into her tone. "Sean, there's no need to rush. I'm truly fine. You have work, and I don't want you to worry too much."

But Sean was resolute. "Work can wait, Mom. You're more important. I'll be there soon."

Lost in thought, his mind consumed with worry about his mother, Sean barely registered the world around him until John's voice snapped him back to reality.

"Sean!" John called out firmly, his voice cutting through the haze. "You were scheduled to work in the External Communications Hub (ECH) today?"

Sean blinked, his thoughts scattering like leaves caught in a sudden gust of wind. "Oh… yes, but I don't remember if it was for today," he replied, though his voice carried a faint undercurrent of distraction, his mind still tethered to the phone call with his mother.

John gave him a knowing look, his usual sternness softened by genuine concern. "There's been a change in the schedule. If you need a moment or some time off, just let me know. I just got a call—they've reassigned your duties for today, so you will be working on the ECH. Also, you will be featured on the news for your latest discovery this afternoon. Do you remember?" his tone uncharacteristically gentle, the words landing with unexpected warmth.

Sean sighed, running a hand through his hair, fingers raking through the tension knotted at his scalp. "That's good news. I've had a complete blank in my head today," he admitted, his voice low, tinged with frustration at his own scattered focus. Glancing at the time, a flicker of urgency crossed his face. "I think I'm already late. I'd better get going now." His cellphone rang again. He checked it, and once again, it was a spam call. He looked at John, shaking his head. "I don't know what's going on—I've had two spam calls today." John looked at him and asked: "Are you on call forwarding?" Sean said, "Yes, I am."

John smiled and said, "Maybe that's the problem. It's better if you leave your cellphone here." Then he nodded before turning to leave Sean's office.

With that, Sean straightened, pushing the weight of his worry to the back of his mind—at least for the moment—and headed toward the (ECH), his steps quick but heavy, each one echoing the thoughts he couldn't quite shake.

He quickly left his office, his footsteps echoing softly in the hallway as he made his way toward the (ECH). Tucked away on the top floors, the room was discreetly positioned, requiring special access due to its unique structure—an extension that jutted slightly beyond the building's edge, crowned with a glass dome ceiling that offered an unobstructed view of the clear sky above. It was a space designed for connection, both literal and symbolic, where the boundaries between Earth and the vast expanse beyond seemed to blur.

Sean stepped into the elevator, the metallic doors sliding shut with a soft hiss. He retrieved his ID, a sleek device resembling a short pen, and from a distance, aimed its built-in flashlight at the scanner near the entrance. Instantly, the flashlight transmitted the information to the security system acknowledged his authorization, signaling to the security cameras. Stepping closer, he pressed his ID card against the door, the plastic cool beneath his fingertips, before sliding it smoothly into the security slot.

A brief pause—then a green light blinked, signaling authorization. His fingers moved with practiced precision as he pressed the keys for the penthouse floors simultaneously, a coded sequence that granted access to only a select few.

With a low, steady hum, the elevator began its ascent, rising smoothly, the faint vibration beneath his feet the only sign of movement. As the elevator reached the top, the back door slid open with a soft whoosh, rather than the front. The entrance to the ECH was revealed as the computer announced, "PH floor. Have a good day, Mr. Morgan."

The corridor beyond was sleek and minimal, the glow from recessed lights reflecting off polished surfaces, drawing his gaze toward the glass-paneled doors that guarded the heart of the hub. Beyond them, the faint curve of the glass dome ceiling hinted at the vast sky waiting just above.

He stepped inside, swallowed by the sterile, high-tech atmosphere of the room. A faint hum of machinery pulsed in the background, mingling with the soft glow of monitors that flickered like watchful eyes, silently greeting him as he braced himself for the shift ahead.

Sean sank into his chair, his fingers instinctively reaching for the stack of messages on his desk. With practiced precision, he began inputting the data into the computer system, his focus sharpening as he selected the star he had been working on for months. But then, he changed his mind, shifting his attention to a new direction— perhaps a new planet among the endless tapestry of celestial destinations.

The complex code required for transmission unfolded under his steady hands, each sequence a testament to meticulous care. Every step was deliberate—calculating fresh distances, fine-tuning trajectories, and scrutinizing details with unwavering accuracy. It was routine for Sean, yet within the rhythm of repetition lay the silent weight of connection, stretched across the vastness of space.

Recently, he had discovered a planet with a high likelihood of supporting life. The atmosphere surrounding it suggested a strong possibility. Now, he was determined to examine the planet—and its sun—even more closely.

Engrossed in typing and meticulously organizing the data, he barely noticed the quiet hum of the room until it was broken by the soft creak of the door. John and his colleague Daniel stepped in, their footsteps whispering against the floor, subtle yet distinct in the stillness.

John stepped closer to Sean, observing him in silence for a brief moment before breaking it with a question, his voice laced with quiet concern. "Sean, how do you feel?"

Sean's fingers froze mid-keystroke. He glanced up, his gaze steady but shadowed by an unspoken weight. "I'm fine," he replied, though the subtle strain in his voice betrayed the truth beneath his words. "Just trying to stay focused."

John nodded, his expression softening with genuine understanding. "If you need to step out or take a break, just say the word," he offered quietly, his voice a gentle anchor in the room's stillness.

"Thanks, John," Sean replied with a faint smile that didn't quite reach his eyes, before turning back to his work.

His focus snapped into place as he navigated seamlessly between the screen, keyboard, and an intricate calculator. His fingers danced across the keys with practiced precision, each stroke a step closer to determining the exact distance to the newly chosen sun. The calculations were unforgiving, demanding flawless accuracy, and the weight of that responsibility settled over him like an invisible pressure.

"How long will the message take to get there?" Daniel asked, leaning slightly over Sean's desk, his curiosity sharp in the quiet room. Then he turned to John and whispered, "I was scheduled to work on the special project today. You know which one, right?" He stared at John, his brows drawn. "Why did they change it?"

John gave a small nod, then shrugged, his expression blank—either genuinely unaware or unwilling to say.

Sean's eyes remained fixed on the screen, his fingers moving with deliberate precision across the keyboard. "I'll tell you in a few minutes," he replied, his voice steady and controlled, layered with the quiet intensity of someone lost in complex calculations. Daniel nodded and stepped back, giving Sean the space he needed, while Sean's mind raced through a labyrinth of intricate calculations, each number a thread woven into the fabric of the message's journey across the vastness of space.

After a tense pause, Sean's fingers stilled. He turned to Daniel, his expression calm but shadowed with the weight of the answer. "It would take eighty-five light-years to get there," he said, his voice steady yet tinged with a quiet, reflective gravity, as if the distance itself carried more than just numbers.

Sean paused, tapping his lips thoughtfully with his finger as he stared at the number glowing on the screen. The sheer scale of the distance, the immensity of time, and the boundless stretch of space pressed on him like an invisible weight. Daniel studied him, curiosity flickering in his eyes. "What are you thinking?"

Sean exhaled softly, his gaze distant yet fixed on the screen. "Just… imagine how much can change on Earth in eighty-five light years. By the time they receive this message, who knows what their world—or ours—will look like?"

He allowed a faint, wistful smile to curve at the corner of his mouth. "Maybe by the time it gets there, we'll have figured out time travel—and reaching them will be as easy as sending a message."

Daniel chuckled, leaning back against the edge of the desk. "Wouldn't that be something? Sending a message across eighty-five light-years only to arrive before it does."

He looked at Sean and asked, "Is it even worth doing that? What would we gain?" Sean stared at him in surprise and replied, "It's not about what it does for us—it's for future researchers."

Daniel crossed his arms and said thoughtfully, "That makes sense."

Sean nodded, a faint smile tugging at the corners of his lips, his eyes gleaming with a blend of wonder and curiosity. "It's strange to think about, isn't it? How the universe might look by then—what we'll have achieved, or even who'll still be around to witness it." His voice carried a quiet awe, as if the vast unknown stretched not just across space, but through time itself.

Daniel grinned. "One thing's for sure—if we figure out time travel, you'll be the first to chart those stars."

Sean chuckled softly, the tension dissolving into the warmth of the moment. But as he turned back to his work, his thoughts lingered, still adrift somewhere in the vast expanse beyond.

Then it came—a series of faint beeps from the computer as the screen flickered off and on, signaling an incoming message. At first, they were subtle, like distant echoes, but they quickly grew louder, sharper, more insistent. Sean's fingers hovered above the keyboard, his frown deepening as he glanced at the screen. Initially, he dismissed it as a minor technical glitch, something easily corrected with a few keystrokes. But the beeping didn't stop. It became more urgent, almost rhythmic, pulsing with an intensity that set his nerves on edge.

A subtle chill crept over him, an unease threading through the familiar hum of the room. This wasn't just a system error. Something was wrong. Terribly wrong. Daniel turned to John, his voice low and tense. "Here we go again."

Sean stared at the screen, his uncertainty morphing into confusion, then spiraling into something far darker. His eyes widened, pupils dilating as lines of data streamed past, each one chipping away at his composure. His breath hitched, shallow and uneven, while his hands hovered, trembling slightly, above the keyboard—paralyzed between instinct and disbelief.

John, sensing the shift, glanced over. The change in Sean was stark and immediate—the color drained from his face, leaving his skin a ghostly pallor, his lips tinged with a grayish hue, the unmistakable mark of shock carved deep into his features. John turned to Daniel and gestured toward the room at the end of the hallway. It was as if they had been expecting this all along.

"Sean?" John's voice was cautious but edged with growing alarm as he stepped closer. "What's wrong? What's happening?"

But Sean didn't respond. His gaze remained locked on the screen, his eyes were moving left to right, eyes glassy, as if trying to see beyond the data, into the terrifying truth hidden within it. His mind raced, battling to process the impossible, yet the numbers remained the same, indifferent to his disbelief.

He couldn't hear John or anyone else around him. He stood like a statue carved from shock—rigid, unblinking, his eyes locked onto the screen as if tethered to the revelation before him, one that was both terrifying and exhilarating.

"Sean! Answer me!" John's voice rose, sharp with urgency, but it was little more than a distant echo, swallowed by the deafening silence inside Sean's mind. Realizing something was terribly wrong, John moved swiftly, crouching beside Sean to follow his fixed gaze. His eyes darted across the screen, parsing the data that had unraveled Sean's composure. The shift in John's expression was immediate—confusion giving way to alarm, and then to sheer urgency.

Without a second's hesitation, John shot to his feet, his chair scraping harshly against the floor. He lunged for the phone, his fingers punching in the number with mechanical precision. The line clicked, and his voice came out tight, clipped, every word weighted with the gravity of the moment.

"This is John McAllister from the External Communications Hub. We have an emergency again—immediate action is required."

The tension in the room was palpable as Sean remained motionless, while John worked swiftly to escalate the situation.

Without missing a beat, John dialed another number, his voice firm and commanding. "Mr. Newman! Stop whatever you're doing and come to the (ECH) immediately." He hung up before waiting for a response, urgency driving his every move.

John returned to Sean, who remained frozen, silent, and visibly shaken. Only his eyes were moving on the computer screen, but then, as if in slow motion, Sean turned his head toward John.

"It's unbelievable—we've received a message from outer space. Where exactly, I still need time to figure out." Sean murmured, his voice trembling. "It happened millions of years ago? It didn't happen six months ago. That's not possible. There's something wrong. There must be something wrong."

John placed a steadying hand on Sean's shoulder, his own unease growing. "Sean, what are you talking about? What did you see?" he asked, trying to anchor him back to reality.

Sean pointed a shaky finger toward the screen, his words barely audible. "The signals... the message! They're not from six months ago—they're from millions of years ago. How is that even possible? Who could reset our world? Did they make a mistake, and that's why they had no choice but to start it all over again? What does that even mean?"

The message on the screen scrolled on, its words seemingly endless. John joined them and read aloud, his voice tinged with confusion.

"Dear Receiver,

We acted swiftly, following your instructions, intending to reshape your world for the better. Yet, after initiating the procedure, we lost contact. At first, we feared the worst—that your world was lost to us. But now, after six months of relentless effort, we have succeeded. We are prepared to try again."

The message kept going.

"I will not reveal everything, but know this: the benefits are real, tangible, and undeniable. Your land, once barren and forsaken, will flourish. Crops will thrive where none could before. Sickness? A relic of the past. Germs and bacteria will cease to exist.

Do not hesitate. The choice is simple—one press of a button. We await your reply. Time is... fleeting. Thank you."

John finished reading and glanced at Daniel, then turned to Sean, their eyes silent but filled with unspoken questions. Before either of them could say a word, the door creaked open, and Mr. Newman stepped into the room, his presence sudden and commanding. Mr. Mark Newman was the Chief Research Officer (CRO).

"There's better be a good reason for summoning me here," Mr. Newman exclaimed, his tone laced with impatience.

"Who are these people?" Sean asked, his voice laced with suspicion.

"Don't worry about it," John replied, his gaze steady. "We'll figure out who's behind these messages."

"But this isn't ordinary, is it? It just appeared out of nowhere?" Sean pressed. "You know better than anyone that no one has access to these computers."

"I know, but I think you're overthinking this. There's nothing to worry about," John said, his voice calm. He paused, then added, "You've been working so hard lately, and with your mother in the hospital, it's no wonder you've become so tense."

Mr. Newman walked over to Sean's computer and stared at the screen. He read through the entire message from beginning to end, then turned to John and asked, "Did you talk to the FBI, CIA, FABI, SMI, or TCI?"

John nodded. "Yes. They said they'll track the origins of the message. They said they receive these kinds of tricks every day." Mr. Newman nodded, then asked again, "When did the last one come?" John replied, "This is the third day in a row."

Sean looked at Mr. Newman, then at John. "Are you kidding me? Read it again. No. This message isn't from this world—or anyone on it. How hard is that to understand? It came from… out there. As you're well aware, this system was never intended for online connections—its purpose lies in the external world. Thus, access is restricted from the public, and not even a hacker could penetrate these systems." Sean tried to calm himself down, then continued:

"They said they tried this six months ago and thought they destroyed us. But here's the thing—our world was destroyed millions of years ago, almost at the same time when no one was here. You know… dinosaurs? Who are these people? How are they, that their six months equals millions of our years? And the scariest part—who sent them a message from here? Millions of years ago?"

Sean glanced between John and Mr. Newman as he continued, his voice steady: "I've started to believe that the discovery in Tisul, deep in the heart of Siberia, wasn't a myth after all. Maybe… it was the truth." Daniel's interest was rising. "I've heard about it, but what's the real story? Do you know about it?" Sean nodded slowly, then leaned forward across the table, lowering his voice like a man about to confess something forbidden.

"It was 1969," he began, his tone steady but ominous. "Somewhere in a coal mine near a place called Tisul, in the heart of Siberia. A group of miners hit something they weren't expecting—solid marble. Perfectly sealed. Perfectly out of place." Daniel raised a brow. "Marble? That deep underground?" "Seventy meters," Sean said, nodding. "They pried it open and found something that changed everything... or should've. Inside was a coffin, and in that coffin lay a woman. Not a skeleton. Not a mummy. A woman. Young, maybe thirty. Her skin was flawless. Her hair was dark and silky. Her eyes... still open. Blue, clear, and somehow alive." Daniel blinked. "You're kidding." John angrily said, "This is a myth."

Sean looked at Daniel when he said, "I wish I were." Sean continued: "She was dressed in white, a gown embroidered in some strange, colorful patterns—nothing anyone had ever seen before. And she wasn't just lying there. She was floating... in a pinkish liquid, like some kind of preservation chamber."

"Preserved?" Daniel whispered. "Like, cryogenics?" Sean nodded. "Something like that. But here's the twist: beside her head was a rectangular object—smooth, metallic. People say it looked exactly like a smartphone." John laughed once, then stopped. Sean wasn't smiling.

"The Soviets came in fast. Shut it all down. Hauled the whole thing off. The miners who saw it were silenced. Some say they disappeared. Others say they were told it was a geological anomaly. But Sean leaned in closer. "There were whispers... that when they tested the materials, the readings came back saying it was 800 million years old."

Daniel froze. "That's impossible. Humans didn't exist then."

"Exactly," Sean said. "That's what they want you to think. Some believe she was a visitor from another world. Others say she was a time traveler. Or a remnant of a forgotten civilization—one more advanced than anything we know." John stared at him for a long moment. "And you believe it?" Sean's eyes darkened with something that looked a lot like certainty. "I believe the world hides more than it shows. And this... I believe it wasn't a myth. It was a cover-up. The message we received today proved it—it was the truth."

Sean turned to look at the message again: "They called her Princess of Tisul," Sean said. "But what if it wasn't a myth? What if it was a warning left behind? A message misread?" He leaned forward, urgency in his eyes. "They say the body was tested. They say it dates back 800 million years ago. Long before humans were even supposed to exist. And beside her head was something strange—something metallic, rectangular. People said it looked like a smartphone... decades before those even existed."

John's voice dropped to a whisper. "Are you saying... she sent the message?"

"I'm saying," Sean whispered back, "someone did. Someone from that time... or even before it. And now the message has finally reached us. But whoever or whatever they were, they knew this moment would come." John glanced at the paper Mr. Newman held in his hand, then nodded approvingly before turning to Sean. "Listen to me, Sean!" John exclaimed, his voice firm. "I know you're under pressure at work and dealing with family issues. Honestly, I think it's best if you take some time off. You need to be with your mother and your family for a while."

John glanced at Mr. Newman, who nodded in agreement. "Sean," Mr. Newman continued, "I heard your mother is in the hospital. "I highly recommend you take some time off and visit her—you truly deserve it. Leave this matter to the professionals."

"Mr. Newman took a prepared document, ...pre-approved by a higher authority within the company...clearly indicating they had been anticipating his temporary leave, and handed it to Sean. This is a formal notice confirming that your two-week paid vacation begins immediately, effective today."

He said, his tone serious. "You won't get this chance again." He placed a hand on Sean's shoulder, his grip firm. "Have fun, son," Mr. Newman said, holding the note in front of Sean, a clear signal that the matter was settled and there would be no further discussion.

Sean took the note, looked at them one by one, then he grabbed his jacket, casting a suspicious glance at them again before rushing out of the building. He was certain the message had come from alien beings—or something even beyond this world or maybe galaxy. He was convinced that the computers inside the building, especially those within the "ECH", were impenetrable. The message gave him a sense of great hope—a hope for a great future. But as he hurried away, one question lingered in his mind: "Why was information being kept from him?"

There must be something that can be done. I have to find out who sent it, he thought, his determination growing. He needed to know if such things could really happen. His mind raced: "Could they really change our world like that? Was it even possible?"

Sean's headache was so intense, it felt as though his brain might explode. The only thing he could focus on was getting home— making an airplane reservation, taking a shower, and then resting, preparing himself for whatever tomorrow would bring.

"I'm going to take the first flight to Toronto. Mom would be surprised to see me," he mumbled to himself. Then, a thought crossed his mind: After all, maybe I really do need a vacation.

He tried to focus on anything other than what had happened today in the (ECH). But then, His mind drifted to Mary, who was relying on him. He reached his car, started the engine, grabbed his cell phone, and dialed her number.

"Hello! May I speak to Mary, please?" he asked. A woman's voice answered on the other end. "Yes, hold on for a second, please." After a couple of minutes, Mary's voice came through the phone. "Hello?"

"Hi Mary, this is Sean," he said. "I just wanted to let you know that I'm going away for a while, almost two weeks. I was wondering if you need anything for yourself or your mother. Please let me know before I depart."

"Oh, I hope it's nothing serious. But thank you for letting me know. If I need any help, I will call you for sure," Mary said. After a brief pause, she added, "Anyway, where are you going?"

"I'm going to Toronto. My mother is in the hospital," he said, his voice trailing off into silence. "Oh my God. Is everything alright with your mother?" she asked, her voice tinged with panic.

"She's alright. I just want to stay with my family for a while, and this seems like a good time to go back," he said, his voice calm.

"I'm glad she's okay, but enjoy your time with your family. I'll see you later," Mary said, her voice bright with happiness. "I will. Bye," Sean said, and they both hung up.

He recalled the first time he had seen her on the street. His mind drifted back, pulled by the weight of an unforgettable moment from his past. He could still hear the little girl's voice, soft yet urgent.

"Hello, Sir. Would you spare me some change? I need it for my mother." Sean frowned, a mix of confusion and disbelief crossing his face. "Can I ask you something personal?"

When she nodded, he continued, his voice softer now. "Why would a beautiful girl like you, barely thirteen, if that, be begging on the street at this time, in this place?"

Her eyes welled with tears, and she looked away, as if trying to shield herself from the question. "I'm sorry to bother you, Sir," she murmured, but before she could turn and walk away, Sean reached out and gently gripped her arm.

"You're not bothering me. I'm just concerned," he said, his tone insistent. "Please, just tell me. Why are you doing this?"

For a long moment, she said nothing. Then, her voice cracked, the weight of her words heavy in the air. "I need money for my mother. She has a fever... a bad one. She needs a doctor."

Tears had spilled from her eyes, her beautiful face flushed with shame and desperation. Her words had struck him like a thunderclap, and in that instant, he had understood—something darker, something more tragic than he had ever imagined.

"How much do you need?" Sean asked, his voice gentle. "Maybe one hundred dollars," she replied, her words coming out in a quiet rush. "She needs medication and soup, too."

"If I give you the money, will you go home where it's safe?" Sean asked, concern flickering in his eyes.

Her face brightened, and she nodded eagerly. Sean pulled out his wallet and handed her two hundred dollars, his gaze steady as he asked, "Where is your father?"

The girl's expression faltered, her voice shaky. "My father died last month. My mom... she had to find a job at a doughnut shop. But when she got sick, they fired her." Her words hung in the air, thick with pain. She was close to tears, struggling to hold them back.

Sean's heart tightened as he processed what she had said. He went quiet for a moment, lost in thought. Then, a warm smile spread across his face, something sincere and reassuring.

"May I ask you something else?" he said, his voice calm but firm. She met his gaze, her eyes wide and trusting. "Certainly, Sir."

"If you ever need money again," he began, "would you promise me something? Before you do something like this... anything like this... would you come to me for help?"

The girl turned bright red, her face flushed with embarrassment. After a long pause, she whispered, "Yes, thank you, Sir."

"What's your name?" Sean asked. "Mary," she replied. Then she asked him: "What's yours?"

"My name is Sean." He handed her his phone number before getting into his car. He glanced at her one last time and asked, "Do you need a ride?"

Mary looked at him with a glimmer of gratitude in her eyes, as though he were her savior, and smiled. "No, thanks. My home is very close."

"Alright," Sean said with a warm smile. "Have a good night, and take care of your mom—and yourself."

Mary gave him one of the most beautiful smiles when she answered. "I will, sir. Thanks."

They exchanged a final wave before each went their separate ways.

Since that day, almost two years ago, Sean had been consistently helping Mary and her mother, sending money each month to support them. He felt a deep sense of relief that nothing had happened to her, grateful that he had been there at the right time.

The evening before his flight, he had a light dinner, then settled down to sleep, the weight of the day's events lingering in his mind.

CHAPTER TWO

"Whispers Before the Storm"

At 7:30 the next morning, the plane touched down at Pearson Airport in Toronto. It was one of those perfect mornings in July, with the weather idyllic and the sun shining brightly overhead, casting its warm glow over the city. The day was so beautiful that it could make anyone feel like singing or dancing, filled with a sense of joy that seemed to lift the spirit.

By the time Sean arrived at the hospital, it was nearly 8:55. He picked up a bouquet of vibrant red roses and a newspaper before heading inside. The nurse at the information desk was engaged in a phone conversation, her attention elsewhere as he approached.

When she finally hung up, the nurse turned to Sean. "May I help you, sir?"

"Yes, please," Sean replied. "I need to know where Mrs. Helen Morgan's room is. I believe its room 306. Could you tell me how to get to the elevator?"

She reviewed the list of patients, then looked at Sean and said, "You're correct. She's in room 306, on the third floor," she said, pointing to her left. "You can take the elevator. Just go through those doors, and you'll see the elevator."

"Thank you for your help," Sean said as he made his way toward the elevators.

He found the elevator, stepped inside, and pressed the button for the third floor. The elevator stopped at each floor, the minutes stretching as he waited. When the doors finally opened on the third floor, Sean walked straight to the nurse behind the desk. She gave him the directions to his mother's room.

The visiting hours began at 8:00 in the morning. Each room was filled with visitors. He scanned the room numbers until he found the right one. "That's it. Here I come," he murmured. "I hope I don't scare her."

He peered into the room carefully. There were several baskets of flowers, a pitcher of water, and a lovely view from the window, all while his mother lay on the bed like an angel. She was over 65, but for her age, she was strikingly beautiful. In excellent shape, with honey-green-colored eyes and brownish hair, her smooth, radiant skin made her both unique and captivating. Helen was also reclining, chatting with a young, attractive woman.

"Hello, would you like another guest?" Sean asked.

"Sean! Oh, Sean! My goodness, is that really you?" his mother asked uncertainly, stunned. "Come, let me hug you, my lovely son. I missed you so much, my darling," she said, hugging and kissing him so fervently that it embarrassed him.

"I missed you too, Mom," he said, hugging her and wiping away his tears, while Helen's face was also streaked with tears. After a moment, she glanced at the young woman standing beside her bed.

"Oh, dear. Where are my manners?" Helen said, then turned her gaze back to her son. "Sean, do you remember Donna?"

Donna was as beautiful as a model. She had blonde, highlighted hair that only added to her striking appearance. Standing taller than the average woman, she exuded an undeniable presence.

Sean jerked his head away from his mother and turned to the young woman. He paused. "Donna?" It felt as though he had seen a ghost. Donna was his cousin and his father's niece, the one who had tormented him and his sister when they were little. She was cruel, and Sean had always hated her. He knew she worked for the government, but he had no idea what exactly she was doing for them. "Maybe they only use her for the interrogation room, so she can torment the victims and extract the information they need through that twisted mind of hers." The thought made Sean chuckle softly. Then he turned to Donna when he said:

"Yes, of course, I remember her. How could I forget her?" he said, his voice laced with sarcasm and shock at seeing her in his mother's room.

"Hello, Sean. It's nice to see you here. It's been a long time, almost since grade six. You've changed a lot," she said, gathering her things and walking over to her aunt. "I have to go, Aunt Helen. I'll see you again. I have to see a patient in this hospital, too."

Helen kissed her again. "I'll be glad to see you again," she said. With that, Donna nodded goodbye to Sean and left the room.

"Are you all right, son?" Helen asked, noticing Sean was still staring in Donna's direction. "Yes, I'm okay. Don't worry," Sean replied, frowning. He then looked at his mother, and his face softened, returning to its usual calm.

"The important thing is that I'm here beside you, the greatest lady on Earth," he said cheerfully. "Sean, dear, would you please open the window?" Helen said, feeling very hot.

"Yes, Mom," Sean replied. He opened the window just a crack, then glanced outside. He saw Donna crossing the street, talking to a man. Sean turned back to his mother, about to ask her about Donna, but then paused. He reminded himself that he was there to cheer her up, not to question her.

"Come here beside me and tell me about yourself and your job. I want to know everything. I'm all yours, and I'm listening," Helen said.

"Oh, Mom, I love my job, and everything is perfect. The only thing is that I miss you, Dad, and Sharon. I miss the old times when we used to be together. I miss everything," Sean said. When he finished speaking, he took a deep breath, his face breaking into a big smile. "Where's Dad?"

"He went to the cafeteria to have breakfast," Helen replied with a satisfied smile.

Although Sean wanted to make his mother feel better, the conversation pulled his mind back to his job. He couldn't stop thinking about the secret behind the message he had received at (ECH). It lingered in his thoughts, distracting him despite his efforts to focus on his mother.

Helen looked at her son, and it was clear that he was struggling with something. "Sean, I'm so happy you're here, but at the same time, it saddens me to see you so disappointed. What's wrong?" she asked, her voice full of curiosity.

But Sean's mind was elsewhere. He couldn't hear Helen; his thoughts were consumed by the puzzle at work, the mystery of the message from.

"Sean! Are you listening? What's wrong? Are you OK? Sean...?" Helen called, her voice growing louder.

He looked at her, noticing the concern in her eyes. "Sorry, Mom. I didn't want to worry you. It's just that I'm very tired. I didn't mean to upset you." He was angry with himself, thinking that he should be helping her feel better, not adding to her worries.

The door swung open, and a middle-aged man appeared before them. He was strikingly handsome for his age, and even without his uniform, it was clear to anyone that he was a police officer. The way he spoke and moved exuded a unique confidence. He had retired the previous year, but he still enjoyed researching everything that piqued his interest.

"Sean! I didn't know you were coming! It's great to see you." He walked toward Sean and embraced him.

Sean stood up and returned the hug. "Dad! I'm glad to see you, as always."

They chatted for a long time, covering nearly everything, before deciding to head to the cafeteria, giving Helen some time to rest.

"Well, Dad, how is she? Was it a heart attack or, seizure? What's the doctor's opinion?"

"Don't worry, Sean. She'll be okay. They still don't know what caused the seizure, but they're running tests to find out."

They sipped their coffee, both trying to look in different directions. James was anxious to ask his son so many questions, but wasn't sure if it was the right time. He glanced at Sean's unhappy face, then couldn't wait any longer.

"Sean, is everything alright at work?" he asked, his concern clear. "Yes, Dad. Of course, everything is all right. Why?" Sean stared at his father.

"Nothing serious, son. It's just very unusual to see you here at this time of year. Honestly, since you moved to the US two years ago, this is the first time you've been here." James kept looking at him

"Yes, I know. I'm here for Mom, and also, I missed you all," Sean answered.

James opened his mouth to ask something when the lights in the cafeteria suddenly started flickering on and off. It lasted for several seconds. During that time, everyone paused, and murmurs filled the air.

One complaint seemed to echo from all corners. "It's happening again. When are they going to fix this?"

"This is the hospital? Damn it!" someone yelled.

A full-figured lady, carrying her plate to a table, stopped in her tracks and stood still. "What's happening?" she cried, then made her way to the first empty seat and waited until the flickering stopped.

"People don't read newspapers," James said with a grin. Sean looked at his father and asked, "What's the news, Dad?"

"You mean, you haven't read about it yet?" James replied, looking at his son in surprise. "Yes, Dad. But I don't know about this one," Sean answered.

"Would you please tell me everything you know about this incident? It must've been big news, and I'm aware of it."

James loved explaining the news. He always prided himself on being the first to know about everything. Leaning back in his chair and crossing his arms, he began to tell Sean the story, as if he were about to announce an important discovery.

"Well, son, it all happened last week in North York. They're calling it the mystery blackout in North York. A ten-year-old boy named Kevin Thomas had some connection to those electrical problems."

"What kind of connection?" Sean asked impatiently.

"Well, it happened a few times before the main incident; this time it was different. His mother, terrified, finally called 911 to request an ambulance. What happened that night is still a mystery, only the boy and his mother know the truth. The police, though, are certain there's a connection between the boy and the electrical problems, but they can't explain it. They're baffled, unable to prove anything, and don't have any answers yet. But rest assured, they're working around the clock to crack this case."

Sean was listening seriously, "You know, Dad, I actually came across this news when I was in the US, but it was just a short, cryptic report. It didn't give much away. But now, I'm dying to know more. Where is the boy right now?"

James looked at him thoughtfully before replying, "They brought him here, to this very hospital, and ever since, we've been experiencing these strange electrical issues, just like the one a moment ago. It's as if his presence is causing it all."

Sean was stunned by the story. "Could it have been just a natural phenomenon? Or was this strange power of a ten-year-old boy some sort of sign from God? Could alien forces be at work?"

His mind raced with questions, each one more perplexing than the last. He had no idea what the answer could be, but the need to find out gripped him. As his thoughts deepened, an unsettling feeling crept over him. "Was this the beginning of the end of the world?" The message he had received yesterday, coupled with the mysterious power that had emerged in the boy just a week ago, could they be connected? Sean couldn't shake the feeling that something much bigger was unfolding. He had to meet this boy. "Can anybody go and visit him?" Sean asked, a hint of doubt in his voice.

"I don't see any problem with that. However, we can always ask his doctor," his father replied. "Do you want to go now?"

Sean nodded, his heart pounding with anticipation. Together, they stood up and left the cafeteria, their footsteps echoing in the bustling hospital halls. The air was thick with excitement, visiting time was still underway, and the hospital was teeming with people. Flowers, boxes of chocolates, toys, and gift boxes filled the hands of eager visitors, each one rushing to see their loved ones. The atmosphere was oddly uplifting, as if the very presence of these visitors had given the patients a renewed sense of hope. They were able to see their families, even if only for a short time each day.

As they approached Room 281, the room of the so-called miracle boy, Sean couldn't shake the feeling that something extraordinary awaited them. It was clear that James had already been involved, as he knew exactly where the room was. The door to the room swung open and closed with an unsettling rhythm, the nurses and doctors moving in and out like clockwork, each of them attending to the mysterious boy. Sean's pulse quickened. "What was it about this child that had set the world spinning in such strange ways?"

Sean peered cautiously into the room. The hospital equipment surrounding the bed was all turned off, and the room had no power, creating a stark contrast with the cold, metallic presence and the boy lying there. Sean stepped closer, his curiosity growing with each passing moment. The bed was positioned next to the window, offering a glimpse of the world outside.

The boy appeared no older than ten, though his frail frame made him seem even younger. His dark hair framed his pale face, and his skin was almost unnaturally white. He was small, far too small for his age, and his eyes were fixed on the window, as though he could see something far beyond it, something that Sean couldn't.

The boy didn't seem to notice anyone else in the room, lost in whatever thoughts were consuming him. Sean's chest tightened. There was something about this boy, something that felt both otherworldly and deeply mysterious.

Sean couldn't shake the feeling that he had known the boy for a long time, even though they had never met. There was something about the way the boy watched the birds and squirrels outside, as if he shared their thoughts, felt their movements, and understood their quiet, fleeting world. It was as if a deep, unspoken connection existed between them, one that transcended words.

Sean felt drawn to him, a powerful need to understand him, to uncover what lay behind those quiet eyes. He would have done anything to get closer, to learn what made this boy so uniquely different from anyone he had ever known.

When he quietly slipped inside for a better view, he noticed a strikingly pretty woman standing by the boy's bed. She was watching him intently, her presence calm yet commanding. Nearby, an elderly doctor, short and frail, with bony fingers that seemed almost too delicate for his profession, was asking the boy a series of questions. The boy, however, appeared to be doing his best to ignore the doctor, his gaze fixed on the window as though he were trying to escape the interrogation. The contrast between the boy's quiet resistance and the doctor's persistence only added to the mysterious tension in the room.

"You said that you didn't touch anything during or before the blackout?" the doctor asked, his voice stern yet probing.

"Yes," the boy replied with a slight grimace, his expression flickering with something unspoken.

"After or before the shock, did you feel any pain?" the doctor asked, his voice still calm but insistent.

"At exactly the same time, but only for a few seconds," the boy answered tiredly, his voice flat and uninterested. "I'm alright now. Can I go home?"

As Sean made a move to approach, a security guard stepped forward, blocking his way. "I'm sorry, sir, you're not allowed to go any further."

"I didn't know that it was a restricted area," James interrupted, his voice steady but laced with a hint of frustration.

Sean slipped his hand into his pocket and pulled out his wallet. He opened his wallet, retrieved a card, and held it up in front of the security guard. The guard examined Sean's ID card, then glanced back at him.

"Yes, sir. I'm sorry to bother you. Please go ahead, but I can't allow anybody else to go in the room with you," the security guard said, his gaze lingering on James as he spoke.

James realized it was better to make an excuse and leave. "Look, son. It's better if you go ahead, and I'll go back to your mom. She'll probably be awake by now."

"Okay, Dad. I'll meet you in Mom's room." Sean thanked him and made his way inside. He approached the lady standing beside the boy's bed. She was one of the most beautiful and captivating women Sean had ever seen in his entire life. Her dark brown hair cascaded over her shoulders, framing her face perfectly. Her large, expressive brownish-golden eyes seemed to hold a thousand secrets, and her smooth skin glowed with an almost ethereal quality. To Sean, she looked like something out of a dream.

His heart was pounding with anticipation. He extended his hand. "Hello, I'm Sean Morgan."

"Hi. I'm Julia Thomas. I'm Kevin's mother, and they shook hands as if they were old friends, the connection feeling instant.

Then, Julia pointed toward her son. "And he's Kevin."

Sean turned to the boy, extending his hand. Kevin looked up briefly before shaking it, his grip surprisingly firm for someone so small.

Julia looked at Sean and asked, "Which agency sent you here?"

Julia's voice was soft and almost girlish, sending a strange flutter through Sean's chest. He felt his heart pounding hard, and, for a moment, he couldn't bring himself to look her in the eyes. Instead, he focused on a spot on the wall as he answered her question.

"Oh no, I just had a feeling that I had to see him." The words felt wrong the moment they left his mouth, and a wave of discomfort washed over him. He could sense Julia's gaze lingering on him, and it only made him feel more uneasy.

Kevin interrupted, his voice calm but surprisingly mature. "Don't worry, Mom. Perhaps you had felt that I needed to see someone whom I could trust."

They both looked at him in surprise. Sean, unsure whether Kevin was being serious or joking, let out a small chuckle, then turned back to Julia. The moment hung in the air, as if something unspoken had passed between them.

They both turned to the doctor as he began questioning the nurse again.

"How long did it take each shock?" the doctor asked, his tone clinical.

"It took 35 seconds this time; last time was shorter," the nurse replied, her voice steady as she took note of the details.

"And the last time?" the doctor asked, checking Kevin's pulse. "Did it take the same length of time?"

"It was almost twenty percent lighter," the nurse replied, her tone measured as she continued to monitor Kevin's condition.

Kevin turned his face to Sean, his eyes glowing with an unsettling intensity. His voice, too, was unlike that of a typical ten-year-old, carrying a depth that felt out of place. Sean couldn't help but notice how different he looked in that moment, there was something almost otherworldly about him, as if he knew the answers before anyone had asked a question.

"Who are you? And why do you want to know more about me?" Kevin asked, his gaze piercing through Sean, leaving him momentarily speechless.

"I'm just a friend, and I would be glad if you'd let me be your friend," Sean replied, feeling an unexpected sense of ease in Kevin's presence. There was something magnetic about him, an unspoken connection that made everything around them feel quieter, more focused. Sean realized, with a strange sense of clarity, that Kevin seemed to understand people in ways that went beyond mere words, he could read the emotions on their faces, the subtle shifts in their voices, as if he saw into their very souls.

"Do you want to ask me some questions too?" Kevin's voice was calm, almost inviting, as if offering Sean a glimpse into a world that only he could comprehend, a world that was both mysterious and enchanting.

"Not really. I just wanted to see you," Sean answered politely, though he couldn't shake the feeling that Kevin already knew he had been thinking of asking more questions. The boy's knowing gaze made Sean feel unexpectedly embarrassed.

"I know," Kevin said softly, his eyes locking with Sean's. "But I mean, do you know what's happening to me?" He paused, his expression darkening slightly. "You know, I had asthma my whole life... but they told me..." He hesitated for a moment, as if gathering the strength to continue. "They told me I'm as healthy as a normal kid now. It's no harder for me to breathe, and I don't have to worry anymore."

With a look of helplessness, Kevin gazed directly at Sean, as though silently asking for reassurance, yet holding onto a deeper, unspoken truth.

"It's the first time he's spoken this long since he's been here," the doctor remarked, his gaze lingering on Kevin before turning to Sean.

"Very interesting." Then, with a curious expression, he asked, "Are you a family friend or relative?"

Sean looked at the doctor, surprised by the question. "No. This is my first time seeing him. Why?"

"Because he talks to you easily, I feel he's comfortable with you," the doctor replied, his voice steady but carrying an underlying note of intrigue. "Not to anyone else."

Sean felt a sudden wave of discomfort wash over him. He hadn't expected the doctor's question to stir something deeper inside him. Realizing he had no answer to give, he felt a slight unease creep up his spine. The way Kevin had opened up to him so easily, so naturally, unsettled him. He could feel his heart rate pick up as the silence lingered, the weight of the moment pressing on him.

The boy looked at him, his expression thoughtful as he continued, "You know, I don't have to carry my medication with me all the time anymore. And you know something else? When I was sick, I didn't have to stay in the hospital, but now, when I'm healthy, they've kept me here almost a week, and I still have to stay."

With a deep sigh, Kevin turned his face back to the window, his eyes following the birds as they fluttered outside, as if seeking answers in their flight. An air of mystery weighed thick around them, pressing in from all sides.

Sean was thrilled when he saw the miracle child, especially his mother. Yet, a sense of puzzlement lingered regarding the child's condition. He couldn't discern whether it was truly a miracle or if there was a hidden secret between mother and son. It was far too soon for patients to be using nanotechnology as treatment. It wasn't even in trial yet. What could logically explain this incident? There is no real cure for asthma, he kept reminding himself.

"Sean!" Kevin called, his voice warm like that of an old friend, pulling Sean out of his silent reverie. "I'm sorry," he added.

"Are you alright?" asked Julia.

"Yes, I am," Sean answered.

The doctor and one of the nurses began to argue. "I have to run some tests urgently," said the doctor.

"Yes, doctor, but as I tried to tell you, there is no power in this room. It might harm the patient," the nurse replied.

The doctor looked at Kevin, smiled, and said, "I don't think a few minutes would harm you. How about we go to my office for a questionnaire?"

"Doctor, do I have to stay in bed? I feel great and I can walk," Kevin's voice was full of life and energy.

"Oh, my son! Of course, you can walk there. I don't see any problem with that," the doctor suggested.

Kevin slid out of bed and then jumped onto the floor. Julia was overjoyed to see her son's apparent miraculous recovery. She kept repeating, "Thank God, thank God, you gave my son his health and happiness back."

Kevin was too busy to get dressed, but he was ready to go when he saw Sean standing beside his mom. He stopped in front of Sean and asked, "Would you go with me too? I think you're okay, that's why I chose you. When you're close to me, I'm not worried."

Sean became more puzzled and asked, "What do you mean by that? You chose me?"

Kevin smiled and walked with the doctor while Sean felt an unusual comfort when he was talking to the little boy. Kevin seemed to radiate a powerful positive energy, an aura that put Sean at ease. *How does he do that?* Sean wondered. *I feel like I could get my answers through him. But how?* He nodded toward Kevin and then gestured to the doctor.

"If the doctor doesn't mind, I'd be glad to join you," Sean said.

"I don't see any problem with that if his mother is okay," the doctor replied without hesitation.

Julia smiled, and as she began to follow Kevin and the doctor, she turned to Sean and said, "I'm more than okay with that, he talked to you longer than he's ever spoken to anyone. Please, come with us."

Later, in the doctor's office, the doctor prepared various instruments to examine Kevin. He checked his blood pressure, measured his heart rate, and conducted a thorough check-up. Once finished, the doctor turned to Kevin and said, "Let's go. The real tests will begin in the next room."

Kevin looked at him, puzzled. "What kind of tests?"

The doctor met his curious gaze and said, "We're going to check if anything's wrong inside your body, or perhaps you unknowingly ingested something harmful. We'll figure out if that's what's happening to you."

"How can you see inside of me?" Kevin asked, his curiosity evident.

The doctor waved Kevin's hair and said, "We are going to use Ultrasound to see, but first we start with EEG to see what's going on with your brain."

The doctor smiled and said, "It's called an EEG. It stands for electroencephalogram. It's a test that shows us how your brain is working by recording the electrical activity inside it. It doesn't hurt at all, we just put small sensors on your head to watch how your brain sends signals."

"After that, can I go home? I'm sick and tired of staying in the hospital," Kevin said.

"Yes, I don't see any problem with that," the doctor said, giving him an assuring look before smiling.

Kevin stretched out his hand, grabbed Sean's, and, without looking at him, followed the doctor.

Julia smiled at Sean and said, "I'm amazed at how much he likes you."

Sean looked at her and smiled. When they got to the exam room, the examination began with the doctor placing small plastic discs onto Kevin's head, forehead, and specific areas on his head. Later, with different colored wires, the doctor connected each disc on his head according to its color.

"Kevin, please listen to me," the doctor said tenderly. "Just explain everything from the beginning to me."

"Oh, I've already told you everything," Kevin replied, his voice tinged with frustration.

"Yes, but this time, I need to record it and see your brain reactions. Maybe your new friend would like to hear it from you," the doctor said calmly. "This way, I won't have to ask you the same questions again."

Kevin hesitated, his expression cautious. "You promise?"

"I promise," the doctor said, his tone unwavering and serious.

"Well, it started almost four o'clock in the morning!" Kevin exclaimed, his eyes wide with intensity. After taking a deep breath, he rushed on, "At first, the shock was so weak, I barely felt it! I didn't want to wake up my mom, I figured I could handle it. But then, it happened again... every half an hour!"

"How long did it last?" Sean asked.

"It was like a flash," Kevin answered quickly. "But after a few minutes, it would come back, again and again, each time with less time between them. And each time, it got more powerful. But I could still handle it. The fifth and sixth shocks were stronger than the first, but the sixth one... I don't remember it. It must've been the most powerful. But I remember my mom was beside me, and after that, I don't remember anything else."

Kevin leaned back, his body easing into relaxation as a wave of relief washed over him, while Julia, tears welling in her eyes, watched her son, her memory suddenly rekindled.

"Which part of your body was more painful? Where was the pain more focused?" Sean interrupted again, and the doctor, however, was pleased with the questions and, along with the others, waited attentively for Kevin's answer.

"At first, it was in my head," Kevin murmured, his voice barely above a whisper. "Then I felt it in my chest, my shoulder, my stomach... and suddenly, it was everywhere."

The doctor rose from behind his desk, his gaze flicking to Kevin's chart before shifting to the computer screen. Leaning forward, he studied the display intently, his lips parting as if to speak. But before a single word escaped, the lights wavered, flickering weakly. In an instant, the hospital equipment erupted into a frantic symphony of rapid, urgent beeps.

Sean looked at Kevin, then walked toward the doctor and shifted his gaze to the computer screen. The lines were moving very fast, and only Sean and the doctor, who were closest to the screen, could see it. His heart raced as he tried to make sense of what was happening.

Julia's screams pierced the room as she frantically yelled at the doctor, her voice raw with desperation. "Save him! Do something!" she cried, her hands trembling as she clung to the edge of the hospital bed, refusing to let go.

The doctor rushed toward Kevin, his voice sharp with urgency as he barked orders to the nurses. "Bring the sedative, now!"

He commanded, his gaze locked on Kevin, whose body trembled with uncontrollable tension. A nurse hurried forward, a syringe of lorazepam in hand, its calming effects meant to steady Kevin's racing mind and ease his distress.

Meanwhile, Sean edged closer to the computer, his eyes narrowing in disbelief. At first, he couldn't comprehend what he was seeing. The images flickered into existence, shifting too quickly to grasp. Were they pictures? A language? Some kind of script? He couldn't tell. Each new symbol was different, morphing unpredictably. But one pattern remained persistent, lines intertwining, undulating up and down like a living waveform. One thing was certain: whatever this was, it wasn't random. It was information.

Luckily, no one else seemed to notice, as they were all focused on calming Kevin down. Sean's heart raced as he studied the screen, the shapes and patterns eerily familiar. He was sure he'd seen them before, but he couldn't place where or when. The mystery nagged at him, but he had no time to investigate further as the chaos around him intensified.

Not wasting a second, Sean slid into the chair in front of the computer. His mind raced, but he couldn't quite grasp what was unfolding on the screen. The images were cryptic, like fragments of a puzzle he wasn't sure how to solve. But something deep inside told him to act fast. Without thinking twice, he hit the print button, watching the paper emerge, each page adding to the mystery.

As the office slowly returned to normal, the doctor and staff focused on Kevin, unaware of what had just transpired. Sean grabbed the printout, his hands trembling slightly, and tucked it securely into his jacket, as if the paper itself held secrets he wasn't ready to share. Something told him that these images held the key to something far larger, and he was determined not to let it slip through his fingers. He knew that if the government caught wind of these messages, they'd bury it all, shutting out anyone else who got too close.

When everything came to a halt and Kevin opened his eyes, the doctor looked at him and asked, "How do you feel, Kevin?" His voice was anxious, his brow furrowed with concern.

Julia's face was streaked with tears, her eyes wide with worry. Nurses rushed in and out of the room, their movements frantic, while outside the door, a crowd of people had gathered, their hushed voices adding to the tension in the air. The scene felt charged with uncertainty, and everything seemed to hang in the balance.

Kevin remained unresponsive, despite the doctor's repeated calls. After a moment of growing tension, the doctor motioned to the nurse to bring another shot for injection. Just as they were about to proceed, Kevin's eyes fluttered open, and he weakly looked at the doctor.

He was barely able to speak, his voice faint and strained. "This time it was painless. I don't know how I managed to control the pain... but I had this feeling, like something was going through my brain."

His words trailed off, and his body went limp, unable to move. Julia's screams filled the room as she desperately called her son's name.

Finally, Kevin, exhausted and barely able to lift his head, slowly turned toward his mother. In a whisper, barely audible, he said, "Don't worry, Mom. I'm okay... I'm just really tired."

Sean looked at Julia's pale, helpless face, her eyes filled with fear and uncertainty. He moved toward her, his steps slow and deliberate, and placed a gentle hand on her shoulder. Julia suddenly burst into tears, her body trembling with emotion. Without a word, Sean pulled her into his arms, offering her the comfort she desperately needed. Julia's sobs softened as she leaned into him, feeling a small sense of relief.

As Sean held her, he studied her beautiful, tear-streaked face, his voice barely above a whisper. "Julia, I know it sounds crazy, but I think someone... or something is... is trying to contact Kevin. There's no harm to him, but you have to promise me, you won't tell anyone about what we've talked about."

Julia pulled back slightly, her brow furrowed in confusion. "How do you know? Is there something I don't know?"

Sean smiled faintly, his expression serious. "I can prove it. Listen, try to take Kevin home tonight. If the intelligence services find out about him, they won't leave you in peace. They might even take him without your consent, he'll become nothing more than a subject for their experiments."

Julia's eyes widened as the weight of his words sank in. She was lost for words, trying to grasp what Sean had just revealed to her.

The doctor's ears were sharper than Sean had realized, and every word he spoke was heard. Without warning, the doctor turned and addressed the room. "Everyone, out," he commanded.

As the last person left and the door clicked shut, the doctor locked it with deliberate calm. He faced Sean, his eyes narrowed with growing suspicion. "What do you mean by 'make contact'? Are you talking about Kevin's body, his mind?"

Sean froze, caught off guard. He had spoken so quietly to Julia, keeping his voice low and careful. But now, with the doctor's penetrating gaze on him, his thoughts spiraled. He glanced at the doctor, his voice steady but carrying an underlying tension.

"I mean... something… or someone, from another world is trying to reach through Kevin. They've found a way to use him. And I'm not sure how or why, but its happening."

The room seemed to grow colder as Sean spoke, the weight of his words hanging in the air. The doctor's expression shifted, disbelief crossing his face, before something more complex flickered in his eyes.

Sean hesitated to reveal the printout, fearing it would be seized for examination, only leading to more trouble for Kevin. He was on the verge of speaking when suddenly, the computer emitted a sharp beep, signaling a new message. Everyone jumped in surprise. Sean's eyes snapped back to the screen, his pulse quickening as a stream of unfamiliar words appeared, each one shifting, changing, written in what seemed like an entirely different language every time.

His gaze shifted to Kevin, a question forming on his lips, but before he could speak, Kevin's mother broke down in tears, her sobs echoing in the tense room.

"Do you mean his body is haunted by ghosts, or some sort of evil spirit?" she cried, her voice trembling with fear.

"Not at all! That's not what I meant," Sean responded quickly, his voice filled with regret. "It was just a suggestion... I'm truly sorry if I frightened you."

He immediately regretted speaking aloud, the weight of his words sinking in as he tried to reassure her, his own discomfort growing.

Julia covered her mouth with her hands, her voice trembling as she whispered, "No! It can't be evil. It must be something good. It gave Kevin his health back. It has to be something special, something positive." She spoke with a desperate hope in her eyes.

Sean moved closer, trying to soothe her. "Julia, I'm sorry if I confused you," he said gently. "I know it's not a demon. We know that because of the power we're seeing. Whatever it is, your son is going to have a long and normal life. You don't have to worry."

His words, though meant to reassure, carried the weight of uncertainty, but he hoped they would bring her the comfort she needed.

The doctor stood there, clearly baffled. He couldn't understand what Sean was doing in the room, especially considering the situation with Kevin. At the very least, he should have been offering comfort, not posing questions about the boy's condition. With growing suspicion, the doctor approached Sean, locking eyes with him, his expression hardening.

"May I ask," the doctor began, his voice sharp, "who you are, what you're doing here, and why you're asking so many questions about my patient?"

Sean felt a flush of embarrassment creep up his neck. Realizing the tension in the room, he took a deep breath before responding. With a formal tone, he introduced himself.

"I apologize," he said. "My name is Sean Morgan. I work for a space research center in the U.S."

The doctor's gaze didn't waver as he absorbed the information, his mind still racing with confusion and doubt.

"You mean NASA? Are you saying Kevin has some kind of connection to aliens, or do you think they might try to abduct him?" Julia asked, her voice rising with a mix of confusion and fear.

Sean looked at her, momentarily taken aback. When Julia was upset, she seemed even more striking, her emotions only heightened her beauty. No one wanted to make her angry, least of all Sean. Her eyes, full of innocence and worry, made him feel protective, and he didn't want to hurt her feelings.

"No, Julia!" Sean said quickly, trying to reassure her. "As I told you, it's just an idea, nothing more. I am here independently, representing neither an individual nor a company. I'm here because my mother is sick, and she's on the third floor. I just came down here out of curiosity, that's all."

His voice softened with sincerity as he hoped his words would calm her, not realizing how deeply his own doubts were beginning to intertwine with the situation.

Sean felt the weight of discomfort pressing on him. His answers only seemed to deepen the tension in the room, and he couldn't help but wonder if they were ready to hear the truth. Maybe I'm not ready to say it either, he thought to himself.

The doctor finally opened the door, and the nurse stepped in, positioning herself beside him. Her gaze quickly landed on the printer, where a stack of freshly printed pages lay. Hesitantly, she picked up the printouts, holding them uncertainly in her hands. Her eyes darted between the doctor and Sean, searching for guidance, as if waiting for someone to tell her what to do next.

Breaking the silence, Sean looked at her and asked, "May I see them?"

His voice was steady, but the uncertainty in his chest lingered. He needed to understand what was happening, but the moment felt like it was slipping further out of his control.

The nurse glanced at the doctor, seeking his approval. The doctor paused for a moment, his gaze intense as he weighed the situation. After a brief silence, he took the papers from the nurse and held them out to Sean.

"I don't think that would be a problem," the doctor said, his tone shifting to one of acknowledgment. "After all, you are one of the best astronomers I've ever known." He paused, then added with a slight smile, "I thought I recognized your face from somewhere. Now I know, it's from the newspapers. I've also read your books about the universe and the future. It's a pleasure to meet you in person."

With that, the doctor extended his hand, shaking Sean's firmly. "I'm Doctor Howard."

Julia, utterly blindsided, fixed her gaze upon him, her eyes wide with astonishment. The others in the room mirrored her reaction, their attention now riveted on Sean, perceiving him in an entirely new light. Kevin's eyes, usually unremarkable, now seemed to bulge with curiosity, appearing almost unnaturally large, as if the gravity of the moment had warped reality itself.

Dr. Howard extended the remaining documents to Sean, and together they scrutinized the printout. Sean's eyes flitted rapidly across the enigmatic symbols and cryptic phrases, his mind racing to decipher the unfolding mystery.

Dr. Howard's voice, tinged with curiosity, broke the silence as he gestured toward the enigmatic images on the printout. Sean leaned in, his gaze narrowing as he examined the cryptic symbols. "I'm not certain," he murmured,

His tone was thoughtful yet laced with uncertainty. "But observe the structure… they're interconnected. It suggests they might form an alphabet or perhaps a language."

Sean's eyes lingered on the intricate patterns, each glance deepening the enigma before him. The symbols exuded an almost supernatural aura, as if whispering secrets from another realm.

"May I keep these, Dr. Howard?" Sean inquired, his voice low but brimming with urgency.

"Certainly," Dr. Howard replied, his tone softening. "You may keep them along with the initial prints that emerged."

A flush of embarrassment washed over Sean; he had believed his earlier actions had gone unnoticed.

Dr. Howard continued, "I trust you to decipher the meaning behind these symbols. Also, I don't want those printouts left here or any further investigation to be initiated in the hospital."

As Dr. Howard turned to leave, he cast a solemn glance back at Julia. "If anyone can help your son decipher these images, it's him," he said, nodding toward Sean with a mixture of respect and uncertainty. Looking at Julia again, he continued, "He's right about a lot of things. Remember your husband. Keep Kevin's situation to yourself."

His words carried the weight of both hope and unspoken concern, as if he sensed that the answers might lie within Sean's grasp. With a final look, Dr. Howard addressed Sean, "Keep me informed of your progress, and if you require my assistance, don't hesitate to ask." He then exited the room, leaving an air of anticipation in his wake.

Sean approached Kevin, standing beside him as his gaze lingered on the enigmatic printout. Kevin, though still weak, exhibited a spark of curiosity in his eyes.

"Could you explain it to me as well?" Kevin inquired, his voice soft yet imbued with a genuine desire to comprehend.

Sean considered Kevin's request, recognizing that while he lacked all the answers, an instinct suggested that Kevin might be pivotal in unraveling the mystery. Taking a deep breath, he nodded, his gaze softening.

"I'll try," Sean replied, his voice steady despite his uncertainty. "We'll figure this out together. But before that, may I ask you a question?"

His tone remained calm, but his eyes briefly flicked toward Julia. Kevin followed Sean's gaze to his mother, who offered a reassuring nod, her expression gentle.

"I guess there won't be any problem," Kevin said, his tone more relaxed now, as if his mother's approval had provided him with a sense of security.

Sean leaned in closer to Kevin, his expression earnest. "Do you remember what you were thinking about before or during those shocks? Did you hear any voices or experience any unusual feelings?"

Kevin's brow furrowed as he searched his memory. "I... I can't recall exactly," he began slowly. "There was a sensation, like a buzzing in my head, and maybe... whispers? But it's all so hazy."

Sean nodded thoughtfully. "It's not uncommon for individuals who've experienced electrical injuries to report sensations like buzzing or even auditory hallucinations, such as hearing voices or noises that aren't there. These phenomena can be linked to the brain's response to electrical trauma."

He continued, "Additionally, some people report heightened emotional states or vivid sensations during such events. Understanding these experiences can be crucial in deciphering the underlying causes and effects of the shocks you've been experiencing."

Kevin listened intently, absorbing Sean's words. The pieces of his perplexing experiences seemed to be slowly aligning, offering a glimmer of clarity amidst the confusion.

Sean offered a faint smile, silently appreciating Julia's unspoken approval. He sensed that the revelations ahead would demand more than mere dialogue, and uncertainty loomed over Kevin's readiness for the forthcoming challenges. Yet, destiny had intertwined their paths irrevocably.

Sean's gaze remained fixed on the cryptic documents, his mind a whirlwind of thoughts as he endeavored to decipher the unfolding enigma. Kevin, driven by an insatiable thirst for understanding, leaned in, his anticipation palpable. His eyes widened, a mix of curiosity and disbelief coloring his voice. "All that writing came from my body?"

Sean's gaze remained fixed on the enigmatic symbols. "Frankly, I'm not sure," he replied, his tone steady despite the uncertainty. "But we will find out. And that's all that matters."

As he spoke, Sean couldn't help but consider Julia as an essential part of the equation. With her cooperation, he might unlock something extraordinary, something beyond his imagination. He knew that without her, the mystery would remain just that: a mystery.

Sean remained by Kevin's side throughout the day, vigilantly observing the boy's condition. The intermittent shocks persisted, but with heightened awareness, everyone felt more prepared. The tension in the air was palpable, yet there was a growing sense of control over the situation.

The most astonishing phenomenon occurred when Kevin approached a computer. As soon as he neared the device, peculiar images manifested on the screen, seemingly linked to him, a visual representation of the unseen forces at play. Sean couldn't shake the feeling that they were on the brink of uncovering something profound, something that could potentially alter their understanding of reality.

While the human body can emit small electrical currents, especially after exposure to electrical injuries, the direct influence of these currents on external devices like computers is not well-documented. Electrical injuries can lead to various physiological effects, including burns, cardiac arrhythmias 2, and neurological symptoms. However, the phenomenon of a person's proximity causing visual manifestations on a computer screen is highly unusual and warrants further investigation.

It's crucial to consider environmental factors that might contribute to such occurrences. For instance, ungrounded or faulty electrical equipment can sometimes cause unexpected behaviors in electronic devices. Ensuring that all equipment is properly grounded and functioning correctly is essential to rule out external causes.

Given Kevin's extraordinary condition, consulting with specialists in neurology and biomedical engineering could unravel the underlying mechanisms at play. Such a collaborative approach might yield groundbreaking insights, but it also risks drawing the attention of scientists and government agencies, entities that would likely demand further proof and potentially treat Kevin as nothing more than a test subject.

Sean, fully aware of the possible consequences, meticulously documented every side effect. He saved all the data onto the computer and printed it out, preserving tangible evidence of some form of contact, an undeniable trace left by Kevin's otherworldly, vibrating body.

The weight of the discovery was settling on his shoulders as the papers piled up. He returned to his mother's room with the stack of printouts in hand. His father, visibly excited by the news, wasted no time bombarding him with questions. His mother sat quietly, her expression unreadable but observant. "Does it excite you that you were able to see Kevin?" Helen asked gently, breaking the silence.

Sean paused, the question catching him off guard. He hadn't allowed himself to consider his own feelings amidst the whirlwind of recent events. A mixture of anticipation and apprehension welled up within him. "Yes," he replied softly, "I am."

His mother's eyes softened, understanding the unspoken complexities behind his simple affirmation. The room fell into a contemplative silence, each of them grappling with the implications of the discoveries and the uncertain path ahead.

Sean began, "I also gave Kevin's mother your home number, mentioned that I'm here visiting you, and that I'm staying at my parents' house..."

Helen interrupted with a knowing look. "Sean, I understand. My answer is yes, and of course, you did the right thing. You don't need our permission, nor do you need to explain everything to us."

Sean felt a wave of relief wash over him. His mother's reassurance was exactly what he needed.

Helen's voice was warm, her eyes filled with trust. She had always believed in her children, Sean and his sister Sharon, no matter the situation. To her, their decisions were always made with good intentions, which was all that mattered.

The night had settled into a deep darkness by the time Sean arrived at his parents' house. He closed the door softly behind him, the silence of the evening wrapping around him. Without a word, he went to the living room and sank into the sofa, his mind racing in every direction. Thoughts collided in his head, and he wasn't sure where to begin.

The weight of the day's discoveries pressed heavily on him. The enigmatic symbols, Kevin's inexplicable connection to the computer, and the profound implications of it all swirled in his mind. He felt as though he stood on the precipice of a revelation that could change everything, yet the path forward remained shrouded in uncertainty.

As he sat in the dimly lit room, the ticking of the clock the only sound, Sean grappled with a torrent of emotions. Excitement warred with apprehension, curiosity with doubt. He knew that the journey ahead would be fraught with challenges, but the potential for discovery was too great to ignore.

In that quiet moment, Sean resolved to delve deeper into the mystery, to seek answers no matter where they might lead. With his mother's unwavering support and the enigmatic connection he shared with Kevin, he felt a renewed determination to uncover the truth.

After a moment of hesitation, Sean picked up the phone and dialed several numbers, but each call went unanswered, leaving him to leave messages. Just as he was about to set the receiver down, an impulse urged him to try one more time. He dialed another number, and a young woman's voice answered, sharp and clear, pulling him from his tangled thoughts.

"Hello?" she said, her voice hesitant.

"Hello, Sharon!" Sean replied, his tone warm but tinged with excitement.

"Sean? Is it you? It's been so long since we've talked. Is that really you?" Sharon's voice carried a mix of surprise and disbelief.

"Yes, I know. I'm sorry, it's my fault. I should've called you sooner," Sean admitted, unable to hide the rush of emotion in his voice. "But I'm so glad to hear your voice again."

After a heavy pause, Sharon's voice shifted, now laced with genuine curiosity. "Where are you now?"

"I'm at Mom and Dad's," Sean responded, the familiarity of the place evoking a tidal wave of nostalgia.

"You mean you're in Toronto?" Sharon's voice quivered, barely able to contain her excitement.

"Of course I am," Sean replied, his tone sharp but urgent.

Sharon sighed deeply on the other end, the sound heavy with frustration. "What's troubling you, Sharon?" Sean inquired, his voice brimming with palpable concern. "Is everything all right?"

"Oh, it's nothing," she replied, her voice soft yet laced with unmistakable disappointment.

"It's just my boss. I'm supposed to stay here and finish my report on my recent research. But the problem is that by the time I finish everything, it'll be too late to see you tonight." Her words lingered in the air, the weight of missed moments pressing down on them.

"Don't worry, I'll be awake as long as it takes, and I'll wait for you," Sean said with his voice full of unwavering reassurance.

"That's marvelous," Sharon replied, her voice a symphony of relief. "It's 9:30 now. I'll see you around 12:45. Is that okay with you?" she inquired, her words laced with a hint of hesitation.

"Absolutely, that would be perfect," Sean responded, a smile tugging at the corner of his lips.

As they ended the call, Sean felt an unexpected surge of elation. It had been so long, and hearing Sharon's voice again rekindled a profound realization, he still loved her deeply. She was his only sister, his twin, and their bond had always been unbreakable.

"Yes, Sean. I'll see you later," Sharon said, her voice warm with affection.

They both hung up, and Sean sat back, the lingering excitement from the call slowly fading. He picked up the newspaper and began flipping through the pages. His eyes landed on an article about Kevin Tomas, who was currently hospitalized. The article detailed his condition, mentioning unexplained shocks he had been experiencing. Sean found himself reading it repeatedly, unable to shake the growing feeling that there had to be a logical explanation for what was happening to Kevin.

"There must be an explanation," he murmured to himself, the words barely above a whisper.

Sean's thoughts drifted back to the hospital papers he had printed earlier. He stood up, walked to the living room, and spread them out on the coffee table, the printouts before him resembling a complex puzzle awaiting solution.

For a long time, Sean gazed at the symbols, his mind racing. The more he looked, the more patterns emerged, apparent and distinct signs that defied immediate understanding. Some symbols resembled pictographic scripts, while others appeared to belong to different languages, perhaps even ancient ones like Akkadian3 or Babylonian cuneiform. He thought it was a language, but why hundreds of different styles?

His mind buzzed with questions as he stared at the enigmatic symbols before him. The patterns seemed deliberate, yet their meanings eluded him. He couldn't shake the feeling that these images were conveying a message, one that he was determined to decipher. The symbols bore a resemblance to ancient scripts like Akkadian or Babylonian cuneiform, hinting at a deeper, hidden narrative. Sean knew he had to piece together this puzzle to uncover the truth.

He leaned back in his chair, the enigmatic images weighing heavily on his mind. Questions swirled: Were these symbols messages from spirits? Aliens? Or perhaps even divine communications? The possibilities spun through his thoughts like a relentless whirlwind. The notion that they could be messages from God startled him, yet he couldn't dismiss it. Why Kevin? Why was he chosen to receive such messages? The mystery thickened, and Sean felt an intense urgency to uncover the truth behind it.

Sean leaned forward, his fingers lightly tracing the enigmatic symbols on the papers before him. His mind raced with possibilities:

Could Kevin possess an understanding of these messages, perhaps awaiting the right moment to disclose their meaning? Sean pondered whether Kevin was waiting for the truth to come to light when he felt ready to share his story. But questions lingered: *Did Kevin truly trust him, or anyone, enough to share something so profound? And why did he say he chose me?*

His thoughts shifted to Kevin's mother, Julia. Perhaps Kevin sensed that she wasn't ready to confront the full truth, which might explain his hesitation in sharing everything. He could likely anticipate her fear and confusion, understanding that revealing too much too soon could overwhelm her. Sean realized that Kevin's reluctance might stem from a desire to protect his mother until she was prepared to handle the information.

His realization struck him profoundly. The mystery was far more intricate than he'd initially perceived, and Kevin appeared to possess a deeper understanding than anyone had anticipated. The boy seemed to hold the key, yet it remained concealed, awaiting the right moment to be unveiled.

He paced into the kitchen, his mind a tempest of unanswered questions, each more confounding than the last. To ensure he stayed up for Sharon, he made coffee. As the coffee maker hummed, he wrestled with the enigma before him, searching for clarity that remained just elusive.

The steaming mug he eventually cradled offered little solace, its warmth unable to quell the unease gnawing at his core.

Suddenly, the phone rang, slicing through Sean's thoughts with a piercing urgency. Without hesitation, he picked up the receiver and answered automatically, "Sean Morgan speaking, how may I help you?"

"Sean? You're supposed to be on vacation!" exclaimed Greg, his deep voice brimming with surprise.

Greg stood tall, his broad frame complemented by an intentionally unkempt appearance that added to his rugged charm. His perpetually tousled hair and bushy beard contributed to a look that was both disordered and captivating. Yet, it was his voice, a smooth, velvety timbre that effortlessly drew people in, its rich resonance leaving a lasting impression.

"Yes, well, it just turned out that way," Sean replied, attempting a casual tone, though his thoughts remained distant.

"How are you, Greg? Thanks for returning my call. You're really the only person I can trust right now," he added, his words heavy with the gravity of his situation.

"Is something wrong, Sean? You seem exhausted, or perhaps disoriented. What's happening over there?" Greg's voice brimmed with concern.

"Did you receive my fax? Do you have any thoughts on it?" Sean's tone was more assertive than usual.

"Oh yes, I received it a couple of hours ago," Greg replied, his tone tinged with apology. "I wasn't home when you sent it. I just got back, saw your message, and called you immediately upon hearing your voice on the answering machine."

"So! What do you think about them?" Sean asked and immediately kept quiet.

After a brief pause, Greg continued, "Yes, I saw them, and my question is, what the heck are these? I skimmed through the materials but couldn't make heads or tails of them. Why are they so important to you?" His voice carried a note of confusion as he grappled with Sean's request.

"Greg, do they represent some kind of language? Just tell me something about it," Sean pressed, his voice tinged with urgency.

"It could be, I don't know yet, Sean," Greg replied, his tone measured. "I need more time to analyze them. Please, just a bit more time." After a pause, Greg's voice softened. "Sean, can I ask you something?"

"Sure. What is it?" Sean responded, attempting to conceal the tension in his voice. "Where did you find these papers? The symbols are... intriguing," Greg inquired, his curiosity evident by now.

Sean hesitated, weighing his response. "I'll explain it to you later, if that's alright," he said cautiously. "But please, promise me you won't discuss this with anyone."

The weight of secrecy pressed upon him as he awaited Greg's reply, "Okay, Sean, as long as I get all the info, I promise. Scout's honor! Well… I was never a scout, but you get the idea. You're my friend."

Greg responded sincerely, though concern tinged his voice, "We'll talk later. Please, be careful."

Greg's voice carried that familiar sense of unwavering support, always striving to shield Sean from trouble, no matter the circumstances.

"Thanks, Greg. I will," Sean replied, his voice now subdued as the gravity of the situation settled over him.

The line went silent, and an unspoken understanding of what lay ahead hung heavily between them. Sean poured himself another cup of coffee and settled onto the sofa, its familiar embrace offering a rare moment of solace. The cushions enveloped him, their softness reminiscent of the carefree days of his youth. As he sank deeper, the burdens of the day began to dissipate, and his thoughts meandered back to his student years, a time when life was unburdened and full of promise. The quietude of the room, punctuated only by the rhythmic ticking of a distant clock, lulled him into a gentle slumber, where past and present intertwined in the tapestry of his dreams.

In his dream, Sean perceived himself as an elderly man, his hands bony and his face etched with deep wrinkles, yet he possessed the vigor of youth. He floated effortlessly through the air, defying gravity, and willed his path through a landscape of lush greenery. Below him, vibrant bushes and trees stood in full bloom, their branches heavy with colorful fruit, creating a serene and picturesque scene.

As Sean drew closer to the trees, he noticed figures dwelling among the branches. They reached out with cold, urgent hands, grasping at him while whispering, "It's all your fault, your fault, your fault." The accusatory words echoed in his ears, laden with blame. He struggled to break free, but his strength waned, and their grip tightened, enveloping him in an overwhelming sense of guilt and helplessness.

Suddenly, a force pulled Sean away from the accusing figures, and the crushing guilt and fear dissipated. A comforting warmth enveloped him, instilling a profound sense of security. Turning, to his astonishment, he saw a light, as powerful as the sun yet as effortless to behold, standing above him and radiating an aura of power and strength.

The light grip was firm, a hand clasping Sean's arm with unwavering assurance. His presence felt almost otherworldly, as if he were guiding Sean through the storm of confusion and darkness. The tension in Sean's body eased as he looked up at it, feeling an undeniable sense of safety in its powerful hold. With all its torment, the dream seemed to fade as the light's strength enveloped him, offering peace and protection. He jolted awake, his heart pounding, cold sweat clinging to his skin like a chilling reminder of the nightmare's grip.

The remnants of the nightmare lingered, casting a heavy fog over his senses. Suddenly, the sharp slam of a car door pierced the silence, pulling him further from the dream's grasp.

Startled, Sean sprang to his feet and rushed to the window, his breath catching in his throat. Outside stood Sharon, transformed into a stunning young woman. In just a couple of years, she had become almost unrecognizable. Her dark, glossy hair cascaded over her shoulder, catching the light as she moved.

Her hair is just like Mom's, Sean thought, a wave of nostalgia washing over him. Time had passed in the blink of an eye.

As Sean watched Sharon, a pang of longing hit him. He hadn't realized how much he missed his sister until that moment. The years of separation rushed back, reminding him of their once-inseparable bond. They had always been two halves of a whole, promising to attend university together, stay close, and let nothing come between them. They joked about remaining together until death parted them.

But then, something changed. Sharon, once so committed to their shared future, decided to pursue a different field of study at university. The decision shook Sean, leaving him feeling abandoned and confused. He couldn't fathom why she had chosen a separate path, why their meticulously crafted plans had unraveled. As he stood by the window, the weight of that shift pressed heavily upon him, and he realized how profoundly it had affected him.

Sean's anger had burned hot and bitter when Sharon made her decision. He felt betrayed, their shared dreams crumbling in an instant. In his frustration, he accepted the first offer from the United States, fleeing to America against his true desires. The distance, both physical and emotional, was meant to provide space, but instead left him with a gnawing sense of shame. He later realized how selfish he had been, allowing pride to push him away from the sister he had vowed to stand by.

As Sean stood by the window, watching Sharon approach, he felt the weight of his past decisions pressing heavily upon him. Beside her walked a handsome man, taller than she, their conversation flowing effortlessly. As they neared the house, Sharon's eyes met his through the glass. Without hesitation, she waved, her smile warm and familiar, a poignant reminder of the bond they once shared. In that simple gesture, laden with unspoken meaning, Sean felt the chasm between them narrow, if only slightly.

Sean's pulse quickened with excitement. He swiftly left the living room, his steps eager as he approached the entrance. By the time he reached the door, their reflections appeared in the glass, and almost immediately, the doorbell rang. He hurried to open it, anticipation bubbling inside him.

As the door swung open, Sean and Sharon locked eyes. Without a word, they embraced, their bodies pressing together as if the years of separation had never existed. Tears welled up in Sharon's eyes, streaming down her cheeks.

"Sean!" she whispered, her voice thick with emotion. "It's been such a long time since we were last together. I've always dreamed of this moment."

Sharon smiled through her tears and motioned toward the man beside her. "Sean, I want you to meet Mark," she said, her voice filled with pride. "He's my fiancé."

Sean's eyes widened, and a genuine smile spread across his face. "That's wonderful news! Congratulations to both of you."

Mark extended his hand, his grip firm and warm and Sean grasped it firmly. "It's a pleasure to finally meet you, Sean. Sharon has told me so much about you."

"All good things, I hope," Sean replied with a chuckle, feeling the initial tension ease.

"Of course, sometimes I felt jealous," Mark said with a grin, making everyone burst into laughter.

Sean offered a proud, warm smile. "Welcome to our family," he said, his voice filled with genuine acceptance.

"Thank you, Sean," Mark replied sincerely. "I'm really happy to finally meet you. Sharon has shared so many wonderful things about you. I also read about your recent discovery of that high-speed exoplanet system, truly fascinating work."

Sean's eyes lit up with appreciation. "I appreciate that, Mark. It's been an exciting journey."

Sharon beamed, glancing between the two out of three most important men in her life. "I'm so glad you two are finally meeting."

"As am I," Sean agreed, stepping aside to usher them into the house. "Come in, let's sit down and catch up properly."

As they moved into the living room, the initial nerves gave way to a comfortable camaraderie, the promise of renewed family bonds evident in their smiles and easy conversation.

As they settled into the living room, the conversation flowed effortlessly. Sean shared stories of his recent astronomical research, his eyes lighting up as he described the thrill of discovery. Sharon recounted her experiences in environmental advocacy, her passion evident in every word. Mark chimed in with anecdotes from his work in renewable energy, highlighting the innovative projects he was spearheading.

Laughter punctuated their exchanges, and the room buzzed with genuine excitement. The initial apprehension melted away, replaced by a comforting sense of familiarity and renewed connection. As the evening progressed, they found themselves reminiscing about childhood memories, their shared history weaving seamlessly into the present.

The warmth of family enveloped them, and Sean couldn't help but feel a profound sense of gratitude. The years apart had been challenging, but this reunion was a testament to the enduring strength of their bond. In that moment, surrounded by loved ones, he knew they were embarking on a new chapter together, filled with hope and shared purpose.

As the evening progressed, Sean couldn't help but notice a subtle shift in Mark's demeanor. While Sharon spoke passionately about her work, Mark's responses seemed curt and distracted, lacking the enthusiasm one might expect from a supportive partner. This observation stirred a sense of unease in Sean, prompting him to reflect on the dynamics he was witnessing.

In relationships, a partner's indifference toward significant aspects of their loved one's life, such as career or personal interests, can be indicative of deeper issues. Emotional indifference often manifests as a lack of interest, concern, or sympathy, leading to surface-level conversations and a sense of disengagement. This disengagement can stem from various factors, including feelings of jealousy, fear of change, or a perceived threat to the relationship's balance.

Sean pondered whether Mark's behavior was a sign of such indifference or perhaps rooted in personal insecurities. Understanding the underlying cause is crucial, as it can impact the relationship's health and Sharon's well-being. However, Sean recognized the importance of approaching the situation with sensitivity. Intervening without a clear understanding or invitation could lead to misunderstandings or strain his renewed connection with Sharon.

For now, Sean decided to focus on rebuilding his relationship with his sister, providing a supportive presence. He hoped that, in time, Sharon would feel comfortable confiding in him if there were underlying issues she needed to discuss. Maintaining open lines of communication and being observant without being intrusive would be his approach, ensuring that he could offer support if and when it was needed.

Mark, filled with excitement at meeting Sean, looked at him intently and asked, "When you say you contacted the blah blah planet, what exactly do you mean? Are you referring to some kind of entity? How can you be sure they're actually there?"

Sean chuckled at Mark's question. "It's a common misconception," he began. "In astronomy, we don't 'contact' stars or planets directly. Instead, we observe the light and other electromagnetic radiation they emit. By analyzing this data, we can infer a great deal about these celestial bodies."

He continued, "For instance, we use radio telescopes to detect radio waves naturally emitted by stars, planets, and galaxies. These instruments allow us to study various phenomena, such as the composition and behavior of these objects."

"Additionally," Sean added, "we employ techniques like Doppler spectroscopy to detect exoplanets. This method involves observing the slight shifts in a star's light spectrum caused by the gravitational pull of an orbiting planet, which helps us determine the planet's presence and characteristics."

Mark nodded, his curiosity piqued. "That makes sense. So, it's more about interpreting the information they naturally send out, rather than direct communication."

"Exactly," Sean replied with a smile. "It's like being cosmic detectives, deciphering the clues the universe provides."

Sean smiled back, appreciating the compliment but sensing a subtle hint of skepticism in Mark's words. He understood that the realm of space research could seem abstract and overwhelming to those not immersed in it.

"It's not exactly like talking to them," Sean replied with a modest shrug. "It's more about interpreting the signals they naturally emit. We use various technologies to detect and analyze these signals, everything from light waves to radio emissions, which allows us to uncover the secrets of these distant celestial bodies."

"Fascinating," Mark said, leaning forward. "It's incredible how much we can learn from signals that are invisible to the naked eye."

"Indeed," Sean agreed. "Each type of signal provides a different piece of the puzzle, helping us to build a more comprehensive picture of the cosmos."

Sean chuckled at Mark's comment, understanding how astronomical research could seem like science fiction. "I get that it sounds like something out of a sci-fi movie," he said, "but it's all grounded in physics and observation."

He continued, "For example, the James Webb Space Telescope, launched in 2021, has been pivotal in advancing our understanding of the universe. It's designed to observe the universe in infrared light, which allows us to see through cosmic dust and study the formation of stars and planets in unprecedented detail."

"Additionally," Sean added, "missions like the Kepler Space Telescope have revolutionized our knowledge of exoplanets. By monitoring the brightness of stars, Kepler has detected the tiny dips in light that occur when planets transit in front of them, leading to the discovery of thousands of exoplanets."

Mark nodded, his curiosity piqued. "It's incredible how much we can learn from interpreting these signals," he remarked.

"Absolutely," Sean agreed. "Each observation brings us closer to understanding the vast complexities of the cosmos."

As their conversation continued, Sean felt gratified to share his passion, hoping it bridged the gap between their worlds.

Sean chuckled at Mark's observation. "It's true," he said, "Sharon and I have always shared a passion for uncovering the mysteries of existence, even if we've approached it from different angles. While I explore the vastness of the cosmos, Sharon delves into the intricacies of the subatomic world."

Mark stared at Sean, then at Sharon, and said with a smirk, "In a different sense, you're basically studying the larger-scale version of what Sharon represents."

Sean glanced at his sister, her eyes alight with enthusiasm. "Both realms are fascinating in their own right. The universe is filled with phenomena like black holes and supernovae that capture the imagination. But the subatomic world is equally thrilling. Understanding particles and their interactions can reveal the fundamental laws governing everything, including the cosmos."

Sharon nodded in agreement. "Exactly. Studying particles isn't just about tiny components; it's about comprehending the forces and principles that shape the universe. For instance, research in particle physics has led to significant technological advancements, such as the development of the World Wide Web at CERN."

Mark raised an eyebrow, intrigued. "I had no idea. So, your work contributes to both our understanding of the universe and practical innovations?"

"Absolutely," Sean replied. "Theoretical and experimental physics often lead to unexpected applications that impact daily life. It's a continuous cycle of discovery and innovation."

As the conversation continued, Mark's appreciation for both fields grew, recognizing the interconnectedness of exploring the vast cosmos and the minute particles within it.

Sean observed Mark's growing enthusiasm for space exploration and couldn't help but smile. "It's true that the cosmos holds a unique allure, capturing the imagination with its vastness and mysteries. Space exploration has a way of inspiring curiosity and wonder, often motivating individuals to delve deeper into scientific fields."

He continued, "However, the microscopic world is equally fascinating. Understanding atomic and molecular structures has led to ground-breaking advancements in medicine, technology, and materials science. Both realms, though vastly different in scale, contribute profoundly to our comprehension of the universe and our place within it."

Sharon nodded in agreement. "Exactly. While space exploration offers insights into the cosmos, studying atoms and molecules allows us to understand the fundamental building blocks of matter, leading to innovations that impact our daily lives."

Mark smiled, appreciating the perspectives. "I see your point. Both fields, though different, are essential in their own right. It's incredible how exploring both the vastness of space and the minuteness of particles can lead to such profound discoveries."

The conversation continued, weaving between the wonders of the cosmos and the intricacies of the microscopic world, highlighting the interconnectedness of all scientific pursuits.

Sean was finally back on Earth and eager to learn more about their lives. He turned to Mark, his gaze steady.

"What do you do, Mark?" Sean asked, locking eyes with him.

Mark's expression brightened, his posture straightening with pride. "I'm a university teacher, and I love it," he replied, his voice filled with excitement.

"That's wonderful," Sean responded, offering a warm smile. "Teaching is such a rewarding profession."

"It truly is," Mark agreed, his enthusiasm evident. "There's nothing quite like inspiring young minds and sharing knowledge."

As the conversation shifted, the earlier tension began to dissipate, replaced by a more relaxed atmosphere.

"I wholeheartedly concur, Sharon and I share the same sentiments. She is a distinguished scientific researcher whose groundbreaking work has garnered universal respect and admiration," Sean asserted, his voice steady as he sought to deflect Mark's critique of Sharon's contributions.

Sharon, sensing the mounting tension, interjected with a nostalgic smile. "Sean, do you recall how I used to mimic everything you did? I wanted the same clothes, the same haircut, even down to your favorite T-shirts."

"Yes, I remember," Sean replied, his gaze flickering between Mark and Sharon, the unease palpable in his shifting eyes.

Mark's brow furrowed, his skepticism unmasked. "So, you believe that emulating Sean's every move qualifies you as a competent researcher?"

Sharon's smile tightened, but she held his gaze. "It taught me the value of dedication and attention to detail, traits essential in research."

Sean cleared his throat, attempting to ease the strain. "Those were formative years for both of us. We learned a lot from each other."

Mark leaned back, arms crossed, skepticism etched across his face. "Learning is one thing; producing results and merely imitating someone is another."

The room fell silent, the weight of unspoken challenges hanging heavily in the air.

Sharon's face flushed with anger, her eyes narrowing as she clenched her fists. Sensing the brewing tension, Sean swiftly intervened, sidestepping Mark's remark with a playful grin. Leaning in, he caught Sharon's gaze and said, "Sharon, remember when you asked me why you always had to dress like me? Why couldn't I, just once, wear what you wore, for your sake?"

Sharon chuckled, the tension easing from her shoulders. "Oh, I remember that. You were relentless."

They both laughed, the shared memory momentarily dissolving the unease in the room.

"Yes, I remember that," Sean chuckled. "We were only about eleven."

Mark glanced at both of them, unable to see the humor. "What's so funny about that?" he asked.

But they continued laughing to themselves. Mark grew impatient and finally asked, "What happened next?"

Sharon went on, her voice tinged with frustration and playfulness. "I was so upset, I told him, 'If you don't dress like me at least once, I swear I'll never speak to you again.'" Her cheeks turned a deep shade of red as she realized how silly her ultimatum had sounded in hindsight.

Sean chuckled softly before replying, "I told her, 'I'm not dressing up like a girl. And just like that, she spun around, her face flushed with anger, and stormed off to her room, slamming the door behind her." A faint grin played on Sean's lips as he spoke, always keen to remember the smallest details as if each moment were a piece of a much larger, unforgettable story.

"Exhaustion weighed heavily on me as guilt gnawed at my conscience. I longed to rewind time, to see her vibrant smile once more. Our connection had always been profound, but now, each day, my love for her intensified, intertwining with my very being. She wasn't just my sister; she was my twin, my mirror, my other half."

Sharon continued, "The next day, the boys started bothering him, just like they always did after school."

Sean interjected, his voice a mix of frustration and determination. "But I was still upset from our argument the day before. Normally, I'd just run from those guys, but that day felt different. When they got closer, I didn't hesitate. Without thinking, I swung and punched one of them right in the face."

Sean's voice grew livelier, his excitement palpable as he recounted the story. Sharon took over, her tone playful, while Mark listened, his laughter growing as the tale unfolded.

"Then he took off running, with the boys hot on his heels, furious and desperate for revenge. He was the first to stand up to them, the first to challenge their dominance."

Sharron paused, her gaze shifting to Sean. "Maybe it's better if you finish the story," she said with a teasing smile.

Sean nodded, his expression turning serious. "I ran with everything I had," he began. "Luckily, Mom was just heading out. I barely had time to say hello before I rushed past her, muttering a quick goodbye as I slammed the door behind me. I ran straight to Sharon's room, grabbed one of her dresses, and threw it on.

As soon as I was dressed, I rushed down the stairs. The kids were already banging on the door, screaming my name. 'Where are you, Sean? Are you kidding around like a girl?" one of them yelled. Another shouted, 'I'm going to kill you, Sean!"

Sean's grin widened as he continued, "And then..." he trailed off, eyes gleaming with mischief.

"I flung open the door, and for a moment, they just stood there, stunned," Sean grinned, the memory still amusing him. "Then, I put on my best girlish voice and started acting the part, 'Well, well.' I said, flipping my hair dramatically, 'What's going on here? It's really not nice for handsome boys like you to scream and yell like that.' I could see their jaws drop as they tried to figure out what was happening."

One of them finally spoke up, his voice cracking with disbelief. "I knew Sean had a beautiful sister, but I never realized she was this beautiful," Sean laughed, clearly enjoying how flustered they had become.

"The boys quickly apologized for their behavior, backing away before rushing off. I shut the door with a sigh of relief and turned to head upstairs to change out of the dress. As I reached the staircase, I spotted Sharon standing there, her face flushed, clutching her stomach as she laughed uncontrollably."

Before Sean could continue, Sharon interrupted, still struggling to contain her laughter. "I said to you, 'Thanks, Sean. You really didn't have to do this for me. But now I get it. I understand why you refused to dress like me. You were the ugliest girl I've ever seen."

Sean pointed toward the door and added, "Not to them!"

They all burst into laughter, the room resonating with their shared amusement. As the mirth subsided, they sipped their coffee, a comfortable silence enveloping them. Finally, Sharon broke the quiet.

"So, how's life treating you now, Sean? Are you enjoying your job?"

Sean took a deep breath, pausing to sip his drink. He glanced up at his sister, curiosity evident in his eyes. "Why do you ask?"

"Nothing serious, really," Sharon said, her voice soft. She paused for a moment, gathering her thoughts before continuing. "It's just... after all this time, you suddenly showed up. I'm just concerned if everything's all right. I want you to know that if you need any help, I'm here for you." Her words carried warmth, a desire to offer him the same support she had in the past.

"Where did you think I'd go? I'll always be here for you," Sharon declared, her voice resolute yet tender, embodying a promise she intended to uphold unwaveringly.

"Thank you, Sharon. Your kindness means the world to me," Sean responded earnestly. "You've been an incredible sister, and I know you always will be. I'm fortunate to have you and immensely proud of you."

Sharon squinted at the clock, then looked up at Sean. "We'd better get going. It's really late, and we all need some rest. I'll call you tomorrow." She stood up, straightening her dress with a small sigh, ready to head out.

Meanwhile, Sean scribbled his new cell phone number on a piece of paper and handed it to Sharon. "This is my new number," he said with a grin. "Just in case I'm not home, or in the hospital, tomorrow."

As they embraced, Sean felt a profound joy, a warmth that lingered as Sharon and Mark departed. Mark extended his hand with a friendly smile. "It was very nice to meet you. I hope this is the beginning of our friendship."

"Of course it is. I'll see you both later. Take care, and have a nice evening," Sean replied warmly. He stood in the doorway, watching until their car disappeared into the night. In that quiet moment, he reflected that, regardless of whom Sharon chose as her husband, he would respect her choice. He lingered a little longer, the stillness of the night enveloping him.

He gazed up at the night sky, a tapestry of shimmering stars scattered across the vast expanse. Each pinpoint of light seemed to whisper possibilities of distant worlds teeming with life. Which of these celestial bodies, he wondered, might harbor intelligent beings gazing back at him with the same sense of wonder? The longer he stared, the more it felt as though some stars twinkled in acknowledgment, engaging in a silent cosmic dialogue. With a contemplative sigh, he closed the door behind him and made his way to his room, his thoughts still adrift among the distant constellations.

CHAPTER THREE

"Whispers of the Unseen"

Sean woke early, grabbed a quick breakfast, and hurried to the hospital. On the third floor, he spotted the same nurse from the previous day behind the reception desk. He approached her with a friendly, "Good morning."

"Oh, hi! Good morning," the nurse replied warmly. "Your mother is a very strong woman. I think she'll be released from the hospital very soon."

"Thank you for the good news," Sean said, smiling. "I'm sorry I didn't introduce myself yesterday. I'm Sean."

The nurse's eyes met his, her expression genuine. "Hi again. I'm Hanna Johnson. It's a pleasure to meet you."

Sean was on his way to his mother's room when he accidentally bumped into Sharon. Both of them apologized at the exact same moment, and they both burst out laughing.

"It looks like we make the same mistake all the time," Sharon said, still chuckling as she shook her head.

"Indeed," Sean replied with a smile, opening the door for her. "Did you sleep well last night?"

"Yes, fine. How's Mom? Is she awake?" Sean asked, his concern evident as he looked at her.

"Oh yes, she's in the bathroom now. She'll be out any minute. Dad is with Mom's doctor and should be back in about fifteen minutes. He asked me to tell you to wait here until he returns."

"Okay," Sean replied, nodding. Then, glancing at her, he asked, "Are you heading to work now?"

"Yes, I'll call you," Sharon replied kindly. "Okay?"

"Yes, of course, it's okay."

"I guess I'll see you later," she said softly.

"Well, see you later," Sean repeated, watching her with a faint smile. Sharon lingered for a moment, as if reluctant to leave, but with a final glance, she turned and walked away, disappearing down the hallway.

Sean peered into the room briefly before moving to the window, where he stood waiting for his mother. Sunlight streamed in, warming his skin. The hospital's yard was lush and vibrant, with well-maintained green grass and colorful plants radiating joy. Vivid flowers added bright splashes of color, evoking a sense of happiness.

Beyond the hospital window, the world bustled with life. Cars glided along the streets, their movements a gentle reminder of the vibrant city beyond. The parking lot brimmed with vehicles, reflecting the day's activity. Overhead, the sky stretched endlessly, a soothing canvas of blue adorned with fluffy white clouds drifting lazily. Birds chirped energetically, flitting from branch to branch, their lively melodies enhancing the serene atmosphere. The view resembled a picturesque scene, as if plucked from a dream and worthy of an artist's canvas.

Sean pondered the profound questions of existence, reflecting on the possibility that life might extend beyond physical death. He considered the idea that, rather than ceasing to exist, individuals might transform into another form, allowing their essence to continue. This perspective provided him with a sense of purpose and continuity, suggesting that life holds deeper meaning beyond what is immediately visible.

He paused, feeling the weight of his thoughts. "There has to be something else," he mused. "Maybe if I'm a good person, I'll come back as a bird, an eagle, or a lion, or even as a human again. But if I'm not, maybe I'll end up as a worm or a slug... or maybe even a human, but one of the unlucky ones." The last thought made him chuckle to himself.

Just then, Sean was snapped out of his reverie by the sound of his mother's voice.

"Sean! How glad I am to see you here!" Helen exclaimed, her voice brimming with warmth. Despite her pallor and the fragility that seemed to deepen with each passing day, she walked toward him with a determined stride. Embracing him tightly, she held on as if never wanting to let go, her arms encircling him with a strength that belied her condition. She grasped his hand firmly, as though drawing comfort and healing from his touch.

Sean pressed a gentle kiss to his mother's forehead before helping her settle back into bed. They spoke for a while, and Sean reflected on his conversation with Sharon the previous night.

"I'm so happy to hear this," Helen said, her voice soft but brimming with warmth. "It brings me such joy to know you two are reconnecting. It's one of the hardest things for a mother, watching her children drift apart. I can't tell you how grateful I am to see you both like this again." Her eyes glistened with emotion, her smile full of quiet relief as she reached out to take his hand.

The door burst open, and James flew into the room, his arms piled high with flowers, coffee, doughnuts, and chocolates.

"Hi, Dad," Sean greeted with a grin, moving quickly to help his father.

"Hello, son," James replied warmly, setting the items down. "Did you sleep well last night?"

"Yes, indeed. Sharon and Mark visited me, and we were up almost until 2:00 a.m.," Sean said, smiling.

"That's good. Sharon mentioned it this morning," James replied. "She was so excited." Sean chuckled. "It was great catching up with them."

James nodded, his eyes reflecting contentment. "Family time is precious." Helen, observing their exchange, smiled softly. "It's wonderful to see you both together."

Sean turned to her, his expression tender. "We're here for you, Mom." The room filled with a comforting warmth as the family shared a moment of unity. "How's everything around here?" Sean asked, eager for an update.

James's expression shifted slightly. "I forgot to tell you about your friend..." Sean quickly interrupted, concern evident in his voice. "What happened?"

"He's still in the hospital," James replied calmly. "Frankly, there's nothing wrong with him. They couldn't find anything, and he's actually doing better than the first day."

James provided detailed information about the situation, his thorough knowledge evident as he filled Sean in.

"You should go see him," James suggested thoughtfully. "He asked about you."

Sean nodded, absorbing the information. "I will. Thanks for letting me know." The room settled into a contemplative silence as Sean considered his next steps.

He turned to his mother, about to speak, but she smiled and nodded before he could get the words out. "I know, Sean. Go ahead. I'm not disappointed," she said softly, her eyes filled with understanding and support.

"Thanks, Mom," Sean replied, his voice full of gratitude. He grabbed his computer bag and slung it over his shoulder. Turning to James, he added, "See you, Dad. If you need me, you know where to find me." With a quick nod, he headed out the door.

As Sean walked through the hospital corridors, the sterile scent of disinfectant filled the air, mingling with the distant hum of medical equipment. He passed rooms where monitors beeped rhythmically, a reminder of the fragility of life. The soft murmur of conversations between doctors and patients created a backdrop of hushed urgency. Sunlight streamed through the large windows, casting a warm glow on the polished floors and offering a stark contrast to the clinical environment. The occasional squeak of a gurney wheel echoed, punctuating the steady flow of hospital activity. Exiting the building, the fresh air greeted him, a welcome change from the controlled atmosphere inside. The sounds of the city, distant traffic, chirping birds, and the rustle of leaves, provided a comforting normalcy and a refreshing breath for him. He lingered outside for a while, breathing in the fresh air to clear his mind, before turning and heading toward his friend's place.

Sean headed straight to Kevin's room, his steps quick. Noticing the absence of the security guard who had been presented before, he peered inside, taking in the familiar sight: equipment humming quietly and monitors emitting steady beeps. Kevin was watching a program on TV, but as soon as Sean entered, his eyes locked onto him.

"Sean! Where have you been?" Kevin blurted out, his voice full of surprise and energy. Sean smiled, relieved to see his friend in good spirits. "I've been around, dealing with some family matters. How are you feeling?"

"Better, actually." Kevin gestured to the machines. "They've run all sorts of tests but haven't found anything wrong."

"That's a relief." Sean pulled up a chair beside the bed. "I was worried when I heard you were still here."

"Yeah, it's been frustrating, but at least the food's not terrible," Kevin chuckled, then immediately added with a grin, "It's horrible." He burst into laughter before adding, "But hey, the nurses are nice." They shared a laugh, the tension easing as they caught up.

As they talked, the rhythmic beeping of the heart monitor provided a steady backdrop, a reminder of the hospital's constant vigilance. The scent of antiseptic lingered in the air, mingling with the faint aroma of the lunch trays being distributed down the hall. Occasionally, the intercom crackled to life, paging doctors to various departments. Despite the clinical environment, the room felt warmer with their conversation, the bond of friendship providing comfort amidst the sterile surroundings.

A nurse entered to check Kevin's vitals. "Good to see you have company," she said with a smile. "Yeah, it's good to have a friend around," Kevin replied, glancing at Sean appreciatively. Sean nodded. "I'll be here as long as you need, buddy."

The nurse finished her tasks and left the room, leaving the two friends to continue their conversation, the hum of the hospital fading into the background as they focused on each other's words.

"Where's your mom?" Sean asked, his eyes scanning the room before locking onto Kevin. "She'll be here after one," Kevin answered, his voice steady and calm.

"Any more shocks since I left?" Sean inquired, his voice laced with a playful undertone as his eyes scanned the room.

"Yes, I still have it, but it's not as strong anymore," Kevin replied with a calm demeanor, his gaze softening.

Maintaining his focus on Kevin, Sean asked, "Do you feel any changes in your body?" His tone bordered on clinical, and he quickly realized he might have overstepped.

"You're just like a doctor," Kevin remarked with a slight smile, "but I don't mind because I trust you." Sean raised an eyebrow, intrigued. "How do you know I'm trustworthy?"

Kevin met his gaze with unwavering sincerity. "I can see it in your eyes and sense your thoughts. And I know you're not here to report on my ability, you're here because you care."

Sean was momentarily speechless, unsettled by Kevin's response. There was something undeniably mature about Kevin's demeanor, a gravity beyond his years. Sean hesitated, his mind grappling to make sense of it.

"Could the boy truly perceive such things? Was it possible to read someone's emotions just by looking at them?" The thought lingered in Sean's mind, but he couldn't find a clear answer.

Sean's gaze shifted to the monitors beside Kevin's bed, scrutinizing the printouts displaying Kevin's vital signs and emotional metrics. Everything appeared within normal parameters.

"Kevin, I don't see any changes here. Have you experienced any more of those unusual shocks?" Sean's concern was evident.

Kevin held Sean's gaze for a moment before deliberately disconnecting a wire from the machine attached to him. "I can sense when they're about to happen," he explained calmly.

"That's why I disconnect it. After a few minutes, they assume it disconnected on its own and rush here to reconnect, but I know its coming." His expression grew more serious. "I want to go home. I don't want to be here anymore." Sean nodded, his mind clearly elsewhere.

Without a hint of hesitation, Kevin turned to Sean and asked, "May I have a glass of water?" His voice was quiet, yet steady, carrying an unspoken resolve.

"Yes, of course," Sean replied, swiftly fetching a glass of water and handing it to him.

Kevin accepted it but didn't drink. Instead, He stared into the water, his gaze deep and searching, as if deciphering a message inscribed beneath the surface, something only he could read. Then, with deliberate precision, he blew softly over it. Sean remained silent, watching, waiting, and unsure of Kevin's intent.

After a long pause, Kevin slowly turned the glass toward Sean, offering it to him. Sean hesitated, confusion flickering in his eyes. He wasn't sure what to make of the gesture, but he took the glass nonetheless, uncertainty settling over him like a shadow.

"I brought it for you, and now you're not even thirsty?" Sean explained, his own words feeling strange as he spoke them.

Kevin's gaze remained steady, unreadable yet profound. "You know," he said slowly, "somehow, and I don't know how, I'm connected to you emotionally."

He locked eyes with Sean, his expression unwavering, leaving a mysterious impact on him. "It's not for you. It's for your mother. I can feel it, you're worried about her. This will fix everything. I promise you that you just have her to drink it. Please!"

Kevin's voice took on a strained, urgent tone. His face glistened with moisture, and his hands trembled slightly, an unusual sight during his usual glass-staring ritual.

"But I don't understand, I need more information," Sean said, confusion evident in his voice. "I can't explain it to you," Kevin replied, his voice firm yet tinged with desperation.

"But please, just do it, for your mother. I know how much you love her." His eyes pleaded with Sean,

His hands were gripping the edge of the bed tightly. "And don't ask me any more questions about this. Would you please? Would you do it for me? Right now?" He added, his tone serious, "Please give it to her and make sure she drinks it all."

Sean set the glass down momentarily, casting a puzzled glance at Kevin, who had reclined back into his bed, attempting to shift the conversation as if nothing unusual had transpired. Still bewildered, Sean eyed the glass of water once more before exiting the room.

He hurried to his mother's room, immediately noticing the tension etched on her pale, almost colorless face. His father was calling her name, but she remained unresponsive. Turning to Sean with urgency, James implored, "Call the doctor quickly."

Sean dashed out, but as he sped down the hallway, Kevin's words and the image of the glass of water resurfaced in his mind. He abruptly turned back, rushing to his mother's side.

"Mom! Please, drink this water," he urged, holding the glass to her lips.

James shouted at Sean, his voice ringing with urgency. "What are you doing? Just call the doctor!" His gaze flickered to his wife, watching as she began to respond to Sean.

At first, she didn't respond, but Sean persisted. Gently, he pressed the rim to her mouth, and slowly, she began to sip.

By the time the doctor arrived, Sean's mother had already begun showing signs of recovery. He quickly assessed her, asking a series of questions, each of which she answered clearly. After a brief pause, he turned to James, a thoughtful expression crossing his face.

"I think it was a false alarm," the doctor said reassuringly. "A temporary episode, but she's fine now. I'll run additional tests and schedule another MRI to see what's happening in her brain right now, even though we already have the one from this morning, which, unfortunately, was taken before the seizure began.

Sean stood frozen, speechless. He glanced at his father, who was staring back at him, eyes wide with surprise. As the doctor left, James finally broke the silence, his voice laced with confusion. "I know she was in the middle of a seizure because the doctor told me about the tumor in her brain, but what was all that about the glass of water?"

Sean looked down at the glass still in his hand, uncertain. He didn't have an answer, not a logical one, at least. Yet, deep inside, something told him that Kevin's strange request was the key. He then turned to his father, a mix of disbelief and hurt in his eyes. "Mom has a brain tumor? You never told me."

A knot tightened in his stomach as he struggled to put his thoughts into words. He turned to James, hesitated, then asked him to keep it between them until he figured it out. Without another word, Sean left the room and headed toward Kevin's. His mind raced, each step pressing him further into the mystery. What had just happened? What role had Kevin played in all of this? The answers felt close, just beyond his grasp, but he had to know.

Sean entered Kevin's room to find him lying back on his bed, watching TV. Taking a seat beside him, Sean felt a wave of uncertainty, unsure how to broach the subject. Sensing the tension, but Kevin spoke first:

"I know your question, but I don't have the answer," He said, his tone firm yet evasive. "All I can tell you is that I rearranged the water and gave it an order."

Before Sean could probe further, Kevin's eyes shifted to the laptop in Sean's hands. "What's that?" he asked, clearly aiming to change the subject.

"This? It's my favorite laptop," Sean replied with a smile, tapping the device lightly. "I carry it almost everywhere."

Kevin nodded, the earlier topic left hanging in the air, as both seemed to silently agree to let it rest for now. "I always wanted to have one," Kevin said, his curiosity piqued. "My father had one, but it was a little bigger than yours. How does it work?"

Sean chuckled at Kevin's enthusiasm. "Well, for example, if someone sends you an email, it comes through the internet. You just check your inbox, and there it is. It's like getting a letter, but much faster."

Kevin's eyes lit up with more questions. "Any kindergarten child knows that, but how do you send something back? How does the message travel?"

Sean smiled at the genuine interest. "I can show you now, if you'd like." Kevin's eyes brightened with excitement, eager to learn more. "But before we start, I have a question about the glass of water," Sean said hesitantly.

Kevin's expression darkened, his impatience evident. He smiled at Sean, then very calmly he asked: "If you can demonstrate exactly how that email travels, then I'll show you. Until then, please stop asking me about it," he replied, his voice strained. "I sense everything, but it's not me. Somehow it comes to me, and I don't know how I know that. Please, don't ask me."

His frustration was palpable, an emotion Sean hadn't seen in him before. Recognizing Kevin's distress, Sean refrained from pressing further. He gently placed the laptop on Kevin's lap, intending to shift the focus.

Before Sean could open it, Kevin touched it, fingers brushing the keyboard. "Hold on," Kevin murmured, his touch lingering on the console. "I can access it. The hardware is like another world."

He closed his eyes briefly, as if concentrating. "Did you say email? It's like navigating through a city to reach the right destination." A moment later, he opened his eyes, a sly smile playing on his lips. "You've got mail, actually, scratch that, three messages."

Sean stared, astonished. "How did you...?" Kevin shrugged nonchalantly. "I don't know. It's like I can sense the pathways, the data streams. I just... connect."

Sean's mind raced, trying to comprehend the implications of Kevin's abilities. The room seemed to hum with unspoken possibilities, the air thick with the weight of newfound understanding.

Sean couldn't discern whether Kevin was jesting or sincere. The notion of perceiving hardware with the naked eye seemed preposterous, yet Kevin's demeanor left little room for doubt. Stunned, Sean found himself immobilized, his gaze fixed on Kevin, searching for any sign of deceit.

Kevin met Sean's eyes, an unspoken challenge flickering within them. His voice, low and deliberate, carried an air of mystery. "You're not sure if you can trust me in this, right?" He leaned in slightly, a subtle smile playing on his lips. "But I can show you. I can prove it."

"Can you read my mind?" Sean asked, skepticism evident in his tone.

Kevin's gaze remained steady, the enigmatic smile lingering. "No," he replied, his voice smooth and assured. "But I can sense your emotions, every ripple, and every shift."

Sean's mind raced, grappling with the implications of Kevin's claim. The room seemed to pulse with unspoken possibilities, the air thick with the weight of newfound understanding.

Sean leaned forward, curiosity and skepticism mingling in his voice. "But how can you prove it to me?"

Leaning back slightly, Kevin's tone turned casual yet loaded with intrigue. "Shall I read them for you?" he asked, the faintest hint of a challenge in his voice.

Sean's mind raced, grappling with the implications of Kevin's claim. The room seemed to pulse with unspoken possibilities, the air thick with the weight of newfound understanding.

"But how can you prove it to me?" Sean leaned forward in the chair beside Kevin's bed, his voice a blend of curiosity and skepticism.

Kevin's eyes remained fixed on the computer screen, his face a canvas of quiet concentration. Seconds stretched into what felt like an eternity before he finally looked up, his gaze sharp and unwavering.

With an unsettling calm, he began, "Your first email is from your phone company. The second and third..." He paused, a flicker of amusement dancing across his features. "...are from someone named Greg."

Kevin leaned back slightly, his tone casual yet laden with intrigue. "Shall I read them for you?" he asked, a subtle challenge lacing his words.

Sean's heart pounded as Kevin's revelation took hold. Disbelief washed over him, how could Kevin possibly know? The mere thought of those emails, especially the ones from Greg, being unveiled sent a cold shiver coursing through his veins.

Kevin was amused by Sean's reaction when he said, "Don't worry, the third one is from someone named Scarlet. Her email included a big red heart." Sean pulled out his laptop and said, "It's okay. I'm a believer." He checked his email and, within seconds, turned to Kevin. "She has no red heart on her email."

Kevin laughed. "I know, but who is she?" Sean glanced at him. "She's a ninety-year-old woman in a wheelchair. I help her get to the park sometimes or pick up groceries for her."

He looked back at Kevin, catching the mischief dancing in his expression, just as their moment was abruptly shattered by a sharp, insistent beeping from Sean's computer. Both men froze, their words suspended in the air as their eyes snapped to the glowing screen.

Sean's gaze shifted to Kevin, suspicion intertwining with unease. "Are you in shock again?" he murmured, his voice barely above a whisper, the question laden with a mix of doubt and foreboding.

"Yes, I am. But don't worry, I can control it now." Kevin's voice was steady, yet a shadow of unease lurked beneath his words. On the screen, the enigmatic patterns from earlier wove and twisted, each line morphing like a living enigma. His crimson eyes, sharp and probing, bore into Sean's with an intensity that demanded truth.

"What are they, Sean? Are they coming from inside me?" The question hung heavy in the air, laden with dread and anticipation.

Sean swallowed hard, choosing his words with care. "Yes, Kevin, they are." Each syllable fell like a stone, marking the gravity of the revelation.

Sean stared intently at the swirling images on his laptop screen, both captivated and unnerved. "They're coming from your body," he said cautiously, his voice a blend of curiosity and dread.

"But don't be scared. I... I feel like I'm starting to understand why people talk about ghosts taking over someone's body. The doctors didn't find anything wrong with you, so I'm not jumping to conclusions, but..."

He hesitated, the words tumbling out as if escaping his thoughts. "It really feels like something, like a ghost, is trying to take over. Not that I believe it, of course! Because nothing like this has ever been documented. At least, not in the way you're experiencing it. But how is that even possible? To me, it's not a ghost because if it were, it would have taken over you already, but it must be something else. It sends you printable information. Why would a ghost do that if it wanted to take over your body? They wouldn't do that. But why does it keep sending these things?"

In this passage, Sean grapples with the mysterious phenomenon affecting Kevin, oscillating between scientific reasoning and supernatural explanations. His internal conflict reflects a broader theme in literature where technology intersects with the paranormal, challenging characters' understanding of reality.

Sean rubbed his temples, his mind a chaotic whirlwind of fear and logic battling for dominance. "I'm sorry. I don't want to scare you, and I don't even know why I'm saying these things to a ten-year-old boy." His voice wavered, betraying the storm of confusion and guilt raging within him.

Taking a deep breath, he steadied himself before speaking in the calmest tone he could muster. He needed Kevin to feel safe, to trust him completely. "Kevin, listen to me," He spoke gently, his gaze steady and reassuring. "The things I'm trying to tell you... You've probably already figured out."

Kevin met his eyes, his voice unwavering despite the turmoil around them. "It's okay, Sean. I trust you. You're the only one who can help me."

The weight of those words settled heavily on Sean's shoulders, but he nodded, determined to be the anchor Kevin needed. Sean's curiosity deepened, his gaze fixed on Kevin. "How do you know I'm the one who can help you?"

Kevin met Sean's eyes, his voice steady. "Sean, when I first felt that pain, back when my mom was calling an ambulance, there was a news report on TV. My mom had been watching it. It was about you, about how you discovered a mysterious planet somewhere in the universe, a million light-years away. And how you're trying to find a way to contact them."

Kevin paused, his intense focus never leaving Sean's face. "I knew if you could do that, you might be able to help me too," he said, chuckling softly at the absurdity of his words before continuing.

"When I was in the hospital, I had a phone beside my bed, and when nobody was there, I went through the phone and found you. Through your phone, I sent you the same messages I was receiving a few times." Kevin tilted his head slightly, a small, wry smile on his lips. "Have you received them, Sean?"

Sean's eyes widened as fragmented memories surged forward. He recalled the cryptic message that had mysteriously appeared on his computer, the one his superiors had swiftly concealed. They had insisted he take a "vacation week," claiming it was for his own well-being. Now, the pieces aligned, revealing a deliberate orchestration.

"I remember the message, Kevin, but it was different from the ones I read here. They probably hid the real messages from me, and the one I saw on their screen came from somewhere else. That message wasn't from you, it was from a higher, stronger source." Sean said slowly, piecing it together aloud. "But wait a minute! My phone is connected to my office line, and they have access to the messages that come through there as well. They probably hid it from me, thinking the message that came through HCT was meant for me, too."

"That's why they sent me away. They didn't want me involved." He paused, a bitter yet curious smile spreading across his face. "But strangely enough, they sent me right to a different source of a different message. Almost as if..." He trailed off, the realization hitting him like a wave.

Sean turned back to Kevin, his expression a blend of wonder and suspicion. "How did you transmit the message to me?"

Kevin shook his head, his voice calm yet certain. "I can't explain; it's complex, and I don't fully understand it myself. But I know I sent you more than one message."

Sean's gaze drifted to the window as he began pacing, his thoughts a tangled web of mistrust and newfound conviction. His manager, they must have intercepted the messages, receiving them all along, yet choosing to keep him in the dark.

Now, he was certain. They had all planned it, but they needed more time to uncover the reason.

As Kevin's words unraveled, Sean experienced an unexpected surge of satisfaction, a deep chord resonating within him. He approached Kevin's bed with deliberate steps, pausing momentarily before addressing him in a tone that was both calm and resolute.

"Kevin," he began, his voice measured and deliberate, "I have a request. What transpired here today, everything you've shared, our entire dialogue, must remain strictly between us. This is our secret."

Kevin nodded without hesitation, his expression unwavering. "That's fine with me," he replied, his voice steady. "It was a secret to me from the beginning. You're the only one I've told." A satisfied smile spread across Sean's face as he whispered, "You're smarter than me."

Just then, the door swung open, and the doctor stepped into the room. Without hesitation, Kevin leaned in, his breath warm against Sean's ear.

"I can keep a secret," he whispered, a mischievous smile playing on his lips, his eyes gleaming with quiet amusement as he pulled back.

Sean held his gaze, his expression unreadable, then offered a faint smile. "I know you can," he murmured, his voice calm, steady, certain.

"How do you feel, Kevin?" Dr. Howard asked, pressing the cold diaphragm of the stethoscope against his chest, listening intently to his heartbeat.

Kevin smirked, his voice ringing with playful defiance. "I'm alright. Want me to somersault across the room to prove it?" His mischievous grin widened, daring a reaction.

Dr. Howard chuckled, shaking his head as he moved on to examine Kevin's ears and eyes. "No, Kevin, that won't be necessary," he said, amusement flickering in his eyes. "But don't worry, you'll be going home very soon." His tone was warm, reassuring.

Kevin's smile faltered slightly. "How soon is very soon, doctor?" he asked, his politeness barely masking the impatience creeping into his voice.

"In a few days," Dr. Howard replied evenly, his expression calm, unwavering.

Kevin's expression darkened, disappointment flickering across his face before settling into frustration. "A few days?" he echoed, his voice rising with disbelief. "There's absolutely nothing wrong with me, Doctor! Why are you still keeping me here?"

The sharp edge in his tone cut through the room, his frustration palpable, hanging in the air like a storm cloud ready to break.

Sean studied Kevin intently, drawn in by the way the boy carried himself. His words, his bearing, the raw intensity in his voice, it all felt far beyond his years. It was as though an adult resided within the frame of a child, cloaked in youthful skin but exuding a depth that defied his age.

Kevin wasn't just intelligent; he was sharp, unnervingly composed, and possessed a quiet sophistication that rivaled even the most seasoned adults Sean had known. A strange sense of fascination took hold of him, compelling him to decipher the enigma sitting before him.

"Doctor, he's as healthy as any boy his age," Sean interjected, his tone firm yet laced with curiosity.

Dr. Howard turned to him, his expression thoughtful, almost hesitant. "Yes, that's exactly why this is so strange," he said slowly. "Kevin had asthma before, one of the worst cases I've ever seen. But after those shocks, his illness didn't just improve, it disappeared. Completely. As if it never existed."

A charged silence hung between them before the doctor continued, his voice brimming with quiet excitement. "If we can understand what happened to him, we might be on the verge of something groundbreaking. Something that could lead to a real cure for asthma."

His eyes flickered with a rare kind of hope. "Imagine the possibilities. Kevin could hold the key to helping countless people live normal, healthy lives. Right now, we don't have a cure. But this..."

He exhaled sharply, his gaze steady. "This could change everything."

Sean's expression tightened, his jaw clenching as he fought to keep his tone civil. "But Doctor," he said, his voice steady yet resolute, "By keeping him here as a lab rat? You're holding him here, stripping him of his freedom, his right to live as a normal child, on nothing more than the hope that you might find a cure for asthma?"

His words hung in the air, sharp and unwavering, challenging the weight of the doctor's reasoning. Sean stepped closer to Kevin, positioning himself protectively beside the boy's bed. His stance was unwavering, his presence a silent shield.

His voice hardened, ringing with quiet authority. "You've taken his blood, run more tests than anyone could count. But you have no right to keep him here, no right to take away his freedom, his childhood, just because you hope to find an answer."

Sean's eyes locked onto Dr. Howard's, unyielding. "He's ten years old. And what if you never find the explanation you're chasing? What if this was simply a healing from God, a miracle beyond your understanding?"

Sean's voice dropped, but the weight of his words only grew heavier. "Kevin is healthy. He's normal. And that's all there is to it. Keeping him here against his will isn't science, it's captivity. You have to let him go. Immediately, as he's requested countless times, it's a violation of human rights."

His eyes burned with unwavering conviction, his words slicing through the tension in the room like a blade, leaving no space for debate.

Dr. Howard hesitated, a flicker of surprise crossing his face. Without a word, he stepped toward Kevin's bed, retrieving the hospital record from the bedside table. The air in the room grew thick with unspoken weight, as if even the walls were bracing for what came next.

But then, something shifted. Sean's gaze flickered toward the doorway, and there she was. Linda! Standing just beyond the threshold, her presence was silent yet unmistakable.

Her face was a whirlwind of emotions, joy, astonishment, and something caught between relief and disbelief. A wide smile stretched across her lips, but uncertainty lingered at its edges.

Her eyes darted between Dr. Howard, Sean, and Kevin, as if trying to grasp the weight of the moment, to make sense of the unspoken tension thickening the air. The scene before her was unraveling too quickly, yet she could feel that something, something was about to change. Just as she parted her lips to speak, Sean shattered the silence.

"Julia!" he said, his voice warm yet urgent. "I'm so glad you're here." His gaze locked onto hers, earnest and unwavering. "Your son, he's as healthy as any boy his age. You can't keep him in this hospital when, for the first time, he has the chance to be a kid to run, to play, and to live like any other child."

His words carried a weight beyond logic, beyond science. It was conviction wrapped in a plea not just to Julia, but to everyone in the room. A call for reason. A call for freedom.

"We're not keeping him here forever," Dr. Howard said, a flicker of impatience creeping into his tone. "We're just asking for a few more days of his time."

His gaze snapped to Sean, sharp and assessing, his eyes narrowing slightly. "What exactly is your interest in him?" he asked, the words pointed, though he clearly wasn't expecting an answer. It was less of a question and more of a challenge, a silent demand hanging in the air.

Julia turned to Dr. Howard and said, "He's a good family friend who truly cares for my son."

Dr. Howard turned to Julia, his tone shifting, softening as he sought to justify his stance. "I've already removed the security guard. There's no need for drastic measures. We just need a little more time to understand what's happening. And then he'll be free to leave. Just a few more days, that's all I'm asking."

The room seemed to hold its breath, thick with tension, the unspoken battle pressing against the walls. The air itself felt charged, heavy with the weight of conflicting wills, as if the next words spoken would tip the scales one way or another.

Kevin's mother stepped into the room, her face etched with exhaustion, every movement deliberate yet weighed down by weariness. Her eyes found Sean first, flickering with a mix of concern and curiosity, searching for answers before she even spoke.

"Look at my son, having to sit here and endure these tests against his will. A few days may mean nothing to you, but for a child, its pain," she asked, her voice soft but laced with tension.

Her gaze flickered briefly to Dr. Howard, catching the frustration tightening his features, before settling back on Sean. She pressed, her voice growing firmer, no longer merely questioning, but demanding an answer.

The room settled into a tense, charged silence, each person entangled in the invisible threads of conflicting emotions.

Sean's gaze flickered to Julia, and in that instant, he became acutely aware of the tremor in his own voice, how, despite his composed exterior, his words had carried the weight of the storm raging beneath.

He exhaled subtly, steadying himself before speaking again, this time softer. "I'm only concerned about Kevin. I asked Dr. Howard why he won't release him, he's not sick anymore."

Moving toward Julia with quiet intent, he reached for the bags and coffee in her hands, his touch gentle, and his concern evident in every motion. He met her eyes with a reassuring smile, an unspoken attempt to ease the burdens she carried, both the visible ones in her arms and the heavier, unseen ones pressing down on her shoulders.

"I am, too," Julia admitted, her voice unsteady, trembling beneath the weight of her emotions. "I'm so worried about Kevin. I keep wondering why they won't release him, and now..." She swallowed hard, her breath hitching. "Now, I wish I had never called for help."

Her hands curled into fists at her sides as if trying to hold herself together, but the cracks in her composure deepened. Her eyes shimmered, the unshed tears reflecting the helplessness pressing down on her, threatening to break free.

"I told you not to call them, Mom," Kevin said firmly, his voice carrying a quiet authority far beyond his years. His gaze was unwavering, almost defiant, as if he had foreseen this moment from the very beginning. There was no hesitation, no wavering uncertainty, only the steady conviction of someone who had known all along what the outcome would be.

"I know that now, sweetheart," Julia whispered, her voice fracturing under the weight of her emotions. "But when I saw you like that... I thought I was going to lose you, just like I lost your father."

Tears spilled freely down her cheeks, her anguish laid bare, raw and unguarded. She clung to the memory of that desperate moment, caught in the agony between remorse and the unrelenting love that had compelled her decision. The fear of almost losing Kevin still clung to her like a shadow, refusing to let go.

"Don't worry, Julia," Sean said gently, his voice a steady anchor against the storm of her emotions. "We'll find a way. I know you're scared, but you don't have to be. I promise you, nothing is going to happen to Kevin. You can count on me."

He stood beside her, solid and unwavering, his presence a quiet pillar of strength. In that moment, he wasn't just offering words, he was offering certainty, the reassurance she so desperately needed to hold onto.

"Thank you. I really appreciate that," Julia murmured, a flicker of hope surfacing in her weary eyes. She straightened, brushing away the remnants of her tears, as if gathering what strength she had left.

Turning slightly, she glanced toward Dr. Howard, only to realize he was already gone. Her gaze shifted back to Sean and Kevin, determination settling into her features. "Let me go and talk to the doctor again," she said, her voice steadier now.

With that, she turned and left the room, her steps firm, resolute. Yet, even as she moved with purpose, the weight of her worry still clung to her, trailing behind like an unseen shadow.

Kevin grew unusually quiet, his shoulders slumping as he stared down at his hands, the weight of uncertainty settling over him like a heavy cloak. The spark of defiance that had burned in his eyes moments ago had dimmed, replaced by a quiet misery that he didn't bother to hide.

Noticing the shift, Sean crouched down beside him, meeting his gaze with a warm, reassuring smile.

"Hey," Sean said gently, his tone light, laced with playful mischief. "Did you know you can go on the internet too? Maybe even teach you a thing or two about navigating it."

A subtle attempt to lift the boy's spirits, to remind him that, no matter how confined he felt, his world was still limitless.

"Do you really think I'm someone important? That I'll be able to help them somehow?" Kevin asked, his voice tinged with something new, something raw and hopeful.

His eyes, once clouded with doubt, now gleamed with renewed energy. A flush of color returned to his cheeks, and for the first time in what felt like forever, he looked alive, vibrant, as if Sean's words had struck a chord deep within him, reigniting a spark that had nearly been extinguished.

Sean knew he had to help Kevin regain his strength, anything less would be unbearable. The thought of leaving the boy in this state, stripped of his confidence and trapped in uncertainty, was enough to break him.

But it wasn't just Kevin. Julia's sorrow clung to him in ways he hadn't anticipated, heavier than he wanted to admit. The pain in her eyes, the exhaustion in her voice, it unsettled him, pressing against his chest like an invisible weight. He couldn't stand by and do nothing. He wouldn't.

Sean was the only one who could truly help Kevin, and he understood the gravity of that responsibility. The weight of it settled deep within him, but what struck him most was the change already unfolding before his eyes.

In just a brief exchange, he had given Kevin something rare, something powerful, hope. A hope that, perhaps, the boy had never truly felt before.

Maybe if his father were alive, he would have done the same, offered the same reassurance, the same steady presence. But Kevin didn't have that. He didn't have a father to guide him the way a son needed, especially at a time like this.

The realization humbled Sean, yet at the same time, it strengthened his resolve. He had to see this through. Whatever happened next, he would stand by Kevin, because, in this extraordinary journey, the boy didn't just need a protector. He needed someone who believed in him.

"Yes, Kevin. I think so," Sean replied, his voice steady and resolute, each word laced with an unshakable conviction.

To Kevin, that answer was more than just words, it was certainty. It felt as solid and reassuring as a mountain, something to anchor him in the storm of uncertainty he had been caught in for so long. For the first time, he felt grounded, seen, and believed in.

As the two spoke, lost in their conversation, the door creaked open, and a nurse entered, balancing a tray with Kevin's lunch. The soft clink of utensils against the plate momentarily broke the moment, pulling them both back to reality.

Sean glanced at the clock and realized his time had run out. With a quiet sigh, he began gathering his things, packing up with careful precision, as if reluctant to leave.

Turning back to Kevin, he offered a reassuring smile. "I'd better get going," he said gently. "But I promise you, I'll be back as soon as I can." His words weren't just a promise, they were a vow.

Kevin shot a sharp glare at the nurse, clearly unimpressed by the interruption, before snapping his attention back to Sean.

His wide eyes, filled with doubt and vulnerability, searched Sean's face, clinging to something unseen. "Are you coming back for sure?" he asked, his voice quieter this time, laced with hesitation.

It wasn't just a question, and it was a test and a reassurance. A fragile hope teetering on the edge of disappointment, as though he was already bracing himself for the letdown, for the possibility that Sean's promise would dissolve like so many before it. The weight of that doubt hung thick in the air, unspoken yet undeniable.

Sean looked at Kevin, and in that moment, he saw past the boy's brave front, saw the quiet loneliness that lingered beneath. It was a loneliness not of circumstance, but of something deeper, something unspoken. Sean pointed at his head and said, "Read it! If you're not sure. And feel my emotion."

He crouched slightly to meet Kevin's gaze, his tone gentle yet unwavering. He moved to Kevin's bed again.

"You know, Kevin," Sean began, "I'm going to give you my cell phone number. And not just mine, I'll also give you my parents' home number in Toronto."

Kevin's eyes flickered with curiosity, but Sean continued before he could respond. "Just in case you need me before I come back from lunch. Or "If anything happens and you need my help..." He let the words linger, watching Kevin absorb them, then added, "You know where to find me."

"Keep it as an emergency number. Call me anytime, you or your mom. No matter what, okay?"

It wasn't just reassurance. It was a lifeline. A promise that Kevin wouldn't have to face this alone.

Kevin's eyes softened, the faintest glimmer of trust flickering back to life. He nodded, holding onto Sean's words as if they were something tangible, something solid in a world that had always felt uncertain.

His wide eyes shone, brimming with an emotion too deep for words. It wasn't just about the number scribbled on a piece of paper; it was about what it meant. For the first time in a long while, he felt something unfamiliar yet unmistakable connection.

This wasn't just another adult passing through his life, offering empty reassurances before fading away. Sean saw him. Sean cared. And in that moment, Kevin realized he had found something he had rarely known.

A true friend. Sean handed him the slip of paper, his fingers lingering for just a moment, silent reassurance, a quiet promise. He offered Kevin a small, steady smile before turning toward the door.

Kevin clutched the paper tightly, his grip firm as if anchoring himself to something real, something that couldn't slip away. It wasn't just a number, it was hope. A fragile but powerful connection, one he hadn't expected, but one he desperately wanted to last.

Kevin nodded, his expression calm but tinged with hope, as Sean made his way toward the door.

"See you, Kevin," Sean said warmly, flashing a reassuring smile as he reached for the handle.

Just as he was about to step out, Kevin's voice stopped him. "Sean!"

Sean turned, eyebrows raised in question.

Kevin pointed to the glass of water sitting on the table. "Don't forget that just to make sure your mom's sickness doesn't rise again."

A chuckle rumbled from Sean's chest, amusement flickering in his eyes. "No, I won't," he said, shaking his head as he turned back to grab the glass.

He lifted it slightly in a mock toast, gave Kevin a playful wink, and then stepped out of the room, leaving behind something intangible yet undeniable, a lightness that hadn't been there before.

Sean headed straight for his mother's room, his pace steady but his mind still lingering on Kevin.

Helen was just finishing her lunch when he walked in. The moment she saw him, her face lit up with warmth, yet beneath her smile, there was something else, something unspoken.

"Oh, Sean! How happy I am that you're here," she said, her voice bright, but laced with an undertone he couldn't quite place.

Sean's brow furrowed slightly. He knew his mother too well to miss the faint ripple beneath her words.

"Is something wrong, Mom?" he asked, his voice gentle but probing.

She hesitated for just a fraction of a second before shaking her head. "No, nothing's wrong. I'm just happy," she said, her tone smoothing into something calmer, more measured.

But Sean wasn't convinced. Something lingered beneath her words, just out of reach, and he couldn't shake the feeling that whatever it was, she wasn't ready to say it yet.

He moved closer, settling beside her and gently taking her hand in his. There was a quiet tenderness in the gesture, a silent reassurance that he was there, not just physically, but in the way that truly mattered.

Reaching for the glass of water, he handed it to her, his expression unreadable. "Could you do me a favor?" Sean asked softly, his voice calm yet carrying a quiet weight. Helen's smile was warm, unwavering. "Of course, Sean. What is it?"

His grip on her hand tightened ever so slightly. "May I ask you to drink this water? Please don't ask me why, simply it's from Kevin," he said, his tone steady but laced with something else, mystery.

The air between them grew heavy, laden with unspoken meaning. Helen studied his face, a fleeting memory surfacing, and she couldn't recall the first time she drank from Sean's glass, as she had been in the midst of a seizure at the time. She sensed that whatever this was, it went beyond a simple request. Yet, without hesitation, she reached for the glass.

Helen studied his face, searching for any sign of hesitation. Finding none, she nodded, her trust in him unwavering. Without question, she raised the glass, her fingers wrapping around it with quiet acceptance. But curiosity flickered in her eyes as she hesitated for just a moment. "What is it, Sean?" she asked, glancing at the water in her hand.

Sean's expression remained calm, but there was something beneath his words, something weightier than the simplicity of a glass of water.

"This is from Kevin," he said, his voice even yet laced with quiet urgency. "He asked me to bring it to you. It's just a glass of water, the same kind that saved you from a seizure once before."

Helen's grip tightened slightly. "Please," Sean added, holding her gaze. "Don't ask me why right now. Ask me later."

The unspoken weight of his words lingered between them, thick with a mystery Helen chose not to challenge. Without a word, she lifted the glass, took a sip.

Helen hesitated for a fleeting moment, uncertainty flickering in her eyes. But then, with a quiet nod, she chose to trust her son. Without another word, she lifted the glass and drank, the cool water sliding down her throat as if carrying something unseen with it.

She handed the empty glass back to Sean, her fingers lingering just a second longer than necessary.

"Say thank you to your friend for me," she said softly, her voice laced with quiet gratitude. Yet, beneath it, there was still a hint of puzzlement, as if she could sense there was more to this moment than met the eye.

"Where's Dad?" Sean asked, his gaze sweeping the room. "He's in the cafeteria," Helen answered, her voice gentle. "He asked me to let you know, in case you wanted to join him."

Sean nodded, offering her a small, reassuring smile. "I'll stay with you."

He lingered by her side, cherishing the warmth of her presence, the unspoken memories weaving between them like a silent melody of the past. Helen seemed to revel in it, her eyes bright with nostalgia. After a while, she reached for his hand, her fingers trembling slightly.

"Your dad is waiting for you," she murmured. "Go on. I need to rest again."

Sean embraced her tightly, as if trying to imprint the moment in his heart. "Thanks, Mom," he whispered. "I'll go see him." As he rose and made his way to the door, Helen watched him go, a soft, knowing look in her eyes, comforted by his presence, even as he left.

Sean strode purposefully toward the hospital cafeteria, the murmur of voices and rhythmic clatter of utensils growing louder with each step. As he reached the entrance, he hesitated, his eyes sweeping across the room. The scent of coffee and faint traces of disinfectant lingered in the air. Then, he spotted his father, seated alone at a corner table, lost in thought, his fingers idly tracing the rim of his cup.

Sean moved toward him, his steps quiet, measured. Pulling out a chair, he met his father's gaze. "May I?" His voice was soft but warm, carrying an unspoken familiarity.

His father looked up, his expression shifting from contemplation to warmth. A slow smile spread across his face as he gestured to the seat. "Yes, please, help yourself, son," he said, his tone laced with quiet relief. "How's everything going?"

Sean settled in, his hands resting lightly on the table. "Okay, I think," he replied, his words careful, thoughtful, as if weighing the emotions behind them.

His father's gaze flickered over the menu, though his mind seemed elsewhere. "How's Kevin?" he asked, his tone casual but laced with quiet interest. "I've heard a lot about him. He's a bright kid, after all." His eyes remained fixed on the menu, never quite meeting Sean's.

Sean studied him for a moment, reading between the lines, the genuine curiosity, and the unspoken thoughts lingering just beneath the surface. "He's doing alright," Sean replied carefully, his voice measured as he watched for any shift in his father's expression.

Sean's words hung between them, subtle yet heavy, stirring something deep within his father. Though his expression remained composed, his fingers stilled against the menu, betraying the quiet storm beneath his surface. Concern shadowed his eyes, faint, but unmistakable.

He was afraid. Afraid that if he encouraged Sean to step further into this path, it might lead to dangers neither of them could predict. Afraid that the deeper Sean went, the harder it would be to turn back. And worst of all, afraid that one day, he might not be able to protect his son from the unseen threats lurking ahead.

Just then, a waitress approached their table, pen poised, ready to take their order. Sean and his father exchanged a brief glance before settling on their choices, their conversation momentarily interrupted. Once the orders were placed and the waitress had moved on, the moment of quiet stretched between them.

Sean leaned forward slightly, his voice soft but deliberate. "How about Mom?" he asked. "When are they going to give us the results of here tests?"

His father hesitated, his gaze drifting to the edge of the table, as if searching for the right words, or perhaps the strength to say them. A slow breath, a measured pause. Then, finally, he spoke.

"They're still running a few tests," he said, his tone steady, almost rehearsed. "But they seem optimistic. Hopefully, it won't be much longer."

He tried to sound reassuring, but Sean caught the subtle tension in his features, the quiet weight of worry pressing just beneath the surface, a fear too stubborn to fade, even in the face of hope.

James studied Sean carefully, his fatherly intuition sharpening like a blade. He knew his son too well, knew the way his words often danced around the truth, how his questions served as veils, concealing the deeper emotions he wasn't ready to voice.

A beat of silence passed between them before James spoke, his tone calm yet deliberate. "You're still thinking about the boy, aren't you?" His gaze met Sean's with quiet understanding, not pushing, not accusing, just knowing.

Sean hesitated, momentarily thrown by how effortlessly his father had seen through him. He parted his lips to respond, but for a brief moment, the words stalled, tangled in the weight of unspoken thoughts. The silence between them felt almost palpable, an unacknowledged truth hanging in the air.

Finally, he exhaled, leaning back in his chair. "As a matter of fact, yes," he admitted, his voice edged with contemplation.

He ran a hand through his hair, eyes distant. "You know, Dad, sometimes I really want to know who Kevin's father was. Is Kevin like him? Or is he something else entirely, someone truly unique, one of a kind?"

He paused, his gaze drifting as his thoughts unraveled, pulling him deeper into the unanswered questions that had taken root in his mind. When he spoke again, his voice carried a quiet intensity, laced with both curiosity and frustration. "And where is his father now? What happened to him?"

The words felt heavier than he expected, as though voicing them made the mystery more tangible, more pressing. He studied his father's face, searching for insight, for reassurance, anything that might lift the shroud of uncertainty. But the silence that followed only deepened the enigma, leaving Kevin's past an unsolved puzzle that refused to let go.

James regarded Sean thoughtfully, his sharp gaze narrowing ever so slightly as he studied his son's expression. A quiet moment passed, heavy with unspoken considerations, before he shifted in his chair, settling in as if preparing for a serious conversation.

"Son," he said at last, his tone careful, deliberate. "Are you saying you want me to look into what happened to Kevin's father? To gather all the information for you? And... use my sources as a retired police officer to find out about him?"

There was no accusation in his voice, only quiet scrutiny, measuring Sean's intent, weighing the implications of such a request. James held Sean's gaze, his expression calm yet probing, searching for the depth of his son's investment in the mystery that seemed to weigh so heavily on him.

Sean didn't answer right away. Instead, he simply looked at his father, his eyes shadowed with an unspoken helplessness that said more than words ever could. The silence stretched between them, thick with meaning, until finally, Sean exhaled and spoke.

"That is exactly my request. You were a cop, right?" His voice was careful, edged with something close to hope. "And getting this kind of information... It's easy for you, isn't it?"

He hesitated for only a breath before leaning in slightly, his next words quieter, almost pleading. "Can I ask for your help?"

His words hung in the air, a mixture of vulnerability and determination, as if he were bracing himself for the possibility of rejection but hoping for the support he so desperately needed.

His father looked at Sean with a glimmer of pride in his eyes, but before he could respond, Sean's phone buzzed to life. He picked it up, glancing briefly at the screen before answering. "Hello, Sean speaking."

"Hi, Sean. This is Sharon," came the cheerful voice on the other end. "Hi, Sharon. How are you? Are you in the office now?" Sean asked, his tone lightening. "Yes, I told you I'd call, and here I am," she said, giggling happily, her energy infectious.

Sean smiled, leaning back slightly in his chair. "Well, it's good to hear from you." "Listen, Sean," Sharon continued, "would you like to have dinner tonight?"

"Yes, I'd be glad to spend more time with you while I'm here," Sean replied warmly. Then he continued: "I'm free anytime, but I know how busy you are with work. So I thought it'd be better to leave the timing up to you, whenever it's most convenient."

"Don't worry about my job," Sharon said, her voice bright and cheerful. "I've got some time off this week. I even told Mark I'd be spending some of it with you." She sounded even happier than during their earlier conversation. "That's great. What time?" Sean asked.

"How about 6:00 o'clock?" She said, "That's fine with me. Where?" Sean replied. "Well, that's a good question," Sharon said quickly, as if eager for his answer. "Do you remember that small café we used to go to when we were students at the University of Toronto?"

Sean smiled, a nostalgic warmth filling his voice. "Yes, I remember. It was Café Elise, right? An excellent choice." He sighed contentedly, then added, "We can refresh those memories again. Do you know if the food is still as good there?"

"It definitely is," Sharon replied enthusiastically. "As a matter of fact, I still go there at least once a week. Sometimes Mark comes with me, too." "Alright, I guess I'll see you there," Sean said, his tone relaxed and agreeable. "Perfect. See you there. Bye," Sharon responded, her voice as lively as ever.

They both hung up, leaving Sean with a faint smile and a spark of anticipation for the evening ahead.

"We're going to see each other tonight," Sean explained to his dad, a faint smile lingering on his face. "Sharon mentioned she wanted to spend more time with me while I'm in Toronto," he added, his tone light but carrying a subtle warmth. His father nodded knowingly, a hint of a smile playing at the corners of his mouth as he listened.

"I'm so glad that you two are spending time together again," James said, a genuine smile lighting up his face. He glanced at his watch, then pushed back his chair with a chuckle. "Well, son, I'd better get going. Your mom must be up by now, and if I'm not there when she needs me. Well, God help me!"

They both laughed, the sound easy and warm. James stood and reached for the bill, settling it with the waitress before giving Sean a quick pat on the shoulder. "Take care, son," he said, his voice filled with quiet pride as he walked away.

"Dad! Wait, I'm going with you, but before we go, you didn't give me an answer?" Sean called out, quickly rising from his chair.

James paused and said, "Okay, then he turned back to his son, his expression shifting to something more serious. "Son," he began, his voice quiet but firm, "before we go, there's something I need to tell you about your mother."

Sean's steps slowed as he caught the tone in his father's voice. "What is it?" he asked cautiously. James sighed, rubbing the back of his neck as though searching for the right words. "I didn't tell you earlier because I didn't want you to worry before I had an answer. But..." He hesitated, the weight of his next words hanging heavily between them.

"What's wrong?" Sean asked, his voice tight with concern. He braced himself, his eyes locked on his father, waiting for the truth. "The doctor told me that your mother has a tumor," James said, his voice barely more than a whisper.

"She had an X-ray and some tests yesterday, and after that seizure, they had to confirm the result, and now they're waiting for the results. They think..." He faltered, his breath unsteady, as though the very words were too heavy to say aloud.

"They think it might be a brain tumor. If it is, she'll need surgery immediately." His voice cracked, and for the first time, Sean saw his father unravel. Tears welled in James's eyes, his composure slipping under the crushing weight of the revelation. Slowly, he lowered his head, his shoulders caving as if the burden had finally become too much to bear. The silence that followed was suffocating, thick with unspoken fears, the terrifying uncertainty of what lay ahead.

Sean's stomach twisted. His pulse pounded in his ears. "That's horrible," he murmured, his voice shaking with a mixture of shock and frustration. "You should've told me earlier." He sucked in a sharp breath, willing himself to stay steady, but the weight of it all pressed down on him.

He forced himself to focus. To act. "Let's go back to her room and wait for the doctor," he said, his concern for his mother eclipsing everything else. Right now, nothing mattered more than being by her side.

Then, after a brief pause, Sean swallowed hard and asked, "Does Mom know?" His voice was strained, barely steady, and his eyes searched his father's face, desperate for clarity, even as the weight of the truth began to settle over him. James exhaled slowly, as if the very question had added to his burden. "Yes," he admitted, his voice thick with emotion. "But we thought it would be better to keep it to ourselves until we had the results. We didn't want to worry you unnecessarily." Sean's chest tightened. He understood, but that didn't make it any easier to hear.

He paused, taking a deep breath as he met Sean's gaze. "I only found out about it this morning when the doctor shared the latest test results. I didn't know how to tell you... Or if I even should, not until we had more clarity." His shoulders sagged slightly, the weight of the decision and its consequences pressing down on him. "I feel so miserable," Sean admitted, his voice low and filled with anguish. "Let's go now," James said firmly as he rose from his seat, motioning for Sean to follow.

The hallway was buzzing with activity as they stepped out. A crowd of doctors, nurses, patients, and visitors moved about, creating a flurry of motion and conversation. Some people waited anxiously in the seating area, while others stood around chatting quietly. The elevators, usually easy to access in the morning, were now packed, requiring a brief wait before they could get inside.

When they finally arrived on the third floor, the scene was calmer. As they walked toward the information desk, they both waved at Hanna, the receptionist, who offered a polite smile in return. Without hesitation, James led the way to Helen's room. He opened the door slowly, stepping inside with Sean close behind him.

"Hi, darling. Did you sleep well?" James asked, his voice warm with affection. "Oh, you two are together. How wonderful to see you both," Helen said, her gaze shifting gracefully from James to Sean.

There was something different about Helen, an unspoken shift in her aura, subtle yet undeniable. James and Sean exchanged a quick glance, both silently acknowledging the change. "Helen, you look... different," James remarked, a note of wonder in his voice. "I can't quite put my finger on it, but I do know one thing, you are the most beautiful woman I've ever seen." "Yes, Mom. Your skin is so radiant and healthy-looking," Sean said, unable to take his eyes off her. "Did you do something different? Maybe put on some makeup or try a new skincare routine?"

"No, but I feel great right now," Helen replied with a serene smile.

Just then, the door swung open, and the doctor stepped inside, followed closely by a couple of other doctors and specialists. He carried Helen's X-rays and medical chart in his hands, his grip firm yet uncertain, as if holding something that defied reason. His gaze shifted cautiously, first to Helen, then to James, and finally to Sean. A quiet, uneasy weight settled over him, visible in the slight tension in his posture, the hesitation in his breath. For a moment, he simply stood there, as though searching for the right words, yet finding none that could adequately explain what he was about to say.

"Mrs. Morgan, I must admit, I don't quite know how to explain this," the doctor began, his voice tinged with disbelief. His fingers tightened around the chart, as though searching for an answer within the ink and paper.

"We have the X-rays from this morning, and we also have the ones taken just an hour ago, as a precaution." He hesitated, his brow furrowing. "The first set clearly shows a tumor, one that required immediate surgical intervention." He held up an X-ray film, pointing to a spot on the brain where a tumor, the size of a walnut, was unmistakably visible. "But the second set, taken just hours later, shows no trace of it. In fact, it indicates that you're completely fine." As he spoke, he displayed another X-ray; this time, the tumor was gone.

He paused, glancing down at the scans once more, as if expecting them to change before his eyes. "We're as puzzled as you must be. Even the X-rays from a few days ago confirmed the tumor was there. I have no medical explanation for this."

His voice dropped slightly, thick with incredulity. "It's as if the tumor has simply… vanished." Taking a deep breath, he continued, "I'll need to run a few more tests to be certain. If those results match what we've seen this afternoon, you'll be free to go home and enjoy the rest of your life. For now, I'd like to proceed cautiously, but this… this is extraordinary. I'll tell the nurse to take you to the MRI room again for another scan, just to be on the safe side." Then he left the room.

Tears streamed down James's face. Sean, overcome with excitement, turned to his mother and hugged her tightly as he said: "Do you remember that I gave you a glass of water?" his voice was tinged with unease. "Yes, I remember," Helen replied, narrowing her eyes. "What was in it?"

"I don't know," Sean admitted hesitantly. "But I do know there was something, and that Kevin was involved." Before Sean could say more, his phone buzzed, breaking the tense moment. He quickly answered. "Hello?" "Sean, I need to see you in my room," Kevin's voice came through, calm but firm.

"Is something wrong, Kevin?" Sean asked, his concern evident. "No, nothing's wrong. But there's something very important I want to show you. Are you coming?"

"Yes, I'll be there in no time," Sean replied, ending the call with a click. He slipped his phone back into his pocket, a determined look crossing his face. "I'll find out what's going on," he murmured, more to himself than to anyone else, before heading toward Kevin's room.

"Oh, Mom! You don't know how happy I am right now," Sean exclaimed, rushing to Helen's bedside. He wrapped his arms around her, holding her tightly as he pressed a kiss to her cheek. His eyes shimmered with uncontainable joy, his relief pouring out in every trembling breath. "I need to see Kevin, if that's alright with you?" Helen's eyes brimming with unshed tears, squeezed Sean's hand and gazed at him with quiet understanding. "Say thank you to your friend for me, darling," she said softly, her voice laced with gratitude.

Sean turned to his father, and they embraced, tears flowing freely. James gently patted Sean's shoulder as they shared a quiet moment of happiness. Without hesitation, Sean gathered his things, preparing to leave. He turned back, his expression shifting to something more serious.

"I will," he assured her, "but please, keep this to yourselves. If the doctors find out, they'll never leave him alone." In his haste, he barely noticed the glance his parents exchanged, their expressions flickering with curiosity and concern. He hesitated again, turning to his parents. "Mom, Dad, please keep this a secret. Don't mention the glass of water to the doctors or anyone else, okay?"

"As you wish, son," Helen replied, her voice calm but tinged with intrigue. "But what was in that glass? Sean recognized that the question was repeating. He looked at his mother and replied, "I told you I'm going to find out." Helen asked: "I just want to properly thank Kevin if he truly had something to do with my healing."

James, who had remained silent until now, arched an eyebrow. "I thought you were going to see Sharon tonight?" "I am," Sean replied, glancing at him briefly. "But I need to see Kevin first, then I'll go." In a brief silence, he continued: "It must have something to do with Kevin," he murmured to himself, his voice laced with thought. Then, looking back at his mother, he added, "Don't worry, Mom, I'll make sure he knows how grateful you are." Before stepping out, he leaned down and pressed another soft kiss to Helen's cheek. Then, pausing briefly, he met his father's gaze.

"See you later, Dad. Take care," he said with a faint smile, then turned and slipped out the door, his heart pounding with urgency. "Something must have happened," Sean thought to himself, a sense of unease creeping over him.

As he approached Kevin's room, he paused at the doorway, catching sight of the boy staring blankly out the window. Kevin's posture was eerily still, his expression vacant. His eyes, devoid of any spark, looked like those of a lifeless statue. There was no movement in his body, no flicker of emotion on his face, only an unsettling stillness that sent a chill through Sean's veins.

"Kevin! Are you alright?" Sean asked, his voice trembling with concern. Slowly, almost imperceptibly, Kevin's eyes shifted toward Sean. In that moment, it was as though a switch had been flipped, life surged back into his face, and his body stirred with movement. The vacant, lifeless expression vanished, replaced by a look of awareness and normalcy, as if he had been pulled back from the brink of some unseen abyss.

"Hi, Sean. When did you get here?" Kevin asked, his voice calm and steady, as if nothing unusual had happened. "Hi, Kevin. I was worried about you," Sean replied, his concern evident. "What happened? Do you need any help?" He hesitated, uncertain of what he truly wanted to ask. It was the first question that came to mind, but his thoughts were a jumble of unease and curiosity.

"No, Sean. I'm great," Kevin said with a faint smile. "You know, I want to show you something. I've been thinking about it for a long time, and I decided this is the perfect time." Sean let out a relieved breath. "I'm glad to hear that. Alright, I'm all eyes and ears. Go ahead and show me whatever you have in mind." Sean pulled up a chair beside the bed, crossing his arms as he leaned back, his curiosity piqued. Kevin sighed deeply, his gaze locking onto Sean's eyes for a long, contemplative moment. It was as if he were weighing the enormity of a secret he was about to share, searching for the right words to begin.

"You know," Kevin finally said, his voice low and deliberate, "I can do whatever I want with my body. Somehow, I've gained complete control, absolute power over it. My whole body. It's what everyone dreams of, isn't it? You name it, I can do it. I can even command my body to die... maybe for a few minutes, or even a few days."

He paused, his expression unreadable. "If you ask me exactly how long, I can't give you an answer. The truth is, I don't know how this happened. But it's real." His voice carried both awe and a hint of unease, as though he was still coming to terms with the scope of his own abilities.

Sean murmured: Oh God! Then he remained silent, his thoughts swirling. Questions and doubts played in his mind. Is he toying with me, or is this really the truth? He wondered, struggling to piece it all together.

But as he studied Kevin's face, there was no trace of deception or humor, only a calm sincerity that made everything he said seem unnervingly real. The way Kevin spoke, with quiet conviction, left little room for doubt.

"You mean you don't believe me? Or you think I made this up?" Kevin asked, his voice edged with frustration, his eyes searching

Sean's for answers. Sean met his gaze, his expression unreadable. "I didn't say that," he replied evenly. "I didn't say anything at all."

Kevin leaned forward, his face flushed with a mix of hurt and determination. "You don't have to say anything, you know that I can feel your emotions," he said, his voice quieter now, tinged with something almost pleading. "You know, Sean, ever since I've had this… feeling, I haven't known who to trust. I thought about telling my mom, but it's too soon for her to hear something like this. Besides, she'd just worry even more."

Kevin's voice grew steadier, but the emotion lingered. "Then I thought of you. I thought you'd understand. But if you want proof, I'll give you proof. I'll prove it to you right now."

His sudden shift in tone caught Sean off guard, leaving him unsure of how to respond. Kevin's upset demeanor was unlike anything Sean had seen before, making the moment feel all the more charged with tension.

"Please, Sean, come closer and sit beside me," Kevin said softly, gesturing to the space next to him. Sean hesitated briefly but did as he was told, sitting down with curiosity and unease. Kevin raised his index finger, holding it in front of Sean. "I don't want to scare you," Kevin said, his voice steady but carrying an unmistakable gravity that sent a ripple of unease through Sean.

He extended his hand, holding it out with quiet confidence. "Just look at my finger, and with this pen, put a dot anywhere on it." There was no challenge in his tone, no theatrics, just a calm certainty that made Sean hesitate, his grip tightening slightly around the pen as he studied Kevin's outstretched hand.

Kevin held a tissue in the palm of his other hand, ready for whatever he was about to demonstrate. Sean drew a dot on Kevin's finger and stared at the dot, unsure of what he was supposed to see. For a few long moments, nothing happened. Then, something extraordinary occurred.

At first, a faint line appeared on Kevin's skin, almost like a seam coming undone. Slowly, the line widened, revealing the flesh beneath. Yet, there wasn't a single drop of blood, not even the smallest bead.

"Can you see it, Sean? There's no blood," Kevin said, his voice steady, as though he had done this a hundred times before. Sean's eyes widened in disbelief. "How in the hell did you do that? Is this some kind of trick?" he asked, his voice trembling with fear and confusion.

Kevin's calm demeanor only deepened Sean's unease. "This isn't a trick, Sean. It's real. Now, look more carefully, Sean. Can you see the wound?" Kevin asked, his gaze fixed on his finger.

Sean leaned in slightly, his eyes narrowing as he tried to make sense of what he was witnessing. Suddenly, blood began to seep from the wound, first as a trickle, then flowing steadily onto Kevin's palm. The tissue in his hand quickly absorbed it, turning wet and crimson.

Kevin remained calm, his tone even. "From my finger," he replied simply. "I wanted to open a wound, and I did. Now, look again, how I control my bloodstream too," he instructed, holding up his hand with quiet confidence. Sean's eyes were glued to the wound as it began to close, the edges slowly knitting themselves together. The blood stopped flowing, and within moments, the cut was gone entirely, no scar, no trace that it had ever existed. The skin looked flawless, as though untouched.

Sean staggered to his feet and sweating, overwhelmed by what he had just witnessed. A wave of dizziness washed over him, and he steadied himself against the wall, his mind racing to comprehend the impossible sight before him. "No, there's no logical explanation for this. How could this happen?" Sean muttered, his voice trembling as he looked at Kevin, then back at his finger. Everything was back to normal. Kevin's finger appeared completely unscathed, just as it had been before.

Sean, unable to process what he had just witnessed, grabbed Kevin's hand tightly. His eyes searched Kevin's face, desperate for answers. "Was that real? I mean… how did you do that? Were you in pain?" he asked, his voice a mixture of disbelief and urgency.

"Honestly, I don't know," Kevin admitted, his voice calm but tinged with uncertainty. "I only know that I can control every inch of my body." He paused, letting the weight of his words settle in the air. After a moment, he looked at Sean with a curious expression and asked, "Do you want to see something else?"

"No, no," Sean said, shaking his head as he instinctively stepped backward, his face pale and his movements unsteady. Slowly, he made his way back to the bed and sat beside Kevin, his mind racing.

"Does anybody else besides me know about this?" he asked, his voice barely above a whisper. "No," Kevin replied calmly, his tone steady and reassuring. "I told you before, you're the second person who knows."

Sean looked at him intently, his voice firm as he asked, "Who's the other person?" Kevin chuckled lightly. "Me, silly," he said without thinking, but his smile faded quickly as he realized how flippant it sounded. "I'm sorry," he added, his tone more subdued. "I didn't mean it like that."

Sean continued to study Kevin, still grappling with the strangeness of the situation. He had no idea what had happened to his friend but felt a growing need to understand. "Kevin," he began slowly, his curiosity edging out his confusion. "Why are you telling me all this? Why me?"

"Because… something, or someone, inside my mind gives me the feeling that I can only trust you," Kevin said, his voice low but filled with conviction. His eyes searched Sean's, seeking understanding. "I don't know why I feel this way, but you have to trust me on this, okay?"

There was no hesitation in his words, no trace of doubt, only an unshakable certainty that sent a quiet chill through Sean. He paused, letting the words sink in before continuing. "If you're looking for an explanation, I have to tell you, there isn't one. Not right now. I just… feel it. I hear it."

Kevin's shoulders slumped slightly, a subtle sign of exhaustion. The weight of Sean's questions, combined with the strain of revealing his secret, seemed to take its toll. He looked at Sean, his expression both weary and pleading, as if hoping his friend would simply accept his words without pushing further.

"May I ask you something, Kevin? It's important to me," Sean said, his voice tinged with hesitation. Kevin nodded, his tone unwavering. "Yes, you can. And as I've already told you, I don't know how it works, I just did it."

Sean took a deep breath before speaking. "Still, I would like to ask you. Do you remember this morning, you gave me a glass of water for my mother? I need to know… what was in there?" Kevin's expression remained calm, unwavering. "I don't know," he said simply. "I just did what I felt I had to do. I commanded the water to wash away what didn't belong to purge the unnecessary, the unwelcome. Then I blew gently across its surface, transforming what remained into a stream of cleansing essence."

His voice was steady, almost serene. "I wanted to free your mind. I didn't want you to be burdened or stressed about your loved one." He paused, his gaze locked onto Sean's, searching for something beneath the surface. "Why do you ask?"

"Do you know what exactly you did to that glass of water?" Sean asked impatiently, leaning forward.

Kevin replied wearily, his voice low. "I changed something in the water so it would help your mother." Sean's brows furrowed as he pressed on. "What did you change in the water? Do you mean the molecules or atoms, or maybe particles? Or something else?"

Kevin sighed, the weight of the conversation clearly taking a toll on him. "I don't know what they're called, but I call them little body, but I reprogrammed them to cleanse anything in her body that doesn't belong to a healthy one." Sean's curiosity only deepened. "What do you mean, reprogram? Like nanobots?" His eyes were wide, and he wasn't even blinking, hanging on to Kevin's every word.

Kevin tilted his head, confused. "What are nannnooo bots?" He laughed because of the last word. "Wait... were they organic?" Sean asked the question tumbling out in his excitement. "Organic?" Kevin echoed, his voice quieter now, tinged with weariness. His exhaustion was beginning to seep through the cracks of his usual composure.

"You mean natural?" He let out a faint breath, as if the question itself was unnecessary. "Of course. Otherwise, how could I feel them?"

Sean froze for a moment, his mind racing to make sense of what he was hearing. But seeing Kevin's drained expression, he realized he couldn't push him much further without causing more strain.

He realized he was expecting a scientific explanation from a ten-year-old boy, clearly, he was still just a child. Sean looked at Kevin's tired face and leaned forward, his tone serious.

"Look, Kevin," he said, his tone unwavering, "if anyone discovers this power of yours, the outcome won't be pretty. They'll want to study you, dissect what makes you so different. You'll be nothing more than a specimen, locked away, never seeing your mother again."

Kevin's face softened, his eyes darkening with the weight of the words. He nodded slowly. "Like what happened to my father?" His voice was calm but filled with an unspoken understanding. "I won't say a word," he vowed. "But you have to promise me the same."

Sean smiled faintly, his gaze warm but resolute. "I promise. But my sister is trustworthy, she's a professional in this field. I need to share it with her, and I trust her with my life," he said, placing his hand over his chest. "I'll keep it right here." He pointed at his heart, a gesture of loyalty that seemed to reassure them both.

Sean felt he had pushed Kevin too far and wanted to do something to lift his spirits. Looking into Kevin's eyes, he said with a playful grin, "You know, Kevin, with this extraordinary power, I'm calling you 'NonaMan7.' How's that? Do you like it?"

Kevin's eyes sparkled as he gazed at Sean, as if looking at a hero. He nodded, his smile radiant, more beautiful than any Sean had ever seen before. "Like Superman, and I'm NonaMan!" Kevin declared, leaping onto his bed and striking a heroic pose, his chest puffed out like a caped crusader ready to save the world.

Sean's curiosity was insatiable, and with plenty of time before his meeting with Sharon, he couldn't resist asking more. He studied Kevin's face carefully, trying to gauge his mood before speaking.

"Kevin, can I ask you something else? Just answer yes or no," Sean said cautiously. "Go ahead," Kevin replied, his tone neutral.

"Can you, for example, grow a hair or make a specific hair fall off? Like, just one in particular?" Sean asked, his voice filled with both disbelief and fascination. Kevin met Sean's gaze and nodded. "Yes. Do you want me to do it now?"

"Would you?" Sean asked, leaning forward, his skepticism battling with intrigue. He still couldn't fully wrap his mind around Kevin's abilities, but he wanted to see for himself.

"Just tell me which hair you want to fall out," Kevin said calmly. "I don't know, maybe one on your hand," Sean replied, his voice tinged with curiosity.

Kevin studied his hand for a moment, and Sean pointed to one of the longest hairs he could find. Kevin seemed to go unnaturally still. His breathing slowed so much that for a moment, Sean thought he'd stopped altogether. But when Sean glanced at him again, Kevin was fine, just breathing very slowly, his focus intense.

Sean leaned in closer, his eyes fixed on the chosen hair. He felt his face practically brushing Kevin's hand as he stared. Suddenly, there was movement. The tiny hair trembled, then began to grow, pushing upward at an unnatural pace. It stretched longer and longer, reaching nearly twenty centimeters before it detached, falling softly like a leaf in autumn. The hair landed on the floor.

Sean bent down, picking it up gingerly, as if handling something fragile and surreal. He turned the hair in his fingers, then looked back at Kevin, his face pale and wide-eyed. "What... how...?" he stammered, unable to form a complete thought.

Kevin remained calm, watching Sean's reaction with a quiet understanding. For Sean, it was as if he had just seen a ghost, or perhaps something even stranger. "How do you do that?" Sean asked, his voice barely above a whisper, his disbelief evident.

Kevin gave him a small smile and asked, "Would you show me your pinky finger?" Sean blinked, surprised by the odd request. "My pinky finger? You want a pinky swear?" he repeated, raising his hand slightly.

"If this solves anything, then here you are," he said, extending his hand toward Kevin, his pinky finger held out. "What does this mean?"

Kevin looked at him with calm composure. "This is your answer. The same way you chose your pinky finger when I asked you to, I chose that particular hair when you pointed it out. It's that easy for me," he explained.

Sean's mind was a whirlwind of confusion, overwhelmed by the sheer flood of unfamiliar events. He stood frozen, his thoughts tangled in the chaos of the moment, uncertain of what to say or do. His gaze drifted upward, searching the sky as if it held the answers he couldn't grasp. Then, turning to Kevin, he asked, his voice edged with both disbelief and curiosity, "Can you fly?"

Kevin burst into laughter, shaking his head. "I can't fly," he said, still chuckling. "Because, unlike some, I have yet to figure out how to defy gravity."

"Why not? You can control it, can't you?" Sean asked, his curiosity deepening.

Kevin fell into a deep, unsettling silence, his eyes clouded with memories. Then, after a long pause, he turned to Sean and said, "I tried… I tried to talk to gravity." Suddenly, his face went pale, his breath hitching as terror crept into his expression. He looked at Sean, his voice trembling. "Sean… it was the scariest thing that ever happened to me. I couldn't escape. Gravity wasn't just a force, it was alive, pulling me into something I couldn't understand. I struggled, I fought, but I was trapped. I thought I'd never get out."

His hands clenched as his voice dropped to a whisper. "That day… my mom found me. I wasn't responding. She panicked and called an ambulance. By the time I managed to return, they were already there. I begged her not to call, but she was terrified."

Kevin's body started to shake uncontrollably, his breathing ragged. Sean rushed forward, wrapping his arms around him, holding him steady. He whispered his name, over and over, his voice low so the nurses wouldn't hear.

Then, just as suddenly as it had begun, Kevin stilled. He took a deep breath, his trembling subsiding. "I'm okay… I'm okay," he muttered, though his voice was far from steady. He exhaled shakily, his gaze distant. "But thinking about that day… It's terrifying. Gravity is terrifying. I don't ever want to go near it again."

Sean nodded, his voice gentle. "Okay. Don't think about it."

Kevin looked at Sean with wide, innocent eyes, his voice barely above a whisper. "Maybe… maybe my dad was trapped there too. Maybe he tried to fly out of that place, and that's why he reached out to gravity," he murmured, His tone laced with a haunting vulnerability. "And that's why he was never able to come back. What if he is trapped there?"

Sean stared at Kevin, the explanation sinking in. The simplicity of it was baffling, yet it made perfect sense in a way that left him both amazed and unsettled.

Sean was at a loss for words, his thoughts tangled with questions he couldn't even begin to articulate. He felt like an idiot, overwhelmed by the extraordinary things unfolding around him so quickly. He glanced at Kevin, a newfound resolve forming within him. "I need to spend more time with him," he thought. Whatever this was, it was too extraordinary to ignore.

The room fell into a heavy silence, and Sean suddenly became aware of the heat rising in his body. His skin felt flushed and uncomfortable. "Your face is wet, Sean," Kevin pointed out matter-of-factually.

Sean instinctively reached for a tissue, wiping the sweat from his face. He looked at Kevin again, his mind still spinning, trying to make sense of the surreal moments they had just shared. "Do you even grasp the magnitude of what you are, Kevin?" Sean said, his voice sharp yet laced with awe.

"You're not just a miracle, you're the embodiment of a human's deepest dream, something that defies reason. For me, it's as if reality itself has dissolved into a dream I can't wake from." He placed his hands firmly on Kevin's shoulders, his gaze intense yet filled with a brotherly warmth. Kevin's brow furrowed, his expression betraying a sense of unease, as though he already knew the weight of the words about to be spoken.

"Do you still feel the vibrations coursing through you?" Sean asked, his tone a mix of curiosity and concern. "Yes," Kevin replied, his voice distant, his thoughts clearly elsewhere. "Every three seconds or so."

Sean's eyes narrowed. "Then why don't we see any lights flickering anymore? No blackouts, no surges. What's changed?"

Kevin met his gaze, a faint, almost enigmatic smile curling his lips. "Because I'm controlling it now, like adjusting a radio, I've turned down the volume of the shocks," he said with astonishing confidence, his words carrying a quiet power. "I can suppress the vibrations, bend them to my will."

"That's unbelievable," Sean murmured, his thoughts scattering as he struggled to process what he'd just heard. "How... how did you even learn to control it?"

Kevin's expression was calm, almost unsettlingly so. "Because I asked them," he said, his tone steady yet laced with something unspoken. "And they told me how to do it." Sean leaned forward, his excitement bubbling over. "Who told you that? And can they actually help you understand the messages coming through you?"

Kevin hesitated, his confidence faltering just slightly. "I don't know who they are, but I know they won't harm me, I can feel that they care. As they said, whatever problem I have, they're facing it too."

He admitted, his voice faltering with uncertainty. "But they said they're part of me." After a brief pause, he continued, his tone heavy with an unsettling realization. "I feel like they think I am God. They're happy because they believe they've found a way to speak to Him. I can understand them, but I have no idea about those prints."

Sean rose to his feet, the words on the tip of his tongue evaporating as the door swung open with an unexpected force. A young woman entered, her presence commanding the room. She was strikingly tall, her soft, silky skin glowing under the dim light. Her naturally pink lips and cheeks added an air of effortless elegance, while her golden hair cascaded in shimmering waves, framing her face and draping over her shoulders like liquid sunlight.

Her gaze locked onto Sean, and his complexion instantly drained of color. Sean's face turned ghostly pale, as if he'd just seen something beyond comprehension. "Hello, Sean," she said, her voice smooth and melodic, yet tinged with an undercurrent of mystery.

"I didn't expect to see you here. But the day I saw you in your mother's room… I was truly pleased to see you again. And now," her lips curled into a soft, knowing smile, "I'm equally glad to see you here."

She glared at him, her eyes narrowing with a sharpness that seemed to pierce straight through him.

Sean, unshaken but guarded, returned her gaze with equal suspicion. "Hi, Donna," he said coolly, his voice carrying an edge.

"I didn't expect to see you here, especially in a place like this. Visiting your sick aunt at the hospital? That doesn't exactly sound like you."

He took a step closer, his tone dripping with accusation. "So, why are you here? And tell me, who's your victim today?" Kevin looked perplexed, his brow furrowing as he glanced between Sean and the mysterious woman. "Do you… know her?" Kevin asked, his tone hesitant.

Sean hesitated, his jaw tightening before he finally replied, "Unfortunately, yes. She's my cousin," the words leaving his mouth reluctantly, as if they carried a bitter taste.

Donna's lips curled into a smile, though it didn't quite reach her eyes. She turned her attention to Kevin, her voice adopting an air of forced friendliness that barely masked its bossy undertone. "Hi, Kevin! How are you feeling today?"

Sean was frozen in place, his mind racing as he managed to stammer, "You… you know her, Kevin?" His voice was shaky, laced with disbelief.

Kevin's expression darkened, his confusion giving way to quiet resolve. "I know her because she comes here every morning," he said, his voice low but steady. "She asks me strange questions and keeps pushing my mom to send me to some special hospital she picked out."

He turned to Sean, his eyes pleading and distrustful. "But I don't trust her, Sean." Sean looked at Donna sideways and said, "Me too."

Kevin added, his smile fading as he climbed onto the bed, his small frame tense with urgency. Grabbing Sean by the arm, he pulled him closer, his voice dropping to a near-whisper. "Sean," he said, his tone carrying an almost desperate weight, "you can't trust her."

"I know that, Kevin," Sean said quietly, though confusion still clouded his face. He turned slowly to Donna, his eyes narrowing with realization.

"Now I understand," he said, his voice sharp as he gestured toward her. "That's why you're here, isn't it?" He stepped closer, his words cutting through the tension in the room. "There must be something here for you. Now I see it, you've got your sights set on something." His tone darkened, dripping with accusation. "What are you hunting this time, Donna? Is your prey Kevin now?"

"Save your breath, dear cousin," Donna said smoothly, her confidence radiating in every word. She was the kind of woman whose every movement and phrase was calculated, slick, and deliberate.

"I come here every morning for one reason only," she continued, her tone calm yet unnervingly sharp. "To see this young man, just as you do." Her gaze flicked briefly to Kevin before returning to Sean.

"And I can tell, you already know something about him, that's why you're here too, isn't it?" She was looking directly at Sean's eyes.

Her lips curled into a faint, enigmatic smile as she leaned slightly closer. "I just need to talk to him," she said, her voice softening, though it carried a razor's edge.

"There are answers I'm looking for, and once I have them, everyone can go home happy." She locked eyes with Sean, her stare unflinching, her words hanging in the air like a quiet storm.

The way she spoke sounded less like a promise and more like a warning. Sean moved to the window and stared out, his posture rigid, refusing to face Donna. Donna simply shrugged, her indifference almost theatrical.

"Try to be reasonable," she said, her tone smooth but laced with quiet insistence. She stepped closer to Kevin, her gaze softening in a way that seemed almost genuine, almost. "We just want to help you," she said, her voice dipping into a coaxing rhythm.

"If something were to happen to you, who would bear the weight of that? The ones who've been confusing you? Misguiding you?" Her attention shifted sharply to Sean as she continued, her words gaining a subtle edge.

"Everyone needs to be cared for. Without support, everything, everyone, will crumble and fade away. Even I need someone to lean on." She paused, allowing the weight of her words to settle in the heavy silence. Sean smirked, his voice dripping with sarcasm. "Yep, lean on victims."

"Our future," she said, her voice quiet but firm, "depends on this balance of support. Think about it, Sean. Think carefully, before it's too late."

Donna cast one last lingering look at Kevin, her expression unreadable but heavy with unspoken intent. With a measured stride, she made her way to the door. Just as she reached it, she paused, her hand resting lightly on the frame. Without turning around, she spoke, her voice smooth and deliberate.

"I'll see you tomorrow morning, Kevin," she said, her tone carrying an almost eerie calm. "Have a good night's sleep."

And with that, she stepped out, leaving an air of tension that clung to the room long after she had gone. After she left, Kevin's gaze remained fixed on Sean, his face pale and uneasy.

Sean turned, immediately noticing the color drained from Kevin's cheeks. "Kevin! Are you okay?" he asked, his voice tinged with concern. Kevin nodded hesitantly, his voice cautious. "Yes... But I didn't know she was your relative. I only know that she has an evil plan."

Sean let out a faint, humorless chuckle. "And I didn't know she's been coming to see you every day."

He fell silent, his expression growing serious as his thoughts churned. "I knew something was off," he muttered, almost to himself. "That's why she's been coming here."

Sean absently stroked his chin, his brow furrowed as he sank into deeper contemplation, the gears in his mind turning with a quiet intensity.

"Kevin, I have to go," Sean said, glancing at the clock. "I promised my sister I'd meet her for dinner tonight."

The hospital had grown eerily quiet, the muffled sounds of footsteps and distant murmurs fading as visiting hours drew to a close.

"Are you going home?" Kevin asked, his voice subdued.

Sean shook his head lightly. "No, we're heading to a restaurant for dinner. After that, I'll head home," he explained, his tone reassuring. He stepped closer, his expression softening. "Anyway, if you need me, anytime, you can call me."

"Yes, I'll remember that," Kevin replied quietly, his voice steady but carrying an undercurrent of hesitation. After a brief pause, Kevin added, "My mom's coming soon."

Kevin frowned slightly, his gaze lingering on Sean, the weight of unspoken emotions flickering in his eyes. He didn't want Sean to leave, not now, not yet. Sean was the first real friend he'd ever had. The first person who listened without judgment, who didn't mock his thoughts or brush them off as nonsense. The first person who never called him weird or a freak. Sean never laughed at him, never called his ideas strange or his abilities ridiculous. He didn't treat Kevin like an oddity but as someone worth understanding. For Kevin, that meant everything.

"I'd love to meet your sister, too. Do you think she'd come visit me?" Kevin asked. "I'm happy you told me that. I think she would like that," Sean said, a soft smile warming his face. He walked to the door, his steps measured. As he opened it, he paused, glancing back at Kevin.

"So, I'll see you tomorrow," he said, his voice carrying a quiet reassurance. He waved gently before stepping out and letting the door close behind him.

Kevin lay back on the bed, his gaze shifting toward the window. The city lights outside twinkled like distant stars, their gentle flicker casting a serene glow that filled the room. For a moment, he allowed himself to relax, the hum of his thoughts blending with the stillness around him.

He focused inward, feeling a growing sense of control over his body, as if the vibrations were no longer foreign but a part of him he could command. Turning his eyes to the ceiling light, he studied its steady glow, his mind drifting to the possibilities of what he could truly do.

"I think I'm more capable than ever before," Kevin murmured to himself, his voice filled with quiet determination. "I'll show Sean tomorrow."

He lay back on his bed, his hands clasped behind his head as he gazed up at the ceiling with a sense of newfound confidence. A slow, satisfied smile spread across his face as his eyes drifted closed, his thoughts dancing with the promise of what was to come.

***

Sharon ordered her second cup of coffee, glancing at the clock once more, 6:45. She tapped her fingers on the table and whispered, "He's never been late before. I hope nothing's wrong."

Pouring a splash of cream into her coffee, she stirred it absently, her thoughts swirling as much as the liquid in her cup. Taking a cautious sip, she shifted her gaze to the window, where Spadina Avenue stretched before her. The rain had polished the street to a gleaming finish, the reflections of headlights dancing like fleeting ghosts.

Outside, pedestrians hurried under umbrellas, their faces set against the rain, while vehicles crept forward sluggishly, their wipers battling the relentless downpour. Sharon watched it all, feeling both connected to the city's rhythm and eerily detached, waiting for someone who was never late.

The view from the window carried her back to the simplicity of her childhood, a wave of warmth washing over her. A faint smile tugged at her lips as memories of carefree days and laughter with her family surfaced. She thought about her parents, kind, supportive, and steadfast- and felt a swell of gratitude for the love they had always shown her. And then there was her brother, her unwavering confidant, whom she adored as the best brother in the world.

Lost in these cherished thoughts, the bustling world outside faded into a blur until a voice pierced her reverie. "Sharon," someone called, pulling her abruptly back to the present.

"Sharon! Hi. I'm so sorry for being late," Sean exclaimed, his breath hitching as he stood before her, drenched from head to toe. Rainwater dripped from his hair and jacket, pooling at his feet. She raised an eyebrow, concern and curiosity mingling on her face. "Sean, what happened to you?"

"I was... somewhere else," he said, his eyes alight with a mix of excitement and wonder. "Something incredible happened, something I couldn't walk away from. It was... amazing. Remarkable. I don't even know where to start."

Sharon leaned forward, intrigued by the intensity in his voice, "Well, you'd better start explaining." Sean began speaking, his words tumbling out in a chaotic rush, fragments of sentences colliding as if his thoughts couldn't keep up with his mouth. He didn't seem to know if he was talking to Sharon, to himself, or to some unseen presence only he could sense.

"Sean, slow down! What happened? Are you alright?" Sharon blurted out, her voice tinged with both concern and exasperation. They spoke over each other then, their words overlapping in a frantic cacophony until they both stopped, startled by the noise they had created. For a moment, silence hung between them, broken only by the soft patter of rain against the window. And then, unexpectedly, they both laughed, a shared burst of release, cutting through the tension like a blade through mist. In that moment, the mystery lingered, but the weight of it seemed a little less heavy. Sharon apologized for the interruption.

When Sean said, "Oh, no problem. It's all right," his voice was steady but distant, as though he were reassuring himself as much as Sharon.

He gestured to her seat, and they both sank into their chairs. For a while, neither spoke. The silence between them was heavy, like the air before a storm, broken only by the rhythmic hum of rain outside.

Sean's gaze lingered on Sharon, his eyes searching, hesitant. He seemed on the verge of saying something, a confession perched on the edge of his lips, but it never fully formed.

Sharon's heart quickened as she studied his face. His unusual quietness, the flicker of something unspoken in his expression, it unsettled her. "Sean," she began softly, her voice laced with a quiet urgency. "What happened? Tell me."

He hesitated, forcing a faint smile that didn't reach his eyes. "Don't worry," he said gently, his tone unconvincing. "I'm fine." But Sharon wasn't convinced. She could feel it, beneath his words, something deeper stirred, something he wasn't ready to share. Sean picked up the restaurant menu and opened it, his eyes scanning the words without really seeing them. His mind drifted elsewhere, far beyond the neat columns of dishes.

"Sean!" Sharon's voice broke through his haze, tinged with a mixture of worry and frustration. "I'm worried. Is there something you need to tell me?" He lowered the menu slightly, his gaze still distant.

"Oh, Sharon," he began, his tone unsteady, as if the words were too fragile to carry the weight of what he wanted to say.

"Everything... everything is perfect. I just don't know how to explain it to you and how to start. "I don't even believe it myself," he whispered. "Even though I was a witness." His hands tightened slightly on the edges of the menu, and his voice trembled as he continued, "Honestly, I don't even know if you'd want to hear my story. Maybe it's too... strange. Maybe it's not what you're expecting."

Sharon leaned closer, her concern deepening with every word. "Sean, whatever it is, I'm here. You know you can tell me anything."

He looked at her then, his eyes clouded with a mix of fear and exhilaration, as if he was about to pull back the curtain on something extraordinary, or terrifying.

"Sean! We've always shared everything," Sharon's voice steady and full of reassurance. "If you saw it and believed it, then I believe it too. And remember, I trust you, no matter what." She reached across the table and gently took her brother's hand, her warmth cutting through the storm of uncertainty he seemed to carry. "Tell me," she urged softly, her eyes searching his. "What did you experience?"

Sean exhaled deeply, as though her words had unlocked a weight from his chest. His tense shoulders eased, and his breath, once uneven and ragged, began to slow and steady.

For the first time since he arrived, Sean felt a sense of calm, as though the turbulent sea inside him had finally begun to settle. His gaze met hers, filled with gratitude and something else, an unspoken promise that what he was about to share would change everything. Sean waved to the waiter and placed their order. "We'll have the special and two chamomile teas, please."

His movements were mechanical, his mind burdened by the weight of what he was about to share. As the waiter walked away, Sean exhaled deeply, his fingers lightly tapping the table. When he finally spoke, his voice was low and deliberate, each word carefully chosen, as if shaping the impossible into something believable. He started with what had happened in Kevin's room. He described the moment with vivid clarity, their mother's tumor, an unyielding shadow over their lives, somehow vanishing after she drank from Kevin's glass of water. Sean's words carried a mix of awe and disbelief, as if he were still grappling with the enormity of it himself.

When he finished recounting that miracle, he hesitated before plunging into the next part of his tale, Donna. His voice grew heavier as he described her involvement, the mysterious air surrounding her, and the inexplicable events that had unfolded. As Sean spoke, Sharon's expressions shifted like a kaleidoscope of emotion. Her initial smile of curiosity melted into wide-eyed surprise. As his story deepened, her face grew paler, her features tightening with exhaustion and disbelief. By the time Sean finished, her shock was palpable, her lips parted as though searching for words that refused to come.

The room seemed quieter now, the clatter of dishes and muffled conversations around them fading into the background, leaving only the weight of Sean's story between them. Sharon leaned back in her chair, her hands trembling slightly as she absorbed the magnitude of what she had just heard. Sharon burst into tears, her emotions overwhelming her in an instant. "I'm so glad about Mom," she managed between sobs.

Her voice trembled, raw and unguarded. "Dad told me about her tumor, but I had no idea about the healing. I guess... I guess that's why Dad couldn't find me in the office today, I wasn't there. I was away." She wiped her cheeks quickly, but couldn't stop the tears from flowing. Her gaze locked onto Sean's, her bright, kind eyes searching his for reassurance, for understanding, for a way to make sense of the extraordinary story he had shared.

"I can't believe this, Sean," she whispered, her voice a mixture of disbelief and gratitude. "It's a miracle. It's... incredible." Despite her tears, there was a warmth in her expression, a glow of hope and relief that only family could spark in such moments of revelation.

When they had finished both their conversation and their meals, Sean glanced at his watch, and his eyes widened. "Oh, my God. It's almost nine-thirty. Can you believe that?" Sharon didn't answer. She sat in silence, her mind spinning with everything Sean had told her. The weight of his story, so extraordinary, so far beyond anything she could have imagined, rendered her momentarily speechless.

Sean leaned closer, concern etched across his face. "Are you okay, Sharon?" he asked gently. She still didn't respond, lost in the labyrinth of her thoughts.

Then, with a deep breath, she finally emerged from her reverie. "So," she said slowly, her voice steady but tinged with lingering disbelief, "when do you plan to see him again?"

"Tomorrow morning," Sean's excitement unmistakable, his eyes alight with anticipation.

Sharon hesitated, uncertainty flickering across her face. "May I come with you?" she asked tentatively, her voice softer now. "I'd really like to meet him in person... if that's okay."

Sean smiled, a hint of relief in his expression. "Of course, you can go with me," Sean said, his tone warm and reassuring.

"You don't have to ask me, you know. In fact..." he paused, a small smile tugging at the corners of his lips, "he'd like to see you, too." Sharon blinked, her brow furrowing slightly.

"Why would he want to see me?" her voice was barely above a whisper.

Sean raised his hands in a gesture of surrender. "Don't ask me why or how, because I don't have an answer for you. He didn't explain it to me, and I didn't press him. That's why he is getting interesting every minute."

He leaned forward, his voice softening, "But he did tell me one thing, he likes you. And he said he trusts you."

"Are you joking, or are you serious?" Sharon asked, suspicion in her voice. Sean met her gaze, as if anticipating her reaction, and replied calmly, "I'm serious. I'm not joking."

Sharon felt a shiver run through her, the kind that comes with the realization that something larger, something unseen, was at play. She nodded slowly, her curiosity now mingled with a sense of responsibility. "Then I'll go," she said, her voice steady. "I need to know what this is all about." They sat in silence for a moment, the air between them filled with unspoken thoughts.

Then Sean broke it, his tone careful. "But... what about your work?"

Sharon looked up, momentarily puzzled by the question. Her expression softened, and a radiant smile spread across her face. "Tomorrow," she said with quiet determination, "I'll go to work a little late. But I have to see this miracle boy myself. If someone has the power to speak to spirits and command his body to obey, then I have to see him." She shifted her gaze from the swirling coffee in her cup to Sean, her eyes gleaming with a mix of curiosity and resolve. "Like every morning, I'll be at the hospital to visit Mom. But this time, I'll wait for you. Then we'll go together." With a playful yet decisive motion, she rested her hand on his shoulder and added, "Deal?"

Sean couldn't help but grin at her unwavering enthusiasm. "Deal," he said, his voice tinged with relief and excitement. In that moment, the room seemed to hum with anticipation, the promise of the next day lingering between them like an unspoken vow. Sean's gaze lingered on the cherry pie behind the glass refrigerator, its glossy crimson filling glinting under the soft light. It was impossible to resist. With a small, mischievous grin, he ordered dessert for both of them. When the slices arrived, the sweet aroma filled the air, and they ate in quiet contentment, savoring each bite until nothing was left. Sean leaned back in his chair, a satisfied look on his face. "I've always loved cherry pie," his voice carrying a hint of nostalgia. His eyes drifted to the empty plate, as if it held memories of simpler, sweeter times.

"It's better if we get going," Sharon suggested, glancing toward the window.

"Yes," Sean agreed, checking his watch. "We've been here for more than three hours."

Outside, the rain had finally ceased, leaving the streets glistening under the city lights. More people now bustled along the sidewalks, their hurried steps weaving through the lively flow of Bloor Street's evening crowd.

"It's a lovely city," Sharon remarked, her voice cutting through the comfortable silence.

"Yes, indeed," Sean said, his tone carrying a hint of pride. "I'm proud of my city. I've always liked it here. And someday... I'd like to come back to live here again. The people are friendly, the energy is warm, and, most importantly..." He paused, his gaze distant but fond. "It's my home."

Sharon smiled, watching the bustling scene outside, feeling a quiet connection to the place Sean held so close to his heart.

"Oh, Sean, that would be lovely," her voice trembling with emotion. "We'd be together again, and Mom and Dad would be so happy." Her eyes glistened, catching the light like the rain-soaked streets outside.

Sean smiled warmly, the depth of his affection for his sister evident in his expression.

"Sean, I had a wonderful time tonight," she said softly and her voice filled with sincerity. "And I'm so happy you're here." Her eyes sparkled, reflecting both the city lights and the emotions that filled the moment.

"Me too," Sean whispered, leaning in to press a gentle kiss to her forehead. "Well, I'll see you tomorrow." As he stood to leave, the warmth of the evening lingered between them, a quiet promise that tomorrow would bring more than just another day, it would bring a new chapter.

"See you," Sharon said softly, her voice wavering as she fought back the tears threatening to spill. She climbed into her car, her hands trembling slightly as they gripped the steering wheel. Sean leaned in, gently closing the door for her with a reassuring smile. He stepped back and waved, his eyes filled with unspoken warmth as she pulled away into the bustling night.

Sean stood on the curb, watching until Sharon's car disappeared into the maze of city lights. Only then did he turn, the quiet streets enveloping him as he walked to his own car. Sliding into the driver's seat, he paused for a moment, letting the evening's weight settle before starting the engine and heading home, the memories of their time together lingering like the faint glow of the streetlights.

Thinking of Kevin filled Sean's mind with a tangle of questions. The boy's unwavering confidence, his remarkable ability to achieve the extraordinary, and the sheer improbability of how their paths had crossed, it all felt too deliberate, too significant to be a mere coincidence.

And then there was Kevin's mother, a breathtakingly beautiful young woman who had been the reason Sean had first approached Kevin. Her elegance and mystery had drawn him in, but now everything had shifted. Kevin's abilities eclipsed everything else, consuming Sean's thoughts.

If Kevin possesses abilities, intellect, or qualities that surpass the average human, whether physical, mental, or even emotional, he could be seen as a symbol of human evolution. Evolution doesn't necessarily mean gaining superpowers; it can also mean adapting in ways that enhance survival, understanding, or interaction with the world.

Is Kevin showing signs of advanced intelligence, empathy, or abilities beyond the norm? If so, he could represent a step forward in human evolution, either biologically or metaphorically. What makes you wonder if he's a sign of evolution?

He couldn't stop wondering what the source of the boy's powers was. Was it a natural evolution of humanity, a glimpse into the next stage of their existence? Or was there a far greater mystery at play, something beyond comprehension? His mind wrestled with questions and answers, each thought colliding with the next in an endless loop of uncertainty.

Sean's grip on the steering wheel tightened as his mind raced with possibilities. He was driving slowly, almost absently, when the sharp ring of his cell phone shattered his thoughts. The sound jolted him back to the present, his heart skipping a beat as he fumbled to answer, unsure of what new revelation or challenge the night might bring. He pulled into his parents' driveway and parked, reaching for his phone as it rang. "Hello?" he answered.

"Hi, Sean. I thought this might be interesting for you," James said abruptly, his tone quiet but eager. Sean frowned in surprise. "Hi, Dad. What's the interesting news? Calling this late, I thought you'd be asleep by now."

"Oh, I can't sleep when I'm on duty," he chuckled lightly, then continued: "It's about Kevin's father," James whispered, his voice barely audible. "You'd asked me to find out what happened to him."

Sean's pulse quickened. "Yes. What's the news?" he asked, his voice rising with excitement.

"Sorry, son, if I'm whispering," James said, a faint chuckle in his tone. "I'm in your mother's room, and she's asleep. I don't want to wake her."

"That's okay, Dad. I understand. How's Mom? Is she better?" Sean asked, momentarily sidetracked by concern for his mother. "Yes, she's doing excellent," James said warmly, then he continued:

"The doctors might release her by the end of this week. They're still amazed by what happened to her tumor. They're calling it the second miracle in this hospital."

"Did you get the new results from her tests? And what's the doctor's opinion?" Sean's voice was laced with both curiosity and concern.

James sighed softly, his voice calm but tinged with disbelief. "They still have no clue what happened to the tumor. It's like, it just... vanished. But the good news is, she's as good as new. They're confident she can lead a completely normal life now."

"That's wonderful news, Dad." A genuine smile spread across Sean's face. "I'm so happy for Mom, and for all of us. I'll come by tomorrow to see you both."

He let out a long, relieved sigh, his heart swelling with gratitude for the miracle that had spared his mother. For a moment, the weight of the evening lifted, but he was unable to contain his curiosity any longer, Sean pressed on. "So, Dad... what did you find out about Kevin's father?" His tone grew eager, the mystery pulling him back into its grip.

There was a brief silence on the line before James spoke again, his voice quieter, as though the weight of what he had discovered required caution. "It's... complicated, Sean. But I think you need to hear it."

"Oh, yes," James began, his voice dropping to an almost conspiratorial tone. "It all happened last year. Ira, Kevin's father, had problems that were eerily similar to Kevin's."

Sean listened intently as his father continued. "When these... episodes occurred, they rushed him to the hospital. At first, the doctors were baffled. After a few days of tests, they couldn't find anything physically wrong with him. But Ira was suffering from something, some kind of vibrations."

"Vibrations? Kevin experienced them too." Sean repeated, his curiosity mounting. "Yes," James confirmed. "But his were far more powerful, and far more dangerous, and, like a seizure, they shook him to his core. They were wild, uncontrollable. Wherever he was, there was no light. It was as if the vibrations themselves disrupted everything around him. The doctors started calling them 'vibrate man."

Sean leaned forward in his seat, gripping the phone tightly. "Vibrate, man? What do you mean?"

James sighed heavily. "These... shocks worried the doctors. Equipment would malfunction, lights would flicker, and sometimes, entire rooms would plunge into darkness. The worst part was, all these were happening in a hospital, and they couldn't pinpoint what was causing it. Ira was a complete mystery to them."

Sean felt a chill run through him, his mind racing. "And then what happened, Dad? Did they figure it out?"

"No," James said softly, the weight of the story evident in his tone. "They never did. After about a week," James continued, "they assigned Ira to a highly reputable doctor, someone very professional and experienced in dealing with unusual cases like his. The only issue..." He paused, his tone growing heavier. "What issue?" Sean was leaning forward as though the weight of the story demanded his full attention.

"The doctor wasn't in Canada," James said. "He was in New Jersey. They offered to transport Ira there, with all expenses covered. They were desperate to figure out what was happening to him, and to contain it."

Sean frowned, the details unraveling in his mind like pieces of a puzzle. "Did he go?"

"Yes," James replied, his voice quieter now, as though the story carried a sense of foreboding. "But things only got stranger after that."

The line went silent, leaving Sean staring into the darkened street, his thoughts consumed by a mystery far larger than he had anticipated.

"Following the offer, the Thomas family received a letter directly from the doctor in New Jersey," James continued. "In it, he personally invited Ira for a free check-up, claiming he was confident he could help. At first, the family was overjoyed, it felt like a miracle, a glimmer of hope in the chaos."

Sean listened intently, already sensing the shadows lurking behind the story.

"But there was a problem," James went on. "They couldn't send Ira by airplane because of the vibrations. They feared the disruptions he caused could lead to something catastrophic mid-flight. So, they arranged for him to travel in a gear car. It was a long, tedious journey, but they made it."

"When they arrived, however, things took a strange turn," James said, his voice lowering. "The hospital staff informed Ira that while his expenses would be covered, the rest of the family would have to pay for their own lodging and needs. It felt deliberate, like they wanted to isolate Ira from his family, perhaps to work on him without any interference."

Sean clenched the phone tighter. "Did Ira agree to stay under those conditions?"

"He did," James replied. "Ira believed it would all be over in a matter of days. But his wife... she insisted on staying with him, no matter what. She wouldn't leave his side, even if it meant hardship for the rest of the family."

Sean exhaled slowly, the tension in the story palpable. "So, what happened next?" James hesitated, as though the next part was harder to say. "That's when things really started to unravel, Sean."

"The treatment ended up taking much longer than they initially expected," James' voice growing somber. "And the hospital imposed strict rules on visitation, they wouldn't let his family see him for more than an hour a day. They claimed it was better for him, that he needed isolation to focus on recovery." Sean frowned, his grip on the phone tightening. "And his wife agreed to this?"

"Reluctantly," James admitted. "But as time dragged on, the expenses of staying there became too much for the family to bear. Ira eventually convinced his wife and son to return to Canada, promising he would call them regularly with updates."

James paused, and his voice dropped to a near whisper. "But Sean... that call never came. Not once." Sean felt a chill creep over him. "He just... stopped communicating? Completely," James said. "And no one, not his family, not the doctors here, heard from him again. It was as though he vanished into thin air." The silence between them was heavy, the mystery of Ira's fate growing darker with each word.

"His wife tried desperately to contact the hospital," James continued, his tone heavy with the weight of the tale. "But every time she called, she was met with vague excuses, claims that Ira was in treatment, that he couldn't talk, or that they were still running tests."

Sean's chest tightened as James paused, the story taking a darker turn. "Then, on the third week of his stay," James said quietly, "the doctor called her directly and told her that Ira's body couldn't handle the strain any longer and that he had passed away. He claimed there was nothing they could have done to save him."

Sean inhaled sharply, the words hitting like a blow. "And the hospital? What did they want?"

"They asked for permission to retain Ira's body," James said grimly. "They wanted to study it, to understand the condition that had plagued him. But his wife... she didn't agree. She demanded that they return his body immediately."

Sean clenched his jaw, the injustice of it boiling inside him. "Did they comply?"

"Not at first," James said. "They refused, insisting that keeping the body was essential for their research. But eventually, they realized they couldn't keep it indefinitely without creating more problems for themselves. His wife's lawyer intervened and forced them to release the body." James went silence, then he continued. "They even offered his wife half a million dollars, but she refused, insisting that bringing him there had been a mistake from the start."

James sighed, the exhaustion in his voice unmistakable. "It was a nightmare for the family, Sean. And even now, there are so many unanswered questions."

Sean sat in stunned silence, the weight of the story settling heavily on his shoulders. "What happened to Ira... it doesn't make sense, Dad," he finally said, his voice low and filled with unease.

"The mystery deepened when the doctors conducted their examinations," James continued, his voice tinged with unease. "They searched for any sign of what went wrong, but they couldn't find a thing. There was no damage, no illness, nothing. In fact, his body was in perfect condition."

Sean frowned, leaning closer to the phone. "Perfect condition? How is that even possible?"

"They said it was as if he were simply asleep," James replied, his tone growing quieter, more bewildered. The only difference was… he wasn't breathing, and not a single vital sign stirred within his body.

Sean felt a chill run down his spine as James went on. "Even a week after his death, his body showed no signs of decay. It was still… normal. No odor, no stiffness, nothing you'd expect. The doctors were baffled. They couldn't explain it."

James paused, his voice faltering slightly. "Sean, they said it was like his body was frozen in time, untouched by death, yet undeniably lifeless."

Sean's breath caught, his thoughts racing. "And no one ever figured out why?"

James sighed. "No. And that's why the doctors were so desperate to keep him. They believed there was something extraordinary about Ira… but they couldn't figure out what it was."

James hesitated before adding, "Even now, when I think about it, I can't make sense of any of it." He became silent, his expression as puzzled as his voice. "Does this have anything to do with Kevin?"

Sean didn't answer immediately, the weight of the revelation settling heavily in his mind. "I don't know, Dad," he finally said, his voice barely above a whisper. "But I intend to find out."

Sean was riveted, his mind racing as he clung to every word of the story. A strange sense of responsibility for Kevin weighed heavier on him now. He recalled Kevin's peculiar confession, how the boy had said he could play dead but didn't understand how or why. For a fleeting moment, an unsettling thought crossed Sean's mind: What if Kevin's father was still alive, somehow trapped in a state beyond comprehension?

Meanwhile, James continued, his tone both awestruck and uneasy. "They said Ira looked like he was sleeping," he explained. "But the most amazing, and shocking, part was that he wasn't breathing. His heart had completely stopped, and there was no movement in his bloodstream."

Sean's brow furrowed deeply, the enormity of what he was hearing sinking in.

James hesitated before continuing, as though the next words defied logic. "Even though his body showed no signs of life, no breath, no heartbeat, nothing, there were no signs of decay. No deterioration. Nothing that would indicate death. His body remained... fresh. Healthy, even. The doctors couldn't understand it."

James paused, his voice almost a whisper. "They said... he seemed to be alive, Sean, even though every vital sign said otherwise."

Sean felt a shiver run through him, his thoughts spiraling. What if this wasn't the end of the story? Something about Ira's condition, and Kevin's inexplicable abilities- felt eerily connected, a mystery far larger than anything he could have imagined.

"But how could they feel he was alive when all of his vital signs were dead?" Sean asked abruptly, the tension in his voice cutting through the stillness of the night.

James took a deep breath, his hesitation palpable. "Because, Sean, his body stayed fresh. There was no stiffness, no discoloration, and most shockingly, his body didn't emit any odor. Not for two consecutive weeks."

Sean's stomach tightened. "Two weeks?" he echoed, barely able to grasp the enormity of what he was hearing. "What... what happened to the body?"

"They cremated it," James said simply, his tone weighted with finality. "It was in his will. He had specifically requested it." Sean exhaled slowly, his mind swirling with unanswered questions, as James added, "I need to go now, son. Your mother's calling me."

"Thanks, Dad," Sean said quietly, his voice steady despite the storm inside him. "But before you hang up, would you kiss Mom goodnight for me?"

"I will, son," James replied, his tone warm despite the gravity of their conversation. "Have a good night."

"Good night, Dad," Sean said, and then the line went dead, leaving him alone with the weight of what he'd just learned, and the unsettling connection it might have to Kevin.

As Sean drove, his knuckles whitened around the phone in his hand, gripping it as if he could wrestle answers from the device itself. His mind churned with fragments of the story, questions colliding with possibilities in a relentless loop.

Pulling into the driveway, he parked the car and stepped out into the stillness of the night. He entered the house, the faint hum of its silence greeting him. Methodically, he hung his damp jacket in the closet and wandered into the kitchen. The routine felt hollow, but he needed something, anything, to ground himself. He grabbed a bottle of water from the fridge, letting the cool surface offer a momentary distraction.

Carrying the bottle of water, Sean slumped onto the sofa and turned on the TV. Channels flickered past, a blur of meaningless images. Nothing held his attention. The noise was only a faint hum against the loudness of his thoughts.

Restless, he got up and wandered to the answering machine. His finger hovered for a moment over the play button before he pressed it. The machine beeped, and the first message began to play, its disembodied voice filling the room. Sean stood motionless, waiting, hoping, for something that might shift the weight pressing down on him.

The answering machine crackled to life, and a warm, slightly hesitant voice filled the room.

"Hi, Helen, this is Norma. I was just worried about you, so I decided to call, but you weren't home. Anyway, if you have any chance, would you please call me? Thank you, dear. I hope you feel better."

The message ended with a soft click, leaving a faint echo of concern lingering in the air. Sean furrowed his brow, staring at the machine as though it might offer more.

The answering machine beeped again, followed by a new voice, formal and measured.

"Hello, this is Angela Collin from the insurance company. I am calling for Helen Morgan. It's about the life insurance. Please contact me at 930-555-0972. Thank you."

The message ended with another soft click. Sean stood frozen, his gaze fixed on the machine as the room seemed to grow quieter around him.

Beep...

Sean had barely taken a step toward the sofa when the answering machine began playing a third message.

"Hi, Sean!"

He froze, his eyes narrowing as he stared at the machine. The voice that followed was unmistakable, dripping with a playful, almost teasing tone.

"Despite our conversation earlier, I'm willing to see you. You know, we're still cousins. Call me!"

The way Donna's voice lingered on her words, girlish and flirtatious, sent a shiver down Sean's spine. Her tone carried a strange mix of familiarity and intrigue, but also an undercurrent he couldn't quite place, something that made him uneasy.

Sean remained still for a moment, processing her words. Why now? And why like this? The timing, coupled with the strangeness of the other messages, made the whole night feel even more surreal.

He let out a slow breath, his mind buzzing. "Donna..." he muttered under his breath, the name hanging in the air like a question he wasn't sure he wanted the answer to.

"Little trickster," he mumbled under his breath, a bitter edge to his voice. Turning away from the answering machine, he made his way back to the kitchen, the faint hum of the refrigerator filling the silence.

"She doesn't know anything about humanity," he muttered, opening a cabinet to retrieve a mug. "She wants Kevin."

Sean paused, gripping the mug tightly, his mind swirling with suspicion. "That's definitely the reason," he said aloud, as though trying to convince himself.

His thoughts were heavy, like a storm cloud gathering on the horizon. Donna's message felt like a calculated move, and the way she had spoken, so casual, so dismissive of their earlier conversation, only fueled his unease.

He poured himself a cup of milk, the white liquid swirling like his restless thoughts. Taking a deep sip, he leaned against the counter, staring into the middle distance. If Donna wanted Kevin, then she was part of something bigger. Something Sean wasn't sure he was ready to face. He was pacing the kitchen, milk cup in hand, still muttering to himself, when the last message played.

"Hi, this message is for Sean. This is Greg. Call me. Thanks."

Beep. Beep. Beep.

The abruptness of the message made Sean freeze mid-step. Without hesitation, he picked up his phone and dialed Greg's number.

"Hello!" Greg's voice came through immediately.

"Hi, Greg. What's up?" Sean asked, his tone laced with curiosity and concern.

"Hi, Sean. I'll call you back in five minutes. I'll explain it later. Bye for now," Greg said hastily before abruptly hanging up.

Sean stared at his phone, the empty line buzzing in his ear. "That was strange," he muttered, setting the phone down on the counter. A knot of unease tightened in his stomach.

"I hope everything's alright," he whispered, taking another sip of his drink, his mind racing with possibilities. He glanced at the clock, counting down the minutes until Greg called back. Something about the hurried tone of Greg's voice left Sean feeling that whatever was coming, it wouldn't be ordinary.

Sean paced back and forth, his cup cradled in his hands. He took a slow sip, savoring the coolness, but it did little to calm the growing unease in his chest.

"Five minutes? Yeah, right," he muttered under his breath, glancing at the clock again. The second hand seemed to mock him with its deliberate crawl. He returned to the kitchen, setting the cup down with a soft clink. Pulling open the sugar jar, he scooped another spoonful into the cup, stirring absently. "One spoon, a bit of cream," he whispered to himself, the rhythm of the mundane task grounding him for a fleeting moment.

The kitchen clock ticked in deafening silence. Seven minutes now. Seven long, drawn-out minutes, and still no call. Sean tapped his fingers against the counter, his mind running in circles.

"Come on, Greg," he murmured, staring at his phone as though willing it to ring. A sense of dread began to creep into his thoughts. What could possibly take this long? What had been so urgent, yet now so delayed?

With a deep breath, he resisted the urge to redial Greg's number, gripping the edge of the counter as if it could anchor his restless thoughts. But in the pit of his stomach, he knew something wasn't right.

He stared at his phone, his frustration bubbling over. "Greg! Ring, please ring!" Sean muttered under his breath, as though willing the device to obey him. Exhausted, he picked up the receiver, his fingers hovering over the keypad. He hesitated, then set it back down.

He thought about Kevin and how he claimed he could reorder molecules. A flicker of curiosity sparked in his mind. Fixing his gaze on the phone, he took a slow breath and whispered, "I order you to ring... RING... RING." Then he got back on the phone.

"Maybe it's not a good time," he reasoned, trying to convince himself. "Maybe he's caught up in something and can't talk right now."

With a sigh, Sean sank into the sofa, grabbing the TV remote. Just as he was about to switch on the TV, the phone rang, its sharp sound cutting through the silence.

Sean shot to his feet, sprinting toward the phone. He snatched up the receiver, his voice laced with impatience. "Hello?"

"Hi, Sean. I'm sorry I couldn't talk earlier," Greg said, his voice tinged with fatigue. "A few colleagues were around, and I didn't want to discuss this in front of them."

"I'm just glad you finally called. What's new? Are you still at work?" Sean asked, trying to mask his impatience. Then he continued:

"I couldn't dig up anything about the pictures you sent me," Greg admitted. "But these printouts... they're strange, Sean. Really strange." He paused, the weight of his next words hanging in the silence.

"Is this some kind of language? Because if it is, well... it's like nothing I've ever seen before. Totally new. One hundred percent unknown." He hesitated for a moment. "Where did you get these?"

"I can't tell you that right now, " Sean replied firmly. "Just keep working on decoding them. Find out what they mean, what they want, and, most importantly, how they can be contacted."

"I'll try," Greg said, a hint of frustration in his voice.

"But as you mentioned, the only real way forward seems to be direct contact. You'll have to reach out and get more information. Unfortunately, there's absolutely no record of anything like this on Earth." He paused for a moment before adding, with a touch of curiosity, "Hey, by the way, if you ever, you know, do make contact with aliens, will you let me in on it?"

Sean gave a small chuckle despite the tension. "Sure, Greg. I'll let you know. But listen, I need you to keep this strictly confidential. No one else can know about this, not yet, anyway."

"You have my word," Greg assured him. "Take care, Sean. I'll keep you posted if I find anything. Bye."

"Thanks, Greg. See you in a few days," Sean replied before hanging up, his mind spinning with possibilities.

The next morning at the hospital, Helen radiated happiness. Her laughter filled the room, and she even sprinkled in a few jokes, lifting everyone's spirits. It was a rare and beautiful moment, her entire family together again, with her dear friends Katherine and Norma joining the joyful gathering.

James, elated by the news of his wife's recovery, seemed lighter than air. He bustled around the room with a contagious energy, serving coffee, muffins, doughnuts, and decadent chocolate candies. His movements were so sprightly it was as if he might take flight at any moment, buoyed by sheer relief and joy.

Amid the cheerful chatter, Sean slowly rose from his seat, his expression thoughtful and reserved. "Mom! I hope you'll be home tonight," Sean said warmly, glancing at Helen as he prepared to leave with Sharon.

Sharon, already ready to go, chimed in, "We have to go. Mom! Dad! I'll see you later."

They both leaned in to kiss their mother, and Sharon added a quick kiss on her father's cheek before they turned and left Helen's room. As they walked down the hallway toward Kevin's room, their lighthearted mood was shattered by the sound of wailing and desperate cries. Just outside the door, they froze, listening as Kevin's mother screamed, her voice trembling with fury and despair.

"No! I told you once and for all, and I'll tell you again—I won't let you do this to him! I won't let my son go there again! I made a mistake once, and I won't allow it again."

Sean opened the door widely, and his gaze landed on Donna, her presence unexpected. Kevin's face lit up at the sight of him.

"Sean!" Kevin exclaimed, his voice brimming with relief.

Sean hurried to Kevin's side. "What's going on, Kevin?"

"They want me to go to New Jersey. The same place where my dad died." Kevin's voice faltered.

Julia, tears streaming down her face, turned to Sean. "They're sending Kevin to the same hospital. I never agreed to this. I won't allow them to do this to him. Not over my dead body. And that's final."

"I'm just asking you if you care about your son," Donna interjected gently.

"I do care about keeping him safe and alive, okay? That's why I can't let you do this to him. I won't let him be sent there," Julia replied, her voice trembling.

Sean stepped closer to Julia, his hand gently resting on her shoulder. "Don't worry, Julia. Kevin is fine, and he's not going anywhere," he reassured her, his voice steady.

He then turned to Donna, his expression hardening as he told Julia, "Nobody—no one—can make you send Kevin anywhere. I promise you that," Sean said firmly, locking eyes with Donna to make sure she understood the weight of his words.

Julia's eyes widened, a silent gratitude filling them. "No, I don't want to send him. I want him to come home with me," she said, her voice resolute.

Donna assessed Sean with a lingering gaze before turning to Julia. "Well, I have to go. I'll be back tomorrow."

Julia rose to her feet, her voice firm. "Don't even bother. We don't want you here—I hope that's clear."

Donna spun on her heels, heading for the door, but stopped short when her eyes landed on Sharon. "Looks like you two are together again," she remarked coldly, her tone sharp and biting.

Sharon looked at her with a warm smile and said, "We've never been apart." Donna shot her a sharp, disdainful look before turning on her heel and leaving the room without a word.

Sean watched Donna leave, his eyes lingering on the door as the tension faded. He turned to Kevin. "That's my sister, Sharon," he said, gesturing to Sharon beside him. Then, with a calm but firm tone, he introduced everyone in the room to one another.

"Don't worry, Julia. We won't let them take your son away," Sean reassured her. Julia's face was clouded with worry. "But if they force us… what can we possibly do?"

Sean stepped closer, his voice unwavering. "Then we will fight back."

He gently took Julia's hand, his touch a silent promise. His words were strong yet tender, carrying the weight of certainty. "I'm right beside you. I'll never leave you in this fight. My father is a retired police officer, and he will help us."

"Why are you doing this, Sean?" Julia asked, her voice steady yet filled with curiosity. Sean met her gaze, then looked at Kevin, a soft resolve settling in his eyes. "Because I will always fight for the truth and the freedom of any individual," he said, his voice strong.

"Your honesty means the world to me. And I knew from the start—there's nothing wrong with Kevin. He's healthier than any other child. Also, without your authorization, nobody is able to take Kevin away from you."

He paused for a moment before adding, "Even if they threaten and intimidate you, they still have no right to take Kevin without your consent. That's why they resort to fear—to force you into giving it willingly."

Julia didn't respond immediately, but satisfaction flickered across her face. Instead, she stepped toward Kevin, gently placing her small hands on his shoulder. "I'm going to talk to the doctor. We're leaving tonight. We're going home, my darling." She gave Sean a small nod of appreciation before hurrying out of the room.

Sean turned to Kevin, his expression soft. "Are you scared?"

Kevin shook his head, but his voice carried a quiet concern. "No, I'm not scared but worried about my mom. I can feel how scared she is." He shifted his gaze toward Sharon, a slight smile tugging at his lips. "Your sister is very pretty."

Sharon finally had the opportunity to introduce herself in person to Kevin. She approached Kevin, smiling kindly. "Hi, Kevin. I didn't get a chance to talk to you before."

Kevin tilted his head curiously. "Do you two work together?"

Sharon shook her head, warmth in her voice. "No. Actually, not only do we not work together, but our jobs are practically opposites."

Kevin frowned slightly. "What do you mean by that?"

Sharon chuckled softly. "Well, my knowledge, studies, and research all focus on what's happening inside our world—the nature of atoms, particles, and all kinds of tiny building blocks. Meanwhile, Sean's work explores what's outside of our world—beyond our galaxy. So, in that sense, our fields couldn't be more different and, in some weird way, similar."

Sean stepped to the window and pushed it open just enough to let a cool breeze cut through the stale air of the room. The crisp morning air brushed against his face, momentarily easing the weight pressing on his chest. He inhaled deeply, allowing the tension to dissipate—until something outside caught his eye.

Pausing, he leaned closer, his gaze sharpening as he squinted into the bright, sunny light on the street below. There, Donna stood with two men. Their conversation seemed hurried and tense, though he couldn't hear a word. Moments later, The men climbed into a waiting car and sped off, vanishing into the daylight.

Donna lingered for a heartbeat, watching the car vanish. Then, with a deliberate turn, she strode back toward the hospital entrance. Sean's breath hitched. The ease he'd felt moments ago evaporated, replaced by a gnawing sense of unease. Something about the scene didn't sit right. What had Donna just been a part of? And why was she back so soon?

"Sean! Are you alright?" Sharon's voice broke through his thoughts, pulling him back to the room. He jerked his head toward her, blinking as if waking from a dream. "I'm alright," he muttered, though his tone was far from convincing. His eyes settled on Kevin, a serious weight behind his gaze.

"Kevin, I need to tell you something," Sean said gravely. "Do not trust anyone. And I mean it—nobody." Kevin met his intensity with surprising calm. "Don't worry, Sean. I know who to trust."

"Are you sure?" Sharon interjected, raising a brow. Her voice held a sharp edge as if testing him. "For example, do you trust the nurse who was here a minute ago?" Her expression turned sly, a touch of triumph in her tone.

Kevin didn't flinch. "I don't have to trust her," he replied matter-of-factually. "She feels sorry for me. She thinks there's no cure for me." His words were steady, without a hint of doubt, leaving Sharon momentarily speechless.

"How do you feel about her, exactly?" Sean asked, leaning forward, his voice low and careful. Kevin hesitated for a moment before answering, his expression clouded. "I feel sorry for her, too. It's strange... like she's about to lose something. I think—I think I saw something moving inside her stomach like intestinal worms. it was moving." His voice faltered as he turned to Sean, uncertainty etched across his face. "Sean?" Kevin said uneasily. "This is new. I could actually see through her."

Sean stiffened, exchanging a quick glance with Sharon, then back at Kevin. "What do you mean, 'see through her'? What are you talking about?" Kevin's voice grew quieter, his confusion mounting. "I mean it—exactly that. It was like looking through glass. I could see everything inside." He shook his head, his hands trembling slightly. "I don't understand what's happening to me." Sean's concern deepened as he studied Kevin, trying to piece together this strange revelation. Whatever this was, it wasn't normal. And it wasn't random.

"Look at me, Kevin. Do you see anything in me?" Sean asked, his voice edged with anxiety.

Kevin studied him for a moment, his gaze strangely intense. "No. I don't understand how I was able to see her, but wait a minute! I can see now. Yes. You need food. Your stomach is empty," he said with unsettling certainty.

Sean blinked, his logical mind brushing it off as a lucky guess. "Wait a second, Kevin. I'm going to call her back and ask her a question. This time, I want you to look carefully, okay?" Kevin nodded hesitantly, still trying to process his strange new ability. Sean walked to the door, cracking it open to peer into the hallway. "She's not here," he said, stepping back, "but we'll wait."

Sharon, curious and uneasy, moved closer. "Sean, what do you think about Kevin's feelings?" she began, but before she could finish, Sean raised a hand, putting a finger to his lips.

"Shh," he whispered sharply, his ears straining as if listening for something. The tension in the room thickened, every second stretching like an eternity as they waited.

"Please, Sharon. The nurse is coming," Sean whispered, stepping away from the door.

Moments later, he addressed the nurse politely as she approached. "Excuse me, nurse. There's something I need to show you," he said with calm urgency.

"Yes, sir. I'll be there in a few minutes," she replied, her tone brisk but courteous before continuing down the hall.

Sean closed the door softly and turned back to Kevin, his expression serious as he knelt beside him. "Listen, Kevin. When she comes in, don't say anything. Not a word. You got that?"

Kevin nodded, his face a mix of nervousness and determination. "Yes," he replied quietly.

Sean placed a reassuring hand on Kevin's shoulder. "Good. Just watch carefully, and we'll figure this out together." The tension in the room was palpable, every eye silently waiting for what would happen next.

They all waited in tense silence, the seconds stretching into what felt like hours. Suddenly, the door swung open, and the nurse stepped inside, her expression curious but composed. "What's wrong? Is everything alright?" she asked, scanning the room then moved closer to Kevin's bed, her tone softening. "Do you need anything, young man?"

When Kevin didn't immediately respond, she turned to leave. But just as she started to step away, Kevin reached out, gently grabbing her hand. His gaze was piercing as he looked up at her. "Do you feel alright?" he asked, his voice calm but unnervingly certain. "I think you're sick, and you need medication right away."

The room went still. The nurse froze, her face flickering with surprise and confusion. "What?" she murmured, her voice barely audible. Before she could gather her thoughts, Sean rushed to Kevin's side. "Stop it, Kevin. That's enough. You're scaring her," he said firmly, gripping Kevin's shoulders as if trying to ground him.

The nurse's face was as pale as the walls around them. Her eyes darted between Kevin and Sean, wide with disbelief. She took a step back, her voice trembling.

"Wait a minute. I haven't felt well since this morning. No one knows about that except me. And... I do feel like I'm about to throw up." She stared at Kevin, her frown deepening with confusion. "How do you know that?"

Kevin said nothing, his gaze steady and unwavering, but Sean looked at the nurse and said, "It's very obvious that you look sick. You'd better see a doctor today."

The nurse looked at him, then at Sean, her expression a mixture of fear and bewilderment. Without another word, she turned and hurried out of the room, the door clicking shut behind her. The silence that followed was deafening.

After the nurse hurried out, Sean's eyes darted to his sister before settling on Kevin, his gaze sharp and unforgiving. "What were you thinking?" he hissed, his voice a low growl of restrained fury. "I told you to stay silent. You've shaken her to the core. Don't you dare pull something like that again?"

"You're about to be released from the hospital. You've already had enough attention, and these doctors are just looking for a reason to keep you here. And now, you're handing them one on a silver platter."

Kevin met Sean's glare, his face pale but resolute. "But I had to," he said, his voice trembling with conviction. "She's in danger. Her life is on the line. I had to warn her. Something in her body isn't right?"

Sean shook his head, his frustration spilling over. "You don't know anything about her, Kevin! You can't possibly predict something like that. It's—" he paused, searching for the words, when Kevin interrupted, "It's impossible?" Kevin looked down, guilt twisting his features, but the determination in his voice remained. "I don't know how Sean, but I *felt* it. I *saw* it. I couldn't ignore it. If something happens to her and I didn't say anything..." He trailed off, his hands tightening into small fists.

Sean opened his mouth to argue further, but Sharon's voice cut through the tension. "Sean," she said softly, her eyes fixed on Kevin, "maybe we should stop pretending this is normal. Clearly, something is happening to him.."

"But I'm certain," Kevin insisted, his voice steady yet tinged with unease. "I saw it—something like a disfigured ball, deep inside her. I don't know how or why, but it was there." His eyes locked onto Sean's, a fierce determination burning within them as he fought to make him believe. "You have to trust me on this."

Sharon stood frozen, as still as a statue, her wide eyes fixed on Kevin. Then, without warning, Kevin jerked his head toward her, his gaze piercing straight into hers. For a fleeting moment, it was as though he could see through her, reaching into the depths of her soul. Yet, instead of fear, an unexpected wave of comfort washed over her, like a quiet reassurance she couldn't explain.

"Sharon! Are you with us? Talk to me, please!" Sean's voice quivered with concern as he clasped her hands tightly, shaking them gently. "Sharon! Sharon!" he called again, his worry growing.

Finally, she blinked and murmured, "Yes..." Her voice was distant, almost dreamlike. Then, her astonished gaze locked onto Kevin.

"He's the most incredible thing that's ever happened to me... ever," she whispered. "Even the first time I looked at atoms and molecules didn't leave me this amazed." Her eyes shimmered with wonder as she stared at Kevin, as though seeing the universe itself reflected in him.

"Yes, I know," Sean said with a nod, his tone resolute. "That's why we're here—to help him out of this mess."

Just then, Julia entered the room, her expression shadowed with worry. She moved quietly toward Kevin, her gaze briefly lingering on him before shifting to the window. "They told me they'd give me an answer this afternoon," she said softly, her voice carrying the weight of uncertainty.

"Whether they'll release him or not." With a weary sigh, she sank into the seat beside Kevin, her hands clasped tightly in her lap as she waited for the unknown. "Mom, don't worry," Kevin said gently, his voice steady and reassuring. Julia's expression gradually softened, a hint of happiness replacing her tension.

"I'm not going anywhere until you get the answer," Sean added firmly, his resolve clear.

Julia offered a small, grateful smile. "Oh, thank you," she replied softly. After a long pause, her expression shifted, her brow furrowing in thought. "That's strange..."

"What's strange, Julia?" Sean asked, leaning in with curiosity.

She hesitated, searching for the right words. "I don't know how to explain it," she began, her voice tinged with wonder. "Every time I feel upset, unhappy, or even worried... if I get close to Kevin, it's like something changes. It's as though I'm on some kind of euphoric drug. I feel this overwhelming happiness like I'm floating on clouds. And then there's this... warmth, this incredible sense of safety and security, like someone or something is shielding me from harm. I can even feel this energy—pure, radiant energy—flowing into me. It's so powerful, so good. I've never felt anything like it before."

Sharon glanced at Julia, a knowing smile tugging at her lips. "I completely understand you," she said softly. "I had the same feeling just a minute ago." Her words hung in the air, and suddenly, all eyes turned to her, curiosity and intrigue etched on their faces.

Julia leaned her head against Kevin's shoulder and closed her eyes, her breathing slowing as if she had drifted into a deep, almost trance-like sleep. Kevin glanced at Sean, guilt flickering in his eyes, and spoke in a quiet, almost resigned tone. "I have no choice," he said, his voice heavy with responsibility. "I have to make her comfortable.

Breaking the silence, Kevin shifted his gaze to Sean, his voice steady but filled with urgency. "Sean, did you find out anything about those... things, pictures or writings that came from my body? You know, those messages you think are connected to the shocks I've been having?" His question lingered, heavy with mystery, as the room seemed to hold its breath, waiting for an answer. "Actually, no. But we're working on it. My friend mentioned something that caught my attention," Sean said.

"What was it?" Kevin asked, his curiosity evident.

"He told me there's never been a language like that before—completely indecipherable. And he suggested the best way to learn more about it was to contact whoever sent them."

"But how? We don't even know where they came from," Kevin said, his voice tinged with sadness.

"That's a fair question," Sean replied thoughtfully. "We do know where the messages originated, but what we don't know is who sent them, what they want from you—or maybe from us—and why they chose you to receive them."

"Sean!" Sharon interrupted, her tone urgent. "Can you show me how you got those messages and what they look like?" Sean glanced at Sharon, then gave a small nod. He reached for his laptop, placed it on the bed, and powered it on. Within moments, the screen came to life, revealing a chaotic array of needles, dots, *Cuneiform script* [9] and intricate lines that seemed to dance across the display like an enigmatic code.

"Look!" Sean exclaimed. "They're just dots, but they vary in size and shape. The way they weave up and down must hold some kind of meaning." Sean paused for a moment before saying, "It's strange because every time I get them, they're different from the ones before."

"You're right," Sharon agreed, leaning in closer. "The waves and dots are positioned differently. And these... they came from Kevin?" "Yes," Sean confirmed, his voice tinged with awe. "And they're absolutely marvelous."

"Well, if they sent the messages to us like this, then maybe we can use the same method to contact them," Sharon suggested.

Sean looked at his sister and said, "You know, Gary said the same thing."

"But how?" Kevin asked, his confusion evident. "It's simple," Sharon explained, her voice steady at first. "If the messages are coming from your body, then we can send messages back the same way. That means... we send messages *through you*."

As the words left her mouth, Sharon froze, her hand flying to cover it as the full weight of what she had just proposed hit her. Sean stood up, pulling Sharon into a warm embrace before planting a quick kiss on her cheek. "You're incredible, Sharon," he said, pride gleaming in his eyes.

Sharon glanced at her watch and sighed. "I'll be late if I don't leave now. But listen—whatever you plan to do, don't do it without me. I want to be there."

Sean turned to Kevin with a playful wink. "What do you think, Kevin?"

"Absolutely," Kevin replied with a grin. "We'll wait for you, Sharon. Promise."

"I love you both. I'll see you tonight. If anything changes, just call me, okay?" Sharon said hurriedly, dashing out the door. "Yes, for sure," Sean replied, watching her leave. "And I'll get everything ready for our first contact tonight." As soon as she was gone, Sean pulled out his cell phone and began dialing.

"Who are you calling?" Kevin asked, his curiosity piqued. "A friend," Sean said with a faint smile. "I have a few questions, and he's the only one who can give me the answers."

"Hello! This is Sean," he said, his excitement bubbling over so quickly that Greg didn't even get the chance to respond. "Greg! I've been thinking about what you said last night about contact." Sean's words spilt out so fast that Greg struggled to keep up.

"Whoa, Sean! Slow down. What's going on? Yeah, I remember," Greg replied, trying to steady the pace. "I need you to do me a favor," Sean said, his voice tinged with urgency. "Anything, Sean. Just name it, and I'll do it," Greg assured him.

"Great. I need the complete English alphabet, a full grammar guide, and a picture dictionary. And I need it sent to me by eight o'clock tonight." Sean's forehead glistened with sweat as he waited for Greg's response, the weight of the moment pressing heavily on him.

"Of course, I can do it," Greg said confidently. "If you remember, we used to send similar information through radio telescopes to communicate with potential life forms in space. I still have just about everything you need. Once I gather it all, I'll send it over."

"Thanks, Greg. Yes, exactly the same info. I knew I could count on you. Thanks again—I'll talk to you later," Sean said with genuine gratitude.

"Alright, but keep me posted and let me know how it goes, okay? Bye," Greg replied.

Sean ended the call, turned to Kevin, and stepped closer. "I need to do some shopping to get everything ready for tonight. I'll be back in an hour or so. "Sean asked, pausing as he noticed the worry in his eyes. "Are you okay?"

"Yes, I'm fine. Don't worry," Kevin said confidently. "You'd better get going—but first, visit your mother. I have a feeling your cousin is trying to distract you from me by doing something reckless... and your mom!"

Sean felt a wave of panic crash through his mind. He gave Kevin a grateful glance, then bolted toward his mother's room. He burst in and found his parents talking quietly. They turned at once, sensing the tension radiating from him. "What's going on, Sean? Are you okay?" they asked, concerned.

Sean, struggling to steady his voice, said, "Yes, I'm fine. But... was Donna here by any chance?"

James nodded. "Yes, she was. Why?"

"Did she give you anything?" Sean pressed. Helen held up a small box. "Yes! She gave us this pack of chocolates." Without hesitation, Sean rushed to his mother, snatched the box from her hands, and passed it to his father.

"Dad! Please run a test on this, just like you used to do with criminal evidence," he urged. James frowned deeply, his expression darkening. "What's going on, son?" Sean quickly explained what Kevin had warned him about and begged his father to take it seriously. Seeing the urgency in his son's eyes, James immediately took the package, turned to Helen, and said, "Do not eat anything from her or anything else, even if it comes from the hospital—until I get back." Without another word, he rushed out of the room.

Meanwhile, Kevin spent his time watching the news and reading newspapers, though his favorite pastime was solving puzzles. Strangely, he often had no idea how he arrived at the answers—he just *knew*. Whenever he focused on something, the answers seemed to unfold effortlessly before him, as simple as counting to three.

Yet, there was one answer that remained elusive, what had happened to his father? Deep down, Kevin knew he hadn't asked the right person. If only he'd had these abilities a year earlier, maybe he could have uncovered the truth. He imagined how, with just a glance at his father's body, he might have been able to extract all the information he needed. But now it was too late.

His thoughts darkened as he considered the possibility of something happening to him. What would become of his mother? The idea weighed heavily on him. She deserved happiness—deserved the very best life could offer. Kevin loved her with all his heart, and no matter what happened, her well-being remained his greatest priority.

His mind was elsewhere when the door swung open, and Sean stepped in, carrying a large bag. He flashed a smile at Kevin before gently placing the bag on his bed with careful precision. He looked at Kevin and said, "Sorry, I'm late. I had to stay with my mom to make sure she was safe, at least until my dad came back." He gave Kevin a look of deep appreciation, then continued, "You were right. My cousin had a devilish plan to make my mother sick—to trap me in worry, keep me by her side, and leave you alone. My dad ran tests on the chocolates she gave my mom—they were laced with something that could have made her ill for weeks, maybe even months. Thank you."

Kevin gave him a satisfied smile, then turned his gaze to the bag full of gadgets Sean had brought back. His curiosity got the better of him as he gestured toward the various parts. "What *are* all these things, Sean? How does this... thing work?"

Sean smiled, clearly excited to explain. "Alright, let me break it down for you. First, this little piece here," he held up a small, flat sensor—"is a *piezoelectric sensor*. It's what picks up the vibrations from your body. Basically, it senses movement or vibrations and turns them into electrical signals." Kevin nodded slowly. "Okay, so it picks up vibrations. What happens next?"

Sean pointed to a small board with wires sticking out. "The signals from the sensor go into this—it's called a microcontroller. Think of it as the brain of the operation. This little guy processes the raw signals and organizes them into something useful."

Kevin squinted at the tiny board. "And this... brain thing connects to what next?"

"Right here," Sean said, holding up a small module. "This is a *Bluetooth module*. It lets the microcontroller send the processed data wirelessly. The data gets transmitted to the portable printer through this." Kevin glanced at the printer. "So that's how it prints? Just through Bluetooth?"

"Exactly," Sean confirmed. "Once the printer gets the data, it prints it out. It's a thermal printer, so it doesn't even need ink—just special paper. Neat, right?" Kevin looked impressed but still curious. "And what about power? How does all this run?"

Sean held up a small, slim pack. "This is a *rechargeable battery pack*. It powers everything—the sensor, the microcontroller, and the Bluetooth module. It's lightweight, so it doesn't add much bulk." Kevin picked up a wire from the pile. "And all these wires?"

"They connect everything together," Sean explained. "The sensor is wired to the microcontroller, which sends signals to the Bluetooth module, and the printer receives those signals wirelessly. It's all one connected system, but it's small and portable." Kevin's curiosity piqued, "How do you locate the source of the vibration in my body?"

Sean looked at him with confidence and said, "Good question. With a small device—an accelerometer, a vibration sensor, and a microcontroller. It detects the slightest movement, converts it into data, and pinpoints exactly where the vibration is coming from."

Kevin looked at him with wide eyes. "So... I wear the sensor, it picks up vibrations, sends them to the microcontroller, and then it prints out the results? That's crazy cool!"

Sean chuckled. "Exactly, and you are a fast learner. We'll place the sensor somewhere on your body where the vibrations are strongest, and the rest will do the magic. Pretty amazing, huh?"

Kevin nodded, a faint smile on his face. "Yeah... pretty amazing. What do you call it?"

Sean looked at him, and a big smile appeared on his face and lips and said, "We are going to call it 'Vibra-Link' for an **Eidolon**[10] friend. How's that?"

Kevin nodded with a smile, though a trace of confusion lingered in his eyes. "Why did you call me *Eidolon*? I thought I was *Nano-man*."

Sean met his gaze, admiration shining through. "You're both. You've gone beyond any one name. You're so extraordinary, and I don't think there's a word good enough for you. But *Eidolon*—that's the closest I've found." A satisfied smile spread across Kevin's face.

Sean carefully unpacked everything from the bag, laying each item neatly on the bed. He began connecting the wires with meticulous focus, his hands moving with precision. Nearly an hour passed as he assembled the setup, occasionally pausing to check his progress. Once finished, he stepped back to admire his work for a brief moment before disassembling it all and packing it back into the bag. "Well," he said, glancing at Kevin, "There's not much else we can do now. We'll have to wait until Sharon gets here."

But the look on Sean's face told Kevin he was eager to start right away. Sensing this, Kevin chose not to say anything, not wanting to make him feel uncomfortable. Instead, he shifted the conversation.

"Will it be painful?" Kevin asked hesitantly, breaking the silence.

Sean looked up, surprised by the question. "Not at all," he said with a reassuring smile. "You won't even feel it. You'll see."

Kevin glanced at Sean again and asked, "Can I say something? Just to kill time?"

Sean responded immediately, "Of course you can."

"Would you come closer to me?" Kevin asked, a sweet smile spreading across his face. Sean moved closer, curious about what Kevin had to say. Kevin pointed at the monitor beside his bed. "Look at this monitor," he said, then gestured toward another one on the right side. "And that one over there—that one shows when my heart is beating. Don't ask me how I know or how they work. I just... know."

Sean listened intently as Kevin explained everything, his excitement growing as Kevin's knowledge poured out. The more Kevin spoke, the more Sean was struck by the boy's extraordinary intuition.

"Now look," Kevin said, his tone calm but instructive. "You need to stick these discs on my heart, my side, and my chest—just like this." He gestured to show the exact placement. "Once that's done, it's ready. All you need to do is turn it on."

Sean looked at the setup and asked, "But which one is the key?"

"The red key, right next to the yellow one," Kevin replied confidently.

Sean nodded and pressed the red key. Instantly, a steady beeping sound filled the room, synchronized with the screen that now displayed wavy lines moving rhythmically up and down. Each peak and dip was accompanied by a beep.

Sean stared at the screen in fascination, then shifted his gaze to Kevin, wondering what he was planning to do next. The anticipation in the room was almost tangible.

"Wait a second, Kevin. You're not planning to do anything reckless, are you?" Sean asked, his voice tinged with concern.

Kevin looked at him steadily. "Not reckless, remarkable. One of a kind." Please, Sean. Everything you've told me, I've accepted without hesitation because I trust you. Can't you trust me, too?" His eyes brimmed with sincerity, so genuine it made Sean pause, and he sighed, guilt creeping in for his earlier words.

"I do trust you," he said softly. "But I'm worried. What if something happens to you? Will you know how to handle it?"

"Thank you for trusting me," Kevin said, his voice steady but gentle. "Here's what I need you to do. First, and this is the most important thing, I'm asking you not to panic. I know exactly what I'm doing because I did it before. Second, whatever you say to me, I'll hear you. I can also see and feel you, too. If you're afraid or unsure at any point, just tell me how you feel. I'll feel it at the same time. "And if you're scared, even for a second, let me know; I promise I'll be back in a flash."

Sean asked anxiously, "You'll be back?" But Kevin didn't respond. He was already focused, pointing toward the screen. "Look at the heart monitor," he said, beginning his explanation. Kevin pointed at the screen. "Watch this—I can make my heart race on command."

The monitor's beeping quickened, the rhythm accelerating with each passing second. Sean's chest tightened as panic crept in, his eyes darting between Kevin and the erratic display.

"Kevin."

Before he could finish, Kevin reached out and clasped his hand. "Don't worry, I'm okay," he said calmly. Gradually, the beeps began to slow, stretching out until only one sounded every fifteen seconds. Sean's panic spiked again, his breath hitching—until, just as suddenly, the monitor returned to its normal rhythm.

Kevin turned to him with a steady gaze. "Sean, don't panic. I'm in control, and this doesn't hurt me. I just want you to understand these abilities… and know me better."

"What are you going to do now?" Sean asked, his voice trembling slightly. "I'm going to die and come back whenever I want to," Kevin replied calmly, his gaze locked directly onto Sean's when his face turned pale. "What? How do you even know you can do that? What if something goes wrong?" His voice rose with panic as he tried to process what Kevin had just said.

Kevin remained composed. "I'm absolutely certain of the result. I give you my word; I have done it many times when I need to calm down," he said firmly. Then, softening his tone, he added, "And if you need proof, I have it. Sean, I love my mom. Do you think I'd ever risk turning her life upside down? What would happen to her if something happened to me? I wouldn't let that happen, I promise you."

Kevin glanced at Sean, searching his face for any remaining questions. When none came, he closed his eyes, drew in a deep breath, and lay back on the bed. "No matter what, do not call a nurse or doctors."

Sean, feeling the weight of the moment, reached over and turned the monitor's volume down to a whisper. "Okay. I trust you. I don't want the nurses showing up," he muttered to himself.

The room plunged into an almost eerie silence. Kevin lay still, his breathing slow and steady, while Sean sat nearby, unable to tear his eyes away from him. The faint beeping of the monitor filled the air, soft yet persistent, each sound amplifying Sean's nervous anticipation.

Time seemed to drag, each second stretching into eternity. Sean's heart raced, but he forced himself to wait, watching Kevin with a mix of dread and hope, bracing himself for whatever might come next.

As Kevin remained deep in concentration, the silence was abruptly broken by the creak of the door swinging open. Julia stepped in, her eyes immediately locking on Kevin, lying still on the bed. Sean startled, instinctively stepping back. Kevin, hearing the commotion, slowly shifted his gaze toward his mother, his expression calm but focused.

Julia's face twisted in panic as she rushed forward. "What happened? Oh my God, what's wrong with him?" she wailed, her voice trembling.

Sean quickly moved to intercept her, his hands raised in a placating gesture. "Julia, listen to me," he said, trying to keep his voice steady. "Nothing is wrong. Everything is under control, I promise. Please, just trust me."

Kevin slowly sat up in his bed, his voice calm and reassuring. "Look, Mom, I'm okay," he said gently. "I was just trying to show Sean this equipment. I wanted to demonstrate how it works. That's all. Calm down, there's nothing to worry about." He reached out, pulling Julia into a warm hug. "I promise everything's fine," he added, pressing a soft kiss to her cheek. Julia's tension eased slightly as she felt the sincerity in her son's embrace.

Julia let out a shaky breath, her shoulders relaxing as Kevin's words reassured her. Her eyes glistened with unshed tears. "Oh, I'm so glad it was nothing," she said softly. "It's just... I love you so much. Without you, I don't even want to live anymore." She glanced down and noticed her bags on the floor. Sean quickly picked them up and handed them to her. "I think these are yours," he said with a small smile.

Julia nodded, taking the bags. "Yes, I've got a tuna sandwich and a corned beef sandwich," she said as she peeked inside. Realizing something was missing, she frowned. "Oh, I forgot the drinks! I must have left them on the counter. I'll go grab them. I'll be back in a minute." With that, she turned and left the room, the door closing softly behind her.

"Well, where were we?" Kevin asked his tone light but focused.

"I have no idea," Sean replied flatly, hoping Kevin had forgotten. The last thing he wanted was to encourage him to repeat what he'd done or try something reckless again.

"I know," Kevin said with quiet determination as he lay back down. "Listen carefully, Sean," Kevin continued, his voice calm but firm.

"I'll go for just five minutes this time. I need you to look at your watch and tell me the exact time. You're the timekeeper." Sean stared at him, uncertain but unable to argue. Kevin re-positioned himself and added, "Remember—five minutes. Don't panic like last time. I can feel everything you're feeling, so stay calm. And we need to hurry; my mom will be back soon."

Sean nodded reluctantly. Kevin closed his eyes again, his breathing steady, and Sean glanced nervously at his watch. His hands trembled as he waited for the second hand to strike twelve. When the moment arrived, Sean swallowed hard and said, very slowly, "Now."

The beeping sound shifted, becoming much slower, each tone dragging out like an ominous signal. Sean's heart pounded in his chest as fear crept in, overwhelming the reassurances Kevin had given him. Despite everything Kevin had said about his ability, Sean couldn't shake the dread—this was the sound of death. Kevin was really gone.

Suddenly, Sean's mind grasped onto a thread of hope. He remembered Kevin's words, *I can hear you, I can feel you.* Desperate, Sean leaned over Kevin's bed and whispered urgently into his ear.

"Kevin! Are you all right? I don't know what to do. Almost two minutes have passed."

His voice trembled as he spoke, hoping for any sign that Kevin was still there, still listening. The room felt impossible still; the faint, flat line of the monitor was the only sound breaking the silence.

Sean glanced around the room, his panic mounting with every passing second. He turned his eyes back to Kevin and whispered under his breath, *"What am I doing? He might be dying, and I'm just standing here, wasting time instead of trying to save him."*

He leaned closer to Kevin, his voice louder this time, though still trembling. "Kevin, are you listening? The sound of that non-beeping means your heart has stopped. You're dead. Do you hear me?"

Sean hesitated for a moment, then steeled himself. "I'm going to check your heart myself," he said, his voice shaking as he pressed his ear against Kevin's chest, hoping for any sign of life, no matter how faint.

Sean pressed his ear firmly against Kevin's chest, desperate to hear the faintest heartbeat—but there was nothing. Then he checked his pulse, and again, nothing. Absolute silence. His breath quickened as he grabbed Kevin's wrist, pressing his trembling fingers against the pulse point again. Still, there was no sign of life.

A wave of panic swept over him, and his face turned as pale as a ghost. He stared at Kevin's chest, hoping, pleading for even the smallest rise or fall to signal breathing, but it remained completely still. Sean's hands began to shake uncontrollably. His mind raced, torn between disbelief and the horrifying reality unfolding before him—Kevin was truly gone.

"Oh, Kevin," Sean whispered shakily, his voice trembling with fear. "It's better if I call the doctor or the nurse—anybody." But then he hesitated, remembering Kevin's plea, *Trust me.* His thoughts spiraled. *What if he's dead? What if I've made a terrible mistake?*

He glanced at his watch again. *"Two more minutes,"* he murmured to Kevin, trying to steady his racing mind. His voice rose as panic took hold. Hovering between a whisper and a shout, he called out, "Kevin! I'm so worried and scared. I'm panicking—I don't know what to do. God, help us." He looked at the watch again. *"One more minute,"* he said under his breath. *I must trust him. I have to trust him.*

The seconds dragged by, each one heavier than the last. His voice climbed urgently as the final countdown began, "Four... three... two... one... now? Now, Kevin! KEVIN!" Sean shouted, his voice breaking with desperation.

But there was no reaction. Sean felt his knees go weak, and his breath caught in his chest. "Kevin! Answer me, Kevin!" he screamed, his voice echoing in the silent room. Sean was on the verge of collapse, shaking uncontrollably, more confused and terrified than ever. He stumbled toward the door, ready to call for help, when a sound stopped him in his tracks. Beep. Beep. Beep. "Sean! Wait," Kevin's voice broke the silence.

Sean froze, his heart pounding as he turned back toward the bed. His eyes widened in disbelief, staring at Kevin as if he were seeing a ghost. He rushed back to his side, his hands trembling. "Kevin, I almost had a heart attack!" Sean exclaimed, his voice quivering. "I don't want you to do this anymore!" His words came out louder than he intended, nearly a yell. He quickly checked Kevin's pulse and heartbeat. Relief flooded him as he found everything back to normal.

"Are you alright now?" Sean asked, his voice still shaking.

"Yes," Kevin said with a calm smile. "I feel wonderful."

Sean looked at him and said, "But I feel miserable." Sean's eyes narrowed with a mixture of relief and disbelief. "How did you do that? What do you feel now? What happened? What did you feel when you... passed away?"

Kevin sat down and leaned back slightly on his bed, his expression serene. "It was like sleeping but far more wonderful. I felt your presence the whole time and heard how panicked you were. I didn't want to scare you, but I needed to finish. You held up well, though."

Sean stared at him, still struggling to process what had just happened, his emotions a mix of awe, frustration, and relief altogether. "Kevin, you can't keep doing this. You scared me to death!"

"For an entire five minutes, you didn't breathe, your heart stopped, and your pulse was gone. How was that even possible? You call this being relaxed?" Sean asked, his curiosity battling with disbelief. "I know you probably don't have an answer right now. Maybe you don't even know how you're doing it, but the fact is— you can, and it scares me."

Kevin grinned, his voice taking on a playful, almost childlike tone. "But I can do it for days if I want to, and it feels amazing after! Look at it this way, it's like a driver who doesn't know how to build an engine but can still handle driving a car flawlessly."

"The way you're saying it makes it sound normal—but Kevin!" Sean burst out, his voice sharp. "That could mean... maybe your father is still alive!"

Kevin's smile faded, and his gaze darkened. "No," he said softly, shaking his head. "He died a couple of weeks after... whatever happened to him. I don't know how it happened, but something must've gone wrong. Something must've happened while he blacked out, something that kept him from coming back to a normal life. I can feel it, Sean. Something wasn't right." He paused, then turned to Sean, his voice lower, more uncertain.

"Do you remember when you asked me if I could rearrange gravity? And I told you what happened? I tried... and it wasn't possible. If anyone goes that far, I don't think they'll ever be able to escape." His gaze darkened as he swallowed hard. "Ever since then, I've had nightmares. If it weren't for my mom, I might never have come back. But what if... what if my dad tried to fly away from that place and got trapped there? What if no one was there to help him... and he was just stuck—forever?"

Sean stared at him, the weight of Kevin's words sinking in. There was so much they still didn't know about Kevin, his father, and the mysterious power that had changed everything.

Kevin sighed deeply, the weight of his words lingering in the air. After a pause, he continued, his voice subdued, "Anyway, he's gone now. We cremated him and then buried his ashes in a place where no one would ever find him again. It was his final wish."

As he spoke about his father, a shadow of sorrow crossed Kevin's face, his emotions slipping through the cracks of his otherwise composed demeanor. He's just ten years old, yet he carries the weight of a ninety-year-old man's sorrow. The way he speaks, the way he thinks there's a maturity in him that feels far too heavy for a child his age. "How do you know about his will?" Sean asked, his eyes narrowing in surprise as he studied Kevin's expression.

Kevin lifted his head, his big, dark eyes locking onto Sean's with an intensity that seemed to pull the room into silence. "Before he left us, he gave us a copy of his will, and the original is with his lawyer," Kevin said, His voice tinged with a mix of bitterness and sorrow. "He told my mom he couldn't bear staying in New Jersey, even though the doctor insisted he remain. He had no access to his phone and no way to reach out. Writing his will was his last act of defiance before going to that hospital as if he knew what was coming—his final attempt to free himself."

Kevin's lips quivered as if he were on the verge of breaking down, his eyes glistening with unshed tears. Sean hesitated, opening his mouth to say something, but before the words could escape, the door creaked open, and Julia stepped in, carrying another bag.

Sensing the tension in the room, Sean decided not to linger. He didn't want to make Julia uncomfortable or intrude on whatever they needed to discuss. Turning to Kevin and then Julia, he spoke gently, "Kevin, I'm heading out for lunch, but I'll be back soon." Then he turned to Julia," If anything comes up, just call me, alright? Otherwise, I'll see you both after lunch." With a reassuring nod, Sean gave them a momentary glance before stepping out, leaving Kevin and Julia alone.

"That's okay. Just don't forget, Sharon will be here after five," Kevin said, flashing Sean a confident smile, though the weight behind his eyes lingered.

When Sean returned from lunch, he found Kevin standing near the door, fully dressed and looking more alive than he had all morning. Before Sean could ask, Kevin broke the news, his words spilling out in an excited rush. "Sean! Guess what? I'm leaving the hospital in a few minutes. We're ready to go. I'm just waiting for the doctor to hand me the release papers. I didn't call you because I only found out right before you got back."

His enthusiasm was palpable, but there was a subtle nervousness in his tone as if he didn't know how to explain everything at once.

"That's very good news, Kevin!" Sean managed to say, though his voice was strained. A knot formed in his chest as he tried to hold back the flood of emotions threatening to overtake him. The thought of not seeing Kevin again felt like losing something he hadn't even realized he cared for so deeply.

He stood frozen, unable to move, just staring at Kevin and Julia. The room felt heavy, as if the weight of the unspoken hung between them, and Sean's heart beat faster with the sudden realization that everything could change in an instant.

After a few minutes, Kevin and Julia were ready to leave. Kevin turned to Sean with an expectant look. The nurse and doctor were still in the room, and Kevin remained cautious, careful not to reveal too much in front of them. "Are you coming now? We're still playing that game, right?" he asked his tone light but his eyes searching for reassurance.

Sean shook his head gently. "No, Kevin. I'll wait for Sharon, and then we'll both come by later. Just give me your address. How about I come by around seven o'clock? Does that work for you and your mom?" Kevin's face lit up instantly. "Yes, of course! That's even better—I'll have time to take a shower, and Mom will have time to prepare dinner." He glanced at his mother, a hopeful smile spreading across his face. "Right, Mom?"

Julia paused, her eyes briefly meeting Sean's as if weighing the sincerity of his words. Then, with a warm smile, she nodded. "Of course, it'll be okay. You're always welcome in our home."

The nurse entered the room, carrying her equipment, ready to take Kevin's blood pressure pulse and monitor his heartbeat before he left. Sean stood nearby, looking pale and uneasy, his mind racing with the possibility that Kevin might try to pull some kind of prank or say something to scare the nurse.

Sean's eyes stayed locked on Kevin as the nurse moved methodically through her tasks. She glanced at the monitor, puzzled, and turned to the doctor. "I think his heartbeat just dropped slightly."

Kevin glanced at the screen, then at the nurse—calm, focused. Within seconds, his heart rate adjusted, rising just enough to appear normal again.

The nurse blinked at the change, then turned back to the doctor and said, "Oh, never mind. It fixed itself." Kevin could feel Sean watching him. He turned—and there was Sean, smiling with a slow, impressed nod. Kevin gave the faintest shrug as if to say, *Control is everything.*

The nurse noted something in Kevin's chart, her expression neutral, before turning to him with a few routine questions. Kevin answered them all calmly and without hesitation.

When the nurse finally left, Kevin turned to Sean, a playful smile tugging at his lips—a smile that, surprisingly, carried no trace of mischief. It was a quiet reassurance, a silent promise that he wouldn't do anything foolish like he read Sean's mind. For the first time that day, Sean felt his tension begin to ease.

"The doctor will be here any minute to see you, and then you can go home," the nurse explained, her voice calm yet tinged with curiosity. She hesitated for a moment as if debating whether to say more. Finally, she took a deep breath and continued, her tone softer now. "You know, Kevin, I went to the doctor yesterday, and... I just found out that I'm pregnant. But it turns out I also have low blood pressure and need to be closely monitored. You were right when you said I was in danger."

The nurse's eyes searched Kevin's face, her expression a mixture of gratitude and disbelief. "Thank you for the heads-up and for saying something. But I have to ask how did you know? Did you really see something in my stomach? How is that even possible? Are you... an angel or something like that?"

Her words hung in the air as she turned to Julia, her voice trembling slightly. "They told me I needed medication to stabilize my blood pressure; otherwise, I might have lost my baby. But thanks to Kevin, my baby is safe." Julia's eyes widened in astonishment, her gaze shifting to her son.

The nurse stepped closer to Kevin, her face lighting up with pure gratitude. "It's been such a long time since we tried to have a baby, and I had two miscarriages, but it never seemed possible—until now. Kevin, you saved my baby." Kevin turned to Sean, beaming with a wide smile. "Did you hear that, Sean? I saved her baby!" Sean smiled and nodded, but in his mind, he quietly murmured, *You have to be careful, Kevin. I hope you understand.* Still gazing at Sean, Kevin softly replied, "I will." For a moment, Sean found himself speechless, lost in the thoughts swirling silently within him.

The nurse leaned in and gently kissed Kevin on the forehead, her emotions overflowing as she smiled at him, tears of relief shimmering in her eyes.

She looked at Kevin with kind, searching eyes, her voice soft and sincere. "I have so many questions I want to ask you. Could I see you again? I know you don't want anyone else to know about... you, and I promise to keep it a secret unless you tell me otherwise. But would you come back here or call me sometime? Just so we can talk?"

Her words carried a quiet plea, a mixture of curiosity and gratitude, as though she couldn't bear the thought of losing this unexpected connection. "Yes. Just give me your number, and I'll call you whenever I can," Kevin replied calmly, his tone steady and reassuring.

The nurse quickly scribbled her phone number and address on a piece of paper and handed it to him. With a warm smile, she leaned in and kissed him gently on the forehead once more. "Take care of yourself, Kevin; if you need anything, I might be able to help you," She said softly before turning and leaving the room, her footsteps fading down the hallway.

The room was filled with a quiet joy. Julia's face was lit with relief. Her son had finally gone home after what felt like an eternity. But Kevin's happiness ran deeper than that—he wasn't just leaving the hospital; he had found something he never thought he would have, a friend like Sean.

To Kevin, having an astronomer as a friend felt like a dream come true. Sean was a scientist, and for someone like Kevin, that meant everything. He had never had a true friend before, and most of his life had been spent in solitude. At school, he was often ridiculed for being one of the smartest students, even outshining his teachers at times.

Kevin's love for learning was boundless. His mind was a sponge, soaking up knowledge, always hungry for more. Science, math, history—it didn't matter. If it were something to be understood, he would master it in no time. But his brilliance often made him a target.

His classmates mocked him relentlessly, calling him names, laughing at his intelligence, and sometimes going as far as throwing his books into the toilet. The cruelty cut deep, and though Kevin often knew the answers to questions in class, he would sometimes stay silent, pretending he didn't know, just to avoid drawing attention. It was easier to blend into the background than to be the boy everyone wanted to tear down.

Once, a teacher told him, "When people are bullied, it means they're unique. Bullies could never see themselves as good as those they target. So, if you have a bully, hold your head high—it might just mean you're so good, maybe even perfect, that they can't stand the light you shine. If someone tries to dim your light, be proud—it only means you shine so brightly, they can't bear the brilliance." From that moment on, Kevin never let those kids bother him. In fact, after hearing his teacher's words, it was Kevin who started feeling sorry for them.

But Sean—Sean was different. For the first time, Kevin felt seen and valued, not mocked. And that small, extraordinary shift filled him with a sense of hope he hadn't felt in years.

Kevin's thoughts were interrupted by the sound of the door opening. "Hi, Kevin. How are you feeling now?" Dr. Howard asked, stepping into the room with a warm smile. "Hello, Doctor. I'm doing okay," Kevin replied politely.

Dr. Howard nodded, his gaze kind but firm. "I know you're a bright boy, Kevin, and I don't want to waste your time keeping you here any longer than necessary. The only thing I'll ask is that you take care of yourself. And if you ever need me, just call."

At that moment, he looked at Sean and then Julia. "My direct number is on your release paper—so you can reach me in case of an emergency. Because I am familiar with your symptoms."

He handed Kevin the paper, then added with a small smile, "This was actually your friend's suggestion. Mr. Morgan thought it'd be better for you to go home and stay away from the hospital for a while."

Kevin glanced at Sean, his heart swelling with gratitude. Sean's care and foresight were further proof that he had found a friend worth holding onto. "I want you to promise me," Dr. Howard said firmly, his tone serious as he looked directly at Kevin. "And don't go to any other doctor for your own safety."

He paused, then added with a small, reassuring smile, "This is also your friend's suggestion. And honestly, I believe him when he says you're the healthiest person I've ever known. Maybe even too healthy." They all burst into laughter

Dr. Howard's words seemed to hang in the air, heavy with meaning, as his gaze shifted to Julia. Her face was streaked with tears, a mixture of relief and emotion she couldn't contain. Kevin nodded silently, his expression calm but thoughtful, as if he was internalizing every word. It was a quiet promise, unspoken yet understood.

Dr. Howard turned to Julia, his voice gentle yet deliberate. "Your son is a very special person, Ms. Thomson. His brain's reaction time is extraordinarily high, something I've rarely, if ever, encountered. I haven't disclosed any information about Kevin to anyone, and I want to thank Mr. Morgan for bringing this to my attention." He hesitated for a moment, then added with a touch of sadness, "I also knew your husband very well, and he was a remarkable man."

Julia's eyes widened in surprise. "You knew my husband? How?" she asked, her voice trembling slightly.

Dr Howard nodded, his expression somber. "Yes, I knew him. And I was deeply sorry to hear of his passing—I could hardly believe it. Before he went to see the specialist for his condition, he came to me. I always considered him to be one of the most intelligent people I'd ever met… second only to Kevin, of course."

He sighed, regret flickering in his eyes. "If I'd known he was planning to go to New Jersey, I would have done everything in my power to change his mind. But by the time I found out, it was too late."

Dr. Howard sighed deeply and gestured toward Kevin. "Take care of him. He's very special," he said, his tone a mix of admiration and caution.

As he turned to leave, his gaze fell on Sean, who had been quietly standing nearby. Dr. Howard's expression softened, and he spoke directly to him. "Kevin is in excellent condition. Also, I've received quite a bit of information about his father's condition. I'm not entirely sure what it all means, but I'm confident they're in very good hands now." With that, he handed a stack of papers to Sean, pausing briefly as a small smile crossed his face. "I recognized you the moment I saw you. You're my son's hero—he talks about you all the time. He wants to be just like you when he grows up."

Dr. Howard extended his hand in a parting gesture. "I hope you have a good day and, find whatever you're looking for, and take care of yourself," he said warmly before turning and leaving the room, the door closing softly behind him.

Sean and Kevin exchanged a knowing glance, a silent acknowledgment of the bond they now shared. Meanwhile, Julia busied herself helping Kevin gather his belongings, her movements filled with maternal care.

Kevin turned to his mom and asked eagerly, "Mom! Can I have a dog?" Julia glanced at him with raised brows. "Why do you want a dog? Don't you know a dog needs to be taken care of?" Kevin replied earnestly, "I want a dog, so if bullies try to hurt me, my dog can protect me."

As the conversation unfolded, Sean stood quietly nearby, his mind drifting as an odd thought surfaced, *you can train your dog and then confuse him.* Kevin caught the shift in Sean's expression and glanced at him, puzzled.

Sean smirked, the thought flickering through his mind, *You can teach your dog to fetch—then toss a boomerang, and he'll keep himself busy for hours.*

Kevin's eyes widened—then, without warning, he burst into uncontrollable laughter. He laughed so hard his whole body shook, gasping for breath between fits of giggles. He turned to his mom and said, "I know how to keep my dog busy now. Can I have a dog?"

Sean watched, amused, silently wondering if Kevin really understood the joke. But to his surprise, Kevin wiped a tear from his eyes and managed to say, still grinning, "That was hilarious. I'll do that to my dog."

Sean grinned back. *Amazing.*

As they prepared to leave, Julia turned to Sean with a warm smile. "Are you coming to our home tonight with your sister? We'd be glad to have you both there. Kevin already invited you, and I'm confirming the invitation." Sean's heart lifted at her invitation, his smile brightening. He had been hoping she'd say it. "Yes, of course. It would be an honor," he replied, his voice filled with genuine happiness.

Julia beamed as she helped her son, her excitement evident. Together, they all walked toward the hospital's main door. But as they reached the entrance, they were met with a surprising sight. The area was crowded with people, their faces filled with anticipation and awe, waiting for Kevin.

To them, Kevin was more than a boy leaving the hospital—he was a symbol of hope, an angel in their lives, a sign of something greater. Their whispers and murmurs carried words of gratitude and admiration, their eyes fixed on Kevin with reverence.

Sean walked alongside Julia and Kevin, ensuring they reached their car safely. Once Kevin was settled, Sean stood back with a warm smile and watched as the car drove away, waiting until it disappeared from sight before turning to leave. A sense of purpose and connection filled him, knowing that this moment was just the beginning of something extraordinary.

Sean re-entered the hospital and made his way to his mother's room. As he opened the door, he was greeted by the sight of his father, James, sitting by Helen's side, gently holding her hands. Both of them turned their faces toward him, their expressions warm.

"What's up? Is everything alright?" Sean asked, his tone curious but cautious. "Yes, of course, everything is alright, son," James replied with a reassuring smile.

Sean raised an eyebrow, glancing between the two of them. "So, what's going on with you guys?" he asked again, a touch of suspicion creeping into his voice.

Helen chuckled softly, her smile lighting up her face. Before she could respond, James chimed in, his voice brimming with joy. "Tonight is our thirtieth wedding anniversary. That's why I brought these flowers and candies," he said, gesturing toward the bouquet and box on the table.

Sean's eyes widened in realization. "Oh, God. I completely forgot! I'm sorry!" he exclaimed, his face flushing. "But that's amazing! Congratulations! I'm so happy for you."

He paused for a moment, studying their expressions, then narrowed his eyes playfully. "But… I think you have more news to share. Am I right?" he asked, his voice tinged with curiosity. "What is it?"

"Yes, there's more," James confessed, his voice tinged with awe. "It shocked all of us, and we still don't know what's going on." Sean furrowed his brows, waiting for the explanation.

James took a deep breath before continuing. "As you know, the doctor was here earlier and told us something incredible. When they took the first X-ray of your mother's head, they found a tumor—it was the size of a walnut. Yesterday, when they took another X-ray, it was still there. But then, when they checked again, the tumor was completely gone, leaving the doctors baffled. They said they'd do one more X-ray to be sure. And today, after lunch, when they did the final scan…" He paused, his voice trembling with emotion. "It wasn't there at all. It's gone. The doctor told her she's free to go." Sean's eyes widened, disbelief washing over him.

"All the doctors came rushing in, rechecking with more X-rays,"

James went on, shaking his head. "But there's nothing—nothing at all. They don't have a clue where it went or how it happened. They can't explain it. They even double-checked to see if there had been any error with the X-ray or if somehow her scan had been mixed up with someone else's—but it wasn't.

Helen smiled softly, her hands still clasped in James's. "They told me there's no reason for me to stay here any longer. As far as they know, I'm completely fine now."

"We'll be home by tomorrow because her doctor will be here tomorrow," James added, his voice brimming with gratitude and relief. The weight that had hung over them for so long seemed to have vanished with the tumor, leaving only a profound sense of wonder behind. Sean rushed to his mother, wrapping his arms around her and planting a kiss on her cheek. She held him tightly, her embrace filled with warmth and relief. "Mom! That's wonderful. I'm so happy to hear it," he said, his voice brimming with genuine joy.

As he spoke, a memory flickered in his mind—*the glass of water Kevin had handed to his mother days ago.* Sean's thoughts raced, connecting dots he hadn't considered before. Now he's positive that Kevin had something to do with this miracle... *There must be something about that glass of water,* he thought, his pulse quickening.

Kevin must possess some kind of healing power, Sean reasoned. It was the only explanation for the tumor's sudden and unexplainable disappearance. Though he said nothing aloud, the idea lingered in his mind, growing stronger with every passing second. Whatever Kevin had done, it wasn't ordinary—and Sean knew this was just the beginning of something far beyond what he had ever imagined.

James opened the candy box, and everyone eagerly took one. "They're delicious, Dad," Sean said, savoring the taste. A smile crept onto his face as a memory surfaced. "I remember you've been giving Mom the exact same candies every year. And after that, you'd always give her a gift. Is there a story behind these candies?"

James leaned back in his chair, his gaze softening as he turned to Helen. His eyes sparkled with nostalgia. "Well, son," he began, his voice warm with reminiscence. "I remember when we were in high school, the first day she moved to our school. From the very beginning, I was in love with her. She was the most beautiful girl I'd ever seen. Every day, I'd watch her walking through the hallway."

A tender smile tugged at his lips as he continued. "The way she swung her hands and twisted her hair, it was so natural, so beautiful and charming, that everything about her gave me a fever. I couldn't take my eyes off her. She was perfect in every way..." He paused, chuckling softly. "Well, almost perfect." Helen raised an eyebrow, amused. "Almost?"

James laughed, glancing at the candy box. "Except for these candies. She loved them *too* much. She'd eat them all the time, and I couldn't stand the smell of them at first. But over time... well, I guess

I fell in love with the candies too—because they reminded me of her."

Helen blushed, laughing along with him. Sean watched them, a warmth spreading through his chest. It wasn't just a story about candies—it was a story about love, devotion, and the little quirks that made their bond so enduring.

Helen interrupted him with a burst of laughter, her eyes sparkling. "Yes, I remember how I loved those candies—the smell, the taste, everything about them. I could never get enough!" She stopped, her gaze softening as she looked at James, encouraging him to continue.

James smiled, a mix of amusement and nostalgia crossing his face. "And I always asked myself, Why does she eat so many of those candies? It drove me crazy at the time."

He leaned forward, his tone growing more animated. "Then, one day, I saw her sitting in the schoolyard with another guy on the bench. I was so jealous, I didn't even know what I was doing. I grabbed my bike and started walking it across the yard, pretending not to notice them. My heart was racing, but I just couldn't bring myself to look at her."

Helen chuckled, already knowing where the story was heading.

"And then she saw me," James continued. "She jumped up, called out my name, and ran straight toward me. 'James!' she said, 'I called you! Why didn't you answer me?" He laughed, shaking his head at the memory. "And I said, 'Well, maybe I don't want to talk to you.'"

Helen burst out laughing, covering her mouth. "You were such a stubborn boy, James. I can't believe I fell for you after that!"

Sean grinned as he watched the two of them. The love between his parents was undeniable, woven into every memory they shared, and it filled the room with warmth and joy.

Helen interrupted again, laughter spilling from her lips. "Instantly, I realized what the problem was," she said, her eyes twinkling with amusement. "I knew the problem wasn't me—it was the boy I was talking to." She paused, looking at James expectantly, urging him to continue.

James chuckled, shaking his head at the memory. "Jealousy had made me blind. But at the same time, I didn't want her to know I was jealous. I tried to play it cool."

He leaned forward, his grin growing wider. "She told me she could explain why she was talking to that boy, but I cut her off and told her that wasn't the issue. I said, 'You can talk to anyone you want to.' But then, out of nowhere, I blurted out the real problem."

Helen raised an eyebrow, already laughing in anticipation.

James smirked. "I told her the real problem was those stupid candies she ate every single day. I told her, 'You're going to turn into a fat and ugly girl if you keep eating them!'" James threw his hands up in mock defense. "I wasn't thinking straight! I was a dumb teenager! But I swear, I regretted it the second I said it."

The two of them burst into laughter, their joy infectious. Sean shook his head, grinning at their playful banter. It was clear that even after thirty years, their love was built on moments like these— imperfect, hilarious, and filled with a lifetime of memories.

Helen, James, and Sean all laughed together, the room filled with warmth and shared memories. "You really said that?" Sean asked, still chuckling, though his disbelief was evident.

James nodded a sheepish smile on his face. "Yes, I did. And later, I realized just how empty-headed I was. I hurt her feelings, and she ran off crying. She left me standing there like the idiot I was, and she went straight home." Helen's smile softened as she chimed in. "I loved James," she said, her voice tinged with emotion. "And it was hard to believe that he ended our friendship over something as silly as those candies. I was heartbroken." She paused, the memory still vivid in her mind. "When I got home, I threw out all my candies in the garbage. Every single one. Then I went straight to my room. I don't even know how I managed to fall asleep that night."

Sean looked at his mother with wide eyes, the depth of her feelings hitting him for the first time. The laughter had subsided now, replaced by a quiet appreciation for the bittersweetness of the story.

Despite the hurt and misunderstanding, their love had endured, turning what once seemed like a foolish moment into a cherished memory of their journey together.

"Oh, yes," James said, his tone turning serious. "Later on, I understood the kind of reaction I caused, and I was ashamed of myself. I realized how selfish I had been."

He sighed, the weight of the memory still lingering. "The worst part was that Helen didn't come to school the next day. Her parents called the school and said she had a fever. The moment I heard that, I knew exactly what I had done. It was my fault."

James leaned back, a wistful smile tugging at his lips. "I couldn't concentrate on anything. So, I left school early that day and went straight to the store. I bought the biggest candy I could find—one of her favorites." Sean leaned forward, captivated by the story.

James continued, his voice softening. "I took the candy to her home. My heart was pounding the entire way, and I couldn't stop thinking about how I had hurt her. I knew I had to make it right, no matter what."

"When her mother opened the door and saw me standing there, she paused, unsure of what to say or do," James began, his voice growing more animated as he recounted the memory.

"But eventually, she led me to Helen's room. And guess what happened?" he asked, his excitement contagious. Sean leaned in, eager to hear the rest.

"When I opened the door," James continued, "I saw her sitting on her bed. Her eyes were puffy and red from crying. Her mom gave me a strange look like she couldn't figure out why I'd shown up at their house in the middle of the day. But I didn't care. I walked right over to Helen and handed her the candy I'd brought."

James smiled, shaking his head at the memory. "I asked her to open it, but she refused and just said, 'Thanks.' I asked again, and finally, she unwrapped it and looked at me—she looked like an angel, even with her swollen eyes."

He paused, his voice softening. "That's when I told her the truth. I admitted I wasn't angry about the candies. I was jealous. That's all it was jealousy." Sean chuckled, watching his father's expression shift between embarrassment and nostalgia. "Helen smiled at me," James continued, "and then she hugged me. She promised me she'd be back at school the next day."

He leaned back in his chair, grinning. "Then I noticed the pictures on her desk—a family photo. And there he was. The same guy I'd seen her in the schoolyard. My face turned as red as a tomato." Helen laughed, her cheeks slightly flushed. "I saw how embarrassed he was," she said, joining in the storytelling. "So I told him, 'That guy is my brother. He went to Los Angeles yesterday to study at the university. He was just saying goodbye."

Sean was laughing loudly and said, "It was Uncle Harry?" James groaned, covering his face with his hands for a moment before looking up with a laugh. "I felt even more stupid than before. But she kissed me and said, 'Next time, just tell me the truth before it becomes a big problem.'" He smiled at Helen, his eyes filled with love. "And that was it. From that day on, our love started to grow. You know the rest." Sean laughed along with them, shaking his head. "And Uncle Harry?"

James let out a sigh, chuckling. "Oh, Harry. For years, he mocked me and laughed about that story. Every single time he brought it up, he called me 'The Candy Fool.' But you know what? I didn't care. Because in the end, it brought me the love of my life."

Helen leaned over and kissed James on the cheek, her smile warm and radiant. Sean watched them, feeling a newfound appreciation for the love story that had shaped his family. The laughter slowly died down, but the warmth of the moment lingered as James poured coffee for everyone. After handing Sean a cup, he leaned back and asked casually, "By the way, Sean! What happened to that boy?"

"The doctor released him this afternoon," Sean replied, taking a sip. "That's good news," Helen said, her voice bright with relief. Then she paused as if suddenly remembering something. "Oh! I forgot to tell you—Donna was here just before you came."

Sean nearly choked on his coffee, quickly setting the cup down. "Donna?" he exclaimed, his voice rising in disbelief. "What did she want?" He turned to James. "Dad, did you get the results from those candies she gave Mom?" Then he looked over at Helen. She raised her eyebrows at his reaction but smiled knowingly. "I'm not sure," she replied in a teasing tone. "She didn't stay long. Just asked how I was doing and left."

James met Sean's eyes and said, "I got the results. They contained a kind of poison—enough to give someone diarrhea for days. Luckily, Kevin caught it in time. We didn't say anything to her, and now she's furious, trying to figure out why nothing happened. We thought this way was better to ignore her." James took a deep breath, then said, "But I won't let her out of my sight until we're safely home."

Sean frowned, still processing the unexpected visit. "Donna," he repeated under his breath, clearly puzzled. His mind raced with questions, but he decided to keep them to himself for now. Instead, he glanced at his parents, who exchanged amused looks, their interest piqued by his reaction. Sean sighed, his frustration evident. "Mom, I know it's rude to say this, but you know I hate her," he admitted, his voice firm. "She's always insulted me and Sharon, and I've never forgotten it. "She even tried to harm you just to keep me away from Kevin—she actually went that far."

Helen's expression softened as she listened, sensing the weight behind his words. She glanced at James, who remained quiet, observing the tension. Sean shook his head slightly, trying to shake off the irritation that Donna's name had stirred within him. "I just don't understand why she keeps showing up," he muttered under his breath.

James was always truthful about his family, which was why Sean accepted his explanation without hesitation. The room fell into a heavy silence. A few moments later, Sharon entered, her face pale but determined. She went straight to Helen, pulling her into a tight embrace. "I'm so relieved you're okay," her voice trembling. "When Dad called and told me what happened, I couldn't believe it. It must have been a miracle. Thank God." She turned to her Dad and congratulated him, too. "I'm so happy, Dad. Mom is going to be alright." James hugged her to calm her down. It took a while, then she looked at Sean and said, "Hi, Sean! Anything new?" Sean had just pulled out his laptop and was engrossed in checking something. He glanced up at her, his face lighting up with excitement. Turning to Sharon, he said, "Yes, there's news. I've been waiting for some information from a friend, and he just sent it to me."

"How about Kevin? Is he alright?" Sharon asked, her voice tinged with concern. "Yes, he's fine. As a matter of fact, he's more than fine—he's good," Sean reassured her. "In fact, he checked out earlier. The doctor has already discharged him."

"That's great! Did he give you his phone number or address?" Sharon asked, her concern evident as she settled into a chair beside Helen's bed. "Yes, actually," Sean replied, his eyes sparkling with excitement as he looked at Sharon. "They invited us to their place for supper tonight."

"How wonderful. What time?" Sharon inquired, her tone softening.

"I told them around seven o'clock," Sean said casually.

"Why so late?" Sharon asked, her concern returning. Sean merely shrugged his shoulders, offering no further explanation.

Helen glanced at her children, her expression thoughtful yet tinged with concern. "I know why that boy is so interested in you." She said softly. James was so excited, too and spoke up before they could respond. "Yes. It's because he's a very special and remarkable boy," he said, his tone measured. "He's drawn the attention of the entire world. I think they're just trying to understand him better and uncover what's happening to him. Who knows? Their knowledge might even prove useful in all of this." A brief silence settled over the room, heavy with unspoken thoughts. Then, James began again.

"I myself am quite interested, too," James admitted with a small smile, his gaze steady on Helen. His warmth seemed to ease her tension, and she exhaled with visible relief. "Does it have anything to do with Donna?" Helen asked, her tone cautious but curious. "Somehow, yes," Sean interjected, his voice quieter. "She's trying to get a hold of this boy."

The weight of the topic seemed to press on him, and with a slight unease, Sean moved to the chair beside Sharon and sat down, his shoulders subtly slumping. "Poor boy. He must have something special. That's why Donna must be involved," Helen murmured, surprised by her own words. She usually kept such thoughts to herself. After a moment, her curiosity got the better of her. "Anyway, what is Donna doing for a living?"

Sean leaned back slightly, his tone cautious but informative. "I think she works for a research company in the U.S., probably operating under the government's authority. They seem to want to keep their work under wraps. From what I've heard, they're scouting intelligent individuals from all over the world, studying them, and, when possible, relocating them to the U.S. for closer observation. Just like they did with Kevin's father." He looked at James. His words hung heavily in the air as he glanced at his father, then at Sharon, carefully sidestepping any mention of Kevin's water and the miraculous disappearance of Helen's tumor. Pushing the thought aside, Sean walked over to his mother and gently kissed her cheek. "Mom, I love you so much," he said, his voice full of affection. Helen pulled him into her arms, holding him tightly. "I love you too, my darling. Be careful." Sean assured her with a soft smile. "I will; we've got to go now. I promised Kevin we'd be there as soon as we could."

CHAPTER FOUR

"The Shock That Spoke"

It was nearly six forty-five when Sean and Sharon pulled up to the Thomas residence. To their astonishment, the house was surrounded by a crowd of people, a line stretching out from the front door and spilling onto the street. Some were standing, waiting patiently to get inside, while others sat on the front lawn, murmuring prayers and pleading for blessings from Kevin—the so-called miracle boy. The front door swung open and shut repeatedly as people entered and exited, yet there was no sign of Julia or Kevin amidst the commotion.

Sean struggled to find a spot to park, unable to stop anywhere near the house. He and Sharon exchanged bewildered glances, their unease growing as they took in the scene. They had no idea what was happening—or how, despite all their efforts to keep it hidden, so many people had discovered Kevin's extraordinary abilities.

"I knew this would happen," Sean said, his voice low and tense. Word of Kevin's miraculous abilities spread like wildfire, carried on whispers and eager tongues. That's why they've gathered here— drawn by hope, yearning for healing. Sharon turned to him, her brows furrowed in confusion. "What do you mean by that?"

Sean hesitated for a moment, then took a deep breath. "It's about Mom's brain tumor," he began carefully. "Do you remember what I told you? How did her tumor disappear without any explanation? The doctors are still baffled—they have no idea what happened."

"Yes, I remember," Sharon said, her voice uncertain. "But... was it really Kevin who healed Mom? Are you saying Kevin did something to the water, and that's what healed her?" "Yes," Sean replied firmly. "I'm positive."

Sharon stared at her brother, still reeling from the revelation. The weight of his words pressed on her, leaving her momentarily speechless. Finally, she took a deep breath, steadying herself. "Sean," she said, her voice resolute. "I want to see him. I need to see him now. Let's go inside. This is it. Maybe we'll finally get some answers." Without waiting for a reply, she began moving toward the crowded house, determination written all over her face.

Sean remained silent, his gaze distant, as if lost in a storm of thoughts. "Sean! What's the matter?" Sharon pressed, her voice tinged with concern. "Are they expecting us tonight? Are you sure it's even tonight?"

She studied his face, trying to gauge what was going on, but he didn't respond right away. Finally, Sean turned to her, his expression a mix of frustration and anguish. "Of course, everything is alright," he said, though his voice betrayed his uncertainty. "But the problem is… I'm not sure we have the right to do this. What if something bad happens to him? What if… what if he dies because of all this attention? I don't know what to do."

His voice grew more strained, and he clenched his fists, visibly angry with himself. I don't even know what I'm searching for in him. A ghost? A god? Aliens? Or is it all just the product of a restless mind grasping at the unknown? What if… what if God is reaching out to humanity through him? Or perhaps—something beyond all reason, something Earth has never witnessed before, something that defies every answer we've ever known?

He paused, his breath uneven. "But I still don't have a real answer. That is a logical answer. There's something happening inside him, something beyond what we understand. I've received so many important messages through him—messages that came directly to my computer. But… am I even qualified to handle this? To jeopardize his life? Do I have what it takes to understand it? Or will I just end up making things worse?"

His voice broke slightly, and for a moment, his vulnerability was laid bare. He turned away from Sharon, his inner turmoil written across his face. Sean's thoughts were tangled in a web of fear and uncertainty. He was desperate for reassurance, a guiding voice from someone he could trust completely. And he was with the right person.

"Sean, you're doing your best," Sharon said gently, her voice steady and soothing.

She placed a comforting hand on his arm. "Always remember that. Even if you don't find an answer or things don't go the way you hope, you'll have done everything you could. You won't have regrets in the future."

She paused, searching his eyes for understanding before continuing. "Besides, what's Kevin's reaction? He's not just an ordinary boy. He can sense things—feel what's right or wrong. If there's any danger, he'll know, won't he?" She looked at her brother and smiled as she said, "You mean the people who killed his father are professionals? He doesn't need that kind of professional; he needs someone who cares. Someone like you."

Sean's tense expression began to soften, a faint light returning to his eyes. A small, genuine smile crept onto his lips. "Thank you, Sharon. I knew I could count on you. You really are the best sister anyone could ever ask for." Sharon smiled back, her presence a calming force.

"Let's go inside," Sean suggested, his voice steadier now, a quiet determination replacing the doubt. With a smile still lingering on his face, they stepped out of the car and made their way toward Kevin's house. The night was serene, the sky a vast canvas of stars that sparkled like diamonds, casting a soft, ethereal glow. The cool, fresh air filled their lungs, and for a brief moment, they allowed themselves to savor its calming embrace. The rhythmic echo of their footsteps punctuated the stillness as they walked.

When they reached the house, they couldn't comprehend how they had managed to weave their way through the dense crowd. Strangers surrounded them, bombarding them with questions.

"Are you here to see the miracle boy?" one asked, eyes wide with curiosity. "Is it true he's a healer?" another voice chimed in. "Of course he is," someone else said loudly. "He healed a lot of patients in that hospital." Sean and Sharon exchanged a knowing glance. With a faint smirk, Sean murmured, "I told you they'd blow it out of proportion; listen to how they exaggerated." The gravity of the moment settled heavily around them.

By the time they reached the door, it had closed again as if sealing them off from the chaos outside. Sharon hesitated for a moment before ringing the bell. They stood there, the air between them thick with anticipation.

A few seconds passed before a shadow emerged behind the frosted glass of the entrance door, its movements slow and deliberate.

"Who is it?" a woman's voice called from inside. A child's voice—Kevin's, it seemed—rose in protest, demanding, "They're my friends! Open the door, Mom!" Sean recognized Julia's voice and stepped back slightly before replying, "It's Sean Morgan."

The sound of the lock clicking echoed through the quiet night. Julia opened the door a crack, peering out cautiously. Sharon stepped forward with a polite smile. "Hi, Mrs. Thomas," Sharon said warmly.

Julia returned the smile and gently closed the door again to unhook the chain. She then opened it fully, motioning them inside. "Hi, Sharon. Please, call me Julia," she said with a friendly nod before turning to Sean. "Hi, Sean. Welcome to our little haven."

As Julia attempted to close the door behind them, her movements were rushed, clearly trying to prevent the crowd from intruding. But she wasn't quick enough. A man shoved his foot in the gap, stopping the door from shutting completely. "Please," the man begged, his voice trembling with desperation. "Let me see the boy. My child is dying, and I need to know if he can help her. Please… I'm begging you."

His words hung in the air, heavy with emotion, as Julia froze, torn between sympathy and the chaos that letting him in might unleash.

Kevin appeared at the door, his presence calm yet commanding. He looked the man over from head to toe, his expression unreadable. Then, in a steady and composed voice, he said, "I'm sorry, but you're not telling the truth. You don't have a child."

The man froze, his eyes widening in shock as Kevin continued. "I think you're an investigator. And, for the record, I know who hired you. His name is Gordon…"

Before Kevin could finish, the man's face turned pale. He stared at Kevin in disbelief, his lips trembling as if he wanted to say something but couldn't. Without another word, he turned on his heel, pulled himself away from the door, and vanished into the crowd, leaving an eerie silence in his wake.

Sean and Sharon exchanged uneasy glances, their shock mirroring Julia's as she slowly closed the door, locking it securely this time. Kevin remained still, his gaze fixed on the now-empty spot where the man had stood, his calm demeanor unshaken.

Sean and Sharon exchanged stunned glances before turning their eyes back to Kevin; disbelief etched across their faces. Kevin met their gaze, and exhaustion etched into his features. "That's the fifth one since we got back," he said, his tone flat and resigned."Each one was from a different agency—except for this guy."

"Who is Gordon?" Sean asked, his voice tinged with confusion and curiosity. Kevin shook his head slightly, his tone weary. "I couldn't catch the last name. If he had stayed just one more minute, I would've been able to figure out who Gordon is, what agency he's with, and what he's up to."

Sean studied him for a moment, then spoke calmly. "You could've pretended to listen to him. Gather all the information you need, then dismiss him afterward."

Kevin looked at Sean, then at Sharon, his tired eyes briefly narrowing. Without a word, he turned and bolted up the stairs, his footsteps quick and determined. Over his shoulder, he called out loudly, "I'll be back down in just a few seconds!"

Sean and Sharon remained standing in the entryway, exchanging yet another look, this time tinged with a mix of intrigue and unease. Julia greeted Sean and Sharon warmly, extending her hand as they shook hands in turn. "Please, come in," she said with a kind smile.

"Kevin has been eagerly waiting for you. Ever since we got back home, he hasn't stopped talking about you—about your talents, your position, and how important you are to him… and to the world. He even said he wants to be just like you someday."

Sean smiled and said, "He can't be like me—he's extraordinary. But in return, I want to be like him." Laughter erupted around them, filling the room with warmth. Julia's words carried a tone of pride and admiration for Sean as she carefully took their jackets and hung them neatly in the closet.

"Please, make yourselves comfortable," Julia continued, gesturing toward the living room. "Sit down and feel at home."

Sean immediately felt at ease in the living room. The space exuded warmth and comfort with its professionally coordinated decor. The colors of the curtains, furniture, and flooring blended harmoniously, creating a cozy and inviting atmosphere. As he took in the room, his eyes landed on the mantel adorned with picture frames. Drawn by curiosity, Sean stood up and walked over to examine them more closely.

Most of the photos featured Kevin, from baby pictures to recent snapshots. There were family portraits and even a striking wedding picture. Sean's gaze lingered on an image of Kevin's father, who was undeniably handsome. Kevin bore a strong resemblance to him, though his striking eyes were unmistakably his mother's.

Another photo caught Sean's attention—a picture of Julia and Ira together. They appeared to be a perfectly matched couple, their smiles radiating happiness and love. Then, his eyes fell on a final frame that made him pause.

It was an older image, and at first glance, Sean thought it might be Kevin in the future. Upon closer inspection, he realized it was a graduation photo of Ira. The resemblance between father and son was uncanny, almost as if Kevin were a mirror of Ira at the same age.

Sean couldn't help but marvel at the striking similarities, his thoughts momentarily drifting as he admired the family's story etched into the photographs. "That's my father," Kevin said, his voice calm but filled with pride. Sean turned around, surprised to see Kevin standing by the entrance to the living room.

"Yes, I realized that," Sean replied with a warm smile. "You look exactly like him." Kevin's face lit up with pride at the compliment. He walked over and settled on the loveseat, his energy both eager and contained. "I'm so glad you came," Kevin said enthusiastically. "I can't wait until we start—you know, the contact!" "Me too," Sean replied, his excitement reflecting Kevin's with equal intensity.

Sharon, however, leaned forward slightly, her tone cautious but caring. "But what about your mom? Is she okay with this?"

Kevin nodded, leaning back in his seat, his confidence unwavering. "I explained the situation to her," he replied. "She understood."

"Did you bring your stuff?" Kevin asked, pointing eagerly at Sean's computer and bag.

"Yes, I did," Sean replied with a nod, his expression calm.

"Can we start now?" Kevin asked his excitement barely contained.

Sean smiled but shook his head slightly. "I think your mom would be happier if we waited until after dinner."

"Yes, she said the same thing; after dinner is the best time," Sharon chimed in, offering her agreement. At that moment, Julia entered the room and sat down beside Kevin, her presence warm and comforting. Sean and Sharon settled together on the couch across from them.

"I'm so glad we're finally home," Julia said with a soft smile, her tone filled with gratitude. "I made some tea. You know, since Ira passed away, we haven't been able to afford a maid. So now I handle everything around the house myself."

Her words carried a hint of weariness, but her resilience shone through. It was clear that, despite the challenges, she cherished these simple, shared moments.

"How long has it been since he died?" Sean asked gently, his voice filled with genuine concern. "It's been almost a year," Julia replied, her tone distant and detached, as though part of her still struggled to accept the reality of his absence. She stood up slowly, walked over to a drawer, and retrieved a small stack of photos. Returning to the living room, she handed them to Sean and Sharon.

"These pictures are from the day before we left home to go to the U.S.," she said, her sadness palpable as she sat back down. Sharon carefully flipped through the photographs, pausing on one of Ira, his warm smile and confident stance frozen in time.

"He was a very handsome man," Sharon remarked softly, her words filled with admiration.

Julia gave a faint smile, her eyes misting as she gazed at the pictures in Sharon's hands. "He was," she said quietly, her voice heavy with both love and loss. She added, her voice trembling, "He was also smart, understanding, and such a good father. He and Kevin were my entire life. Ira meant so much to me."

Julia's eyes began to glimmer with unshed tears, her emotions surfacing as she spoke. She glanced at Kevin, who sat silently beside her, his expression a mix of pride and sadness. The weight of her words filled the room, and for a moment, the silence was profound, wrapped in the shared grief of love and loss.

"I'm going to check and see if dinner is ready," Julia said, her voice catching as she quickly stood up and made her way to the kitchen, clearly needing a moment to herself.

Sharon watched her go, then turned to Kevin with a sympathetic expression. "It must have been very hard for your mom to lose such a good husband," she said softly. Kevin nodded, letting out a heavy sigh. "Yes," he replied, his tone unusually mature. "They were really in love."

For a moment, Kevin's demeanor shifted. His posture straightened, and the weight of his words carried a wisdom far beyond his years. It was as if an adult's soul was trapped inside his young body, a complexity and understanding that left both Sean and Sharon momentarily speechless.

Sean noticed the deep sadness lingering in Kevin's eyes, and he decided not to dwell on the painful memories any longer. They had a significant task ahead of them, and he didn't want to burden Kevin further.

"You'll be very popular at school now," Sean said, attempting to lighten the mood. "There are several stories about you in different newspapers." Kevin looked at Sean, his expression calm but shadowed by a hint of resignation. "Not really," he replied quietly. "I don't have any friends there. Who'd want to be friends with a freak?" He paused for a moment, then added, "And the bullies don't care. In fact, they'll probably come up with a new idea to mess with me."

His words hung in the air, stark and heavy, revealing more about his loneliness than he likely intended. Sean and Sharon exchanged a glance, their hearts aching for the boy who seemed to carry so much on his young shoulders.

Sean realized his previous question hadn't landed well, so he tried a different approach. "You know, Sharon is a scientist too. She's researching atoms and particles—her work is truly remarkable."

"What are really atoms and particles?" Kevin asked curiously.

Seeing an opportunity to draw closer to Kevin, Sharon leaned in with a pleased smile and asked, "Do you want to know who discovered them first, or are you just curious for some other reason?"

Kevin looked at her and said, "Now that you mention it, I'd actually like to know who discovered them first." Sharon smiled and stated, "Yes, it's truly fascinating how *Abu Rayhan Biruni*[4], a Persian genius, conceptualized the idea of tiny fundamental particles over a thousand years before Einstein. His term *"Particles of Tenderness"* beautifully captures the delicate and profound nature of these invisible building blocks. Centuries later, Einstein and other physicists expanded on this knowledge, leading to the discovery of atoms and subatomic particles.

Biruni's insights show how Persian scientists were far ahead of their time, laying the groundwork for modern physics while under immense political and cultural pressure."

"Are those particles in everything?" Kevin asked, his curiosity piqued.

Sharon gazed at him with warm, affectionate eyes and said, "Yes, in everything—from liquid to gas, from solid to soft, and even in the air."

Sean smiled and looked at Kevin when he asked, "Do you feel any more vibrations since you got back home?" he asked, his tone gentle.

Kevin nodded. "Yes," he said, his face briefly thoughtful. "But they don't bother me anymore. I lowered them, just like lowering the volume on TV or radio." Then, with a sudden shift in demeanor, his expression grew more focused. "Do you want to check your computer?" he asked, his tone almost challenging.

Sean nodded and reached for his laptop, placing it on the table in front of him. He opened it, quickly typing a few commands, his fingers moving with practiced precision. For a few seconds, the screen remained still, processing. Then, as something loaded, Sean's eyebrows lifted slightly in surprise. "Oh, yeah," he said, turning to Kevin, his voice filled with intrigue. "They're certainly here."

"Look!" Sharon exclaimed, pointing at the screen. "The last part is completely different from the others. If these are languages, comparing them is like putting the Chinese alphabet next to the English one—totally different."

"Are they changing again?" Kevin asked as he leaned in, his eyes fixed on the shifting patterns. "Yes," Sean replied, his voice tinged with both fascination and certainty. "When one pattern finishes, a new one begins. I think… I think it's a language."

Kevin's eyes widened as he studied the intricate shapes and sequences flashing across the screen, while Sharon leaned closer, her curiosity piqued. The room grew quiet, save for the faint hum of the laptop, as they all tried to decipher the strange, evolving patterns.

"They're utterly distinct... fascinating," Sharon murmured, her voice laced with awe as she stared at the evolving patterns on the screen. Her eyes traced the intricate shapes and shifting sequences, struggling to grasp the depth of the complexity unfolding before her.

Kevin nodded, his face serious yet intrigued. "It's almost like they're alive," he said softly as if speaking his thoughts out loud. Sean remained focused on the screen, his mind racing. "It's as if each set of patterns is trying to say something new," he added. "We're just not equipped to understand it yet."

The air in the room grew thick with curiosity and anticipation, the three of them captivated by the mysterious languages taking shape before their eyes.

"You mean they might be ghosts with different languages?" Kevin asked, his tone both curious and cautious as he continued to stare at the screen.

"We don't know yet," Sean replied, his voice steady.

"We don't know exactly what they are." He paused, his gaze settling thoughtfully on Kevin. "But… your body might be generating them somehow, and there's a chance they aren't coming from any intelligent source—they could just be internal vibrations. That's why we need to understand what's happening inside you."

Kevin's eyes widened slightly, the idea both intriguing and unsettling. "You think I'm making them? Like… It's coming from me?"

"It's a possibility," Sean admitted. "The patterns are tied to you, and they only started appearing after you became part of all this. But whether they're created by your body, your mind, or something else entirely, we're still in the dark." The room fell silent for a moment, the gravity of Sean's words sinking in as the strange patterns continued to shift and evolve on the laptop screen, almost as if they were alive.

Julia's warm voice echoed through the house, calling everyone to the dinner table. The atmosphere was nothing short of magical—the soft, golden glow of the lights, the inviting aroma of the meal, and the overall sense of comfort and care made the room feel more beautiful than ever.

The dinner table was a masterpiece. Julia had prepared an exquisite meal and arranged it with a royal touch. Every detail, from the perfectly plated dishes to the neatly folded napkins, reflected her effort to create a flawless experience. The food was delicious, a feast that satisfied both the palate and the soul, and everyone savored every bite. Laughter and conversation flowed freely, and for a moment, it felt as though time had slowed, allowing them to enjoy the warmth of the moment.

After dinner, the group returned to the living room, still carrying the contentment of the meal with them. The air was lighter now, filled with the camaraderie of shared time together, though an undercurrent of anticipation lingered for what was to come.

"Sean! When are you going to start?" Kevin asked, barely able to contain his excitement. His eagerness was palpable, and he shifted in his seat as though he could hardly sit still.

Before Sean could answer, Julia interjected, her tone curious but cautious. "Kevin mentioned you're planning to do something tonight. Is that right?"

Sean nodded, meeting her gaze with a calm but serious expression. "Yes," he said. "But before we get started, I need to explain something to you."

Julia's face shifted slightly, a hint of concern creeping in as she sat forward, giving him her full attention. "Go ahead," she said softly, her voice steady but tinged with unease, clearly bracing herself for what Sean had to say.

"As you know, we've been receiving many signals from Kevin's body," Sean began, pulling out a stack of printed papers and showing them to Julia. "But we still don't know exactly what they are or where they're coming from. Tonight, we're going to attempt something different. We're going to send some messages similar to the ones we've used in space exploration—to see if we get a response."

He paused, glancing at Julia to gauge her reaction. "I asked a friend to provide the specific data we need, and I'll try sending it to the same location we suspect these signals are originating from. But before we can do that, we need to pinpoint where the messages are actually coming from." Sean's gaze shifted from Julia to Kevin and back again. "I want to assure you—there's no danger or discomfort involved. If it helps, I'm willing to use my own body first to show you it's completely safe."

Julia's fingers dug slightly into the sofa, her apprehension evident. "You are so sweet and kind. No hurting, you're sure of it?" her voice tight with worry, then she asked, "And, what happens next? What will it do to Kevin?" Sean's expression softened, his voice calm and steady. "No, it won't hurt. And nothing permanent will happen to Kevin. All we're doing is observing and experimenting to understand the signals better. It's completely non-invasive, I promise."

Julia's grip on the sofa relaxed slightly, though a shadow of uncertainty lingered in her eyes. "Alright, if Kevin's okay with it, then so am I," She said finally, her voice quieter. "But please... be careful."

Sean maintained his steady gaze on Julia, his tone reassuring as he continued. "As we discussed earlier, it's not going to hurt him," he said confidently. "Kevin has a unique ability. He can control his body's reactions in ways other people can't. He's capable of managing virtually every function of his body, which is why he's not in danger."

Julia's expression softened slightly, though a trace of worry still lingered. Sean's calm demeanor seemed to ease some of her concerns as he spoke with certainty about Kevin's extraordinary capabilities. Kevin, sitting nearby, nodded slightly, a quiet affirmation of what Sean was saying.

"Mom! I want to do this," Kevin said firmly, his voice steady but filled with emotion. "I asked them to come here for that reason. If we can figure out what's happening in my body, then maybe... just maybe... We'll understand what went wrong with Dad."

Julia's eyes widened at his words, a mix of shock and heartbreak crossing her face. She looked at Kevin, seeing the determination in his young eyes, and her lips parted as if to protest, but no words came. Instead, she simply sat back, her hands clasped tightly in her lap as if weighing the enormity of what he had just said.

"Kevin..." she began softly, her voice trembling. But she could see he was resolute and that this meant more to him than anything else. After a moment, she nodded, a silent gesture of both acceptance and support, though her heart clearly struggled to let go of the fear.

"Or perhaps... nothing was wrong," Sharon suggested gently, her voice calm, though the weight of the moment lingered.

Sean nodded and took a deep breath. "We just need everyone's cooperation," he said, his tone steady and reassuring. "I don't want anyone to panic—just try to stay calm." Julia glanced at Kevin, then back at Sean. After a brief pause, she spoke, her voice quieter but resolute. "Alright. I want to find out what's going on, too. How, exactly, do you plan to make contact?"

Sean straightened slightly, his expression focused as he explained. "Since the signals originate from Kevin's body, we have to transmit the same way—using a similar frequency or method. It's the only way to ensure the messages reach the same source. But first, we need to pinpoint the exact location."

His explanation was brief but clear, leaving no room for unnecessary worry. Julia nodded slowly, digesting his words while Kevin sat upright, eager and ready to begin. The atmosphere in the room shifted, filled with anticipation and a quiet determination.

Sean turned to Kevin with a steady gaze. "Are you ready?" Kevin grinned, his voice brimming with excitement. "I was ready yesterday."

Sean smiled back, pulling a cord from his bag and holding it up for Kevin to see. "This is a specialized computer cable. Normally, it's used to connect two computers, allowing them to send and receive data. But in this case, I've modified it to create a connection between a computer and your body. I combined a standard computer wire with a unique attachment on the end—a metal clip that looks like a crocodile's mouth."

He paused for a moment, then added, "I call it the *Neuro-Link Clasp*. With it, I'll connect my computer to you and transfer information back and forth between the two." Kevin's eyes widened with curiosity, his excitement growing as Sean explained. The name seemed to add a layer of intrigue to the process, making the moment feel even more extraordinary.

Sean carefully opened the Neuro-Link Clasp and placed Kevin's finger inside, ensuring the metal clip closed gently around it. The device held firm but not tight enough to cause discomfort.

Julia watched them with a composed expression, though her eyes betrayed a hint of unease. Sharon, standing beside her brother, assisted him with quiet focus.

Sean met Kevin's gaze, searching for any sign of hesitation. "How do you feel, Kevin?" he asked, his voice steady. Kevin looked up at him, his expression unwavering. A small, confident smile formed on his lips. "I feel good," he said without hesitation. "Go ahead. I'm not afraid."

Sean settled into his chair, positioning himself behind the computer. Sharon stood just behind him, her gaze fixed on the screen, eager to see what would unfold. Kevin, fully focused, stared at his finger, his expression one of quiet determination. Julia, unable to sit still, shifted her gaze between Sean and her son, her hands clasped tightly in her lap.

Kevin met Sean's eyes and gave a small, confident nod. Taking a deep breath, Sean typed a series of precise commands, his fingers moving swiftly across the keyboard. Then, he reached for a disc and inserted it into the drive, the hum of the machine breaking the tense silence.

Everything was in place. Sean hesitated for the briefest moment, casting one final glance at Kevin. Then, without another word, he pressed Enter.

"I think we have to wait for their answer, but I don't know for how long," Sean explained, his eyes locked onto the screen, scanning for any response. The air was thick with tension, and everyone was holding their breath in anticipation. Suddenly, before Sean finished his sentence, a series of sharp beeping sounds erupted from the computer. The screen flickered, the data shifting erratically.

Kevin let out a small gasp and leaned back abruptly, his eyes rolling toward the ceiling as if drawn to something unseen.

Julia's heart clenched in terror. The color drained from her face as she bolted forward, her voice rising into a frantic wail. "Kevin…! Kevin…!" she cried, panic consuming her. "What's happening to him?! He's dying! Please, help him!" Her hands trembled as she reached for her son, her fear overwhelming any sense of logic. Sean and Sharon sprang into action, but Kevin remained motionless, lost in something none of them could yet comprehend.

The entire house plunged into darkness. The hum of the computer cut off, the lights flickered out, and even the distant streetlamps seemed to dim as if the entire world had momentarily lost its power. Outside, an eerie silence settled over the crowd. For a few seconds, no one moved, no one spoke. Then, like a ripple of fear spreading through water, panic erupted. People shifted uneasily at first, whispering among themselves before their voices rose into frightened shouts.

"What is happening?" someone cried.

"God help us all!" another wailed.

Some dropped to their knees, hands clasped in desperate prayer, while others turned and bolted, running blindly into the darkness. A few, more aggressive in their fear, rushed toward the house, pounding their fists against the door and rattling the handles. Several others pressed their faces against the windows, trying to peer inside, their frantic voices merging into a chaotic chorus of dread. They had come seeking a miracle—now they feared they were witnessing a curse.

"Kevin, answer me… Are you alright?" Julia pleaded desperately in the darkness, her voice trembling. Sean barely heard her. His eyes darted to the window, his stomach twisting as he took in the scene outside. The entire neighborhood was blacked out. Not just the house—everything. The streetlights the distant glow of other homes, were all swallowed by an unnatural darkness. He turned back toward Kevin, barely making out his silhouette in the dim light. Then it hit him. He remembered what had happened at the hospital when Kevin had played dead. Kevin could hear them. He wasn't unresponsive— he was somewhere else.

A thought flashed through Sean's mind. Moving swiftly, he turned back to the laptop, fingers flying over the keys. He typed, "Please stand by. This is an emergency." The moment he hit Enter, everything stopped.

The house remained dark, but outside, the chaos stilled. The pounding on the doors ceased. The panicked murmurs fell into an eerie silence as if an unseen force had pressed pause on the world.

Sean didn't hesitate. He rushed to Kevin, heart pounding, and grabbed his wrist. A pulse. Normal. Steady. He exhaled sharply, relief flooding him. Kevin wasn't dead. But whatever had just happened, it wasn't over yet.

"Kevin...? Do something," Julia pleaded through her tears, her voice barely more than a whisper. Sean quickly stepped forward, placing firm hands on her trembling shoulders. "Julia, look at me," he said, his tone steady but urgent.

"Kevin is all right. I promise you. He can hear you—that's why he's a miracle boy." Julia's sobs slowed as she looked up at Sean, her red, tear-streaked face searching for reassurance. His confidence anchored her, but the fear in her chest refused to fully settle. Sean turned back to Kevin, his voice firm yet pleading. "Kevin! Please answer me. I know you can hear me. Just say something!" But the silence stretched on. Julia's breath hitched as the panic returned, gripping her chest like a vice. Her hands clenched into fists. "KEVIN!" she cried out again, her voice breaking. "Why wasn't he responding?"

The weight of uncertainty filled the room, pressing down on all of them. Sean swallowed hard, refusing to accept the worst. Something was happening, but Kevin was still here. He had to be.

Julia's face was flushed and wet with tears. Panic surged through her again as she saw no reaction from Kevin. Her breath came in sharp, uneven gasps. "I have to call 911," she announced, her voice breaking with fear. She bolted toward the phone, snatching up the receiver with trembling hands. She quickly pressed **9**, her finger hovering over the next number when—she heard him. "Mom! Mom!" Kevin's voice rang out, strong and clear. Julia froze, the phone slipping slightly from her grip. Then, without hesitation, she slammed the receiver back onto the cradle and ran to her son. She wrapped her arms around him, holding him as though she would never let go. "Are you alright?" she whispered, her voice thick with emotion.

Kevin gently patted her back, his voice calm and steady. "Yes, Mom. Sean was right—I could hear you the whole time. I'm perfectly fine." He pulled back just enough to look into her tear-filled eyes. "Please don't cry. Just trust them. Let them do whatever is necessary."

Julia exhaled shakily, her heart still pounding, but something in Kevin's unwavering expression reassured her, and she felt extremely calm. He was still her son. Still here. Still the same, Kevin.

Sean and Sharon exchanged a glance of relief, but they knew this was only the beginning. Julia hugged and kissed Kevin again and again, her relief pouring out in waves. She could hardly believe he was alright, but feeling his warmth and hearing his steady voice reassured her.

"Mom," Kevin said gently, pulling back just enough to look her in the eyes. "I don't want anyone except Sean and Sharon to know what happened tonight. Or anything about me, for that matter." He was looking into Julia's eyes with confidence.

Julia's expression softened with understanding. She could see the seriousness in his eyes, the weight of what he was asking. Pulling him into another tight embrace, she whispered, "If that's your decision, I promise I won't tell anyone."

Before anyone could say more, a sudden, loud banging rattled the front door. "Boom! Boom! Boom!"

"Is everyone alright in there?" a deep voice called from outside. Julia stiffened, instinctively pulling Kevin closer. Sean and Sharon exchanged wary glances. Outside, the murmurs of the restless crowd grew louder. They were still out there. Watching. Waiting. Demanding answers.

"Maybe they figured out that the blackout started from here," Sean murmured, his mind racing through the possibilities. "Don't worry," Julia said firmly. "I'll tell them to go away." She looked at Kevin with a smile, and without hesitation, she walked to the door, taking a deep breath before facing the crowd. Sean turned his attention back to Sharon, who had been unusually quiet. The faint glow of the computer screen illuminated her face, but she wasn't reacting to anything around her. Her eyes moved rapidly from left to right, scanning something with an almost unnatural intensity.

"You okay, Sharon?" Sean asked, concern creeping into his voice. She didn't respond. She just kept staring at the screen, her pupils darting, tracking something only she seemed to understand.

"Sharon, what's wrong?" Sean asked again. He rushed to the computer, his heart pounding. His breath caught as he saw what had captured her attention images. Endless images. One after another, flashing too fast to fully comprehend. They never stopped. Without thinking, Sean quickly began saving them all, his fingers flying across the keyboard. He had no idea what they were or where they were coming from, but they were important.

Sharon, her face pale, finally tore her gaze from the screen and sank onto the sofa as if the energy had been drained from her. She said nothing, but her wide eyes told Sean everything. Something big was happening. And whatever it was, it wasn't over yet. Kevin's eyes widened with anticipation.

"What's happening, Sean?" he asked eagerly. Sean shook his head in disbelief, his voice barely above a whisper. "It's… unbelievable. It's incredible."

"What is it?" Kevin pressed again, leaning in closer. At the door, Julia was still talking to the neighbors, trying to calm their suspicions about the blackout. Meanwhile, Sean remained fixated on the computer screen, his fingers scrolling back through the message.

Kevin was growing impatient. "Sean, what is it? Tell me!" Sean took a steady breath. "Just wait a few seconds. I need to go back to the beginning." His eyes flicked over the text before him, and then, in a measured voice, he began to read aloud,

"Dear Messenger, Thank you for contacting us. It took us nearly five years to fully understand the meaning of your message. Our specialists have learned your language, and we are now sending you information about ourselves and the world we inhabit.

Our galaxy is among billions of stars. Our planet orbits a beautiful neighboring sun, which is protected by 20 energy planets, and 20 other planets orbit around our sun. Two of the planets are inhabited.

Translating our language into yours is difficult, but we are doing our best. We call ourselves **Masonaar A**. *The inhabitants of the second inhabited planet—sharing our orbit—are known as* **Masonaar S**.

We possess advanced knowledge of other galaxies. We have discovered other life forms beyond our own and have successfully made contact with them. We exchange knowledge and share discoveries across vast distances. Now, tell us about your planet. Where is it located?"

The room was silent as Sean finished reading. Kevin's mouth fell slightly open. Sharon, still seated on the sofa, looked as if she hadn't yet processed what she had just heard.

Sean turned to Kevin, his heart pounding. "Kevin… we just received a message from another world." "What does it mean?" Kevin asked, his voice filled with astonishment.

Sean stared at the screen, his mind racing. Before he could answer, Sharon, still wide-eyed, spoke up. "The message said it took them five years to understand our language… yet it only took us five seconds to receive their response." She turned to Sean, her expression one of pure awe. "How is that possible?" She went into deep thought and turned to Sean again and said, "May I have a copy of the messages, and I have to study on it?" Sean accepted and immediately sent a copy to Sharon's email and said, "It's done."

Kevin's breath quickened. His thoughts spiraled. "What does that mean? Does it mean they have short lives?" he asked again, his voice almost a whisper. "Are they… aliens from somewhere else?"

Sean exhaled slowly, his fingers drumming on the keyboard as he considered the implications. "It could mean a lot of things," he admitted. "Maybe time works differently for them. Maybe their perception of reality is completely different from ours. Or…" His voice trailed off, his mind struggling to grasp the enormity of the situation.

"Or…?" Kevin pressed, his heart pounding.

Sean looked at both of them, his expression unreadable. "Or maybe they're a lot closer than we think." He looked at his sister, exhaling sharply. "Well!" he said as if inviting her to take the lead.

Sharon turned to Kevin, her expression softening. Like a caring older sister, she spoke gently but firmly. "No, Kevin," she said. "They're not aliens from another planet or galaxy. And yes… you're right. They do have a short life."

Kevin's eyes narrowed slightly, trying to process her words. "But… how can that be?" he asked, confused. Sharon glanced at Sean before continuing. "The way they perceive time must be different from us. If five years for them feels like just seconds for us, then their entire existence could pass in what we'd consider an instant. To them, an entire lifetime could be happening right now while we're just sitting here, talking."

Kevin's lips parted slightly in shock. "So… they could be born, live, and die all in the time it takes us to have a conversation?" Sharon nodded solemnly. "Exactly."

A shiver ran down Kevin's spine. The concept was overwhelming. A civilization existing at a completely different speed, reaching out across time and space. Sean leaned forward, his voice thoughtful. "And that means… if we respond, we could be speaking to generations of their people within a single night."

The weight of that realization settled over them like an invisible force. The connection they had just made wasn't just with a single entity. It was with an entire history unfolding before their very eyes. Sharon glanced at her watch, her breath hitching. "Look! It's five minutes past our initial contact."

Her voice trembled as she did the mental calculation. "That means… that means each second is one year for them. Every minute is sixty years. We've been sitting here for five minutes… which means three hundred years have passed in their world."

Kevin's face paled. "So… there's no way for us to contact the same person twice?" Sharon swallowed hard, nodding. "They're gone by now. Whoever sent that message… they're long gone. Entire civilizations could have risen and fallen in the time we've been talking." She hesitated, her voice almost breaking. "In my opinion… they have the lifespan of some molecule. I mean… they're living molecules."

The room fell into a profound silence. Nobody spoke. Nobody moved. Kevin's hands clenched into fists as the weight of that revelation settled over them. They weren't just communicating with another species… they were communicating with something beyond human comprehension.

Sean let out a slow, unsteady breath, staring at the screen as if expecting another message to appear. But nothing came. Because whoever had written to them was already dust in the wind.

Julia returned from the front door, her footsteps light but her expression serious. She had been listening carefully, absorbing every word. Kevin scanned the faces in the room, his mind brimming with thoughts he could barely put into words. Finally, he turned to Sharon.

"Why is it only *my* body that receives those messages?" he asked, his voice filled with both curiosity and unease. Sharon hesitated for a moment, then answered thoughtfully. "Well… I think your body is the only one that's upgrading itself."

Sean leaned forward, his voice steady but laced with awe. "Kevin, you know every inch of your body. You can control anything—your heartbeat, your blood flow, even the way your body responds to pain. You can stop yourself from bleeding or breathing or make a wound disappear." He smiled at Kevin and then continued, "You don't need medicine. You don't need a doctor. You are a hundred percent pure human, and you're beyond anyone else's imagination the next evolution of humanity.

"People fear Aliens, robots and AI taking over our civilization, but humanity is already upgrading naturally. This way, we remain in control. You are living proof of that. He paused for a second, then continued again:

"You have the power to command computers to manipulate electronic systems effortlessly. You are not just human; you are the future." Kevin stared at him, his breath shallow.

"And do you know what that means?" Sean continued, his voice rising with realization. "Your body is entirely free of disease, Kevin. Not a single harmful virus, bacterium, or trace of illness remains. It's as if you've eradicated every threat from within, achieving a level of purity the rest of humanity can only dream of. You're not just healthy. You've transcended the limitations of the human body. Perhaps what we're witnessing is the emergence of something new. A redefined human. An evolution. Maybe we should call this upgraded form Neurogen." Silence hung in the air.

"As a matter of fact," Sean added, his words coming faster now, "you healed your asthma on your own. No treatment, no medicine, just you. You healed yourself." Julia inhaled sharply, her hands gripping the edge of a chair.

"You are the first human who will bring hope to people who never had hope, and you are a Neurogen." Sean went on, his voice barely above a whisper now.

"You are the most complete person that has ever existed in human history. And the most important part?" He paused, heart pounding, a faint smile playing on his lips as he said, "You chose me. Not someone else." He had a big smile on his lips, but the room remained silent; no one caught the humor, and no one responded.

The weight of his own words hit him so hard that, for a moment, he couldn't breathe. Kevin didn't move. He simply stared, unblinking. Julia's hands trembled. Sharon's mouth parted slightly, but no words came out. The realization was too immense.

Kevin wasn't just extraordinary. He was something else entirely beyond extraordinary, beyond comprehension. No word could truly define him, but perhaps Neurogen comes closest. "A human Neurogen."

"It is every person's dream to be like you," Sharon continued, her voice filled with a mix of admiration and concern. "You've created a miracle, Kevin. Scientists will spend their lives trying to understand why you are. They'll be mystified by it."

"And that's exactly why we have to keep it quiet," Sean added, his expression darkening. "If they find out, they'll do anything for answers. They'd open every inch of your body just to figure out what makes you different. And they would never give up."

Julia's breath hitched. Panic flooded her eyes as she clutched Kevin's arm. "I don't want that to happen to him," she said, her voice shaking. "What should we do? Do we have to run away?" Sean quickly shook his head. "Oh no, you don't have to do that. Just keep it quiet. That's all."

Julia swallowed hard, still visibly unsettled. Kevin remained silent, absorbing the weight of what had just been said. They had uncovered something extraordinary something the world wasn't ready for. And now, keeping it a secret was the only way to keep Kevin safe.

"I'll do it. I'll do it for Ira and Kevin," Julia burst out, her voice trembling as tears spilled down her cheeks. The weight of the decision was heavy, but she knew she had no choice Kevin's safety came first.

Sean, sensing the tension in the room, decided to shift the mood. He forced a small smile and turned to Kevin. "May I ask a few questions from your planet, Kevin?" he teased, his tone playful. Kevin smirked, catching onto the joke. "Go ahead, Earthling," he said, crossing his arms.

"But this time, it'll be different," Sean continued, his voice growing more serious. "I'm going to ask them to respond in order first to Masonaar A. and then to anyone else. In this case, no interruptions from others in your body. You'll be in control, and you need to stay focused, making sure nothing interferes with any external power sources." Kevin nodded, listening intently. Sean continued: "I'll also ask them how they were able to contact us in the first place," Sean went on. "And I'll tell them to lower their power so the blackouts never happen again. However, I'm going to pinpoint their location and determine exactly where they are in your body."

"But you said they're gone by now turned to dust? And there are no more shocks now?" Kevin asked curiously.

Sean gave him a friendly smile and explained, "There are no more shocks because I asked them to stop until I notified them. Besides, they might already be in their new generation. The ones now are the children of the original ones. You've been experiencing shocks for such a long time, and they kept sending messages.

Heraclitus is famous for saying, 'No man ever steps in the same river twice, for it's not the same river, and he's not the same man.' It's exactly your situation. We're not talking to the same person twice, but they keep growing, and we keep our contact." Sean kept smiling at Kevin and added softly, "They're there, just waiting for our approval."

Kevin looked at his mother when Julia wiped her tears and took a deep breath. "It's okay with me," she said, her voice steadier now. "As long as Kevin wants to do it again." Kevin sat up straight, excitement lighting up his eyes. "Yes, of course," he said with a grin. "I'd love to do that again."

Sean created a device and named it ResoScope9. He placed the ResoScope on the table, its sleek surface humming with a soft pulse of light. The device, no larger than a tablet, projected a faint holographic grid above it, forming the shape of a human figure.

Kevin, Sharon, and Julia watched as Sean activated the scanner, its interface shimmering with intricate data streams. He glanced at Kevin before speaking, his voice steady and sure. "I built this for you, Kevin." Sean ran his fingers across the device's control panel.

"This isn't some hospital-grade medical scanner. The ResoScope is different. It doesn't just detect physical changes it traces the resonance of energy, the unseen vibrations running through your body." Kevin frowned. "Vibrations? Like sound waves?"

Sean looked at him, a half-smile forming. "You know, Kevin… you understand more than someone your age should. It's starting to make me uncomfortable." Laughter erupted around the room. Then he shook his head. "More than that. Every cell, every nerve, even your thoughts they all generate frequencies. Some are weak, barely detectable, but whatever is happening inside you? It's different. It's powerful. I needed something capable of detecting those frequencies at their source."

With a quick swipe, Sean activated the scan, and a holographic image flickered to life in the air. Sharon leaned in with curiosity. "Can I try it?" she asked. Sean nodded and handed her the device.

As Sharon's scan began, a few small light dots blinked across her holographic silhouette. She smiled, then turned to Sean. "Your turn." Sean ran the scan on himself. A few more light points appeared than Sharon's, and he glanced around with a proud look. Julia, however, declined. "Let Kevin try it instead," she said firmly.

When Kevin slipped on the wire and docked the sensor to his finger, the room fell into a hushed stillness. Instantly, the holographic projection of his body ignited every inch, illuminated by countless shimmering points of light. The radiance was so profound it bathed the entire room in a golden glow.

Then, as the image sharpened, golden filaments began to weave through the hologram, pulsing rhythmically in sync with Kevin's heartbeat. At key points, his hands, the base of his spine, and deep within his chest, the light intensified, forming radiant nodes of concentrated energy. Everyone remained motionless, transfixed by the extraordinary sight.

"See that?" Sean pointed at the glowing regions. "This is where it all begins. The ResoScope maps out the exact origin of your internal resonance down to the finest molecular level."

Sharon's eyes widened. "So, it's like an MRI, but instead of scanning tissue, it scans energy?" Sean smirked. "Something like that. However, an MRI only looks at physical structures. This goes deeper. It detects invisible biological frequencies, neural patterns, and even signals that might not be human. And the best part?" With a quick tap, Sean zoomed in on one of the energy pulses, slowing it down. The pulse wasn't random it followed a pattern, almost like a coded message.

"It's not just vibrations, Kevin," Sean said, locking eyes with him. "It's communication. Your body isn't just reacting. It's responding to something." Kevin's breath caught in his throat. "Responding to what?" Sean exhaled, studying the shifting patterns on the screen. "That's what we're going to find out." Sean nodded, rolling up his sleeves. "Alright, then. Let's do this. Let's see where are Masonaar. A located in your body."

Julia sat beside Kevin, holding his hand tightly as if her touch alone could anchor him to reality. Kevin gave her a reassuring squeeze, sensing her unspoken fears.

Sean scanned the setup one last time, ensuring everything was in place. The Neuro-Link Clasp was securely connected, the system was running smoothly, and Kevin looked ready. Satisfied, he turned back to the computer, his fingers poised over the keyboard. He took a deep breath and began typing:

"To the attention of Masonaar A,

We acknowledge the complexity of our current circumstances and recognize that words may fall short of fully conveying our understanding. However, we will endeavor to articulate our observations as clearly as possible.

It has come to our attention that you may not be distinct, separate entities in the conventional sense, as initially presumed. Our latest analysis suggests that you are molecular-based life forms, potentially existing within or integrally connected to the biological structure of Kevin, a human male aged 10.

We seek further clarity regarding your nature and the precise nature of your connection to Kevin.

In an effort to deepen our understanding of your world, your physiology, and the nature of your existence, we respectfully submit the following inquiries. Your responses will be invaluable in facilitating clearer communication and mutual comprehension between our species.

1. Do diseases, pathogens, or any form of physical ailments exist among your people? Additionally, are conditions such as physical impairments, blindness, or disabilities present within your population?

2. What is the typical lifespan of an individual of your kind? How do you perceive the duration of existence relative to your experience of time?

3. How prevalent is illness within your species? In the event of sickness, what are its effects, and how does it impact your biological or molecular structure?

4. Could you describe the environment in which you exist? Do you experience variations in atmospheric or environmental conditions (such as weather), or are you unaffected by external factors?

5. Regarding sustenance, are you herbivorous or carnivorous, or do you obtain energy by other means? How do you nourish and sustain yourselves?

6. Lastly, we seek to understand the mechanism by which you transmit high-frequency signals capable of reaching and interacting with Kevin, which means your universe. What form of energy or technology enables this form of communication?

We greatly appreciate any insights you are willing to provide. Your cooperation will help us bridge the significant gap between our worlds. Respectfully, Kevin's team."

Sean finished typing and glanced at Kevin. "Ready?" he asked. Kevin nodded firmly. "Send it." Sean brought the keyboard closer to Kevin and asked: "Kevin! They're your bodies, so press the Enter."

Kevin felt so excited and he pressed the enter, and the message was launched into the unknown. The screen flickered. The air in the room felt charged as if something unseen had awakened.

Kevin pressed the enter button, and before his finger had even lifted fully from the keyboard, the computer erupted in a sharp, rhythmic beeping. A slow smile spread across his face. "There they are," he murmured. "All the answers we need."

The Moment of Discovery – The ResoScope Reveals the Truth. Sean stood over the ResoScope, his fingers steady as he adjusted the device's precision settings. The holographic image of Kevin's body flickered, its outline glowing softly as streams of pulsing light mapped every inch of his internal structure. The others watched in silence, waiting.

Then it happened.

A spike in the readings.

Sean's eyes narrowed as the data shifted. The ResoScope picked up a concentrated pulse, a rhythmic vibration originating not from his nervous system, not from his organs, but from something much smaller.

"There," Sean muttered,

zooming in on the hologram. The image dissolved layer by layer through skin, muscle, blood, veins, and even down past the atomic level. And then, deep within Kevin's molecular structure, one singular particle glowed brighter than the rest. Sean froze. His breath caught in his throat.

"It's not coming from outside. This is the prof" He looked up at Kevin, his voice barely above a whisper. "It's coming from you, and we have evidence now." Kevin frowned. "What do you mean?"

Sean rotated the projection, isolating the source of the resonance. "Your body isn't reacting to an external signal. It's generating one." A hush fell over the room.

Sharon leaned in, her voice cautious. "But that would mean…" Sean nodded. There won't be a doubt anymore. "It means, as I told you before, your body isn't just human anymore. It's something else something more."

He tapped the device, enhancing the scan. The molecular structure expanded, revealing a single, pulsating unit within Kevin's body, a particle unlike any known to science.

"Your molecules… at least one of them… isn't normal, and I mean, all of them are super, but one is very advanced," Sean said, his mind racing.

Suddenly, the hologram of Kevin flared to life, pulsing with new energy. More spots of light began appearing, first a few, then dozens, then everywhere. His head, chest, hands, feet each part of him was alive with radiant brilliance.

The glow intensified, spreading like a celestial fire, until Kevin's entire holographic form shimmered with an otherworldly light. He no longer looked human. He looked like something beyond human. Like an angel, forged from pure energy, standing between the known and the unimaginable.

"It's transmitting a signal outward, sending something beyond what human biology should be capable of." He looked at Kevin. "You're not evolving into something else, Kevin. You already are something else."

Kevin swallowed hard. The vibrations hadn't been a mystery from the outside they were a message, a signal, and the source was himself.

Sean took a step back, staring at the glowing projection in disbelief. "As I told you before, Kevin, you're not merely human anymore. You're Human Neurogen. You've transcended humanity as if you've graduated to a higher plane. Simply, you are above human."

His eyes darted over the messages once more. His breath came shallow, his vision blurred. His face was damp, and a strange weakness crept through his limbs. He sank onto the sofa, gripping the edge as he read aloud, his voice barely above a whisper:

"We are impressed. Now we know. We are Kevin, and Kevin is us. We wish to see his picture. He is our God now.

As for diseases, I must tell you there is no such thing in our world. Millions of years ago, we suffered from sickness and disease, but now, we are healthy. We are strong. We can live for hundreds of years or for as long as we desire."

Compared to the distant past, that rate has improved by ninety-nine percent. And we will continue to improve for our God.

We devote everything we have to a better existence, knowing that knowledge is the key. Knowledge is our salvation. And with it, we will shape a perfect life."

"We can help you reach this point. We can guide you toward a life free of sickness and disease. Imagine air so pure it carries no trace of pollution, land so rich it yields endlessly, sustaining all who walk upon it. You will no longer struggle to grow what you need everything will flourish effortlessly under your hands.

Long ago, in the records we unearthed from millions of years past, we found a time of suffering. Hunger gnawed at our people, the disease claimed them, and the very air they breathed poisoned their children before they had even taken their first steps. Our world was drowning in filth, choking on its own ruin.

But now now, our world is what you would call 'paradise.' This is the dream your people have longed for. I do not know when you will answer me. Time moves differently between us. But do not be troubled. My great, great, great grandchild will be born within a few seconds by your measure. And if you cannot reach me, you may speak to him… or to his grandchild."

"Tell me, are you merely an atom within another body? A fragment of something greater, a piece within a vast design? We cherish science, and through it, we have conquered what once seemed impossible. No problem is beyond our grasp. No question too great. Remember this: we can help each other. If you seek answers, we will find them. If you need solutions, we will create them. All we ask is that you listen."

Sean finished reading and fell into silence. His gaze drifted toward his sister, his expression clouded with something unspoken. He pressed his hands together, his fingers tightening as if trying to ground himself in the moment.

"Sean!" Sharon's voice cut through the stillness, laced with concern. "What's wrong? Do you want to share something with us? Are you feeling alright?"

Her questions came rapid and urgent, but Sean only stared, caught between the weight of what he had just read and the uncertainty of how to put it into words.

Sean stood up, his movements slow and deliberate. He walked over to Kevin, resting a hand on his shoulder, then turned to face Sharon. His eyes held a weight she couldn't yet understand.

"You know what, Sharon?" His voice was calm, but there was something unsettling beneath it. "Do you know the real reason I came to Toronto? Do you know why they gave me two weeks off?"

Sharon blinked, caught off guard. "Because Mom was in the hospital?" she answered hesitantly.

"That's what they wanted me to believe," Sean said, his fingers pressing lightly against Kevin's shoulder. "But Dad told me on the phone that she was fine. He said there was nothing to worry about."

Sharon's stomach tightened. "If that wasn't the reason, then what was? Or what was the problem?" she asked, her voice quieter now.

She knew her brother too well. He wouldn't have come all this way without something serious weighing on him. And now, standing before her, his expression unreadable, she realized whatever had brought him here was far worse than she had imagined.

Everybody was watching Sean now, their eyes filled with expectation, curiosity, and a hint of unease. He could feel their silent demand for answers pressing against him. What he was about to reveal was a mystery he had kept hidden, even from Sharon, Julia, and Kevin.

He exhaled slowly, his gaze shifting from one face to the next, searching for trust before he finally spoke. "The day before I arrived in Toronto," he began, his voice steady but low, "I was stationed in Virginia, on duty as usual, monitoring the skies, adjusting the radio telescope to new coordinates, and listening for any sign of life beyond Earth. It's what we do every day, tuning in to the vast silence of space, hoping it might speak back." He let the words hang for a moment, watching their reactions. "But that day," he continued, his fingers tightening on Kevin's shoulder, "something listened back."

"That's awesome, Sean! What was it? Was it the one I sent you? You must've loved your job." Kevin interrupted, his excitement breaking through the tension.

Sean gave him a small smile. "Yes, Kevin, I do love my job, and no, it wasn't the one you sent me. But that day… something happened. Something that changed my life forever."

Sharon leaned forward, her worry deepening. "What happened?" Sean took a slow sip of his drink, letting the moment settle. He needed them to listen truly listen. "I'm going to tell you," he said, setting the glass down with deliberate care. "But you need to listen closely." He swept his eyes over everyone in the room, making sure he had their full attention before he began. The room fell silent as he continued. "We received a message. A transmission from somewhere unknown."

Kevin interrupted his voice firm. "I told you, Sean. I sent you the message." Sean's gaze softened, a look almost paternal as if a father studying his son. "That wasn't your message, Kevin. I never received yours." His expression darkened. "I think they hid your message from me." He paused, his mind drifting back, piecing together the fragments of memory before continuing.

At first, I had no idea what they were talking about. Their words were strange, almost surreal. They said they attempted to contact us about six months ago, but something went wrong, and the connection failed. Now, they're determined to reach us to share their knowledge and for us to do the same. I'm not sure whether the message comes from outer space or from something higher, like the Masonaar. I mean, a higher entity.

If five years for the Masonaar equals five seconds for us, then six months for these others must span back to the time when the dinosaurs were wiped out on Earth in our world. I need to know how we can reach them if there's a safer way. I don't want them to destroy our world again."

His voice dropped lower, his eyes scanning their faces. "They didn't know... what had happened to our world."

"What do you mean, Sean?" Sharon asked, her confusion deepening.

Sean took a slow breath, choosing his words carefully. "I mean... they can't be atoms. If they were, they wouldn't be able to contact us like this. Communication between atoms and molecules doesn't work that way. They can only establish contact between larger worlds in space, not between microscopic particles." Sharon's brow furrowed as she tried to make sense of it.

"But," Sean continued, his voice growing more intense, "if molecules wanted to reach us if they truly had a message to deliver it would have to be through a medium we could perceive. The same way Masonaar A. did." He turned to Kevin. "Through your body... or through someone else."

A heavy silence filled the room. The weight of his words sank in, a realization neither comforting nor easy to grasp. Sean's face was damp with sweat, his breath coming in shallow, uneven gasps. His chest tightened as he struggled to put his thoughts into words.

"Masonaar A. can't change our world," he said, his voice barely above a whisper. "They're not that powerful. The only thing they can alter… is a single person's body." He swallowed hard, glancing at Kevin, then back at the others.

"But Masonaar A. made me see something something bigger. Just as Masonaar A. is an atom inside Kevin's body… then what if our entire galaxy is the same? What if we are just an atom inside something greater, something beyond our understanding?" His hands clenched into fists, his mind racing. "They have the power," he murmured. "And they can do it."

Sean paused, his mind a storm of thoughts, but no one dared to interrupt. The weight of his words hung in the air, pressing down on them all. After a moment, he took a deep breath and continued.

"Just imagine," he said, his voice steady but laced with urgency, "a world without hunger, without disease. Picture vast lands, rich and fertile, where anything could grow effortlessly. No more food shortages, no more reliance on corporations or governments. Every person would be independent able to cultivate their own fruits, their own vegetables, whatever they desired."

"We're all living the best way possible for as long as we choose. This isn't survival. It's life in its purest form. If that's not heaven, then what is?" His eyes darkened with intensity.

"Think about the billions we pour into researching cancer, HIV, and other diseases. What if that money didn't have to be spent on survival? What if we had focused on science on progress instead of pouring our time and resources into politics and war? Imagine a world where knowledge was used to unite us, not divide us. If, throughout history, we had chosen discovery over conquest, spared innocent lives instead of taking them, and lifted others up instead of enslaving them, we'd be thousands of years ahead of where we are in science today." He clenched his jaw, his frustration surfacing.

People shouldn't be forced to march into war and die just to satisfy the egos of leaders desperate to prove their power. If dignity is what they seek, let them fight for it themselves. Why should entire nations bleed while those in control remain untouched, hidden behind castle walls, safe from the devastation they command? "In the end, those very leaders sit down to share meals, negotiating their ambitions, while young, innocent soldiers pay the price for wars they never chose. Families lose their homes, becoming homeless. Many are left disabled. Cities are reduced to piles of rubble." His voice dropped, almost a whisper now.

"If everyone had true independence... if everyone respected each other's right to live... war wouldn't steal everything from us. We wouldn't have to lose the people we love. We wouldn't need forces like the police or the army to control society, enforcing rules we should already follow naturally to reach the true essence of humanity and no borders at all.

And the most important of all is everybody has their own job to take care of their own garden, trees full of fruits and, etc." He looked through the window and then continued: "Isn't this what Zoroaster and Jesus sought to teach us through these simple yet profound life lessons: be kind to one another, love one another, and help one another? If all of humanity truly adhered to these principles, would there still be a need for priests, mullahs, or rabbis?"

Julia opened her mouth to speak, but before she could, Kevin cut in, his voice filled with a mix of wonder and disbelief.

"You mean... disabilities would be meaningless? That hunger, pain, and pollution would be gone?" Sean's eyes flickered with cautious hope. "Maybe even violence would disappear, and we'd be living a dream life? "All the evil in our world would be banished because when there is no one to follow, there can be no gang members. Every single person would have a normal life, no more suffering, no more struggling?" He hesitated, his mind racing as he tried to grasp the enormity of it all.

"Maybe these changes would erase the dark side of life," he said slowly as if weighing his own words. "Maybe they'd bring something else... happiness. A never-ending happiness." His voice dropped, almost questioning. "But how is that possible? In today's world with so much chaos?"

"Yes! Yes!" Sharon exclaimed, her excitement building. "Maybe you need to explain it to them. Still, I'm certain you'll be stopped before you even begin. This goes against everything the world of the wealthy stands for."

Sean let out a weary sigh, rubbing his temples. "That's the hard part," he admitted. He hesitated for a moment before continuing, his voice lower now, more uncertain.

"I feel like they already know. They've known for a long, long time. But they don't want these changes. They've had this information for who knows how long, yet they've never revealed it." His gaze darkened. "But this time… I was in the room by mistake. I wasn't supposed to be there. I was just doing my job, searching frequencies, when I saw the message."

He swallowed hard, the memory of that moment still fresh, still raw. "I was lost. I started to panic. What are they going to do? I asked myself." By now, Sean's exhaustion was evident. The weight of everything he had uncovered was pressing down on him, draining him.

Kevin, however, was too caught up in the revelation to notice. He leaned forward, his eyes gleaming with anticipation. "What did they say?" he asked eagerly.

"They told me there was no message," Sean said bitterly, his hands tightening into fists. "They called it a satellite accident. They told me I was just confused… that I was upset because Mom was in the hospital. That's why I imagined it, they said." His voice grew sharper, laced with frustration. "And then, they told me I needed some time off."

His laugh was hollow, disbelief still lingering in his eyes. "Time off? A vacation? Just like that?"

The anger surged in him again, but he forced himself to stay calm. "They issued a vacation order immediately on the spot. No discussion. No explanation. Just 'take a break, Sean.' Like they were doing me a favor." His jaw clenched. "But I knew better. They weren't giving me a vacation."

Sharon's face darkened as realization struck. "On the contrary," she said slowly, "they got rid of you. They didn't want you around." Sean met her gaze, his expression grim. "Exactly," he said.

Sharon looked at Sean, surprised, and asked, "I'm still confused. What exactly are they planning to clean? Our planet? They can't even see our planet."

Sean met her gaze and replied, "You never know maybe a supernova is a kind of cosmic disease, or a black hole is another form of infection. Perhaps when a star explodes somewhere in the universe, it's not an end at all, but the beginning of something else entirely like the birth of a celestial cancer or the onset of a heart attack in the vast entity we inhabit."

There are millions of problems out there in the universe, and if all the destructive, negative ones are removed, it might affect our planet or every other planet. Maybe that's what they mean by cleaning."

"Ok, now listen!" Sean's voice was urgent now, his eyes scanning their faces. "This is very important. I'm going back to Virginia tomorrow. If they ask why I've returned so soon." He stopped suddenly, pressing his hands to his head as if trying to contain the storm of thoughts crashing through his mind. "I have to find out what's going on," he said, his voice heavy with determination.

"I need to know if there's anything I can do to make this world a paradise. We've dreamed of this for as long as human history itself. But this time... this time, we have to make sure it happens." He let the words settle, his heart pounding with conviction.

Sharon nodded, her face set with resolve. "I'll help you too," she said firmly. "I promise. I want the best for Mom and Dad for everyone. They deserve it. We all deserve a good and decent life."

"I'm afraid," Julia admitted softly, glancing at Sean, "but I'd like to help, too. Because of Ira and Kevin."

Sean turned to Kevin, but before he could say anything, Kevin spoke up with an unusual maturity in his voice. "Sean, you don't have to ask for my help. You already know you're my best friend and my hero. Just remember that."

For a moment, Sean was speechless. He looked at each of them, his chest tightening with gratitude. He had braced for resistance, prepared for doubt, but instead, they stood beside him, unwavering and resolute.

His gaze settled on Kevin, and he placed a steady hand on his shoulder. "You're a big boy and an important part of all this," he said with quiet conviction. "You know what to do when the road gets rough, and the choices get hard."

Then, turning to Julia, he continued, "If you want, you and Kevin can go back with me to Virginia for a while. Stay away from all of this, from them. You can stay at my place. It's safe there." Julia smiled, her expression filled with both warmth and determination. She stepped forward, wrapping her arms around Sean in a brief but heartfelt hug. "I appreciate your offer," she said. "I'll let you know if things take a turn for the worse."

The next day, Sean left Toronto on the next available flight to Virginia. He arrived at 2:30 in the afternoon, stepping into a world bathed in golden sunlight. The weather was perfect: clear skies, a gentle breeze, the kind of day that would usually lift his spirits. But today, it felt distant, unimportant. His mind was too tangled in the events of the past few days to appreciate any of it.

As soon as he got home, he checked his messages. Most were routine, but a few caught his attention, especially the ones from Melissa, a woman he had dated on and off. He lingered on her name for a moment, then shook his head. There were more pressing matters to deal with.

He remembered he needed to call his parents, Sharon and Kevin Julia, too, of course, to let them know he had arrived safely. Reaching for his phone, he dialed Kevin first.

"Hello?" Julia's familiar voice came through the line. "Hi, Julia. This is Sean. Is everything alright?"

"Hi, Sean! Yes, everything's fine. Kevin was here just a few minutes ago. Let me go get him."

Sean heard her call out, "Kevin! Sean is on the phone!" In the background, he caught the distant sound of Kevin's voice, though it was too far away to make out the words. "He's coming, Sean," Julia assured him. "How was your flight?"

"It was okay," Sean replied, though his mind was still preoccupied. "Have you talked to Sharon since I left?"

"Oh, yes," Julia said cheerfully. "She's coming over on Friday for dinner." Sean nodded to himself, relieved to hear that things were normal at least for now. "Kevin's here now," Julia added. "It was nice talking to you."

"Same here," Sean said. A slight rustling came through the receiver, and then Kevin's voice, bright and eager, filled the line. "Hi,

Sean!" Kevin's voice came through, but there was something off about it he sounded tired. "Hi, Kevin! Are you okay? You sound exhausted."

"No, don't worry," Kevin reassured him quickly. "I was just doing some exercises. That's all." Sean smiled slightly. "In your age? Good to hear. So, what's up?" There was a brief silence before Kevin asked, "Is there anyone else on the phone?" Sean frowned. "No, I'm alone. Why?"

Kevin hesitated. "I… I don't feel right talking on the phone. It feels like someone is listening." Sean's fingers tightened around the receiver. "Maybe it's coming from your end?" he suggested carefully. But Kevin was certain. "No, I think it's your phone line," he said with quiet assurance. Sean's stomach twisted. He trusted Kevin with his life, and Kevin had never been wrong about things like this. If anyone had been listening, discussing Kevin's capabilities over the phone would have been highly unwise. Whoever was on the other end… they couldn't let them know what Kevin was capable of. "Hey, I think we should discuss this some other time," Sean suggested, keeping his voice casual. "Maybe I'll call you tomorrow. How's that?" At the same time, in his mind, he added: For security reasons.

There was a brief pause, and then Kevin responded, his tone steady. "I understand you completely, Sean. Well, I guess I'll talk to you later." Sean exhaled slightly, relieved that Kevin had caught on. "But if you ever need me, call me on my cellphone. You still have my number, right?"

"Yes," Kevin confirmed. "And if I can't reach you, I'll call Sharon."

"That's a solid plan I was just about to say the same," Sean replied. "Take care of yourself." Kevin smiled, even though he knew Sean couldn't see him, then said, "Thanks. You too, Sean."

They both hung up. Sean sat there for a moment, gripping the phone in his hand. If Kevin was right and he had no reason to doubt him, then someone was listening. And that meant he had to be even more careful.

Sean sat still, his thoughts racing. Kevin's concern lingered in his mind like an echo. Was someone really listening? Was his house bugged? Are his calls monitored? If so, who was behind it?

His pulse quickened as he reached for the receiver again, hesitating only for a second before dialing a number. He listened to the rings, each one stretching his nerves tighter. No answer. He took a breath and left a message. "Hello, Greg. This is Sean. Call me when you get home. Call me on my cell phone. Bye."

He hung up and stared at the phone for a long moment. If someone was listening, then they'd know he was onto them. And if Greg was in any danger Sean needed to find out before it was too late.

CHAPTER FIVE

"The Cipher of the Hidden"

The alarm clock jolted him awake at six in the morning. As he rubbed the sleep from his eyes, he realized Greg still hadn't called him back, and a flicker of unease crossed his mind. Pushing the thought aside, he stepped into the shower, letting the warm water wash away his grogginess. After shaving, he felt refreshed, his face smooth, his expression calm, and his mindset for the day ahead.

Dressing quickly, he wandered to the window and glanced outside. A stunning dove perched on the opposite ledge, its feathers pristine in the morning light. He hesitated, then slowly pushed the window open. Strangely, the bird didn't startle or fly away. Instead, it turned its head slightly, fixing him with an inquisitive gaze as if it had been waiting for him all along.

"Hello, bird," Sean said aloud, his voice soft with curiosity. "You know, they say that if a dove comes to your window, it means you're a very lucky person. Some even believe it means your wish will come true." He tilted his head slightly, studying the bird. "Is that right?"

The dove remained still, its dark eyes glinting with something almost knowing. A faint breeze stirred its feathers, but it did not move as if it understood the weight of his words.

As the bird stared at Sean, he couldn't shake the feeling that it possessed a quiet understanding, as if it had its own thoughts, its own message meant just for him. Or perhaps it was just his imagination, a fleeting trick of the morning stillness.

Then, without hesitation, the dove broke its gaze and spread its wings, lifting effortlessly into the air. It soared higher, gliding with quiet confidence, carried by an unseen current. Sean's eyes followed its graceful ascent into the endless blue, watching until it became a mere speck against the sky. The rising sun, golden and unyielding, blurred his vision, forcing him to blink as the dove vanished beyond sight as a whisper carried away by the wind.

The sky gleamed with a brilliance that made everything feel subtly transformed as if the world itself had shifted in some imperceptible way. Sean found himself speaking to the sunshine as though it, too, could understand. He had always loved long walks, losing himself in the quiet rhythm of nature. He reached out to touch every plant and flower along his path, drawn to their delicate existence, aware that within each of them lay an unseen world pulsing with life.

When you truly know you are not alone, everything around you takes on a deeper significance. Every leaf, every stone, every fleeting moment matters. Perhaps it was Kevin. Perhaps something had changed in these past few days, but the meaning of life no longer felt as distant or abstract as it once had.

He thought about the vastness of existence, about the paradox of scale. If entire galaxies could fit within the point of a needle, teeming with countless living creatures, then what was the true nature of the world he walked through? If life stretched infinitely inward as well as outward, then perhaps understanding wasn't about seeing more; it was about seeing deeper.

Nevertheless, with every rupture of an atom, countless life forms perish beings that, in their own existence, cherish life as dearly as humans do. Each one looks forward to its future, unaware of the forces that could erase it in an instant.

For humanity, knowledge holds the power to build rather than destroy, to preserve rather than annihilate. But what if some distant, incomprehensible force sought to shatter Earth's sun, reducing it to cosmic dust? What would become of humankind then? Would they be mere casualties of an indifferent universe, or would they find a way to endure?

If each atom holds entire worlds within it, teeming with unseen life, then is it so far-fetched to wonder if we, too, are merely atoms within some vast, unknowable being, an infinitesimal fragment of a greater reality? And if entire civilizations can be lost within the collapse of a single microscopic world, how many millions of years would it take for the galaxy to breathe new life into what was once destroyed?

Sean recalled Masonaar A.'s words about making the world better. Was that truly possible? It had to be, he thought. If change wasn't possible, then what was the point of striving at all?

And violence? Violence thrived in a broken environment, Sean reasoned. Perhaps if the environment itself changed, if the world healed, then everything else would follow. Conflicts, divisions, suffering…all of it might fade like a shadow before the rising sun.

If life on Earth were truly advancing, shouldn't the future be one of peace? A world without crime, without violence, without war, a world where every person has an equal chance, where no one is left behind or cast aside. It would be a dream world. But perhaps, just perhaps, dreams are not merely to be wished for; they are meant to be built. This is not like the communist world, which carries many problems. Though it claims to offer a good system, it often keeps people under pressure and holds humanity back. I believe people naturally learn to understand their duties: each one working their land, growing crops, and helping one another. Everyone becomes responsible for their own well-being, and when someone needs help, it is given freely, not by force. After all, half of the world's society shouldn't have to stay home cleaning up the mess someone else made. It should be a simple place full of happiness and respect to call home for real."

Sean snapped his head toward the clock. "Oh, my God! I'm really going to be late again." He threw on his clothes, grabbed his jacket, and dashed outside into a world that always felt new to his eyes. The moment he stepped into the building, warm smiles and cheerful greetings welcomed him. A sense of belonging swelled within him this place wasn't just work. It was his life.

Sean settled into his desk, but almost immediately, a strange sensation crept over him, the unmistakable feeling of being watched. Lifting his head, he found Greg standing in the doorway, blocking the exit.

"Hi, Greg!" Sean greeted, forcing a casual tone. "I left a message on your answering machine last night."

Greg's expression remained unreadable. "Good morning, Sean," he replied flatly. "I got your message when I got home, but it was too late to call you. It was nearly four-thirty a.m. I was out of state yesterday that's why."

Then, stepping fully into the office, his demeanor shifted, his voice softening. "So, what's up, buddy? Is everything alright back home?” He looked different too different. There was something in his stance, in the way his eyes lingered, that made Sean uneasy. It felt as if Greg either knew something or was fishing for answers.

“Yes, as a matter of fact, everything is excellent,” Sean said, his voice carrying just enough force to make sure everyone within earshot heard him. He wouldn't give them another excuse to push him away. Not again.

Greg folded his arms. “You had nearly two weeks off with pay why come back so early?” he asked, while Sean hesitated, pressing a finger to his lips as his eyes darted toward the office door and without a word, he looked up at Greg, studying him. Greg didn't miss a thing. His eyes narrowed slightly.

“You look very upset and uncomfortable, Sean,” he remarked. “Is it because of what they've been saying behind your back?”

“What news?” Sean asked, startled. Greg lifted his hands in a vague gesture. “I don't know exactly. I just heard it on my way to your office,” he explained. Sean's expression darkened. His jaw tightened as a flicker of frustration crossed his face. “What's going on here?” he demanded, his voice edged with rising anger.

Greg took a step closer, lowering his tone. “I just told you,” he said, his voice barely above a whisper, almost a hiss. “I'm your best friend. I don't want to upset you, but I think you should know.”

"I'm sorry, Greg. But please, tell me what exactly did you hear?" Sean regretted the sharpness in his tone. Greg sighed. "Well, I heard it from John. He was telling Russ that you befriended a young boy someone who was a patient at the same hospital where your mother was. They say he suffered from delusions, believed he had some kind of powerful mind, and was... unstable. Weird."

Sean felt the heat rise to his face. "Who started this nonsense?" he demanded, his voice low but furious. "I don't know," Greg admitted, his tone unwavering. "And honestly? I don't care what they say about you. I know you better than that. Even if you told me it was true, I'd still believe you over them."

Sean exhaled slowly, the tension in his shoulders easing just a little. "What you said doesn't make sense, but thanks," he murmured, a faint edge of sarcasm curling at the corner of his mouth and lowering his voice even further; he added, "By the way... do you remember those symbols? The ones that looked like some kind of language pattern? The ones I sent you?"

Greg nodded. "Yeah, I remember. But I still have no idea what they mean. They almost resemble some form of binary language."

Sean's eyes flickered with excitement as he leaned in slightly. "But I do now." Greg's eyes widened with curiosity, his eagerness unmistakable. "Tell me."

Sean shook his head slightly. "That would take time, and I need to tell you in private. Just keep it between us for now." His voice was firm, almost cautious. Greg gave a short nod. "Got it. When can we get together?" Sean tapped his fingers against the desk, thinking. "How about tonight?" Greg's face lit up. "That works for me." Sean leaned forward slightly. "Seven o'clock sharp?"

"Same restaurant?" Greg asked. Sean nodded. With that, Greg gave him one last look before slipping away, disappearing down the office corridor.

They both arrived at the restaurant right on time. A warm sense of familiarity passed between them as they greeted each other, exchanging a few lighthearted words before finally settling in. For a moment, they spoke about other matters small talk, catching up but the anticipation in the air was undeniable.

Sean leaned in slightly, his excitement barely contained. "Okay, I can't wait any longer to tell you all about what I experienced back home," he began, his eyes gleaming with something just short of revelation. Greg mirrored his enthusiasm, a smirk tugging at the corner of his lips. "And I can't wait to hear all about it. I'm ready to explore."

Sean recounted everything, from the very beginning to the end. With every word, Greg's expression shifted his face lit up with excitement, darkened with anger, or gleamed with happiness. At times, his jaw simply hung open in stunned silence, unable to process what he was hearing.

When Sean finally finished, he leaned forward, his tone serious. "That's why I need your help, Greg." Greg blinked, still processing. "How? What do you want me to do?" he asked, his voice laced with surprise.

"Your part is crucial," Sean said, his voice low and firm. "I need you to search the confidential File Department for me. I have to find out who sent that information and how I can contact them." He locked eyes with Greg, his expression unwavering. "Will you help me?"

Greg exhaled, running a hand through his hair. "Of course. Do I have any other choice? I will. But you do realize it's a highly protected area, right? It's not something you can just break into. Do you understand what you're getting yourself into?" Sean fell silent for a few seconds, his mind racing.

Greg studied him, then added cautiously, "I hope that didn't offend you."

"I know what I'm doing," Sean said firmly. "And I also know there won't be any regrets neither for me nor for anyone else in the future. Just tell me if you're in or not. Your decision matters to me, whether you want to be involved or not."

Greg studied him for a moment, then shrugged in acceptance. "Just remember, those files aren't easy to access. But you can count on me, that's for sure."

His voice steadied with conviction. "I'll go with you not just because of this, but because I know you. And because we're friends. And friends don't walk away when one of them is in need." Sean nodded with a slight smile. "I know. I'll do my best."

"But remember," Greg pointed out, his tone firm, "whatever we do has to be precise. No mistakes." Sean met his gaze with unwavering determination. "I understand." Greg exhaled and leaned back slightly. "Okay. I'll let you know tomorrow once I figure out a way to get into the CCFD."

"Thank you," Sean said sincerely. "I promise no one will ever know where I got the information. But I have to see this through… for the sake of a better future." His voice was heavy with conviction, his eyes unwavering.

Greg looked at Sean and said, "I really wish you were normal, like my other friends. But what can I say? I like you too much." Sean narrowed his eyes suspiciously. "You're not gay, right?"

Greg gave a slow, amused smile. "No, I'm not, but you care too much about people you don't even know." He sighed, then added with a raised brow, "So… where's the boy now?"

"He's living in Toronto, as I told you, with his mother," Sean replied. Greg suddenly jerked his head toward Sean as if something had just clicked in his mind. "Oh! I forgot to tell you about John." Sean's eyes sharpened. "What about him?"

"It's about that story going around about you," Greg said, his voice laced with excitement. Sean frowned. "Yes? So what?"

"I found out who started it." Greg shot him a sideways glance. Sean immediately leaned forward, his voice low and urgent. "Who?"

Greg took a sip of his coffee and then met Sean's gaze. "Someone named Donna Madison told him that story." Sean stiffened. A wave of shock passed over him, his face paling. His fingers clenched against the table. "She's my cousin."

Greg's brow furrowed. "What? What's going on, Sean? Maybe she can help you out too ever thought of that?"

Sean exhaled sharply, his mind racing. "Absolutely not. She's trouble. Either she's following me, or she's tracking the story; I can't tell which. But whatever the case… keep your eyes open. She's clever, and she plays dirty." Greg gave a reassuring nod. "Sure. Don't worry."

"I'm wondering, how do they know each other?" Sean asked, uncertainty creeping into his voice. Greg leaned forward slightly. "I saw her once in John's office. They're co-workers. I mean, they work together on special files, unsolved cases, to be exact. That's their job, researching unresolved files." He hesitated, then added, "I know because he's my boss now… and I just started working for him." Sean's eyes widened. "That's your new position? Why didn't you tell me this before?"

Greg shrugged. "Because I didn't know she was your cousin. And besides, I'm not supposed to be nosy about my boss's meetings or who he brings in."

"Anyway, let's get out of here," Greg said, gesturing toward the door.

CHAPTER SIX

"The Unauthorized Entry"

The Next Morning. Sean arrived at work earlier than usual, his nerves on edge. He waited for Greg all morning, resisting the urge to call him for fear of drawing suspicion. As the hours stretched on, impatience gnawed at him, but he forced himself to stay calm.

By lunchtime, unable to sit still any longer, he decided to step out and grab something to eat. He was halfway to the restaurant when his cell phone rang. "Hello, Sean Morgan speaking."

A familiar voice came through, low and hurried. "Hi, Sean. It's Greg. I can't talk right now, but your stuff's ready. I'll call you at home. Bye."

The line went dead before Sean could even respond. He sighed but felt a rush of confidence. If there was one thing he was certain of, it was that Greg was more than capable of handling anything he took on.

After work, Sean went straight home. He wasn't about to miss Greg's call. As soon as he stepped inside, he checked his messages first. There was no telling how long he'd have to wait. As he listened, he absentmindedly sifted through his mail, his mind racing with possibilities.

Sean checked his emails while the answering machine played his messages in the background. His mind was restless, bouncing between thoughts when suddenly, the phone rang. Without hesitation, he picked up the receiver. "Hi, Sean!" Greg's voice came through on the other end.

Sean's heart leaped with relief, but he knew he had to be careful. Without missing a beat, he cut in before Greg could say another word.

"Hi, Peter! I'm in a hurry right now. I need to go pick it up a package from the post office. I'll call you later." Without waiting for a response, he hung up. Sean rushed to his car and drove straight to a specialty store to buy a new cellphone. Wasting no time, he paid for it, activated it, and immediately dialed Greg's number.

Greg glanced at the unfamiliar number but answered anyway. "Hello?"

"Greg, it's me. Sorry, I couldn't talk earlier. While I was away, someone bugged my home line, and I'm not sure if they did the same to my house."

Greg's surprise was evident. "So that's why you called me Peter! I thought you were crazy. I was completely thrown off I thought something was seriously wrong. Now it all makes sense." He let out a short laugh before adding, "Anyway, the stuff you requested is ready for pickup, but I need to see you before I hand it over."

A strange mix of relief and unease settled over Sean. "Alright, whenever you say."

"Tomorrow's Saturday. How about that coffee shop with the amazing cappuccino?"

"Sounds good. Would two o'clock in the afternoon work for you?"

"Perfect. See you tomorrow, then." They exchanged goodbyes and hung up.

The next day, Greg took a slow sip of his cappuccino before leaning in. "That's the tricky part," he said. "The CCFD is buried deep underground, beneath layers of security, but strangely, cellphones and devices are working perfectly down there. We're talking biometric scans, reinforced steel doors, and armed personnel at every checkpoint. It's one of the most secure locations in North America, hell, maybe even the world."

Sean's fingers tightened around his cup. "So, how does someone get in?"

Greg smirked. "Officially? You don't. Unofficially… that's where things get interesting." He glanced around the café, lowering his voice. "There are a few ways, but none of them are exactly legal. And all of them come with risks." Sean leaned in, his pulse quickening. "Tell me everything about all of them."

Greg took another sip of his cappuccino, his eyes sharp with intrigue. "Every week, they gather intelligence from various departments, cities, and even across international borders. All of it is stored down there. Tomorrow is filing day."

He paused, letting the weight of his words sink in. "And guess what? My friend Simon is one of the few people with access to the CCFD." Sean's grip on his cup tightened. "And?"

Greg smirked. "A while back, Simon asked if I wanted to head over and get familiar with CCFD. He also said I should learn the filing process for future assignments. I turned him down and figured I'd do it later. But tomorrow, I could walk into his office, play the part, and ask to tag along."

He leaned in, voice dropping. "Once I'm in, I can get you exactly what you need. I'll have the key to everything. I can see how we can enter and how the procedure is." Sean's heart pounded. This was the break he needed, but it also meant stepping into dangerous territory. He exhaled slowly, meeting Greg's gaze. "Are you sure about this?"

Greg took a measured sip of his coffee before setting the cup down. His voice was steady but firm. "Tomorrow, just stay in your office. Don't go anywhere until I contact you." Sean nodded. "Okay, I'll wait for you." Then, in his excitement, he blurted out, "Do you want more coffee?" It was a reflex his mind racing, his hands itching for something to do. Greg smirked but shook his head. "No, thanks." He studied Sean for a moment, his expression turning serious. "But I'll ask you one last time: are you absolutely sure you want to do this?" Sean met his gaze without hesitation. "Yes. One hundred percent. I'm sure of it."

Greg exhaled, his fingers tapping lightly against his cup. "Alright, then. Tomorrow, we move." Sean had a hard time sleeping that night but still woke up not feeling tired. The next morning, Sean was in his office and checked the time 10:30 AM sharp. His phone buzzed, and he answered immediately.

"Hi, Sean. Are you alone?" Greg's voice came through low and firm.

Sean sat up straighter, tightening his grip on the phone. "Yeah, I'm alone. I was actually thinking if it's okay with you I could go instead." His tone was calm, but tension crackled beneath the surface.

"Good," Greg replied. "We'll talk when I'm on my way."

A few minutes later, Greg arrived at Sean's office, closing the door behind him with quiet precision. He wasted no time, his expression serious as he pulled a key card from his pocket and handed it over. "This is the card, and this is the code," Greg said, slipping a small note into Sean's hand. "You'll have exactly ten minutes to get in, file the documents in the right place, and get out. No mistakes. If you're still in there when the time is up, alarms will go off, and they'll know someone unauthorized is inside." Sean nodded, gripping the card as his pulse pounded in his ears.

Greg's voice dropped even lower. "This card will only work once. Each time, the computer generates a new key or, in this case, a new pass card. If there's any problem, if the scanner rejects it or if something doesn't feel right, don't push it. Don't try again. Just walk away and return everything to me. Do you understand?" Sean swallowed, nodding. "I understand."

Greg studied him for a long moment, then exhaled. "Alright. It's all up to you now." Sean's pulse quickened, and looked into Greg's eyes and said: "Don't worry. If I get caught somehow, I'll just say I used our friendship to steal the key from you." He took a deep breath, bracing himself. Whatever was about to happen, there was no turning back now.

Sean didn't waste time. He went straight to the elevator and pressed the down button. As soon as the doors opened, he stepped in and selected SB for the basement. The ride down felt longer than it should have, the air thick with tension.

When the doors slid open, he quickly stepped out, moving down the dimly lit hallway. At the very end, he found a door. Without hesitation, he pushed the door open and found himself at the top of a dimly lit staircase. Peering down anxiously, he scanned for any sign of a security guard and, to his relief, saw none.

He descended immediately, turning twice before stopping in his tracks. CCFD. The bold letters on the sign confirmed he was in the right place. "Too easy", Sean thought. It didn't sit right with him.

Beside the reinforced door was a small screen with a keypad beneath it. He placed the key card face down on the scanner, his pulse hammering in his ears when a computerized voice responded instantly. "Greg O'Neill, Research Manager. Thank you. Please enter your security code."

Sean's fingers tightened around the slip of paper Greg had given him. This was it. No turning back. With a steady breath, he began entering the code. Sean entered the code with precision, his fingers steady despite the tension coiling in his chest.

"Thank you. Please stand by. Your security number is under process," the computerized voice announced. Seconds stretched unbearably long. Then Click. The door unlocked with a soft metallic hiss. The computerized voice announced: "You may enter, Mr. Greg O'Neil."

Sean stepped forward, and as he crossed the threshold, a red light flickered on above him. His stomach tightened. He knew what it meant to be an automatic security measure. If more than one person tried to enter at once, the alarm would blare immediately, sealing him inside with no way out.

Each card was coded for a single or multiple individual's passage. No exceptions. No second chances. Sean inhaled sharply, forcing himself to stay calm. He was alone. He was fine. He just had to move fast. Ten minutes. No mistakes. He pressed on. Sean stepped inside, his pulse quickening as he scanned the front wall. Twenty buttons. Each is labeled for a different sector.

His eyes darted across them, searching for Contact Files and Received Files, but there was no easy access. Those rooms would be heavily monitored, and if Greg's ID was logged there instead of the International Room, it would raise immediate suspicion. "Think, Sean. Think."

His options were limited, and time was slipping away. He had no choice. He pressed the button for the International Room the only location Greg was cleared to access. As he moved past each door, small red lights flickered on, one after another. Only the light above the International Room glowed green. With a soft mechanical whirr, the door slid open. Sean stepped inside, scanning the cold, sterile walls. Two sections caught his eye: "Recordation Files."

"Patient Files." He hesitated. Patient Files? A flicker of memory surfaced: "Kevin's father." Sean's breath hitched. "If there was anything about him, it had to be here." Forgetting the risks for a moment, he took a step forward. "He had to know."

Sean's gaze flicked to another button, "SRD." He frowned, trying to decipher what it could stand for, but there was no time to dwell on it.

Instead, he scanned the area above the doors, each one marked by a red light. His eyes locked onto one that was flickering in the International Files Room. "That's it." He moved swiftly toward the door. As he approached, he noticed another small red light blinking just beneath the main panel.

A cold wave of tension passed over him. Every step was monitored. Every move mattered. The computerized voice returned, sterile and emotionless: "Please insert your card." Sean swallowed hard and placed the card against the scanner. "Click." The door unlocked instantly. He stepped inside, his pulse hammering in his ears.

The moment his foot touched the cold floor, the voice spoke again, this time with an unmistakable edge of urgency: "You have ten minutes." A pause. Then, the warning came again. "You have ten minutes."

Sean took a deep breath. No time to waste. He had to move now. Sean's eyes darted across the aisles, each labeled with a different number and code. The room was massive, stretching farther than he expected.

He quickly pulled out the files Greg had given him, scanning for the matching codes. Just then, a green arrow appeared on the floor, shifting toward a nearby aisle, its endpoint marked by a flickering green light. He followed it without hesitation, and it led him straight to the exact spot where the file was meant to be placed. "Nine minutes left."

His heart pounded as he moved down the aisles, checking each number. Now, he has to find the exact file number. "Nothing." He turned another corner, his breath quickening, heart pounding in his chest. He had no idea how long he'd been searching for the file number when he heard it again a voice, cold and mechanical: "Three minutes."

Finally there. The right filing cabinet. Sean yanked it open, shoved the files inside, and slammed it shut. "Thirty seconds left."

Without thinking, he spun around and sprinted for the door. His pulse roared in his ears.

"Twenty seconds."

The door loomed ahead. He lunged forward, throwing himself through the threshold just as Click.

The door was sealed shut behind him. His chest heaved, adrenaline surging through his veins. Greg's card was still sticking out from the scanner. He yanked it free. No time to breathe. He bolted for the main door, and with one final push, he threw himself out of the secured area and slammed the door shut behind him. "I made it."

"Thank you for your cooperation. Goodbye," the computerized voice announced, its tone cold and indifferent.

Sean exhaled sharply, pressing his back against the wall. He glanced at his watch. "eight seconds." That was all the time he had left when he signed out. "Too close." He ran a shaky hand through his hair. "God, I was lucky."

His mind raced as he thought about Greg. "If something went wrong, Greg could talk his way out of it." It was his job, after all. "No real penalty. But me?"

Sean wasn't supposed to be there at all. If they found out, there would be no excuses, no second chances. He swallowed hard, pushing himself off the wall. He needed to get out of there "Now."

He wasted no time heading straight to his office. He shut the door behind him, his heart still hammering. "No sign of Greg."

Without hesitation, he picked up the phone and dialed Greg's number. "Hi, Greg. Can I come to see you now if you're not busy?" Greg's voice came through, casual but firm. "Yeah, of course. Simon is here, too. You know him, right?" Sean's breath hitched slightly. Simon? That complicated things. "Yeah, I know him," Sean replied quickly, forcing his voice to stay even. "I'll be there in a minute."

He hung up and grabbed the key card, slipping it into his pocket before rushing toward Greg's office. His mind raced as he walked. "Why was Simon there? Did Greg need the card back immediately? Was something wrong?"

He pushed those thoughts aside and knocked twice. "Come in," Greg called out. Sean took a deep breath and stepped inside into the office, keeping his expression neutral. Simon was already seated across from Greg, his posture relaxed but his eyes sharp. As Sean entered, Simon turned to him with a polite nod and extended his hand.

Sean shook it firmly, offering a brief smile before glancing around the office. His gaze landed on Greg's jacket, hanging from the coat rack. Without hesitation, Sean slipped the key card into the jacket's inner pocket in one swift motion.

Greg, ever perceptive, caught the movement but didn't react. Instead, he continued listening to Simon, nodding along as if nothing had happened. Sean turned back, his expression unreadable. Now, it was up to Greg to handle the rest.

"If you're busy, I can come back later?" Sean offered, keeping his tone casual. Greg glanced at him, his expression unreadable, but there was a flicker of understanding in his eyes. He had noticed the card. "Oh, that's okay with me, Sean," Greg said smoothly, then added, "I'll see you later. Thanks for coming."

Sean gave a small nod and turned to Simon. "Nice to see you, Simon." Simon returned the gesture with a polite smile, seemingly unaware of the silent exchange that had just taken place. Sean didn't linger. He walked out at a steady pace, resisting the urge to look back. "It was done."

A few minutes later, Greg walked into Sean's office. Sean barely had time to react before Greg shut the door behind him, his usual calm demeanor laced with urgency. "You were just in time," Greg said in a low voice. "If I hadn't given Simon the card, we would've both been in trouble."

Sean exhaled slowly. "So, did he check it?" Greg shook his head. "Not yet. But it's logged now, so we're in the clear for now."

Sean leaned back, tension still thrumming beneath his skin. "How did it go down there?" Greg asked, crossing his arms. Sean smirked, but it didn't quite reach his eyes. "Let's just say... I had thirty seconds to spare." Greg leaned back against the desk, rubbing his chin. "Well, I told you it's almost impossible to look for other files." His voice was calm, but Sean could tell he was already thinking.

Sean, however, wasn't ready to give up. "I don't know," he muttered, frustration creeping into his tone. "The only thing I know is that I've been there, and I have to go back." Greg studied him for a moment, then sighed. "You're really not letting this go, are you?"

Sean ignored the comment. Instead, he asked, "Can I ask you a question?" Greg shrugged. "Go ahead." Sean leaned in slightly. "If there were a blackout, what would happen to the security system?"

Greg's expression shifted instantly. His usual composure cracked for just a second as he looked at Sean like he had just asked an impossible science question. Silence hung between them. Then, Greg exhaled slowly, his eyes narrowing. "Are you suggesting what I think you're suggesting? And when exactly did you come up with that?" Without hesitation, Sean replied, "It just came to me."

Greg let out a sharp laugh, shaking his head. "Impossible. You're talking about something that's never happened before. Not once in the history of this building."

Sean crossed his arms, listening carefully while Greg continued, "Even if and that's a big if one percent of the power went out, the backup system would kick in within thirty seconds. And trust me, that system is dead accurate. No gaps. No vulnerabilities." Sean cut Greg off with a smirk. "So there is a way."

Greg's amusement faded slightly as he realized what he had just revealed.

Sean leaned forward, his confidence growing. "I knew it. Now, instead of figuring out how to make a blackout happen, let me ask you something else." Greg sighed, already wary. "What?"

"Would it be possible for you to find the file for me? Just to save time." Sean's gaze remained fixed on him, unblinking and steady. Greg's brows furrowed. "You want me to steal the file for you?" Sean shook his head. "Not steal. Just locate it. That way, when I go back, I don't waste time searching." Greg exhaled, rubbing his temples. "You really won't stop, will you?"

Then he answered flatly. "No, But I can tell you where it would be, along with the time of contact and the year." Sean frowned, intrigued. "What do you mean?" Greg leaned forward slightly, his voice lowering. "The system follows a pattern. For example, "If the contact happened this morning, the file code would end with something like ANL93003152005.""

Sean raised an eyebrow. "And that means…?"

Greg smirked, his tone almost too casual. "It means the contact occurred at 9:30 a.m. on March 15, 2005. The final sequence always records the exact time and date of the event. I know this because Simon once told me how the system works."

But Sean didn't blink. His gaze dug deeper, waiting no, demanding more. Greg hesitated for a moment, then added, his voice lower, tinged with something darker.

"ANL means it was authorized… but no location was found. It's like a signal that vanishes into thin air. If they had pinpointed the source, the code would've changed to ALC. That one means the location was confirmed."

He paused, then met Sean's eyes. "One tells you something reached us. The other tells you where it came from. ANL… leaves us in the dark." He sat back, looking pleased with himself. "So, if you give me the date and approximate time, I can at least tell you what to look for. That way, you don't waste time searching when you're down there."

Sean's mind raced as he murmured, "This changes everything." He nodded thoughtfully. "That's good guidance." Greg narrowed his eyes. "What exactly are you trying to do?" Sean flashed a sly smile. "I'm going to need Kevin's help. I'll call you later."

Without another word, he grabbed his jacket and strode toward the door, leaving Greg sitting there, staring after him in confusion. Once outside, Sean wasted no time. He pulled out his phone and dialed Kevin's number. The call rang twice before Julia picked up. "Hello?"

"Hey, Julia! It's Sean," he said, keeping his tone light.

"Oh, Sean! It's been a while. How have you been?"

A soft smile touched Sean's lips one that always appeared when he spoke to Julia. "I'm doing okay, just caught up with work. How about you? Everything alright?"

There was a warmth in her voice, contentment woven between the words. "Can't complain, can't complain. I have everything I need. When Kevin's home and close to me, I feel whole."

Sean smiled deeper, his voice quiet with admiration. "It's incredible how much mothers sacrifice just to stay close to their children." He paused, then added, his tone shifting ever so slightly, "Listen… is Kevin around?"

"Yeah, hang on." Sean waited as she set the phone down. This was it. If Kevin was on board, things were about to get interesting.

"Hi, Sean! How's everything?" Kevin's voice brimmed with excitement. He knew Sean wouldn't call unless something intriguing was unfolding. And if Sean needed him, there was only ever one answer: "Yes."

The funny part? He didn't even know what the question was yet.

Sean chuckled. "Hello, Kevin. How are you?"

"I'm okay," Kevin replied, his tone light. "But let's be honest you want me to do something, don't you?" Sean smirked. "Maybe."

Kevin laughed. "That's fine. But I still need to hear the question first."

Sean wasn't surprised. Kevin had always been like this quick, sharp, and fearless. And the best part? He had already agreed before even knowing what Sean was about to ask. That alone made Sean feel more confident. He wasn't in this alone.

Sean took his time explaining everything that had happened that morning, every risk, every close call. Kevin listened in silence, absorbing every word. When Sean finished, his voice grew more serious. "I need you here to help me. I need your power and your advice. We can get results by working together." Then, silence.

Sean waited, his own thoughts drifting. He couldn't help but chuckle internally at the irony a thirty-year-old man relying on a ten-year-old for help. Yet, somehow, it made perfect sense. Finally, he broke the silence. "So? What's your answer? Are you going to help me?"

Kevin didn't hesitate. "I already gave you my answer at the very beginning," he said, a flicker of amusement dancing in his voice. "And now you're chuckling because you need help from a ten-year-old kid? That's hilarious." Sean smirked. He had chuckled but only in his mind.

Then Kevin's tone shifted, his confidence giving way to something else. Concern. "But what about my mom?" he asked, his voice quieter now, almost hesitant.

"I'll talk to her shortly after you hand her the phone," Sean said, his voice steady despite the wild energy coursing through him. "But before that, you should talk to her first. You already know what I'm going to ask. I'll call you back tomorrow at the same time." His nerves felt like they were on fire, and Kevin, however, was as cool as ever. "Don't worry, Sean. I'm going to help you, and you don't have to jump wildly." He chuckled. "Bye for now; hold on, I'll call my mom." Sean heard Kevin put the phone down and then yell at the top of his lungs

"MOM... MOM... SEAN WANTS TO TALK TO YOU!"

A few seconds later, Julia's cheerful voice came through the receiver. "Hi, Sean again. How can I help you? Is everything okay?"

Sean took a steady breath. "Hi, Julia. Yes, everything's fine. Thanks for asking. But I need you and Kevin to come here it's important. And I can help you uncover the truth about what really happened to Ira."

Silence. A long, heavy pause filled the space between them. Then, at last, Julia spoke, her voice softer yet resolute. "Okay. I'll come."

Sean's heart surged with relief. "Great! Thank you. I'll send you the ticket and all the details." A warmth lingered in Julia's response. "Thanks, Sean. See you soon." They both hung up, the energy between them electric. Things were finally moving.

Sean was still gripping the receiver, lost in thought when his fingers instinctively began dialing another number. He didn't even realize what he was doing until he heard her voice. It was Sharon. But before he could speak, the familiar monotone message played:

"Hello. Unfortunately, I can't answer the phone right now, but please leave a short message after the beep. Thank you. Beeeeeeeeeeep".

Sean hesitated for a second before saying, "Hi, Sharon. I hope everything is all right. Call me." He hung up, exhaling slowly. Something about that voicemail unsettled him. But he didn't have time to dwell on it. He immediately dialed another number. The moment the call connected, he didn't waste a second. "Hi, Mike. Did you finish the job I gave you?"

Mike's voice came through, confident and clear. "Hey, Sean. Yeah, it's done. There were three spy cameras in your house: one in the living room, one in the kitchen, and one outside facing the front door and driveway." Sean's grip tightened. Three cameras. Someone had been watching him. Mike continued, "We set them up so that, whenever you decide, you can connect them to a computer and let them watch you. Also, I left the access code for when you're away so you can monitor your home or control the cameras remotely from a distance. Otherwise, the feed will just show an image of the empty room where the camera was installed. The computer is in your bedroom, along with instructions."

Sean nodded to himself, his mind racing. "What about the rest of the house?"

"The bathroom and bedrooms, the hallway, and the back entrance had no cameras," Mike confirmed. "You can talk freely in those areas without being recorded. By the way, are you planning to do anything for your home phone? They are bugged."

A wave of relief washed over Sean. "Thanks for being concerned, but I'll keep them busy and use it only for regular conversations. I don't want them to know that I hired someone. I want to keep them feeling like they're doing something. Thanks, Mike. You really did a great job."

"No problem. That's a good idea. Oh, and Sean, there were three thousand dollars on your bathroom counter. I'm taking $1500. That's more than enough."

Sean smirked. "If it's not, let me know." Mike chuckled. "Nah, this is fair. If you need anything else, you know who to call."

"I do," Sean said, feeling a sense of control returning. They both hung up. Now, Sean knew exactly where he could speak freely. And that was everything. He arrived home, his mind still buzzing with everything that had happened. He went straight to his room and checked the computer Mike had set up. The screen displayed a guideline paper left for him detailed instructions on how to manage the surveillance trick. For now, he left everything running. There was nothing suspicious happening inside his house, and that was exactly how he wanted it to appear.

He moved to the sofa and sat down, staring into the distance. His thoughts drifted. "The only way to get through those security doors was with Kevin's help." There was no other option. He knew it. Kevin was the key.

Sean stretched out on the sofa, letting time slip by. But he wasn't idle. His hands moved to the printout data from Kevin's body. He read through them carefully, absorbing every detail. The numbers, the readings it was unlike anything he had ever seen. Kevin wasn't just special. He was beyond extraordinary. Sean was impressed. No stunned. But he buried it deep. No one could ever know. Exposing this truth would open doors better left closed-stirked questions with no safe answers. It wouldn't just endanger Kevin. It could unravel the very future they were struggling to shape.

His world had changed. Everything felt different now. As he looked around his room, he realized something unsettling. It all felt... alive. Like the walls, the objects, even the silence itself, were watching. Sean stared at his hands, turning them over slowly. "How many lives would be in my hands... in my body?" he murmured. The weight of what he was about to do pressed down on him. He wanted to change the world desperately. But at what cost?

His fingers curled into fists. "What if Kevin refused to help because of his mom?" That thought unsettled him more than anything. Julia was his only weakness. If she said no, if she convinced Kevin to stay out of this, Sean would have no way forward. He exhaled sharply. He couldn't afford to fail.

And yet, a deeper question gnawed at him. "What if Kevin was right to refuse?" Sean leaned back, his eyes fixed on the ceiling as his thoughts spiraled. "Julia." He cared about her more than he was willing to admit. And the last thing he wanted was to hurt her or force her into something she didn't agree with.

His mind became restless, calculating. "How will I get that information if Julia refuses to involve Kevin?" She had every right to protect her son. If she said no if she put her foot down... that would be it. A cold sweat prickled across his skin. His body tensed. "What then?"

Would he let it go? Would he walk away? Or would he have to find another way? "Am I capable of finding a way to reach them?" Sean muttered to himself, unaware he was speaking aloud.

His mind raced. "Those files were the key." They would help him send his message, connect to the right source, and, most importantly, get an answer. His thoughts drifted into a vision of a perfect world. A world where people cared, where they worked together for something greater than themselves. A world where everyone wanted the best for all. For a fleeting moment, he let himself believe in it. He whispered: "One for all and all for one."

Then Riiiiiing!

The sharp sound of the phone shattered his thoughts. He jumped, heart pounding. For a second, he just stared at the ringing phone as if it had pulled him from another reality. Then, without thinking, he grabbed it and blurted out "Hello!"

Sean swallowed hard, still catching his breath. The voice on the other end said: "Hi. You seemed nervous." He forced his voice to steady. "I'm not nervous." A brief silence.

"Really?" the voice on the other end teased. "Because you sound like you just saw a ghost." Sean exhaled, running a hand through his hair. "Just... lost in thought."

"Must've been some serious thoughts," the caller remarked. "So, are you gonna tell me what's going on, or do I have to guess?"

"Oh, Kevin? Nothing important." Sean quickly regained his composure, leaning back against the couch. "What news do you have for me?" Kevin didn't buy it. "Uh-huh. Sure, 'nothing important.' You always say that when something's up." Sean smirked, impressed. The kid was sharp unbelievably mature for his age.

"Fine," he admitted. "My mind's just been running in circles. But let's not talk about that right now. Did you get anything for me?"

Kevin sighed dramatically. "I always have something for you, Sean. The real question is, are you ready for it?"

"I talked to my mom," Kevin said, his voice more serious than usual. "She's really scared, Sean. But…"She said the only way I could join you is if she comes with me wherever you take me." Sean's stomach tightened. "Oh no, Kevin. That's too dangerous. You know that, don't you?" Kevin didn't answer right away. Instead, he muttered, "How should I know? I'm just a ten-year-old kid, but I know this is serious, and that's why I love it."

Then he stopped. "Hold on. My mom wants to talk to you." Sean braced himself as he heard the receiver being passed. Then, Julia's voice came through, calm but firm. "Hello, Sean. We need to talk." Julia's voice was steady, but there was an undeniable edge to it. "I know it sounds crazy, but I'm afraid my decision is final. If Kevin goes, then I go."

Sean closed his eyes for a moment, weighing his options. This wasn't what he wanted. Bringing Julia along meant more risk and more uncertainty. But arguing wouldn't change her mind.

Finally, he exhaled and said, "Julia! If anything happens, Kevin is just a child he can get away from it. But if you're involved, you'll be in trouble too." Julia paused for a moment before replying, her voice steady. "I'm willing to take that risk if it means finding out what really happened to Ira, but I won't leave Kevin alone."

Sean said, "Alright then. When can you get here? Once you're here, we'll sit down and talk. Either you'll change my mind, or I'll change yours." Julia didn't hesitate. "As I said before, we can leave as soon as possible."

Sean nodded, even though she couldn't see him. "Okay, thanks, Julia. That's good," he added. "I'll speak to you as soon as I confirm the tickets and to give you flight details."

"Ok. Thanks, Sean, and see you soon," she replied. "Bye now."

Sean hung up, the weight of the conversation settling over him. Things had just gotten a lot more complicated. Sean sat in silence, his mind buzzing with the weight of it all. This wasn't just an adventure. It wasn't some reckless mission driven by curiosity or personal gain. This was real. His actions would ripple across the world, shifting the balance of power and uncovering truths that had been buried for too long. He wasn't just chasing a dream. He was about to change everything. His heart pounded with the realization. This was happening. No turning back. No second-guessing.

The world was about to change. And he was the one making it happen. Sean didn't hesitate. He picked up the phone and confirmed the reservation, his mind laser-focused on the task. Everything was moving forward. Once it was confirmed, he jotted down the details and immediately dialed Julia's number.

She answered on the second ring. "Hello?"

"Julia, it's Sean. I've got everything set. Here's the info." As he read out the details, he could hear her scribbling everything down. "Got it," she finally said. "Good," Sean replied. "Thanks, Julia. I'll see you tomorrow."

"See you tomorrow, Sean," she said before they both hung up.

Sean exhaled, staring at the phone in his hand. Everything was set in motion now. There was no stopping it. Shortly after making the reservation for Julia and Kevin, Sean picked up the phone and dialed Sharon's number. The call rang a few times before she answered. "Hello?"

"Sharon, it's me." His voice was steady, but there was an underlying urgency. "Just wanted to let you know Julia and Kevin will be here tomorrow. Also, I reserved and confirmed a seat for you too. You can change the date if you can't make it tomorrow."

A brief pause. "Tomorrow?" Sharon repeated, her tone shifting. "That's sooner than I expected, but I'll think about it."

"Yeah, things are moving fast," Sean admitted. "I'll fill you in when I see you." Sharon sighed. "Alright. Just be careful, Sean."

"Always."

They hung up, but Sean could still feel the weight of her words lingering in his mind. "Careful". That was easier said than done.

The next day, Sean arrived at Washington Dulles International Airport, his eyes sweeping across the bustling terminal, taking in the swirl of travelers, announcements, and hurried footsteps. The hum of voices, the rolling of suitcases, the distant echo of announcements it all faded into the background as he focused on one thing. He made his way to the Arrivals screen, double-checking the flight number, still on schedule. His pulse remained steady, but his mind was restless. This was it. The moment he had been waiting for. Excitement surged through him at the thought of seeing them again. Beyond his admiration for Kevin's incredible abilities, his heart belonged entirely to Julia. The mere thought of her sent a thrill racing through his veins, quickening his heartbeat in a way nothing else could.

Julia and Kevin were about to step into something far bigger than they realized. Was he really ready for this? Were they? Sean took a deep breath, glanced around, and murmured, "Too late for doubt now."

All he could do was wait. "They'll be right on time," Sean murmured to himself, glancing at the Arrivals screen once more. He paced back and forth in the waiting area, his hands in his pockets, his mind racing. He felt like an expectant father, restless, anxious, and unable to sit still. Finally, he forced himself into a seat, but his eyes never left the gate. Every second felt stretched his anticipation mounting.

Then, the announcement came. "Attention, passengers: flight CA1206 has now landed," the announcement echoed through the terminal. Sean straightened, his heart quickening as he turned toward the arrival gates. He looked at the board, and Julia and Kevin's flight number was green. Passengers began to file out, some briskly, others slowly, weighed down by heavy luggage and heavier expressions. Sean's eyes swept over every face, his impatience mounting with each passing second. Then there they are. A familiar figure stepped through the crowd, and in that instant, Sean's breath caught in his throat. Without thinking, Sean bolted forward, weaving through the sea of people. "Julia. Kevin." They were finally here.

"Hi. Finally, You made it here?" Sean asked, his tone edged with suspicion as he eyed Sharon, who was walking beside them. She smiled, unfazed. "I know. It's weird. But here I am." Before Sean could question her further, Julia and Kevin appeared behind her. His focus immediately shifted. "They made it."

They all exchanged greetings, the tension of travel easing with familiar faces. When Sean shook hands with Kevin, he did it firmly like a man. Kevin returned the gesture with confidence, grinning up at him.

Sean took a deep breath. There was so much to say, so much to explain. But he knew now wasn't the time to overwhelm them.

"There are so many things I want to share with you," he admitted. "I don't even know where to start." He glanced at Julia and Kevin, then at Sharon. "But first," he added with a small smile, "let's take a moment to relax."

Sean felt like he was ready to explode with information. Every part of him wanted to spill everything the mission, the risks, the discoveries but he knew he had to pace himself. The excitement in the air was undeniable. They were all here, finally together. But their roles in this journey were vastly different.

Julia had no real idea where she fit into all of this. She was simply happy to be with Kevin, her son her priority above all else.

Kevin, on the other hand, felt useful. He knew he held the most important piece of the mission. Without him, there was no way forward. Sharon was the researcher. She worked behind the scenes, digging into truths most people wouldn't even dare to consider. And then there was Sean. The weight of the real action fell on him. Every risk, every move, every step into the unknown.

Every other day, Sharon made sure Kevin connected to Masonaar A. She had gathered many answers, some more unsettling than she had expected. But now, a greater question loomed over her. "Could the world even accept these truths?"

Sean's emotions swung like a pendulum. One moment, he felt invincible; the next, a creeping fear gnawed at him. He longed for everyone to have a good life, believing this was his one and only shot at making it happen. That evening, the four of them went out for supper, and afterward, Sean drove them home.

"Where are we going to stay?" Kevin asked, his voice laced with uncertainty. "That's a good question, and I've got the answer," Sean said with a confident smile. "I have a three-bedroom bungalow, one room for your mom and you and another for Sharon. If that works for you two?" He glanced at them, waiting for their response.

"I guess that would be alright with me," Sharon said with a small nod. "Me too," Julia added, glancing at Kevin before answering. "Great!" Sean said happily. Julia studied him for a moment. "You prepared everything for us, didn't you, Sean?" Sean gave a knowing smile but said nothing.

"But why do we have to stay together when we could just book a hotel?" Sharon asked, crossing her arms. "That's not a good idea," Sean replied firmly. "This is just a temporary situation. We've gathered here for something important. Remember, we need to make a plan and prepare ourselves for anything that might come our way." They arrived at Sean's home, and before getting closer to his driveway, Sean quickly reset the cameras to playback mode, ensuring that no one would know Kevin was there.

When he pulled into the driveway and turned off the engine, stepping out, he helped everyone with their luggage before leading them inside. As they crossed the threshold, they were met with a cozy warmth, the faint scent of pine lingering in the air. The house was simple but welcoming, its soft lighting casting a golden glow over the neatly arranged furniture.

Sharon didn't know what to say. It was her first time seeing her brother's house, and the sight of it left her momentarily speechless. It was warm, inviting, almost surreal. She had spent so much time wondering about Sean's life, and now she was sitting in the middle of it.

Once everyone was settled, they gathered in the living room, sipping coffee by the flickering glow of the fireplace. The rhythmic crackling of the flames filled the silence between their words. Sharon finally spoke, her voice laced with curiosity. "I've been thinking a lot about what I discovered... about the lives inside Kevin's body."

She glanced at Kevin, then at the others. "When those life forms truly exist within him, then what if we could reach out to any life form within anyone or even anything? What if life isn't limited to what we know? Imagine... life inside crystals. It would be unimaginably extraordinary."

A quiet hush settled over the room as her words lingered, the weight of the unknown pressing against them. "Alright!?" Kevin yelled with joy, his eyes gleaming. "All of this knowledge comes from my body?" he added proudly.

"Of course," Sean said, "Kevin, your body is the only one that has retained this level of knowledge. You are the greatest life form that has ever existed. Your father was the first, but he never had the chance to understand or unlock what was inside him. But you your body is evolving. Your very atoms are strengthening and adapting. You don't even realize yet what you will be capable of in the future." Kevin stared at him, his excitement giving way to wonder.

"You're changing every day," Sean continued, his voice steady with conviction. "Becoming stronger, more intelligent. You've already conquered the very disease you were born with, something no one else or no scientists have ever done. You've achieved an unprecedented level of control over your own body. Kevin, you're a miracle. The future dream of humanity. You are the one rewriting the course of history."

Kevin felt a flush of shyness creep over him. He didn't know how to respond to Sean's overwhelming praise, so he simply muttered, "Thank you."

Sean smiled but didn't press further. "Well, I think everyone's getting tired. It's almost bedtime for Kevin. You all traveled a long way, and you need to rest. After I come back from work tomorrow, we'll talk."

Kevin hesitated for a moment before speaking. "Sean!" His voice carried a trace of urgency. "Do you remember when we were talking on the phone? I told you I felt like someone else was listening... I even asked if there was another person on the line."

Sean's expression darkened. He met Kevin's gaze, his tone serious. "Yes, I remember. That's why I got help from my friend I hired someone to check my home. They searched every inch of it."

He paused, letting the words sink in. "And they found three cameras." A stunned silence fell over the room. Kevin's breath hitched. "Three?"

Sean nodded. "They took care of it. But that means someone's been watching… and we still don't know who. The phone line's still bugged. If you need to make a call about the mission, use your cell. But if it's just a personal call, friend, or family, feel free to use my home phone."

Sean looked at everyone and said: "I'll teach you all tomorrow how the cameras work here in my home. Right now, it's on a different program and we are okay."

"But who might have done that?" Sharon asked, her voice laced with worry. Sean remained calm, his tone matter-of-fact. "I don't know," he admitted. "But the house is clean now. That's all that matters."

Sharon frowned, unconvinced. "But if someone went through the trouble of planting cameras, they won't just stop because you found them." Sean met her gaze evenly. "Maybe not. But we're prepared now. And whoever they are, they've lost their advantage. Thanks to Kevin."

"But we have to be very careful, Sean," Sharon stressed. "Someone is spying on you, and you need to find out who that is." Everyone nodded in agreement, the weight of the situation settling over them. Sean looked at everyone with confidence and said, "We will."

Early the Next Morning, At the office, Sean wasted no time. The moment he arrived, he headed straight for Greg's desk.

"Can we have lunch together?" Sean asked, his tone casual yet unmistakably firm. Greg looked up, surprised to see him so early. He blinked, then smirked. "Sure, just as long as you're buying."

Sean was anxious to speak with Greg again and accepted. Once they arrived at the restaurant, they exchanged greetings and engaged in some small talk, but Sean quickly grew impatient. He leaned forward, lowering his voice.

"Look, Greg. They arrived yesterday. I need to ask you some questions regarding the filing department."

Greg gave him a knowing look. "I figured this had something to do with that." He took a sip of his coffee before raising an eyebrow. "By the way, who are 'they'?"

"Kevin, his mother, and my sister, Sharon," Sean explained.

Greg nearly dropped his fork. "They're here? You're kidding?" His surprise was evident, his eyes widening as he processed the news. "No, I'm not kidding. They're here, and we need your help. You've got to help us," Sean said urgently. Greg leaned back, nodding without hesitation. "I will. What's a friend good for? I'll be with you until the end."

Sean exhaled, relieved, but Greg suddenly hesitated. He studied Sean for a moment before asking, "By the way, I have a question. That picture on the bookshelf in your living room the one I saw the other day is that your sister?" Sean gave him a puzzled look. "Yes. Why?"

Greg smirked slightly. "She's got to be the most beautiful young woman I've ever seen. I can't wait to see her." Sean's expression darkened instantly. "Yeah," he said, crossing his arms. "And she's got a handsome fiance, too." Greg's smirk faltered, replaced by a thoughtful look. "Are they happy?" he asked, tilting his head slightly.

Sean shot him a knowing glance. Greg caught on quickly, sighing in resignation. "That's okay," he muttered, stirring his drink. "I'd still like to meet her. She's engaged, not married." His voice held a hint of disappointment, but his curiosity remained. "Anyway, can you come to my house tonight? We're going to talk about our plans there," Sean asked.

"Yes, certainly. I wouldn't miss it. What time should I be there? Greg replied, a subtle smile playing on his lips. "Around six? Can you make it? And no funny business, you know what I mean." Sean hesitated slightly, a flicker of uncertainty crossing his face.

Greg grinned. "Yes. I'll be there for sure whether the world is on fire or it's the end of days." Then he looked at Sean's eyes and said: "I'm not going to ask her out or for a date. Don't worry." Both burst into laughter, the tension momentarily easing. "Alright," Sean said, shaking his head with a smirk. "Let's order lunch now."

When Sean returned in the afternoon, he was greeted by the comforting aroma of home cooking, mingled with the rich scent of freshly brewed coffee. The warmth of it all wrapped around him like a familiar embrace, stirring memories he hadn't visited in a long time. For a fleeting moment, it felt like old times, like stepping through the door of his parent's home, where the air was always thick with the scent of a meal lovingly prepared.

His mother had always been an exceptional cook, and she still was. Back then, the house would be alive with conversation, the sound of laughter and chatter filling every corner. Among the people you love, loneliness never found a place to settle. As long as a family stayed together bound by love, by shared memories, and by the simple act of caring, you were never truly alone.

But time had a way of shifting things, of pulling people apart. Only when you leave them or lose them do you fully understand the depth of what you had. And in that realization, you would give anything to have it back.

Sharon walked to the door, greeting him with a warm smile. "Hi, Sean," she said, pressing a light kiss to his cheek. "Hello, Sharon," Sean replied, setting his keys down. "How's everything?"

Sharon beamed. "Everything's perfect. I'm so happy I took two weeks off. I get to spend it with the best brother anyone could ever have." Sean chuckled, shaking his head. "Flattery will get you everywhere. "

Sharon took Sean's arm, and together, they walked into the living room. Julia and Kevin greeted him warmly, their smiles adding to the cozy atmosphere of the house. Sharon, always attentive, brought Sean a steaming cup of coffee and settled beside him, eager to share what she had learned that day. Her knowledge was expanding at an astonishing rate, and the excitement in her voice was unmistakable.

As they spoke, Sean took a moment to soak it all in the warmth of the home, the company of his family, and the rare peace that filled the space. Every moment felt like a new beginning, a fresh breath of life. He was happy, truly happy, relishing each second. They all stopped talking as a sudden knock echoed through the house. Sean looked at the time, and it was exactly 6.00 o'clock.

"Who is it? Are you expecting anyone, Sean?" Sharon asked, glancing toward the door. "Yes," Sean replied, standing up. "That must be Greg. I asked him to come because we need him for our plan. I'll explain everything later."

He walked over and opened the door, revealing Greg impeccably dressed, as if he were attending a formal event, a wedding, or an exclusive gathering of great significance.

Sean smirked. "Hello, sir, are you here for a royal party?" he teased.

Greg, momentarily tongue-tied, peered past Sean into the house before turning back to him. "Come on, Sean," he muttered. "I'm just trying to be nice and polite." He straightened his jacket. "But hey, I also want to look good. You know, for no one." Sean chuckled, stepping aside. "Well, you definitely put in the effort. Now get in here we've got things to discuss."

Sean led him inside, introducing him to everyone. Greg greeted them all politely, though his gaze lingered just a moment longer on Sharon. After a hearty dinner, they all gathered around the fireplace, the flickering flames casting soft shadows across the room. The air was thick with anticipation tonight, they had plans to discuss, and the future felt closer than ever.

The two chatted for a while, but Greg couldn't seem to take his eyes off Sharon. She, however, appeared completely oblivious.

Meanwhile, Kevin sat quietly, observing everything with an intensity that didn't go unnoticed. His gaze lingered on Greg, sharp and knowing, as if he could see right through him. Greg finally noticed and turned to the boy. "What's wrong, Kevin? The way you're looking at me is making me nervous." Sean flashed a wicked smile at Greg and said, "Kevin can feel your emotions and hear your thoughts."

Kevin blinked as if snapping out of a trance. He hesitated before saying, "I'm really sorry, but…I want to make sure you are a good friend of Sean."

Greg stiffened. He shot Sean a quick, incredulous look before turning back to Kevin. "How can you tell?" His tone carried both skepticism and unease. "Sean and I have been friends for over two years."

Kevin looked at him blankly and said, "So… I've known a lot of my classmates for six or seven years, but that doesn't make them good friends."

Greg stared at him in disbelief, saying nothing. But Kevin, still eyeing him with a peculiar curiosity, continued, "You should see a dentist tonight. The nerve around your left gums is inflamed on the verge of bursting at any moment." Greg turned to Sean and asked: "Is he for real?"

Sean leaned back, watching Greg's reaction. "As I told you, he feels the pain of others, Greg. Especially their thoughts." Greg's mouth opened slightly, but no words came out. For the first time that night, he was completely speechless. Sean smiled, rubbing his hands together. "So… let's get back to business."

Sharon nodded, her expression turning serious. "According to Masonaar A., their longest lifespan ranges from five to seven hundred years."

She began. "And what's even more astonishing is that their longevity keeps improving. Their scientific knowledge is about seventy percent more advanced than ours."They've already discovered light-speed travel and alternative energy sources for transportation things we still struggle to grasp."

Greg looked at Sharon, shaking his head. "That's impossible. Light-speed? According to Einstein, nothing with mass can reach the speed of light. Only light itself can travel that fast. If we tried, our mass would become infinite, and it would take unlimited energy; plus, theoretically, we'd turn into pure energy ourselves. That's why, in our understanding, it just can't happen."

"With the right equipment, it is possible," Sean said quietly, his voice steady, almost too calm, as if he'd seen something Greg hadn't.

Everyone leaned in, listening intently as she continued. "They're willing to send us information detailed reports, along with images. But there's a problem. They found our equipment completely obsolete. They say our technology is almost thousands of years behind theirs."

Greg exhaled sharply. "You've got all that information from them? A thousand years?"

Sharon nodded. "Yes, but they're willing to help. They said they'll guide us in developing a computer advanced enough to communicate with theirs. Once we have it, they'll transmit everything images, data, and knowledge beyond anything we've ever encountered. And what's even more intriguing is that we have a significant chance to contact the bigger entity exactly as they reached out to us."

Greg looked stunned, his eyes widening in disbelief. He turned to Sean, his voice rising with excitement. "Sean! You never told me anything about this. You've been in contact with aliens, and it never crossed your mind to mention it to me?"

He studied Sean for a moment before adding, "Now I understand why you won't give up."

Sean smirked at Greg's reaction, leaning back in his chair. "Well, I figured you'd find out sooner or later. And just to correct your perception, they're not aliens from our world; they're from one of Kevin's galaxies." He said casually.

Greg threw up his hands. "Sooner or later? This is the kind of thing you tell your best friend immediately!"

He shook his head in amazement. "I mean, come on, aliens? Actual communication? Advanced technology a thousand years ahead of ours? This is insane!" He looked at Sean again, puzzled. "What do you mean by Kevin's galaxy?" Sean only nodded, a quiet smile playing on his lips, his eyes alight with something that needed no words.

Sharon looked at Greg and chuckled. "Yeah, well, now you know what had happened." Greg exhaled, still processing everything. "Okay, okay. So… what else I should know?"

Sean looked around the room and then met Greg's bewildered gaze. He took a deep breath. "Greg… they're not the kind of aliens you're thinking of. They're not from another planet, not from our universe. They're from…Ah…how they say… well, I don't even know how to explain it." Sean looked at Greg and continued, "As I told you, not aliens. They're in Kevin's body, one of billions of galaxies within him." Greg wasn't sure if he heard right. "Inside Kevin? Galaxies? What did he eat? Maybe that's the problem?"

He hesitated, then turned to Sharon, who immediately understood. She looked at Greg, her expression calm but serious. "Greg, you know I'm a biochemist. I've spent years studying life and existence at the molecular level I know this field inside and out." She paused, choosing her words carefully. "What we discovered is beyond anything we ever imagined. The aliens you think are from some distant galaxy… they're actually from Kevin's body." Greg's eyes widened. "What? I thought you were just mistaken."

Sharon continued, her voice steady. "Everything that exists contains galaxies within it. Just as our universe holds planets, stars, and life, Kevin has an entire universe woven between his cells and molecules, a universe teeming with life forms, civilizations, and beings whose knowledge surpasses ours by thousands of years. And the most fascinating part? There are billions of galaxies within him, just as there are within everyone and everything that exists."

Greg blinked, struggling to comprehend. "You're telling me Kevin's body has an entire universe inside it?"

"No, I'm telling you, his body has billions of galaxies inside him. It includes everything that exists, no matter if it's a human or a rock." Sharon's voice trembled, not with fear but with awe.

Greg narrowed his eyes, trying to decipher her words. "You mean… metaphorically?"

"No," she whispered. "I mean it exactly as it is. His body is not a body in the way we understand it. It's a vessel a universe within a shell. Each cell is a dimension. Each beat of his heart creates motion across star systems. When he breathes, entire planets evolve."

Greg took a step back, his pulse quickening. "That's impossible. That would make him Not human," she finished for him. "Or at least, not only human and evolve human or future of humanity."

The room fell into silence, the hum of the machines suddenly sounding distant, like echoes from another realm.

Sharon confirmed. "And because their civilization is so advanced, they've developed the technology to communicate beyond their own universe to reach out to him and us, the universe above theirs. That's why they can contact us. It's incredible, Greg. We're standing at the edge of something groundbreaking something that changes everything we thought we knew about life, science, and existence itself."

Greg smiled, shaking his head in disbelief. He turned to Sean, his eyes narrowing playfully. "Are you testing me? Is this some kind of joke? Maybe aliens did something, but whatever you're saying doesn't make sense." Then, as if unable to contain his excitement, he looked at Sharon, his curiosity sparking like wildfire.

Sean, still calm and composed, met his friend's gaze with a knowing smile. "Of course, it is unbelievable because it's unique and a new discovery. I wouldn't joke about something like this, Greg. You know me better than that." His voice carried quiet confidence, leaving no room for doubt. "Greg Kevin is the boy who was in the hospital, the one from the newspaper, the one who went through all those shocks."

Greg stared at him, his skepticism wavering under the weight of Sean's conviction. "You're serious," he muttered, almost to himself. "You really believe this... that the boy's body contains entire galaxies?"

"I don't believe it," Sean replied, stepping closer. "I've seen it. I've witnessed the data. And more than that... I've felt it. When you stand close to him, it's like standing at the edge of a black hole and a sunrise at the same time. There's gravity in him, Greg, something that pulls you, something that knows more than we do." Greg rubbed the back of his neck, searching for logic for a reason, finding none.

"Then who is he?" Greg asked finally, his voice lower, more reverent now. "If he's not just a child… then what is he?"

"He is a highly evolved human with advanced cognitive abilities, and I would call him Human Neurogen and this is the only word I can come up with," Sean said with a friendly voice.

Greg exhaled, rubbing the back of his neck again. "This is insane… but at the same time, I can't help but feel like it makes sense. If this is true, if there's an entire universe inside Kevin, then we're not just discovering new life. We're discovering a whole new reality." Sean looked at him and replied: "Exactly."

Kevin, who the whole time was listening leaned in a little while he looked at Greg and said: "Galaxies." Everyone burst into laughter. Sharon nodded. "Exactly. And we have only scratched the surface."

Everyone noticed how excited Sharon was as she recounted all this, her enthusiasm practically radiating from her as she continued: "They've already given us some information to upgrade our systems, and we've received a few pictures, but we couldn't download them properly because our systems aren't compatible. However, the writings are here."

Sean brought his laptop and, held it in front of Greg and said? "We made a few changes to our system and managed to receive some of the images. Have you ever seen anything like this before? Their pictures are… life-sized, somehow. But here's the incredible part: it's not just a snapshot frozen in time. Each image unfolds, revealing what happened moments after it was taken. It plays out like a five-minute scene… showing who took the picture, what they were doing, even the emotions they felt."

Sean paused, eyes locked on the projection as the still image began to stir, shifting ever so slightly.

"But according to them," he continued, his voice lowered, "these images are meant to answer our questions. Not all of them, but enough to guide us. The only problem is… our system still doesn't work properly. We're only catching fragments. Just pieces of the answers they're trying to give us. The amazing part is that when no one's looking, it's just a picture but the moment your eyes meet it, it comes alive, moving, speaking, and answering your questions.

He glanced at Sharon, who stood frozen, transfixed by the image that now showed a figure approaching the camera an expression of both wonder and warning on their face.

Greg's jaw nearly dropped. "Wait… are you saying their pictures move? Like a recorded memory?"

"Exactly!" Sharon exclaimed, her eyes shining with a mix of excitement and disbelief. "But it's not just the memory. When you ask them questions, they respond based on that day, that moment in time; it's like a video chat… only it's flat and still like a photograph. Small, yes, but alive."

Greg took a cautious step closer to the display, staring at the image as the figure within turned, as if sensing their presence.

"But… how is that possible?" he whispered. "How can a picture know what we're saying now and respond from the past?"

"It's not time travel," Sean said, his tone firm but thoughtful. "It's memory. Stored not just in pixels but in something deeper. Some kind of encoded consciousness. Like each image is a window to a preserved moment trapped, but aware."

Greg swallowed hard. "This isn't technology," he muttered. "It's something else entirely." Sharon nodded. "Or maybe it is technology, but so far beyond ours, it looks like magic."

"It's like stepping into a moment frozen in time, except it's not frozen at all. They told me that once we receive them, we'll finally understand what that truly means."

Sean folded his arms, deep in thought. "That kind of technology is beyond anything we've ever imagined. If they can do this, who knows what else they're capable of?" Sharon nodded. "And we're about to find out." Sharon's excitement only grew as she continued. "And that's not even the most unbelievable part. They told me they could help us build a spaceship using the lightest material imaginable something completely unbreakable, absolutely untouchable."

Greg's eyebrows shot up. "Unbreakable? That's impossible."

Sharon shook her head, her voice brimming with conviction. "Not for them, not anymore. The spaceship would be as large as North America yet as light as a minivan. Can you even begin to imagine that?" Kevin stepped in again and faced Greg: "And unbreakable."

Greg leaned forward, struggling to wrap his mind around it. "That defies everything we know about engineering and physics."

"Exactly," Sharon agreed. "But their technology is beyond our understanding. And get this, the ship will be capable of speeds up to 250,000 kilometers per second."

The room fell into a stunned silence. Sean finally spoke, his voice low with awe. "When did you find out this info? But If that's true, we're talking about something that could completely redefine space travel... even reality itself."

Greg ran a hand through his hair and said, "So, as I said before, if something were moving at exactly 300,000 km/s, it would be traveling at or just slightly beyond the speed of light, which isn't physically possible for anything with mass, according to Einstein's theory of relativity. Only massless particles, like photons, can reach that speed.

Greg paused a little, then faced Sharon: "But if something were actually faster than light, it would shatter our entire understanding of physics... which means it's impossible, right?"

Sharon looked at Greg and answered: "Not with the right equipment." Then she turned to Sean and nodded, a triumphant glint in her eyes. "While you were at work, Kevin and I tried it again, and that's how I have more info now, And more interesting is that they're willing to help us make it happen."

Then she looked at Greg again and said, "They've already done it. They're traveling at that speed right now."

She paused, letting the weight of her words settle in his mind, then continued, "Impossible doesn't exist in science. The proof is right here: they found a way to make it possible."

Greg looked suspiciously at Sharon, narrowing his eyes. "How do you know they really moved that fast?" he asked.

Sharon gave a confident smile and gestured toward a sleek device on the table. "That's a biometric positional scanner. Sean designed it to track micro-movements on Kevin's body in real-time. I monitored the readings, and in an instant, the signal shifted from one side of his body to the other. No delay, no transition."

Greg was stunned. Not a word came out of his mouth he was completely speechless.

Sharon's voice grew even more animated. "You know, they've already built a spaceship, one as big as half their planet. And get this, there are two million people on board." Greg's mouth fell open. "Two million? Living on a spaceship?"

"Yes," Sharon confirmed. "It's not just a ship; it's a self-sustaining world. It embarks on life-long journeys, traveling farther than anyone any species has ever gone before."

Sean exhaled sharply, his mind racing. "That means they aren't just explorers… they're pioneers of the unknown. They must have knowledge of entire regions of existence we can't even comprehend."

Sharon nodded. "Exactly. They've seen places and encountered phenomena we can't even dream of. And now, they're offering to share some of that knowledge with us."

She paused again, careful not to overload him with information, then continued: "They helped other planets and galaxies do the same, and together, they fixed all the materials, suns, asteroids, anything that might harm their planet or others. I believe that's when Kevin's asthma was healed."

Sharon looked around at everyone and added, "That's how they managed to reach Kevin's brain and send us messages. They tested everything, pinpointed the exact location, and discovered it had to be an energy source, and they found out they could come into contact with it. Now they know it's his brain. That's how they did it."

Greg ran a hand through his hair again. "This is insane. It changes everything. If they've been to places no one else has ever seen… then maybe, just maybe, they've found answers to questions we haven't even thought to ask."

Sharon reached down, grabbing some printouts to consult. As her eyes scanned the pages, they lit up with excitement. "And get this,"

she continued, her voice brimming with awe. "They discovered DNA a couple of million years ago by their time. Long before we even knew what it was,"

Sean said, his voice low with awe. "And they've mastered it in ways we can't even begin to imagine. Not just sequencing or altering it… but understanding it as a language. A universal language."

Greg listened, motionless, as Sean continued.

"They found something buried deep within their DNA. And not just theirs across galaxies, in every form of life they've encountered. A shared code. A pattern. A signal that proved they were all connected."

Sharon added softly, "That's how they knew, not through exploration or communication, but through the very building blocks of existence. They didn't discover others. They recognized them. Because they were part of the same origin."

"The same origin?" Greg echoed, barely able to grasp the scale.

Sean nodded. "Every galaxy… every species… every spark of life. All connected through that ancient thread. A thread they believe didn't evolve but was placed."

The silence that followed was thick, charged with the weight of a truth too vast for words.

Greg leaned in, intrigued. "Like what?"

Sharon's smile widened. "For starters, they can alter their hair color just by modifying their DNA. The change isn't temporary it becomes their natural hair color for life. And it doesn't stop there. They can even change their hair type curly to straight, straight to curly without altering their genetic origins. They can alter anything in their bodies, from height to skin color anything."

Greg blinked. "You're saying they can rewrite their own physical traits?"

"Exactly," Sharon said. "They've also perfected the ability to change skin tone and eye color at will. They can transform their appearance on a molecular level adjusting only specific parts of their DNA while keeping everything else intact."

Sean raised an eyebrow. "And there are no side effects?"

"None," Sharon confirmed. "They've refined the process to perfection. No health risks, no complications just seamless, natural changes. And here's the best part: they're willing to share their formulas with us."

Greg let out a low whistle. "This is unreal. If this kind of DNA manipulation becomes possible for us, we'd be looking at the most revolutionary advancement in genetic science... ever."

Sean nodded slowly, his mind racing with the possibilities. "And if they're offering this knowledge, imagine what else they might be willing to share." Julia's eyes widened with amazement as she asked, "Do they look like us?"

Sharon hesitated for a moment, then glanced at her printouts again before answering. "Yes and no." She looked up, her expression thoughtful. "Their basic structure is similar to ours. They have a head, limbs, eyes, and a body. But their evolutionary path has made them... different."

Greg leaned forward. "Different, how?"

Sharon's voice grew more excited. "For one, their skin isn't limited to a single tone. They have the ability to shift it, almost like a natural camouflage. Their eyes are far more advanced than ours, able to see spectrums of light we can't even comprehend. And their physical composition? It's stronger and more adaptive. They can survive in extreme environments without needing protective gear."

Julia exhaled in awe. "So they're like an evolved version of us?"

Sharon nodded. "In a way, yes. But they don't see themselves as superior. They just had a head start on thousands of years of advancement. And now, they're willing to share some of that with us."

"Can they change their height, too?" Kevin asked, his curiosity sparked a new thought. Sharon glanced at her notes and nodded. "Yes, they can. But you won't need it. You're destined to stand tall." Kevin's eyes widened. "Seriously?"

Sharon smiled. "They have complete control over their DNA modifications. Just like they can change hair, skin, and eye color, they can also alter their height. If one of them wants to be taller or shorter, they modify specific genetic markers, and their body adapts naturally over time without any artificial surgery or implants. Their bones, muscles, and proportions adjust perfectly."

Greg shook his head in disbelief. "That's insane. No growth hormones, no bone-lengthening procedures, just... natural transformation?"

"Exactly," Sharon confirmed. "And the changes are permanent unless they decide to modify their DNA again." Kevin grinned. "That's so cool. Imagine being able to decide your own height." Sharon looked at Kevin and said: "You are already there." Sean chuckled. "And here I thought getting a haircut was a big change."

Greg glanced at Kevin, uncertain whether it was proper to ask: "Kevin! Can you change your hair color, skin tone, or eye color?"

Sean cut in, adding, "Actually, I think he's already starting to change. Maybe their advanced science is affecting him, too. He can already see through anyone's body."

Greg looked from Sean to Sharon, his brows furrowed in confusion. "Wait a minute, how do you know their speed of light is the same as ours? How do you even know their kilometer equals ours? What if their entire system of measurement is completely different?"

Sharon smiled warmly as if she'd been waiting for that question. "That's exactly what I asked them," she said. "We used Earth as our base reference. We already know Earth's rotational speed and how long it takes a commercial airplane to circle the globe. So we used that as our comparative constant."

She paused, letting the thought settle before continuing. "When I asked them, they gave me their planet's mass, radius, and orbital duration with astonishing precision. Once we had their rotational speed and how long it takes for a spacecraft to orbit their planet, we had everything we needed."

Sean chimed in, "From there, it's just physics. We translated their units by using shared universal constants: mass, gravity, and time. No matter where you are in the universe, gravity acts the same. So once we had matching values, we could convert their numbers into our measurements."

Greg blinked, astonished. "So... you translated their entire system of speed and distance using nothing but flight time and planetary mass?" Sharon nodded. "Exactly. And guess what? Their speed of light matched ours, down to the last decimal."

Greg hesitated, letting his mind absorb the flood of new information. His gaze drifted, unfocused as if he were trying to rearrange the entire universe inside his head. For a moment, the room was silent, heavy with the weight of discovery, before he slowly turned to Sean.

"I believe you had some questions for me," he said quietly. "Why don't you start now?" A flicker of surprise crossed Sean's face, quickly replaced by a nod of respect. Sharon leaned forward, her voice carrying a gentle spark of humor. "You mean… you're one of us now?"

Greg met her gaze and smiled, the hesitation gone from his eyes. "I guess I am," he replied, nodding. "Let's find out what that really means."

Sean nodded, his tone straightforward. "Okay. We're heading to the CCFD tomorrow. We need your guidance." Greg's expression darkened slightly. "The CCFD?" Sean continued, "I need to know again if the alarm goes off; what happens in the CCFD?"

Greg regarded him strangely. "Well, as I told you yesterday, the power must go off to trigger the alarm. If the alarm goes off, which has never happened before, after thirty seconds, the emergency alarm will activate automatically. Keep in mind that emergency power can last for an entire year. Once triggered, everything goes into lockdown. No one can get in or out unless the issue is resolved. The system is extremely precise. There's no bypass, no margin for error." His gaze swept across the room, studying each person in turn.

"Is there a hidden camera around there? I mean around CCFD." Sharon asked. Greg turned to her, a hint of satisfaction in his eyes at her participation. "Yes, but no one knows where they are. Not even Mr. Hagman himself has a clue."

Greg shifted uncomfortably, feeling as though he was suddenly the center of attention like he was being prosecuted. It was as if he were on live television, a prisoner under interrogation. Sean narrowed his eyes at him. "What's going on, Greg?"

A wave of heat surged through Greg's body, his face flushing red. He was trying to keep his composure, especially in front of Sharon. Embarrassed, he chose to ignore Sean's question.

Instead, he asked, a hint of incredulity in his voice, "What's your plan? Are all of you really planning to go there tomorrow?" "Oh, no. Just Kevin and me," Sean answered calmly.

Julia was sipping her coffee when she heard Sean's answer. She suddenly choked, coughing as she set her cup down. "No, I'll go too," she said firmly. Sean shook his head. "We need you somewhere else, Julia," he replied. "We need you to guard and watch over us. I'll explain everything later." Sharon crossed her arms. "What about me?" she asked, her tone unwavering. "You'll need me too. I can be useful. I have more experience with Kevin than you do I've spent more time with him than you."

"But what if you get caught?" Greg interjected, his voice edged with concern. He hesitated for a moment before adding, "What will become of you all?"

"Listen," Sean began, his voice steady but filled with conviction. "We are the only ones who can change the world for a better future. We have to do this. People deserve a fair life. Our people deserve a chance to live like normal human beings. Greg smiled and said: "You mean changing everything in DNA stuff is normal human?"

Sean looked at him and ignored his answer. "Just look around you. What do you see? There are people making more in a year than they could ever need, while others work day and night just to put food on the table for their families. Think about these two realities. Which one truly represents a human life?" Greg hesitated, his thoughts turning over the weight of Sean's words. Finally, he answered, "Neither."

"Well, of course, neither of them," Greg admitted. He leaned forward slightly, his gaze sharp. "But what will those people do with your so-called revolutionary idea?"

"It's obvious if we succeed, everything will change for the better. Our planet will become the best place to live. We will bring heaven to Earth. The land will be available to anyone who wants it, and people will be free to grow whatever they desire.

But it won't stop there. Our bodies will evolve. They will protect themselves against sickness against weakness. And the most astonishing part? Our lifespan.

According to Kevin's body, or perhaps I should say Masonaar A, our lifespan could extend from 100 to 300 years, maybe even more. And during most of that time, we would remain young and healthy. Only in the final twenty years would we begin to age. Everything would change. Just imagine it." Sean stopped and looked at everyone, his gaze finally settling on Greg, who sat in stunned silence, trying to process the weight of what he'd just heard. Then, after a moment, he met Sean's eyes and said, "If you're really doing this, then I'm in. I can help you with all the information you need. You need me anyway."

Sean smiled and said: "I've gathered everything we might need for tomorrow: a walkie-talkie, some tools, and a van I rented this afternoon. Now, the only things we need are hope and luck. And we've already got the first one. We'll start tomorrow at eleven o'clock."

Greg smiled and asked, "Why a walkie-talkie? Don't you have cell phones?" Sean nodded, his expression turning serious. "We do. But listen, every cellphone is tied to our office number. If someone's monitoring that line, even a single call could give us away."

Sharon scanned the piece of paper that had just been printed, her eyes flicking over the text. She looked at Kevin and said, "Here's the answer to your question about the height."

"What is it?" Kevin asked eagerly. Sharon giggled as she read aloud, "They say it's as easy as one-two-three."

"That's amazing," Greg said, his eyes lingering on Sharon. Sean smirked. "You mean the answer or Sharon?" Greg blinked, momentarily caught off guard. Realizing what Sean meant, he quickly composed himself and replied, "I mean the answer." Sean chuckled, leaning back slightly. "Yeah… I got it."

Greg looked at Sean in disbelief. "Everything makes sense except this. Why do you need Kevin? He's just a ten-year-old boy." Sean's eyes lit up as if he'd been waiting for that moment. "Greg, give your phone to Kevin." Greg raised a brow, caught off guard. "Why?"

"Just do it," Sean replied with a calm smile. Reluctantly, Greg handed the phone over. The moment Kevin's fingers touched the screen, the device came to life with a soft chime unlocking instantly. Greg's eyes widened. "How did he do that? I have a security code on it!" Without hesitation, Kevin began reading aloud the most recent text messages.

"Greg, don't forget the 3 PM meeting... Your bank transfer has been confirmed... Need more time for the files."

"That's enough!" Greg barked, snatching the phone back. He stared at Kevin as if seeing him for the first time, not as a child, but as something entirely unfamiliar. Something impossible. Then he turned sharply to Sean. "How did he do that?"

Sean's smile deepened. "Greg," he said quietly, "he's the whole point. He is the key. I need him there to uncover security systems, decode layers we can't even see... and gather as much information as possible. He doesn't break the rules... he simply exists outside of them."

Greg's expression darkened. "You want a ten-year-old to ask about a security code? Are you insane?"

Sean shook his head, amused. "You still don't get it, Greg. He doesn't have to ask. He's a mind reader. Without saying a word, he can pull the information straight from someone's thoughts."He glanced at Kevin with undeniable pride and caught Kevin smirking at him as if he knew exactly how he felt about Sharon, then shifted his gaze back to Sean.

Greg blinked, feeling utterly foolish. "Ah... wow... Are you real?" Sean smirked. Greg turned to Kevin, suddenly realizing something. "That's why you were staring at me? What do you think about me now?" Kevin smiled mischievously and answered, "I'll tell you tomorrow." Greg looked puzzled and asked: "Why tomorrow?" Kevin smiled. Then, with a knowing grin, he turned away.

Greg looked at Sean and asked, "How do you explain Kevin going with you? Isn't that going to be suspicious?" Sean smiled again and replied, "That's where you come in. I'll say he's my nephew, eager to see the place, and you'll confirm it. I need you to talk to Simon or John about everything, and that's it. Kevin can read everything straight from their minds."

CHAPTER SEVEN

"Into the Forbidden Sector"

It was five minutes to eleven when Sean received a call from security. "Do you have two visitors?" the guard asked. "We need your permission to let them enter the building." Without hesitation, Sean replied, "Yes, they're my sister and her son. They're here to visit me."

Ten minutes later, his office door swung open. Sharon and Kevin stood in the doorway before stepping inside and shutting the door behind them. Sean wasted no time. He grabbed his computer along with several Neuro-Link Clasps he had prepared the day before. Swiftly tucking everything into his jacket, he handed the computer to Sharon. "You'll need this to contact Masonaar A," he told her.

Kevin left his hand on the phone on Sean's desk: I can't get to CCFD files. There is nothing by that name here." Sean looked worried. Suddenly, the door opened, and Greg appeared in front of it. "What are you doing here?" Sean asked, caught off guard.

Greg met his gaze, unfazed. "I'm here to help you. You need me to find the files." Sean's expression shifted to astonishment. "You mean you know exactly where they are?"

"Yes," Greg said with a sigh. "I was hoping you'd forget all about that atom business. But after last night and Sharon's explanation, I realized you weren't going to change your mind. So, I decided to change mine."

He glanced between them, his voice firm. "You believe it. It's not just a story. It's the truth. And obviously, none of us are in the business of denying the truth. Not you. Not Sharon. And not me."

Greg spoke seriously, his voice firm and convincing, but Sean couldn't shake the flicker of doubt threading its way through his thoughts. Was Greg here because he truly believed in their mission... or was it because of Sharon?

A heavy silence settled over the room, thick and motionless. Then, as if drawn by an invisible current, everyone slowly turned to look at Kevin.

Sean glanced at Sharon, who looked just as puzzled. Their eyes met, silently asking the same question: Why Kevin?

Greg shifted under the weight of their gazes, his discomfort mounting with each passing second. The tension clung to the air like static. He tried to ignore it, but the pressure was mounting, building like a wave about to break. Finally, he snapped. "Why are you all looking at him?" he demanded. "Because he can catch me if I'm lying?"

Kevin, unfazed, tilted his head slightly and looked up at Sean with a quiet, amused smile. "He truly wants to help us," he said, his tone gentle but sure. "And not for the other reason." Sean and Kevin chuckled, the tension momentarily easing between them. It was the kind of laugh that said more than words a quiet acknowledgment of something only they seemed to understand.

Sharon, however, stood still, her brows furrowing. "What?" she asked, glancing between the two. "What did I miss?"

Kevin tried to hold back a grin. "It's nothing," he said, though his eyes sparkled with mischief. Sean gave her a reassuring smile. "Just one of those moments, Sharon. Don't worry you'll catch up soon."

Still puzzled, Sharon narrowed her eyes at them but didn't press further. "You two are starting to sound like you share a secret language." Kevin tilted his head. "Maybe we do," he said softly then Sean and Kevin both looked at Greg with a smile.

The air grew quiet again, but this time, it was different. Not heavy, not tense. Just the calm before something important. Greg blinked, stunned into silence. Sean gave Kevin a long look, part gratitude, part reverence, then turned to Greg and simply nodded. "All right," Sean said softly. "Let's move."

"Greg and I will go together," Sean continued, his voice steady and measured. "Sharon, this is your walkie-talkie. We'll take the second one. You two go first. After five minutes, Greg and I will follow."

He handed the small device to her, then looked around the group, his expression serious. "When we're down there, I'll reach out using the walkie-talkies only. No cell phones for security reasons. Understood?" Everyone nodded, the tension rising in the air like a current.

Sean then turned to Kevin. "And Kevin, after the first contact, your job is to trigger a blackout. Sharon knows what to do. Exactly two minutes later, restore everything to normal. After that, repeat the blackout every ten minutes until I reach out to you again." Kevin didn't flinch. He simply nodded once, eyes focused and strangely calm for someone his age. "Got it."

Greg looked from Sean to Kevin, then back again. "You're really trusting a kid with that much power?" Sean gave a half-smile. "He's not just a kid, Greg. You saw that yourself."

Greg didn't respond. He just took a deep breath, adjusted the strap on his shoulder, and prepared to follow Sean into the unknown.

Sharon and Kevin took the iPad, which displayed the building's map downloaded by Sean. Kevin held it without even looking, effortlessly navigating the hallways and staircases as if he had memorized every turn. His movements were natural, drawing no suspicion, while Sharon followed closely behind, carefully studying the highlighted path that would lead them to the power and electricity room. With a final nod, they prepared to move.

"Good luck, everyone," Sean spoke into the walkie-talkie, his voice steady. Then, turning to another channel, he asked, "Julia, are you ready?"

"I bet I am!" Julia responded confidently. "That's good. Good luck." Greg and Sean headed toward the elevator when Greg suddenly stopped. "We can't go in together," he warned. "They'd get suspicious." Sean frowned. "What do you suggest?" "Do you know where the fire north exit is?" Greg asked. Sean nodded. "Yes, I do."

"Good," Greg said. "I'll meet you there. I can get into the basement and open the door from the inside. That way, it'll be easier to access the restricted area without drawing attention." Sean paused, weighing the risks. "But won't the alarm go off?" Greg gave a slight grin and held up a sleek, metallic card between his fingers. "Not with this card."

Sean's eyes lit up part surprise, part admiration. A slow smile crept across his face as he gave a firm nod. "You're right. I'll see you there."

Without another word, they moved into action, the plan silently locking into place between them. Sean left the building and circled around, his footsteps quick but calculated. It took him nearly five minutes to reach the fire exit. He positioned himself behind the door, waiting in silence.

Minutes passed. Five. Then ten. A gnawing unease crept in what had happened to Greg? Was he caught? Was he hurt? Suddenly, his walkie-talkie crackled to life. "Hello?" Sean answered immediately. "Sean, wait another five minutes," Kevin's voice came through.

Sean stiffened. "What are you talking about? Where are you?"

"You've just got to trust me," Kevin said, his tone eerily calm.

Before Sean could demand an explanation, another voice came through this time a hurried whisper. "Come on! Hurry up!" Greg's voice cut in, breathless but urgent. "What happened? Why were you late?" Sean asked Greg, his voice sharp with concern.

Greg exhaled, glancing around to make sure they were still alone. "There was a guard near the basement entrance. I had to wait until he left. I couldn't risk being seen." Sean narrowed his eyes. "And Kevin? How did he know to warn me?" Greg hesitated for a split second before answering. "I don't know, but if he told you to wait, then he must have seen something we didn't." Sean let out a frustrated sigh but nodded. "Alright. Let's move. We don't have time to waste."

"Also, I saw John, and he asked me a few questions. That's another reason why I was late. I passed through two dangers," Greg said, his voice still a little tense. Sean's eyes narrowed. "Was he suspicious?" Greg shook his head. "No."

They moved through dimly lit hallways, each illuminated by the soft glow of yellow lights, with only two or three doors lining their path. Greg led the way, navigating the familiar corridors with the ease of someone who knew them like the back of his hand. They halted before a door marked Confidential Contact File Department (CCFD) the very place Sean had visited just the other day.

"Well, here it is," Sean announced. "Alright, enter your code and insert your card. Once the door opens, our little friend will cut the power, giving us a window to slip inside. When the emergency power kicks in, we'll do the same to get through the next room."

"Okay, but how will we get out when we're done?" Greg asked. "The same way we got in; remember I told Kevin every ten minutes?" Sean replied, his gaze fixed on the door. Greg whispered. "I'm ready. Go ahead and contact Kevin and Sharon. Tell them to get set."

Sean reached out and spoke to the communicator. "Sean?" Sharon's voice crackled through. "Are you ready?" Sean, surprised, asked, "You're already there? Okay, just wait for my signal." He turned to Greg and gave him a nod, motioning for him to insert his card.

"Please wait," the computerized voice announced. "Your code has been verified, Mr. Greg O'Neill. Please enter within the next thirty seconds." With a soft click, the door unlocked. "Now, Sharon! Now!" Sean hissed urgently, his voice barely above a whisper.

On the other end, Sharon wasted no time and gave a signal to Kevin that his fingers were held by Neuro-Link Clasps, and Sharon was contacting Masonaar A. Her fingers flew across the controls through the iPad he was holding as he executed the command.

Sharon typed, "Please send us a message at high frequency," then muttered under her breath as she pressed ENTER. Kevin knew exactly what that meant. They had planned for this in advance. The response came almost instantly. Barely a second passed before the blackout hit.

Sean wasted no time he slipped inside just as the door sealed shut behind them.

For security reasons, the system was designed to lock the doors automatically during a power failure, ensuring that once the blackout occurred, there was no way in or out.

"Sharon! We're in," Sean said. "Be ready again."

Greg moved swiftly, repeating the process exactly as before. "I don't think they hear you from here because it's a vault, and no communication is available here." This time, however, the computer remained silent. "What's happening?" Sean asked, a hint of urgency creeping into his voice.

"I don't know," Greg admitted, frowning at the unresponsive system. "It's not working with the emergency power."

"Wh…at'….s h..a….p……eni..ng, Se……an?" Sharon's broken voice crackled through the line. "I don't know," he replied, frustration mounting. "It's just not working with emergency power."

"W…ai….t," Sharon said. "I can turn the power back on. I see the switch."

"Try it," Sean urged. "Okay, just wait," she responded, already moving into action. The power flickered back on.

Greg quickly re-entered his code, and this time, the computer accepted it without hesitation. The door unlocked with a soft click. As soon as Greg stepped inside, the power cut out again.

They moved swiftly, repeating the exact sequence from before. Fifteen seconds later, the lights returned, and the system stabilized everything was back to normal. After Sean stepped into the CCFD, they shut the door behind them. "When was the last time they made contact with us?" Greg asked. "A week ago Monday," Sean replied. "What was the date?" Greg asked. "Monday, March 13, 2025."

"Then you need to find file number ANL0313202511," Greg instructed. Sean gave him a puzzled look. "What are the last two digits for?"

"That's for the morning," Greg explained. "For the afternoon, it would be 99." Nodding, Sean turned and began searching for the file.

"120286, 062741," Greg muttered as he scanned the file numbers. Sean joined in, running his fingers along the labels. "I don't know why I can't find it," Greg finally said, frustration creeping into his voice. Greg glanced around. "I think we're in the wrong aisle," he suggested. "We should check TOW." They moved to that aisle. "Hey, that's it. This is the one!" Sean exclaimed, pointing at the file. "This is the formula they're trying to help us with." Greg flipped it open and began reading, but his brows furrowed in confusion. "I don't understand any of this."

"Maybe we don't," Sean said, "but the little friends inside Kevin do." Without wasting a second, he reached for his communicator and contacted Sharon.

"Sharon! I need you to write down these formulas and pass them on to our friends. Ask them to check if they're correct and if they would actually work for our world. We need confirmation: are these formulas reliable?" Sean walked over to Greg, who was still engrossed in the file.

"Look! You were right," Sean said, pointing at a section. "According to this letter, they tried the formula about six months ago, well, six of their months and realized it wasn't the right one. Since then, they've been working to correct their mistake."

Greg's eyes darted over the lines as Sean spoke. "They have no idea what happened to our world. Since then, they've heard nothing, no messages, no signals. No one ever reached out." Greg slowly lifted his head, his expression darkening with confusion. A cold weight settled in his chest. "The real question is," he murmured, his voice barely above a whisper, "who contacted them?"

His mind raced. "If our world is just an atom inside the other world or better, we say an entity, then six of their months would translate to millions of years on Earth."

"That would mean..." Greg's face paled. "The last time they heard from us was when dinosaurs roamed the Earth."

Shock gripped him, and he kept rambling, trying to make sense of it until Sean finally cut him off. Greg lifted his head, his expression clouded with confusion. "Then... who contacted them?" he asked, his voice barely above a whisper. Sean looked at him and said: "Maybe the real aliens did that." Shock gripped him, and he kept rambling, trying to make sense of it until Sean finally cut him off.

Sean stood frozen, the weight of the revelation crushing him. "One mistake... one mistake destroyed everything," he murmured.

Greg's breath came in short gasps. "But what if it happens again?" His voice wavered as he stared at Sean, his face drained of color. "We're going to die. All of us. Vanish without a trace just like before."

"But it's not going to happen this time," Sean said, trying to steady Greg.

Greg looked at him, his expression filled with doubt. "How do you know?" he asked, his voice laced with sadness. "Because of

Kevin's little friends and their knowledge," Sean replied firmly. "They understand that if anything happens to our world, it will affect theirs too. They will help us. And they will find a way."

For the first time in his life, Sean had never felt more certain more trusting than he did at that moment. "Sean! Sean!" Sharon's voice crackled through the walkie-talkie, laced with urgency. "Yes, Sharon. What is it?" Sean responded quickly.

"The little friends just contacted me," she said, her voice unsteady. "They said everything checks out except for the third part of the formula. It has to be changed. Otherwise..." She hesitated, then forced herself to continue. "Otherwise, we won't get the right result. We won't die, but our world will turn into a disaster." She paused for three seconds and continued: "They gave us the correct formula." Her voice trembled, the weight of the warning heavy in the air.

"Hold on for a second," Sean said to Sharon before turning to Greg. "Where's the main computer used to contact the outer world? Not the one I was using I know there's another one, a stronger one. Where is it?"

Greg exhaled sharply. "It's on the fifth floor," he answered, his tone laced with frustration. "Do you think Sharon could send the formula to that computer by the time we get there?" Sean asked.

Greg shook his head. "No. To send or receive a document, you have to know the access code. And I don't have it," He admitted grimly. "Even if we could send a message, we'd still need the code to retrieve it."

Sean said: "There would be no problem that's why Kevin is here. But we need to go there as soon as we leave this room."

He rifled through the files, his frustration mounting. There was nothing no code, not even a trace of one. He turned to Greg to ask: "Where exactly is the room on the fifth floor?"

Greg answered: "The fifth floor has three doors and is called Contact Station Alpha, Nexus-7." He contacted Sharon: "Find a place to hide and wait for us." With a sharp exhale, he slammed his fist against the box containing the documents. The impact sent it tumbling to the floor, scattering papers everywhere.

Then something caught his eye. A glimmer of something metallic, half-hidden beneath the fallen sheets. Frowning, he flipped through the papers one by one until he found it. Carefully, he plucked it from the mess, holding it between his thumb and index finger.

It was unlike anything he had ever seen. A small, triangular object with a deep red hue so dark it was nearly black. But as he turned it in his hand, it began to shift. Its edges softened, reshaping itself into a perfect square. As it changed, a small window embedded in the surface revealed a sequence of numbers. Sean held his breath as he watched. The moment it reverted to its triangular form, the numbers shifted again. "What do you think it is?" Sean asked, turning the strange object in his hand. Greg stared at it, completely dumbfounded. "I have no freaking idea." Sean's grip tightened around the shifting device. "We have to get to the contact room." Without wasting a second, he called Sharon. "Sharon, can you head to the fifth floor? I can guide you there."

"Yes," Sharon answered immediately. "We're on our way now. Kevin says he knows where it is. Don't worry about us. We'll meet you there." "But before you go there, just get us out of here," Sean said desperately. After their conversation, two more sudden power outages struck before the system finally stabilized.

Sean and Greg wasted no time, slipping out through the emergency exit while Sharon and Kevin emerged from the electrical room. Their timing couldn't have been better. It was nearly lunchtime, and the building buzzed with activity, including the blackout in the building made chaos. People were preoccupied, moving in and out, preparing to leave. In fact, the crowd seemed even larger than usual, providing the perfect cover for their escape.

Sharon and Kevin arrived on the fifth floor earlier than expected. They exchanged uneasy glances what were they supposed to do now? Where were they even supposed to go? And, more importantly, what if someone saw them?

But luck was on their side. The security room was in utter chaos. Guards and technicians frantically scoured the screens, shouting over one another as they struggled to pinpoint the cause of yet another power failure. The confusion was their cover; no one spared them a glance.

Kevin, however, seemed completely at ease. He strolled down the hallway as if he belonged there. There were only three doors, and two of them were equipped with a high-level security system. They looked for Contact Station Alpha, Nexus-7 room and without hesitation, he placed his hand on the doors, one by one, almost as if he were feeling something as if he were trying to understand them. Communicate with them. Then, he paused. His gaze locked onto one of the doors. Slowly, he stepped closer, his movements deliberate, almost instinctual. He placed his hand gently on the doorknob, his fingers barely grazing the metal.

Then, without a word, he turned to the security keypad. He ran his fingers over it, pausing only to press his index finger firmly against its surface.

Meanwhile, Sharon was busy looking for a place to hide, something anything to keep them out of sight until Sean arrived. But as she scanned the area, her eyes landed on Kevin. She froze. Something about the way he was touching that keypad sent a shiver down her spine.

"What are you doing, Kevin?" Sharon whispered urgently, barely audible. Her heart pounded if someone spotted them, she had no excuse, no explanation that would make sense. Kevin didn't even glance at her. His fingers still rested lightly on the keypad, his expression calm, almost serene.

"Don't worry, Sharon. Just trust me," he said with unsettling confidence. "Nothing's going to happen right now. I promise, okay?" Sharon hesitated but nodded silently, deciding to trust him at least for now. She turned her attention back to the hallway, scanning the area once more.

"Where are they?" she muttered under her breath, her patience wearing thin. Sean and Greg slipped back into the building, moving with purpose but trying not to draw attention. They headed straight for the elevators. Sean pressed the UP button, keeping his expression neutral as he felt the weight of the security guards' presence near the entrance. The elevator doors slid open. A few people stepped out, chatting casually as they passed. Sean and Greg stepped inside, but before the doors could close, another man entered with them. He glanced at them briefly before asking, "Which floor?" Sean exchanged a quick glance with Greg before turning to the man. "Fourth, please," he said casually. "Me too," Greg added, keeping his tone even. The man nodded, pressing 4 and then 3 for himself. Sean felt a wave of relief. He stole a sideways glance at Greg, but neither of them spoke.

When the elevator stopped on the third floor, the man stepped out without a second glance. As soon as the doors slid shut behind him, Sean swiftly pressed 5. They stepped out onto the fifth floor. Sean scanned the hallway cautiously, his heart pounding. There was no sign of Sharon or Kevin. A cold wave of fear crept over him. "Where are they?" he murmured impatiently, his voice barely above a whisper.

Greg glanced around as well, his expression tense. "Maybe they're on their way," he offered, though even he didn't believe his own words. Sean looked around to make sure nobody was there and, slowly, opened the walkie-talkie and whispered: "Hello!" Sharon immediately answered: "Oh God, I'm happy to hear you. We are in the door on the left of the elevators waiting for you guys."

Sean exhaled, feeling a bit more confident. "Alright," he said. "When I get there, I'll knock two short, two long. That way, you'll know it's us."

Kevin let out a sharp laugh, his voice slipping effortlessly into Sean's mind. "Seriously, Sean? You don't need a walkie-talkie or some secret knock. Just think it, and I'll hear you." Sean felt a little stupid and didn't know what to say: "Oh! We can do that too." after a second pause then, he said: "Kevin, come out, we are here."

"But before they get here, let's figure out how to get inside the room," Greg said. He reached for the doorknob, but before his fingers could grasp it, It started turning on its own. Greg recoiled instinctively, his hand jerking away as if the metal had burned him. Sean caught the movement out of the corner of his eye and turned sharply. His breath hitched as he watched.

The doorknob continued to turn slowly, deliberately, as if something on the other side was letting them in. "What's going on?" Sean whispered, his voice barely audible. Before Greg could answer, he instinctively grabbed Sean's arm and pulled him back.

The door creaked open just a fraction. A shadow shifted behind it. Then, slowly, someone peered out. Sean and Greg froze, barely daring to breathe. The figure's head tilted slightly, and then Two large, mesmerizing eyes locked onto them, wide and unblinking.

Beautiful. But unnatural. Neither of them moved. Neither of them spoke. For a long, tense moment, all they could do was stare back.

It was Kevin. "Oh, my God! What are you doing in there?" Sean gasped, his voice filled with shock. Greg's eyes narrowed. "How did you manage to open the door?"

Kevin grinned as if nothing was out of the ordinary. "Hi, guys. We couldn't wait outside it was too dangerous and I asked Sharon to move here in this room because it's safer. She accepted," he added casually. "Also, the ID card you gave us? Yeah, it doesn't work for the fifth floor." Sean and Greg exchanged a stunned glance. Kevin stepped aside, pushing the door open wider. "Come on in," he said, as if they were just stopping by for a friendly visit.

"What are these things?" Kevin asked, his gaze sweeping across the unfamiliar devices in the room. "I don't know," Greg admitted. "But the real question is where does this go?" Sean reached into his pocket and pulled out the triangular object they had found in the CCFD. The deep red, almost blackish hue shimmered under the dim lighting as he held it up.

Sharon stepped closer, her curiosity piqued. "What is that, Sean?" she asked, her voice barely above a whisper. She leaned in, eyes narrowing as she examined it. She had never seen anything like it its shifting shape, its eerie glow. It felt wrong… yet important.

"This is the key to everything," Greg said before Sean could answer. His voice carried a certainty that sent a chill through the room. "Practically everything we're looking for is in this. This thing is the most valuable clue we have."

Kevin frowned, his curiosity deepening. "But… how does it work?" Sean exchanged a look with Greg before answering. "We're still trying to figure that out," Greg admitted. Kevin looked at Sean and asked: "If you don't know how it works, how do you know if this is the key to everything?" Sean pretended he didn't hear Kevin. "But we do know one thing," Sean added, holding the object up between his fingers. "This thing… it changes shape."

"What?" Both Sharon and Kevin cried out in disbelief. Sean gave them a firm nod. "It's true." They searched the room, scanning every surface, every piece of equipment, hoping to find something anything that matched the triangular disc. But there was nothing.

Then, without warning, Sean stopped. His gaze shifted to Kevin, who stood eerily still, his eyes locked on something across the room. Frowning, Sean stepped closer. "Kevin... are you okay?"

Kevin barely moved. His voice was calm, but there was something strange about his tone. "Yes, but correct me if I'm wrong. Look at that black box very carefully. Then tell me what you see." Everyone turned, their eyes locking onto the black box in the corner of the room.

They stared. Squinted. Looked at it from different angles. Nothing. Sean shrugged, puzzled, and turned back to Kevin. "There's nothing there," he said. But Kevin didn't take his eyes off the box. Not even for a second. "There's only a black box, nothing more," Sean said, still confused.

Kevin shook his head. "Maybe you're standing at the wrong angle. Come here and look again." Without hesitation, they gathered beside Kevin, crouching down to align their gaze with his, drawn by a shared urgency and curiosity. Then, as one, they turned their gaze back to the black box.

Sharon's eyes narrowed. "Wait... is that a triangle shape on the box?" Kevin exhaled, relieved. "Yes! That's what I mean. It's calling for the triangle key." Greg glanced at Sean, his expression uneasy. "It's weird. He's weird, and he creeps me out." Now that they were looking from Kevin's perspective, they could all see it a faint, almost imperceptible triangular outline subtly embedded in the surface of the box. It hadn't been visible before, but now... Now, it was unmistakable.

Sean stepped forward, heart pounding, and cautiously reached out to align the triangular object with the faint outline etched into the box's side when Kevin suddenly grabbed his sleeve and yanked it back. Sean looked at him and asked, "What is it now?"

Kevin whispered, "Don't move. Just hold it up." Sean hesitated, confused, but did as he was told.

A sudden wave of buzzing erupted between the black box and the triangular key, vibrating through the air with a frequency that defied description. The moment the key hovered near its mark, an invisible force surged forward. In the blink of an eye, the triangle-shaped slot shimmered, transformed into a perfect square, and swallowed the key whole and returned it back to Sean's hand again. He looked at everyone in surprise.

Everyone exchanged startled glances. Sean approached the box and placed the key there again; grinning, they said, "It fits perfectly." He held his breath for a moment, anticipation tightening in his chest, but nothing happened.

Frowning, he twisted the triangle to the right, then back again, hoping for some kind of reaction. But the box remained still, lifeless. He turned to Kevin with a helpless shrug. "It's not doing anything."

Kevin's eyes widened in sudden realization. "Turn it over! Turn it over and push it with your thumb!" he shouted, urgency cracking through his voice like lightning. Sean flipped the triangular object over and pressed it back into the slot. "Click."

Everyone held their breath as the faint outline on the box shifted then, slowly, it began to open. Sean exchanged a wary glance with the others before carefully placing the object into the revealed slot.

The moment it settled into place, the panel snapped shut on its own. A low hum vibrated through the air. From deep within the black box, mechanical clicks and whirring noises echoed. Then two drawers slid open beneath the box. The first held a regular keypad, the kind they had seen before. But the second... The second looked like a keypad, but it was different. Intricate. Far more complex.

It had extra layers, hidden symbols, and shifting panels like a secret interface designed for someone who knew exactly what they were doing. Before they could react, a computerized voice crackled to life from within the box.

"IDENTIFICATION REQUIRED."

The robotic voice repeated itself once more:

"PLEASE ENTER THE SECURITY CODE IN THE NEXT TWO MINUTES. THANK YOU."

Sean turned desperately to Greg. "Do you have any idea about security codes?" Greg met his gaze, equally lost. They exchanged helpless glances, both realizing they had no answer. Then before either of them could react The computer voice spoke again: "THANK YOU. PLEASE WAIT WHILE THE SECURITY CODE IS VERIFIED."

Sean and Greg stared at the machine, their mouths hanging open. "What the hell just happened?" Sean blurted out, turning sharply to Kevin, whose fingers were still poised over the keyboard. Greg, eyes wide with admiration, asked, "Kevin, what exactly did you press?"

Kevin withdrew his hands from the keys, glancing between them before answering. "I just touched the keyboard and looked inside the slot. I could see the code written in that triangle... so I did what needed to be done." His gaze shifted from Greg to Sean. "Did I do something wrong, or that was the right thing to do?" Then, with a triumphant smile, he added, "I told you I can see through everything if I want to." Sean looked at Greg and said: "I told you he can do anything."

From the back of the box, a monitor screen smoothly rose into view.

"YOUR CODE HAS BEEN VERIFIED. THANK YOU. PLEASE CHOOSE ONE OF THE FOLLOWING OPTIONS:"

1. CHANGE THE MENU
2. SELECT E.S.B
3. SELECT A.T.R
4. SELECT S.T.M
5. SELECT R.T.M
6. SELECT E.T.M

"What do the letters mean?" Sean asked, glancing at Greg as he lowered his head in thought. "Maybe number four is the right choice," Greg suggested. "It could stand for 'Send The Message?'" Without hesitation, Sean pressed the key. The screen flickered, then cleared, revealing a new prompt:

"PLEASE ENTER YOUR MESSAGE NOW."

A cheer erupted from everyone as excitement surged through the room. Kevin turned to Sean, his face pale with horror. "Sean! They're coming. They've found out we're in this room!"

He hesitated for a moment, then added urgently, "I can see the scanner it's starting to search." Greg smirked, glancing at Sean. "Wow. I think I'm starting to like him more every minute." Sharon moved to the door, ready to block anyone who might try to enter. Sean didn't waste a second. His fingers moved swiftly over the keyboard as he entered all the details of their formula, carefully explaining the section that needed modification. Then, with precision, he input the new formula the one they had received from their contact through Kevin. He exhaled softly, his gaze sweeping over the others. "Wish us luck," he murmured. Just as he pressed his finger to the send key, the door burst open with force, slamming into Sharon and knocking her aside. "Don't do it, Sean."

The urgent voice cut through the tension as John Newman tall, strikingly handsome rushed into the room. His professional, well-built frame, neatly groomed gray hair, and meticulously trimmed beard lent him an undeniable air of authority.

Everyone turned to face him. Sean's vision swam for a moment dizziness and shock gripping him as if the world had tilted beneath his feet. He blinked hard, trying to ground himself.

"From whence did you emerge?" he demanded, his voice laced with suspicion and awe. How did you gain entry into this chamber and activate the apparatus?" John asked, his voice unsteady as he took a measured step forward, his expression unwavering. "Please, Sean," he said firmly. "You have no idea who you're dealing with. This isn't a game. If you send that message, there's no undoing it. You won't be able to stop what follows you'll never know what's coming for you... or for anyone else." His tone was calm, but there was an undeniable urgency beneath it.

"I know who they are," Sean said, his voice steady but laced with defiance. "I know what's going to happen. And I know that you're trying to stop us." His face burned with anger, his pulse pounding as he locked eyes with John.

John shook his head, his expression grave. "No, Sean. They tried this before... and look what happened to Earth." His voice dropped, heavy with the weight of history. "It was deserted for millions of years. No life. Nothing but silence after their experiment. "They don't care about our galaxy none of this matters to them! They have no regard for our world. Only God knows where they came from... or what they intend to do what nightmare they're about to unleash. Their origin remains unknown and their intentions, even more so." He took a slow, almost reluctant step forward, his voice hollow with pain and edged with quiet intensity. "You know what happened that time... and so do I."

"I know what happened," Sean countered, his jaw tightening. "But that was an unauthorized experiment, as they explained."

John's eyes darkened with disbelief. "How can you say that? How could it have been unauthorized? Who would have had the power to authorize it then? And more importantly who could authorize it now? Wait a minute, how do you know if it was unauthorized? Where did you get this information?"

He took a step closer, his voice measured but urgent. "In any case, it was a mistake. A catastrophic one. If this happens again, who will bear the responsibility for the future of our world? For billions of lives?" His gaze bore into Sean's. "Think hard about what you're about to do," John warned.

"I've thought about it for a long time, and this time, I promise you that will never happen. We checked the formula," Sean said with conviction. "This time, it's different. This time, we got it right. We're going to change the world for the better." Sean explained with pride.

John took a step closer, his eyes locked on Sean's finger hovering over the Enter key, his expression desperate. "Sean, I know how you feel. I know it breaks you to see people suffer. And I know you're shocked to see me here. You don't want to listen to me I get that. But please... just hear me out. Try to understand this time."

Sean froze, confusion flickering across his face. The voice hadn't come from John. It was a woman's. Everyone went still, eyes widening in disbelief as Donna stepped into the room.

"Donna!" Sean gasped, his mind spinning. He couldn't believe what he was seeing.

Greg glanced at him, tilted his head slightly, a sly glint in his eye, and said with a teasing smirk, "Are all the women in your family this gorgeous... or are the ones I'm looking at the masterpiece?"

"But Sean didn't respond. His eyes were locked on Donna, unmoving, as if the rest of the world had vanished. "Yes, Sean, it's me," she said calmly. "Please, leave this to those who know better." Sean immediately said: "You mean like you?"

Her gaze flickered toward Kevin. "Kevin is my client. Ever since his father died, we've been monitoring his file, tracking every move he made. They chose me for this case because I never lose. I always win." Her voice carried an edge of pride.

She took a step closer. "Kevin is my responsibility. My true client. I have to protect him, guide him, and ensure he works with us. He has power the kind of power that must belong to us. We need to use it for good. This research is mine. I've spent three years working on it, and I won't let someone like you ruin everything."

Her expression darkened slightly. "We've been watching you too, Sean. You were too clever for your own good. I know you figured out the microphones and cameras in your house… but it didn't change a thing."

Donna continued moving toward Sean, her voice steady and measured. "Stop right there." Sean's voice cut through the room like a blade. His finger hovered over the key even stronger. "If you or your men come any closer, I will press it." The air grew thick with tension. No one moved. No one dared breathe too loudly. All eyes were on Sean, waiting, watching for the slightest motion that could change everything.

Sean's gaze locked onto Donna's, who stepped back. "You mean to tell me you want to experiment on Kevin. As always, you're wrong. And this time, I'm going to prove it. This time, I let you down. This time, I won. And you? You lose. You lose big." His voice burned with anger.

Donna remained calm, unfazed. "Look, Sean," she said gently, her tone almost persuasive. "It's not logical. It's just a dream, a beautiful, human dream to create a better life. But how do you know that this time, it will work?"

"I know," Sean said firmly. "Because it has been corrected by some of the greatest scientists scientists I trust. They are the best of their kind in the whole universe. They already changed their own world, and it's amazing." His conviction was unwavering.

Donna paused, and then she shook her head. "Even if it works, Sean, it's not worth it. Have you thought about the consequences? It's not realistic. Please, be logical." Her voice carried both urgency and plea.

Sean's eyes darkened with intensity. "Well, for your information," he said, his voice rising, "We stand on the brink of a transformation unlike anything humanity has ever known. Can you truly fathom a world without hunger or disease, without the divides of wealth or power, without the boundaries of good or evil?"

His gaze burned into hers."I guess this is the end of the line for you. After all, without witnessing the suffering and pain of others, how could you ever enjoy your life? Step aside."If you don't understand these sciences, then this isn't your place to interfere. Leave it to those who actually know what they're doing." he looked at her to see her reaction. "We're bringing heaven to our world," he declared. "And when that happens, people like you and your kind will have no place, no power, and no respect here."

His voice grew stronger, brimming with confidence. "This is it. This is the future. And for the last time Kevin is not your client. We will not allow you or anyone else to strip people of their freedom."

"Just think about it, Sean," Donna said her voice steady, firm, but softening with a touch of kindness now. "How can science progress if there's no disease? How can people truly be rich if wealth has no meaning? How can anyone appreciate the taste of something good if they've never known the absence of it?" Donna tried again to change his mind

She took a slow step forward. "There will be no joy in life if everyone has everything. Ambitious will be gone, and there is no place to grow. You feel proud of your success, don't you? You love your expensive car and your beautiful house not just because you have them but because not everyone does. When you drive your BMW, you feel important and powerful because others look at you with envy. But if everyone has the same, then what makes yours special?"

She exhaled, her eyes pleading. "Sean, we already live in a world that is fair in its own way. Competition drives ambition. It makes people strive for more, push themselves, and achieve greatness. Without it, what would be left to live for?"

Donna locked eyes with Sean, sensing that her words had struck something deep within him. But instead of softening, his anger flared.

"Do you hear yourself? Yes, what you say is true," Sean admitted, his voice low but seething. "Without disaster, hunger, and disease, how can science advance? But if I replace 'science' in that sentence with 'Donna'… hmm… it suddenly makes perfect sense." His lips curled in bitter realization.

"You're right about science, and in a way, that is the truth. But there's another truth, too." His eyes darkened with intensity. "How do you know how they feel? What about their pain? Why should I have to associate science with suffering when I can imagine it without it? Why should I accept that knowledge must come from misery when I know there's another way?"

His voice grew sharper. "You, Donna, you and people like you flourish because of others' suffering. How could you possibly enjoy your life knowing that people are starving, sick, and broken? Oh, wait… that's exactly how you enjoy it, isn't it? Your good life is built on the shattered hearts of others. That's the foundation of your so-called success." He paused, watching her closely, searching for a reaction. But Donna didn't flinch. She met his gaze, steady and unwavering. He continued: "I can't expect you to understand me, Donna," Sean continued, his voice unwavering. "That's why we're not on the same side. I don't want to be on your side. And that's exactly why you and your people stand on the NO side while my people and I do. We stand on the YES side." A bead of sweat traced down his temple, but he didn't waver.

Donna's eyes burned with frustration. "SEAN!" she screamed. "Do you really think you know people? That you can feel their pain? You who grew up in a wealthy family? How could you possibly understand their hunger or pain?"

"You're right. I didn't feel it." Sean's voice was steady, but there was fire behind his words. "But I have eyes to see and ears to hear. I have a heart to feel and a mind to think things you clearly lack. I know right from wrong because my parents taught us well. But do you?"

He locked eyes with Donna and asked, "Correct me if I'm wrong. You don't feel or see other people's pain, do you? I know why. You grew up in wealth, and that's your excuse."

Sean held her gaze, his voice unwavering. "But even if you had been born into a poor family, you'd still be the same. Because you were never born with a heart."

His fists clenched at his sides. "I've seen people suffer. I saw a beautiful little girl, barely more than a child, willing to sell her body so that she could buy medicine for her sick mother. And you ask me how I can feel their pain? How can I be proud to drive a BMW when I live in a world where that happens? I'm ashamed of this world and the cruel differences it upholds."

His glare bore into her. "I despise those so-called scientists, the ones who took Kevin's father, not out of compassion, but to satisfy their own selfish thirst for knowledge. They tore him away from his son and treated him like an experiment just to dissect his power. And now, Donna, you want to do the same to Kevin."

His breath came heavier now. "This world has turned into hell, a place where everything revolves around power and violence. A place where those who have more green paper, the things we call 'money,' dictate the lives of everyone else."

He took a step forward, his voice thick with fury. "It was never about people. It never was, and if things keep going this way, it never will be. You say everyone gets what they work for? You say that world is fair?" He let out a bitter laugh.

"Who do you think the real victims are in this world? You? Hardly. The only true victims are the innocent they always have been, and they always will be."

"No, Sean. Let's talk about this. Don't do it!" Donna pleaded, her voice rising in desperation. Sean met her eyes, then glanced at John. He inhaled deeply, forcing himself to steady his emotions.

"Either we all die together, so at least the victims won't suffer anymore… or we live a better life together." With that, he spun around and locked his gaze onto the keyboard.

"No!!!" Donna shrieked, lunging toward him. Her eyes darkened, flashing with something almost inhuman. But when she looked at him again, her expression shifted, calculating.

A slow smirk curled on her lips. "You didn't press Enter," she murmured. "Maybe you've finally come to your senses, or maybe it's just like before when you were a loser who couldn't do anything."

Sean turned to her, a knowing smile creeping onto his face. "You're right." His voice was calm, almost amused. "I didn't press it… because I already pressed it before you walked into the room. I just needed a little fun."

Donna's face twisted in rage. "Arrest them!" she screamed. John barked a command, and in an instant, security personnel swarmed toward Sharon, Sean, Kevin, and Greg. "You're all in trouble," Donna said coldly. "Do you even realize what you've done? Do you have any idea what this means for the people?"

Sean met her gaze with unnerving calm. "I know exactly what happened. I think you're the one who has no idea what really went on."

Donna's expression twisted in fury. "You're under arrest!" she screamed. Sean tilted his head slightly, taunting her. "On what charges?" Her lips curled into a vicious sneer. "I'll make sure your life is miserable," she hissed. Sean chuckled softly. "I'm innocent until proven otherwise. By the way, very soon, your life would be miserable."

Donna let out a sharp, humorless laugh. "Maybe in a court of justice, you could say that. But not in our court." Sean squared his shoulders, standing tall. "Then I have never felt prouder in my life."

John stepped forward, his voice heavy with authority. "You are charged with breaking into a restricted area." Greg scoffed. "Breaking in? What exactly did we break? Do you see anything stolen or destroyed? We are employees here." John's expression darkened as he turned to Greg. "You really disappoint me, Greg. You had a bright future ahead of you, but now? You've ruined everything. You're finished."

Sean stepped in, unwavering. "No, he's not. You have no proof, so you can't arrest him. He saw me here and came to warn me."

"He will be dealt with just like you," John said angrily, his patience thinning. Sean didn't flinch. "No, you won't. Because I'll explain everything before the courts and take this case to people's court." He met John's glare with steady confidence. "I'll testify that Greg only came to warn me."

"This is a restricted area, and everybody knows that," John repeated, his frustration mounting. Sean remained unfazed. "No, I didn't know that, but is there any sign on the door saying that? Any warning?" John hesitated, then growled, "No. But tell me, smart boy, what exactly are you doing here?"

Sean's expression remained calm, but his words were sharp. "Well, my sister, along with her friend's son, got lost in the building. I searched everywhere but couldn't find them. When I couldn't locate them on the lower floors, I figured she might've come up here instead of stopping on the fourth floor."

He gestured around the room. "She was looking for my office. The door was wide open. No security, no warnings, and nothing stopping anyone from entering. So, if anything would be in trouble, I'd say you're the one in."

John's face darkened as Sean pressed on. "Your so-called restricted area was left completely unattended. My sister, who has never been here before, mistook this for my office because my office is directly beneath this room. I can prove it." Sean was ready to keep going, but before he could say another word, Donna cut him off.

"This room is a restricted area," Donna snapped. "You know exactly what we do here. We also know why you came; you were trying to send an unauthorized message. This area must remain secret, and you, as a part of this organization, should understand that. That's why I'm going to make your life miserable."

Sean crossed his arms, his confidence unwavering. "You can't. Because I never even knew what was on the fifth floor, despite working here for a long time like every other employee. If it's so secret, why was I never informed? Why my sister easily could open the door and enter it?"

He took a step forward, his voice steady. "And tell me, Donna, can you even explain to the court what kind of message I was supposedly trying to send? Who was the receiver? Where is your proof?" A slow smirk formed on his lips. "Because I've got more proof to ruin your life than you have against us."

"WHAT?" Donna's voice wavered, her confidence cracking. She eyed Sean uneasily. Sean didn't hesitate. "I have all the evidence I need against you right now. I can prove my innocence, along with everyone else's."

Donna's breath hitched, but she forced herself to remain composed. "Maybe this is just one of your dirty tricks." But her voice lacked its usual edge. For the first time, she felt something unfamiliar creeping in 'doubt." Sean smirked. "Listen to this, Donna." He lifted his walkie-talkie close to his mouth. "Julia, are you in a safe place?"

"Yes, Sean, just like you told me," Julia said, her voice brimming with joy. "That's great, Julia. Don't forget, after this conversation, turn it off. Now, would you please play the tape for us?" He raised the device in the air so that everyone could hear. "Absolutely, Sean. It would be my pleasure." Julia's voice came through, smooth and assured. A brief static crackle filled the air, and then the damning recording played back word for word, undeniable.

Sean's voice was steady as he said, "Thanks, Julia. Send a copy exactly the way I told you, to the places I mentioned. If we're not home in two hours, send another copy to Judge Andrew W. Masion, the Toronto Star, U.S. News, and the other names I gave you. Thanks."

Donna and John's expressions darkened, their eyes narrowing in silent rage. Donna clenched her jaw, then snapped her head toward John. "Go. Find out where she is. Now." John didn't argue. He spun on his heel and bolted from the room. One of the security guards rushed out of the room just as another entered, his expression tense. "Sir," he said, addressing John. "Mr. Sullivan has ordered a full stop on everything. He wants to see you in his office immediately."

John's eyes flickered with suspicion. He turned toward Sean, his face twisted in frustration. "You little deceiver. What have you done?" Without waiting for an answer, he stormed out of the room. A short while later, John returned, his expression unreadable. He glanced at Donna first before shifting his gaze to Sean and Greg. "Let's go." His tone was clipped, urgent. The security guards moved swiftly, opening the door and motioning for them to exit. Sean narrowed his eyes with a little smile: "Where are we going?" John barely looked at him as he answered. "Mr. Sullivan wants to see all of you, including your sister and the boy."

Sean had never seen Mr. Sullivan before. He was one of the senior figures in the research program, a name spoken with both authority and mystery. Sean had always been curious about meeting him but not like this. In fact, no one had ever seen him.

They walked out into the hallway in tense silence, heading toward the elevator. As they descended to the third floor, Sean stole a glance at Sharon and Kevin, his mind racing. Upon reaching the far side of the building, outside Mr. Sullivan's office, accessible by a separate hallway connecting the two structures, they were instructed to wait in the visitors' room.

Kevin glanced at Sean and asked telepathically, "Is my mom okay?" Sean smiled, his response slipping into Kevin's mind. "Don't worry, she's safe. But stay alert, okay?" Kevin gave him a small, relieved smile. John disappeared inside first. Minutes later, he emerged, his face unreadable. "Mr Sullivan wants to see you two now, along with the little boy," he announced.

Sean glanced at Sharon, offering her a small, reassuring smile before stepping forward. He and Greg, followed by Kevin, entered the office together. Sean froze. The man standing before him wasn't at all what he had expected. He was one of the customers in the restaurant they used to go to with Greg.

Mr Sullivan wasn't an ageing, frail scientist tucked away in a research facility. He was handsome, with dark, neatly styled hair, a clean-shaven face, and thick, commanding eyebrows. He looked to be in his mid-forties, radiating both confidence and control. And then there were his eyes, sharp, penetrating, and assessing.

Sean had no reason to feel it, but standing in front of Mr. Sullivan, respect came naturally. "Please, sit down." Mr. Sullivan gestured toward the chairs in front of his desk. Sean and Greg exchanged a brief glance before taking their seats.

Mr Sullivan then turned his gaze toward John, who stood rigidly behind them. "I need to be alone with them." John hesitated for a second before nodding. "Yes, sir." He turned and exited, closing the door behind him.

A heavy silence settled over the room. Mr. Sullivan leaned forward slightly, his piercing eyes locked onto Sean. "As you know, you've done something that goes against our rules. You broke into a restricted area. I don't know how, but somehow, you managed to open the door and bypass security without knowing the access code for the CCFD."

His voice remained calm and measured, but the weight of his words was undeniable. "Not only that, but you took the Triangle CD and proceeded to enter another restricted area. Again, you somehow gained access without authorization." Mr. Sullivan paused, studying

Sean's face for any sign of a reaction then looked at Kevin with a friendly smile.

"And yet… there is no evidence against you." He let the words linger. "Because during the break-in, something highly unusual happened." He looked at Kevin again with a sweet smile. He leaned back slightly, his hands clasped together. "All electrical power was lost. Security feeds were wiped out. No camera footage. No recordings. Nothing."

His gaze sharpened, boring into Sean. "That's quite the coincidence, don't you think?" Sean and Greg exchanged a quick glance, their faces glowing. No evidence. That was the best news they could have hoped for.

Mr. Sullivan studied them both before continuing. "On top of that, you managed to record Donna and John's voices, giving you leverage against us. And despite our efforts, we haven't been able to track down your accomplice. We have no idea where she went." There was a big smile on Kevin's lips.

His tone was matter-of-fact, but his eyes carried something deeper, calculated intrigue. "I can't arrest you without concrete evidence, Mr. Morgan, but don't think you're off the hook. I have something on you. The day before, you used Greg's ID and security code to break into the CCFD. I saw it myself, and I've got it recorded in my files. Access to those records requires my authorization. No one else has clearance for those cameras." Sean remained silent, his expression unreadable.

Mr. Sullivan leaned back slightly. "You see, this idea of yours, this vision, it's not new. It was actually mine, too, about fifteen years ago. I was about your age then." A flicker of something unreadable passed across his face before he continued. "But regardless of all that, our policy is clear. We don't allow revolutionary activity to spread in this facility. And while I can't charge you…" He paused, letting the weight of his words sink in. "…Due to your unauthorized break-in, I have no choice but to dismiss you from your position effective immediately. You are relieved of all duties until further notice."

Silence stretched between them. It wasn't an arrest. But it was exile. Sean was astonished. He had never expected Mr. Sullivan to be this calm, calculated, and almost… understanding. More than anything, he had just confirmed something crucial. They had no evidence.

Sean wasn't sure if Mr. Sullivan had slipped up or if he had done it intentionally, but either way, the message was clear. At any rate, Sean accepted the decision for now.

Mr Sullivan then shifted his gaze to Greg, his sharp eyes assessing him carefully. "Well, Mr. O'Neill," Mr. Sullivan said smoothly, shifting his gaze to Greg. "I've heard many good things about you. You're a very smart man." Greg sat up a little straighter, wary but listening intently.

"I know Sean is your friend, so I'd expect a similar explanation from you." He paused, then continued, "I believe you were there to help him to find his sister and the child perhaps you warned him about the restricted area. Given that, I won't dismiss you." Greg's shoulders loosened slightly, but Mr. Sullivan wasn't finished. "However, consider this your only warning. Next time, before something like this happens again, come directly to me. Otherwise, you'll find yourself in serious trouble." Greg immediately said: "Yes, sir. I will."

He let the words hang in the air, his sharp gaze flicking between the two men before settling on them with a sense of pride. Sean had no words.

"Any questions?" he asked confidently when he was looking at Greg, waiting for their response. "No, sir," Greg replied, his voice steady but tinged with a hint of melancholy.

Sean paused for a moment, then he said: "I just want you to know that I had always dreamed of seeing and talking to you… but not like this."

There was a quiet sincerity in his words, a reflection of the admiration he had once held. Mr. Sullivan met his gaze and said, "I feel the same. I knew you were different."

Sean's gaze lowered slightly as he finished, "Anyway, I appreciate what you've done for us." His tone grew gloomy with those final words, a mixture of disappointment and resignation lingering in the air.

"Thanks, sir," Greg said, nodding respectfully. "I'll never forget what you just said. Thanks." Mr. Sullivan gave a slight nod. "You may now leave."

Sean and Greg rose to leave, but Mr. Sullivan's voice cut through the moment, halting them mid-step. He gestured toward Greg."You leave." Then he turned to Sean and, called his name, and waited till Greg left the room. "Sean." Sean turned, his heart tightening slightly. Mr. Sullivan looked at Kevin kindly and gestured toward the seat, then turned back to Sean. "You are a brave man," Mr. Sullivan said, his piercing eyes softer now, as if something unspoken lingered just behind them. "The world will appreciate you... later."

There was a flicker in Mr. Sullivan's expression as though he wanted to say more but hesitated. Then, after a brief pause, he turned to Kevin: "Hello, Kevin. You don't remember me, but I saw you when you were a toddler. You are a very smart boy, and your father was very proud to have you. Keep up with good things, and you have a very good friend here." He gestured to Sean. Then he turned to Sean again. "Sean... about your friend Kevin." Sean's eyes narrowed slightly, suspicion creeping into his voice. "What about him?"

Mr. Sullivan's tone dropped to almost a whisper. "Nothing serious. I just want you to know that he's very brave too, just like his father. His father was the greatest man I've ever known." Sean's breath hitched for a fraction of a second. Mr. Sullivan's gaze grew distant, his voice softening, almost like a secret meant for Sean alone. "Take care of him, would you? He's... the key. Just between us."

His eyes lingered on Kevin as he continued, "I knew Kevin was in the hospital in Toronto. I also knew your parents are in Toronto and that your mother is in the same hospital. The opportunity presented itself that day when we received the message, and you happened to be there. "You weren't there by accident I chose for you to be there."

Your vacation weeks I approved them personally in advanced. There was an opportunity to send you there to see just how sharp you are. You might wonder why I didn't assign it to you. The truth is I wanted to see whether you'd take the initiative... or walk away. I'm very proud of my decision. You're every bit as smart as I expected. You surpassed everything I imagined. You went beyond what I ever expected."

The words hung in the air, heavy and cryptic, as Mr. Sullivan's eyes met Sean's one last time. Mr Sullivan locked eyes with Sean. "Ira was one of my old friends. I only found out about him when it was too late, when I could no longer help him. If he had come to me first, he'd still be here."

He fell silent for a few seconds, the weight of his words lingering in the air. Then, his expression hardened."I don't repeat mistakes. I'll suspend your employee for nearly six months, but this time, it's personal, and it will be a paid suspension. I have no children or close relatives, so I'm considering making you my partner in the future. But for now, you must face the consequences of violating company policy. I'll be in touch." With a curt nod, he pointed at the door. "You're free to go."

Sean felt a surge of excitement, but uncertainty gnawed at him. Was Mr Sullivan helped him somehow, or was this just a warning? He nodded, and before they left the room, he looked at him and asked: "What about my sister and friends?"

Mr. Sullivan gave a small, dismissive nod and smiled. "As I told you, we couldn't find anything against you and your friends. They're free to go, too." He paused, meeting Sean's eyes directly: "But I want you to remember I'm not firing you, only suspending your employment. I can't afford to lose someone like you. "You're dismissed until further notice," Mr. Sullivan said loudly, making sure everyone around could hear him. Reaching into a drawer, Mr. Sullivan pulled out a manila envelope and handed it to Sean.

Sean hesitated for a moment before taking it. "What's this?" he asked, his fingers tightening around the envelope. Mr. Sullivan's expression remained composed, though his eyes held a flicker of something " Regret? Nostalgia?"

"This is all the information you need to know about Kevin's father. After I found out what happened to him, I demanded for report." Sean's heart skipped a beat. He tucked the envelope carefully into his jacket, feeling its weight not just physically but emotionally.

Sean looked at Mr. Sullivan and asked curiously, "I have a question for you. Why did you let John team up with Donna? Did you ever know Donna was involved?"

Mr Sullivan met his gaze calmly and replied, "You know, Sean, I knew Donna was your cousin. I found out when we got married. She told me about you, and that's how I came to offer you this position. She was right. You're intelligent, and I'd like to see you work with me in the future. Donna isn't involved here, and I know the two of you don't have the best relationship. But I'm here. If you ever need help, just keep me posted. And no more questions." Mr. Sullivan stood up, extending his hand.

Sean rose to meet him, gripping his hand firmly. There was something in that handshake, an unspoken understanding, a silent message that lingered long after their hands parted. Mr. Sullivan then did the same with Kevin, offering the same steady grasp. Meeting Sean's gaze, he spoke to them both with quiet conviction: "Good luck." Sean caught between confusion and pride, looked back at him and replied, "Thanks."

He stepped out of the office while his hand was on Kevin's shoulder with a big smile on his face, his expression unreadable. Sharon hurried to her brother, her eyes filled with concern. "What happened in there?" she asked anxiously. Sean gave her a reassuring smile. "I was suspended. I'll explain later. We're free to go, though." Kevin, his baby-faced innocence betraying his curiosity, blinked up at Sean. "We are? You know something important, but I can't get it out of your mind. What is it?" he asked, his voice tinged with disbelief.

Sean smiled at him, and telepathically, he said: "You're right because I haven't read it yet. It's in the envelope. We will open it when we're home, and your mother is there too."

John stormed into the room and emerged shortly after, his face flushed with fury. Words seemed to catch in his throat, his anger simmering just beneath the surface, ready to erupt. Without a glance at anyone else, he marched straight to Donna, leaning in to whisper something into her ear.

Whatever he said made Donna stiffen. Then both of them turned their cold gaze toward Sean."You deserved what you got losing your job."

Sean smiled and said: "You know, for the first time, we actually agree on something. I know… and I'm glad it happened." Sean replied calmly, his words only fueling Donna's anger further.

"You can go," John snapped, his voice clipped and sharp. "But come back tomorrow and pack up your things." Sean replied with a cheerful grin, "Gladly."

Then he met Donna's eyes, a faint smirk tugging at the corner of his lips. "Goodbye, Donna. I hope we never see each other again. And if we do, it'll be embarrassing for you." Sharon, Kevin and Greg looked at each other and burst into laughter. They had just started to walk away when Kevin halted abruptly. John and two security were walking with them. Kevin's eyes narrowed as he studied John, his usual innocent demeanor replaced by something unsettlingly serious.

"By the way," Kevin said, his voice calm but cutting, looking directly at John: "I suggest you see your doctor before it gets worse. It's about your heart." John spun around, his hand shooting out to grip Kevin's shoulder. "What are you talking about?" Before the tension could snap, Greg stepped in, prying John's hand away from Kevin with firm resolve. His gaze was steady, his words deliberate. "Believe me," Greg said quietly, his eyes locked on John's, "Just go to your doctor today. This time, I understand why last night, I was in the emergency room with severe tooth pain, and he warned me the night before."

As they stepped out of the building, the tension finally eased. John and security were gone. Greg turned to Kevin, his curiosity piqued. "Kevin, what's wrong with his heart?" he asked, raising an eyebrow.

"Noting, really," Kevin said with a calm, cool voice. Greg was surprised and asked him: "If there was nothing, then why did you tell him that?"

Kevin answered: "He doesn't have any heart. That's the problem." Everyone burst into laughter, realizing Kevin had been toying with John, planting just enough doubt to rattle him.

Amid the fading laughter, Sean's gaze drifted to the sky, his expression thoughtful. "Sharon, do you know where our galaxy is located in the outer world?" he asked suddenly.

Sharon tilted her head, intrigued. "No, but since we look into both outer and inner worlds, I've always wondered about that. If you know the answer, can you tell me now?"

Her voice carried a blend of curiosity and anticipation as if the answer might unlock something more than just a cosmic coordinate. "Yes, of course I will," Sean replied, a mischievous glint in his eyes. "According to the outer world, our galaxy is located on the brain of a male body."

There was a brief silence as the words sank in, and then Sharon burst out laughing. "Oh, my goodness! That explains why males think they're so powerful. That's why they call our world a man's world. Now we finally have a logical explanation for that."

The group erupted into laughter, their voices echoing down the street, the tension of the day dissolving into easy, carefree amusement.

Kevin looked at Sean and Sharon with wide, curious eyes and asked, "So if women get stronger in our world and men get weaker... does that mean the guy who has our galaxy inside him will turn gay?" Sean and Sharon froze, exchanging bewildered glances. For a moment, neither of them knew what to say. The question hung in the air, absurd and innocent all at once, leaving them both speechless. Then Sean shrugged, trying to suppress a laugh. "I... I don't think that's how it works, Kevin." Sharon chuckled, shaking her head. "Yeah, pretty sure the universe doesn't have that kind of switch." The group burst into laughter again, Kevin's question adding another layer of unexpected humor to their already strange day. Sean and Sharon exchanged surprised glances, momentarily speechless, caught off guard by the unexpected question. After a brief pause, Sean placed a reassuring hand on Kevin's shoulder, a faint smile tugging at the corner of his mouth. "We'll find the answer," Sean said gently. "I promise you that." The group continued walking, their laughter fading into thoughtful silence, the question lingering like an unsolved riddle woven into the fabric of their curious world. Sharon looked at Sean and asked, "What now?" Sean glanced up at the sky and said, "If each of our years equals a minute for them, then we'll have to wait a couple of years to see any results."

Sean smiled, resting one hand on Kevin's shoulder while holding Sharon's hand with the other. He met Julia's gaze with unwavering determination. "We keep going," he said. "We'll go back to Toronto. I'll sell my house, and from there, we'll figure out the next step.

People need to know about our discovery they have the right to know. And we will change the world. I promise you that."

CHAPTER EIGHT

"The Reshaping Begins"

Sean moved into his parents' home, needing the money from his house to fund the devices he was creating. The Neuro-Link Clasp he had designed for Kevin required an upgrade, so he developed a more convenient and advanced version. This new device combined the Neuro-Link Clasp with a holographic interface capable of pinpointing locations in the body that harbored advanced life. He named it the Neuro-Vista Beacon6.

They advertised it, but at first, no one showed interest. Years passed, and success remained elusive. Sales were low, but those who did purchase it became living proof of its potential. Those who used the Neuro-Vista Beacon stayed youthful and healthy, and their gardens flourished with abundant vegetation.

The years passed, and five years after his discovery, Sean asked Julia to marry him, and she accepted. Decades went by, and fifty years after Sean's breakthrough, the world had changed but he had not. Those who had once been younger than him had grown into senior citizens, yet Sean remained as he was frozen at thirty, untouched by time. His ageing had halted entirely, leaving him strong and youthful. Sharon and Sean remained as young as thirty. Helen and James now appeared to be in their fifties. Julia still looked no older than twenty-five, while Kevin, now a grown man, still looked no older than twenty, his body just as healthy and resilient as ever.

The media began to take notice of Sean and his family along with his discovery, but they were still not permitted to report on it openly. Meanwhile, powerful corporations approached him with billions of dollars in offers to buy his creation, yet he refused every time. To Sean, the Neuro-Vista Beacon was not a luxury for the wealthy; it was a breakthrough meant to be affordable and accessible to all, even the poorest individuals. He knew that if the big companies gained access to the Neuro-Vista Beacon, they would make it inaccessible to the public, and that wasn't his plan.

CEO of major companies sought to claim it for their own benefit, but Sean stood firm. His only offer to them was simple: if they truly valued it, they could provide it to their employees, but it would never be for sale to the highest bidder. Even though the Neuro-Vista Beacon didn't have a majority of buyers at first, it still made Sean and his team among the richest people on Earth. As word spread, people began to ignore the media's silence and kept ordering the device. Sales skyrocketed, climbing higher with each passing day.

With the effects of the Neuro-Vista Beacon keeping users youthful, the beauty industry began to evolve. Hair salons transformed, offering permanent hair color and texture changes as ageing and greying became obsolete. Those who pioneered this new kind of salon business found themselves amassing fortunes in record time.

New clinics emerged, catering to those who wished to alter their height or change their skin type, all working under contracts with Sean. Even eye doctors re-branded themselves as Advanced Eye Clinics, offering permanent eye color transformations. As the impact of the Neuro-Vista Beacon spread, the world itself began to change. Cities became greener, teeming with lush vegetation. Almost everyone had their own thriving gardens, producing fresh, nutrient-rich food packed with energy, vitamins, and everything needed for daily sustenance. The line between nature and technology blurred, ushering in a new era of health and abundance.

Grocery stores had little left to offer. One by one, they either shut down or transformed into dairy shops, the only business still thriving since dairy products remained one of the few essentials people couldn't produce on their own. Unemployment rates dropped among those who still lived in the old ways, while the rest of society embraced a self-sufficient lifestyle, fully immersed in their own gardens and sustainable living. There was nothing left for the media to offer everyone had their own universe, built on different technologies but yielding the same results.

Now, in 2125, a century later, humanity had evolved into a civilization of boundless energy and creativity. Homelessness, poverty, ignorance, illness, allergies, cancer, disability, old age none of these hold any meaning in the world anymore. But still, many religious people refused to follow, believing it was against God's will. In response, Sean told them, "If God didn't want this, He wouldn't have allowed this knowledge to exist. In truth, it's you who are disregarding God. Knowledge is a gift from Him for us to discover and use for our own good."

People remained youthful and vibrant, dedicating their time to the arts, music, dance, singing, seeing the world, carpentry, and countless other crafts. Science reached unprecedented heights, and technology advanced at an astonishing pace. Discovery became second nature, an everyday habit rather than an occasional breakthrough. With more time, clarity, and relaxation, scientists worked faster and understood the mysteries of the universe better than ever before. The world had entered a golden era of progress, where knowledge and innovation flourished like never before.

They had an incredible reputation among the people, so much so that they didn't even need bodyguards. Anyone who knew them became their protector, standing by them out of admiration and respect.

Creativity flourished like never before. People began cultivating entirely new kinds of fruits and vegetables, crafting unique hybrids that had never existed before. The environment of the world transformed, teeming with life and abundance. Everyone was engaged in meaningful work, driven by passion rather than necessity. Each day felt like a new beginning, another beautiful day in a world that had never been more alive. Crime rates dropped to zero violence had lost its appeal. People no longer saw the conflict as a solution; life had taken on a new meaning. Stress itself had become obsolete, its purpose fading into history.

In every city, communities came together, creating vast gardens overflowing with every kind of fruit and vegetable. They learned to work in harmony, supporting one another without competition or greed. Even those who remained stubborn, refusing to fully embrace the new way of life, were still welcomed. They were free to take whatever they needed from the communal gardens, ensuring no one was left behind.

The world had transformed beyond recognition. Even those who didn't follow Sean's path or adopt his way of living found themselves granted extraordinary longevity, living well beyond a century with unparalleled strength and vitality. But still, they were not immortal eventually, even if they faced the end of their lives. This was their decision, and everyone respected it. Even traffic had transformed. There was no rush to get to work, no frantic commutes. Most people preferred walking over driving, moving at a peaceful, unhurried pace.

War became a relic of the past. Even when governments tried to force them into battle, people refused. They had come to understand that life was far more valuable than fighting over borders or lands. They realized that the Earth had more than enough land for everyone to grow, to live, and to thrive together in harmony.

A new kind of traveler emerged, those who roamed the world simply for the joy of exploration. With food abundant and freely available, they never had to worry about survival. Wherever they went, public gardens welcomed them, and there was no fence offering all they needed. The world had become a place of peace, unity, and endless discovery.

No one was forced to do anything. Freedom had become a way of life, and technology had advanced beyond imagination. Scientists had perfected the creation of high-quality, sustainable meat products, eliminating the need for hunting. Vast reserves were established for wildlife, where fresh meat was provided daily in one area while another was filled with fruits and vegetables. Lions, bears, eagles, tigers etc., gathered in the same place, sharing fresh meat in harmony. The meat strengthened their immune systems, enhancing reproduction and restoring balance through childbirth. Even the animals seemed happier and more playful as if peace had softened their instincts.

Sean and his family didn't even need to hire security guards; people simply wouldn't allow anyone to violate another. Police departments stood empty.

Even the fiercest predators, lions, tigers, wild dogs, and bears, no longer pose a threat to humans. With food always available, they had no reason to hunt people or other animals. Thanks to technology, meat could be created from DNA, eliminating the chaos of the past. The predators simply passed by, heading straight to the food sources prepared for them. All the animals, from lions and bears to mice and beyond, ate from the same place without disturbing one another.

The world had become a place where fear no longer ruled. Dark places and dense jungles were no longer dangerous. There was no struggle for survival. Every person and every creature had enough to eat, coexisting in a balance that had never been seen before.

Scientists developed specialized food and seeds for smaller animals squirrels, rats, mice, rodents, birds, and others that naturally regulated their reproduction rates. These innovations didn't stop them from giving birth but ensured their populations remained balanced, preventing overpopulation while maintaining the ecosystem's harmony. With this breakthrough, nature flourished in perfect equilibrium. Cities and forests alike thrived, free from the struggles of over-breeding and scarcity. Every creature had its place, and the world had never been more peaceful or sustainable.

Sean stepped outside, taking in the sight of joyful faces all around him. He lifted his gaze to the sky, eyes filled with wonder, and whispered, "God, I think we've created heaven on Earth. Some may say You don't exist, but their knowledge isn't even a speck in the vastness of the universe compared to Yours. Yet, You helped us… and for that, I thank You." A satisfied smile spread across his face as he added, "I'll see You in a few centuries."

CHAPTER NINE

"A Birthday in Paradise"

The radio blared with urgency, its volume cutting through the air like a sharp blade. The announcer's voice was tense, carrying the weight of breaking news that demanded attention. Every word echoed around them, drowning out their thoughts and conversations, pulling their focus to the unfolding story they hadn't expected to hear.

The radio crackled to life, its volume sharp and clear, as the announcer's voice filled the room with an almost surreal cheerfulness.

Good morning. Today is May 25, 2175. Today is a very special day for everyone. Today marks the birth of life itself and of the one who made that life accessible to all. Today is Sean Morgan's birthday. On behalf of the entire world... Happy Birthday, Sean Morgan, father of life. Suddenly, a joyful yes! Erupted across the globe.

Earth has undergone profound and continual change transformations so frequently that they've become part of daily life. Scientists remain astounded by the scale of evolution. The disease has become nearly obsolete as the human body has advanced to a state where it can autonomously neutralize harmful germs, bacteria, and illness.

The words hung in the air, a testament to a world unrecognizable from the past, where humanity had conquered what once seemed unconquerable.

The screen continued its broadcast, the announcer's voice steady and confident. At every bus stop, sleek screen TVs flickered to life, seamlessly integrated into the futuristic landscape. Every hour, without fail, they broadcast updates on the latest scientific breakthroughs or announcements about local activities.

The screens displayed vibrant visuals, captivating passersby with news of discoveries that once seemed impossible advancements in human health, environmental restoration, and technological marvels.

People paused, even if just for a moment, drawn in by the constant stream of knowledge, a testament to a world that never stopped evolving.

Current statistics reveal that only two hundred individuals remain incarcerated worldwide clinging to what is now regarded as an obsolete way of life. Some are driven by unstable minds, while others remain consumed by bitterness and defiance.

A century ago, a single state held over ninety-five thousand inmates. This dramatic shift stands as undeniable proof that violence has all but disappeared, giving way to a new era defined by peace, collaboration, and mutual respect.

Moreover, disabilities have become a thing of the past. Advances in science and technology ensured that every living being, human and animal alike, was now completely healthy, free from illness, ailments, or physical limitations. The world had reached a state where suffering was no longer a part of life, and every creature thrived in perfect well-being.

The President of the United States has nominated Mr. Sean Morgan for the hundredth time, recognizing his consistent success each year in advancing the groundbreaking technology he introduced to the world.

The screen flickered, seamlessly transitioning to the final segment of the broadcast. The announcer's voice softened, carrying a reflective tone. "Ladies and gentlemen, with the way life is today, it seems we will have to wait much longer to see Him and to return home."

The words lingered in the air, mingling with the quiet hum of the city a subtle reminder that even in a world perfected by science, the mysteries of existence remained untouched, waiting patiently beyond the reach of human understanding. "Ladies and gentlemen, that concludes our latest science update. Thank you for listening. I'm Peter Shade-field, and we'll see you tomorrow."

The transmission ended with a soft, static hum, leaving behind an eerie sense of awe at how profoundly the world had changed followed by a swell of majestic music that pressed heavily on the hearts of all who listened.

Sean glanced at the mirror and smiled. "At age 180, I'm still in good shape," he mused, a hint of pride in his voice. With a flick of his hand, he turned off the radio and stood squarely in front of the mirror, adjusting his collar. His reflection revealed a strikingly handsome young man, appearing no older than thirty-five, with sharp features and a physique that radiated health and vitality.

As he busied himself with getting dressed, the doorbell chimed, its sound echoing softly through the house.

"Julia, could you please answer the door?" Sean called out, his eyes briefly drifting to the cherished photo above the fireplace a picture from their wedding day. He looked at it every morning a simple ritual that filled him with gratitude, a quiet reminder of the love that had remained constant through the years. Beside it stood a photo of Kevin in his graduation gown, and next to that, a portrait of a beautiful sixteen-year-old girl the daughter of Sean and Julia.

"Yes," Julia replied warmly from the other room, her voice carrying the familiar comfort that had been the anchor of Sean's long, extraordinary life. Julia opened the door to find Greg standing there, a friendly smile on his face. "Good morning, Julia," he greeted warmly before glancing past her. "Hey, Sean!"

But Liana, the daughter of Sean and Julia, ran straight to Greg and jumped into his arms for a hug.

"Hi, Uncle Greg!" she said, planting a quick kiss on his cheek before returning to her cell phone.

Greg barely had time to respond, smiling as he said, "Good morning, sweetheart Liana."

Sean appeared at the door, adjusting his jacket. "Are you ready to go?" Greg asked. "Yes, let's go," Sean replied with a nod.

They walked down the path toward the car, the sun casting long shadows on the ground. But just as Sean was about to open the car door, he froze. His eyes locked on someone across the street, a young man walking toward them with an unmistakable spring in his step, his face lit up with excitement.

The young man smiled broadly and waved, quickening his pace. Sean's heart raced. His mind struggled to process what his eyes were seeing. As the young man reached them, they shook hands, and an unspoken recognition passed between them as if time had folded in on itself.

They began talking, their words flowing with the ease of old friends reuniting after years apart, though Sean couldn't shake the feeling that this meeting was far more extraordinary than it appeared.

"Hi, Walter," Sean said, a mix of surprise and warmth in his voice. "I didn't recognize you at first. You've changed a lot. I'm very happy to see you again."

Walter's face lit up even more, his eyes reflecting genuine gratitude. "Hi, Sean! I'm very happy to see you, too. I found your address from one of my friends yesterday and thought to myself, We should see each other again. You were incredibly helpful to me, and I wanted to thank you personally for everything."

Sean smiled, the memories flooding back, and for a brief moment, it felt as if no time had passed between them.

"No, it was you who helped yourself," Sean replied with a warm smile. "Are you working now? Married? Tell me everything." Walter chuckled, his eyes gleaming with a mix of pride and nostalgia.

"Do you remember how my life was before? After you introduced me to the Neuro-Link Clasp and gave it to me at no charge, I started being interested. After thirty years, I found out I was still young, and when I was 105 years old, I realized I was a very healthy man. All I needed was self-confidence. So, I started school. It took me almost 20 years to graduate from high school and to me was worth it. Time wasn't important anymore. After that, I went to university, and it took me eight years to become an engineer." He paused, taking a deep breath, his smile widening.

"Meanwhile, I moved to Canada, married a wonderful woman, and we started a family. We have a son and a daughter, and, funnily enough, my wife is an engineer too."

Walter refreshed his mouth, his breathing easing as he continued, his voice steady and filled with gratitude.

"I never wanted to remain homeless after you gave me that kit and personally taught me how to use it. I don't know why I've survived this long, but I do know one thing: the life I live now exists because of you. Everyone speaks of a man named Sean Morgan, the one who saved the world from unimaginable harm. When I saw you on television, I recognized you instantly. That's when I realized only the first hundred years were difficult. After that, I was finally ready for something better."

When Walter finished, he was beaming at Sean, his face glowing with admiration and joy. The connection between them was undeniable, woven together by the invisible threads of resilience, gratitude, and the passage of time.

"I'm very glad to hear that, Walter, especially about the changes you made in your life," Sean said, his smile filled with genuine warmth. "You know, today is my birthday. I'm 180 years old. We're going to celebrate it at our favorite restaurant." At that moment, Julia stepped out of the house, joining Sean and Greg, her presence adding a soft glow to the moment.

"Walter, this is my wife, Julia, and my best friend, Greg," Sean said, his voice filled with pride. Walter smiled warmly, then turned to Greg. "I remember you. It's good to see you both again." Sean nodded with a smile. "My family's waiting for us at the restaurant. I'd be happy if you joined us."

Walter's face lit up with joy at the invitation, but he shook his head gently, his smile tinged with a hint of regret. "I'm so happy to hear that, Sean. But my wife is expecting me because there is a party and it is very important to her, for that reason I can't. Thank you for the invitation, though."

Sean nodded, understanding completely. They shared one last handshake, firm and filled with unspoken gratitude, before parting ways, each carrying a piece of the past woven seamlessly into the present. "That's okay," Sean replied warmly.

"Listen, I'll give you the address, and perhaps you could come later with your wife and family. I'd be happy to see you there." He pulled out a small piece of paper, scribbled the address, and handed it to Walter.

Walter took the note, his eyes scanning the words. A sudden flash of recognition crossed his face as he read aloud, "Aryan Restaurant."

His expression shifted from surprise to delight. "We'll be there," he said with a broad smile, clutching the paper as if it held more than just an address. "I don't know what to say. I'm so glad I came here today. I guess we'll see you at your party."

Sean smiled, his heart full, as they exchanged one last handshake. Walter waved goodbye, and everyone went their separate ways, the promise of reunion lingering in the air, as light and certain as the morning sun.

When they arrived at the restaurant, everyone was already there, eagerly waiting. Cheers erupted the moment Sean walked in, the room bursting with excitement. He embraced and kissed his parents, and then his eyes landed on Mr. Sullivan and his wife, Donna, who appeared to be a decade older than him. She smiled warmly and said, "What can I say? I got a late start, but you did a wonderful job."

With heartfelt gratitude, he thanked each person individually as music began to fill the air, wrapping the celebration in warmth and joy.

While Sean and Julia were deep in conversation at the table, Sean's gaze drifted across the room and landed on Walter's wife. His expression shifted, and he stood up abruptly. "Hello, Walter. I'm so glad you could make it. This must be your wife," Sean said warmly.

"Yes, this is my beautiful wife " Walter began, but Sean cut him off, his eyes narrowing in disbelief. "Mary?" Sean asked, his voice tinged with surprise. "Yes, Sean. I recognized you too," Mary replied with a gentle smile.

Walter froze, unsure of what to say, his gaze shifting from Sean to Mary. Mary reached for her husband's hand and softly said: "Walter, do you remember when I told you about the gentleman who helped me when my mom was sick? The one who saved me from a life on the streets? That's him." Walter's face lit up with amazement and heartfelt appreciation.

"You know! You saved me and my wife. Sean, this is my wife's restaurant and today is your birthday. Let us thank you properly. Everything's on the house. This is the happiest day of my life. As soon as I saw the address, I called Mary and told her the story. I rushed home, changed my clothes, and here I am."

Sean looked at them with a happy smile and asked, "How long have you had this restaurant?" Walter exchanged a glance with Mary before replying, "After working for so many years, we decided to retire and open this place. But, truth be told, Mary runs it most of the time."

With that, Walter stepped forward and shook Sean's hand firmly, his gratitude evident. Sean was speechless for a moment, emotion tightening his throat. Finally, he managed to say, "No, I can't accept that. It's my party I can't let you pay for me."

Walter chuckled softly, his grip warm and insistent. "I understand, but please let me have this joy. It's the least we can do for you, my friend. Besides," he added with a playful grin, "you have no other choice. It's already down." Sean smiled happily and asked Mary: "Where is your mom? Is she okay?" Mary smiled and pointed somewhere and said: "She is there and happy. Thanks to you."

Without waiting another minute, Walter signaled to the musicians, and the soft strains of a waltz filled the room. He turned to Mary, gently taking her hand and leading her onto the dance floor.

Sean watched them for a moment, his heart swelling with unexpected warmth. Turning to Julia, his eyes softened, and he said with a smile: "I'm the happiest man alive because I've got you the most beautiful woman on Earth."

With that, he offered her his hand and escorted her to the dance floor, their steps soon blending with the rhythm of the music and the soft glow of a night filled with serendipity.

James and Helen were on the dance floor, too, laughing heartily as they danced with the carefree energy of a young couple, their joy infectious. Meanwhile, Sharon and Greg remained at the table, watching the others sway to the rhythm.

Greg had never married. He loved Sharon deeply so deeply that no one else ever came close to the way she made him feel. The connection he had with Sharon was irreplaceable, and in its absence, he never found a reason to walk down the aisle.

Sean caught Greg's eye and flashed him a playful wink before glancing at Sharon, who sat alone, her gaze following the dancers with a soft smile. She had recently ended her fifty-year relationship with Mike, a man with whom she had a wonderful son but never a perfect fit. And yet, despite it all, her face radiated warmth and contentment, genuinely happy for her brother and the life they had built.

Lost in thought, Sharon's mind drifted until Greg's voice gently pulled her back. "Would you do me the honor of this dance?" he asked, his hand extended, his eyes warm with quiet sincerity.

Sharon looked up, surprised but pleasantly so. A smile curved her lips as she placed her hand in his, allowing herself to be led onto the dance floor, her heart lightening with each step.

In no time, Greg and Sharon were gliding across the dance floor, their movements growing more natural with each step, laughter slipping between them like soft notes in the melody.

Sean and Julia were lost in their own rhythm, swaying to the music, when a sudden tap on Sean's shoulder broke the moment. Sean turned, curious, and the instant he saw who it was, his face lit up with surprise and joy.

Both he and Julia let out delighted screams. "Kevin!" Julia exclaimed, her eyes wide with excitement. "I thought you weren't going to make it tonight! We thought you'd be here tomorrow!"

Kevin grinned, his presence like an unexpected gift, and the room seemed to shine a little brighter with his arrival.

"Kevin! I'm so glad you're here with us tonight. You've made my birthday party a hundred times better," Sean said, his face glowing with excitement.

Sean and Julia both wrapped their arms around Kevin in a warm embrace, and Kevin hugged them back tightly, his voice filled with genuine affection as he spoke.

"I'll always be at your parties because you're my hero. Remember that, and how in hell I could miss my best friend's birthday party?" Kevin said with a heartfelt smile. "And no matter how important my science and research are, you are the most important part of my life."

The sincerity in his words wrapped around them like an invisible thread, binding their friendship even tighter amidst the laughter and music of the night. "Kevin! You're one of the most powerful scientists on Earth, maybe even in the universe, and we're so proud of you. Just keep going with your research," Sean said, his voice brimming with admiration.

Kevin looked at both of them and, with a happy smile said: "You know guys, I didn't come alone, my friends Clara and Frank with me." Sean welcomed them and Suddenly, Liana jumped on Sean and

Julia and said: "Mom, Dad! I am so happy we all are here. I love you all."

Without waiting for a response, Sean grabbed Liana, Kevin, and Julia by the hands and pulled them into the center of the dance floor. With a grin, he motioned for Frank and Clara to join them. Kevin wrapped an arm around Clara and began to dance while Frank turned to Liana and offered his hand with a playful bow. The music swelled, and soon, the room was alive with movement, laughter echoing, joy radiating, and the energy utterly infectious.

In the middle of it all, Sean glanced at Julia and Kevin, his heart full, and exclaimed, "Oh my God, this is the best time of my life, and I hope in the next hundred years of my life, it just keeps getting better and better!"

The room erupted with laughter, the joyful sound blending seamlessly with the music as everyone joined in, their spirits high and hearts light, creating a memory that would linger long after the night had faded.

***

GLOSSARY

1. Nanotechnology

The concept is known as nanotechnology or. In the future, scientists envision creating tiny robots at the scale of molecules or cells, often referred to as nanobots or nanorobots. These microscopic machines could be programmed to perform specific tasks inside the human body, such as targeting cancer cells, repairing damaged tissues, or delivering precise drug treatments.

Nanobots have the potential to revolutionize medicine by providing highly targeted, non-invasive treatments. For example, they could be designed to destroy cancer cells without harming surrounding healthy tissue, offering a more efficient and less harmful alternative to traditional treatments like chemotherapy. These technologies are still in the early stages of research and development, but the idea is gaining attention in scientific communities.

2. Arrhythmia's

An arrhythmia is an irregular heartbeat that occurs when the electrical signals coordinating the heart's beats don't function properly. This can cause the heart to beat too fast (tachycardia), too slow (bradycardia), or with an irregular pattern. Some arrhythmias are harmless, while others can lead to serious health issues.

Symptoms of arrhythmias can vary and may include:
- A fluttering, pounding, or racing heartbeat
- Dizziness or lightheadedness
- Shortness of breath
- Chest pain
- Fainting or near-fainting spells

It's important to note that some arrhythmias may not cause noticeable symptoms but can still be detected during a physical examination or through diagnostic tests like an electrocardiogram (ECG). [cite] turn0search0[]

If you experience any of these symptoms or have concerns about your heart rhythm, it's advisable to consult a healthcare professional for proper evaluation and management.

3. Akkadian3

The Cyrus Cylinder, an ancient clay artifact associated with Cyrus the Great, is inscribed in the Akkadian language using Babylonian cuneiform script. This script comprises wedge-shaped characters pressed into clay, a writing system that originated in Mesopotamia. The cylinder was created following Cyrus's conquest of Babylon in 539 BCE and reflects the administrative and cultural practices of that region.

4. Al-Biruni

Al-Biruni and Avicenna (Ibn Sina) were among the greatest Persian scientists, making groundbreaking discoveries centuries ahead of their time.

Al-Biruni was the first to accurately estimate the Earth's radius over a thousand years ago using the most basic tools available. His calculation of 6,340 km was remarkably close to today's known value of 6,371 km a difference of only 31 km, an astonishing achievement given the era.

Long before Einstein, Al-Biruni also discovered that light consists of extremely delicate particles, which he poetically called "Particles of Tenderness." A thousand years later, Einstein identified the same concept and named them photons.

Furthermore, 600 years before Galileo, Al-Biruni had already determined that the Earth was round. Even more impressively, 500 years before Copernicus, he understood that the Earth orbits the Sun, challenging the dominant geocentric model long before it was widely accepted.

These discoveries prove that Persian scholars were far ahead of their time, shaping the foundation of modern science despite the challenges of their era.

5. "Neurogen"

(noun) A highly evolved human with advanced cognitive abilities, enhanced biological functions, and a seamless connection to technology.

Origin: Derived from "neuro-" (relating to the brain and nervous system) and "-gen" (meaning generation, genesis, or evolution).

Example usage: "He's not just human anymore. He's a Neurogen, the next stage of evolution."

6. "Neuro-Vista Beacon"

It combines "Neuro" (for its neural-link capabilities), "Vista" (meaning a view or vision, referencing the holographic projection), and "Beacon" (symbolizing its ability to detect and highlight advanced life within the body).

7. Nano-man

A blend of Nano and a human-sounding suffix. I made this name to represent Kevin with his ability.

8. "Kaleidoscope of emotion" is a metaphor that describes a rapidly shifting and complex mix of feelings, much like how a kaleidoscope constantly changes patterns and colors when turned. It conveys the idea of experiencing a wide range of emotions: joy, sadness, fear, excitement, and more, all blending and shifting dynamically.

For example:

"As she stood on the stage, a kaleidoscope of emotion swept over her nervous anticipation, exhilaration, and a deep sense of fulfillment."

9. "Cuneiform script" (مخیخی خط) is indeed one of the oldest known writing systems in the world, and it was used in ancient Persia, especially by civilizations like the Elamites, Akkadian s, and later the Achaemenid Empire. It was written by pressing a wedge-shaped stylus into clay tablets, which is why it's called cuneiform (from the Latin cuneus, meaning "wedge").

10. "Eidolon" The word Eidolon comes from the Greek Eidolon, meaning image, phantom, or ideal form. In ancient literature, it often referred to a ghost or spirit image of a living or dead person. Over time, it came to symbolize the perfect or ideal version of something

As AI Rises, So Do We

AI Is Advancing, But So Are We

In a world gripped by fear of artificial intelligence surpassing human control, few noticed the quiet evolution unfolding within humanity itself. Sean and Kevin are part of a daring mission bridging communication between generations, not just human, but something stranger and older, whose signals have pulsed through shocks for years. As contact deepens, Sean reminds Kevin that, just as Heraclitus once said, no one steps into the same river twice; they are no longer speaking to the same beings they once knew; the entities have evolved, and so, silently, have humans. While the world obsesses over machines rising, no one realizes that mankind, too, is changing, adapting, and awakening to something far beyond the fears of AI: the next stage of human connection and transformation.

- "We Rise As They Rise"
- "The Song of Two Evolutions"
- "In the Shadow of Steel, Humanity Shines"
- "Not Fear, But Flight We Evolve Too"

About the Author

Susan Shakeri is a passionate science fiction author based in Canada. With a vivid imagination and a deep curiosity about the unknown, she creates thought-provoking stories that explore human evolution, emotion, and the mysteries of the universe. Susan's writing blends wonder with realism, inviting readers to journey beyond the limits of imagination.

www.ingramcontent.com/pod-product-compliance
Lightning Source LLC
Chambersburg PA
CBHW051139300726
48978CB00011B/338